The Dark Side of a Blazing Passion...

"I'll warn you, I'm not your kind of man."

Now Faith knew the truth. He was violent. Dangerous. She couldn't forget. He even warned her. But the warning disappeared, and the words seemed to drum excitement into the heated flow of her blood.

"Let me go. You don't really want me, Delaney. You've made your feelings plain enough."

"I have, haven't I?"

The fractional move he made against Faith stroked her in a long shuddering caress. His breath mingled with hers, and she parted her lips as if he had commanded it. It had been so long since someone had held her. She didn't want to think, or reason. Her warnings to herself were forgotten. A warmth unfurled inside her, spread slowly to every nerve ending, and Faith heeded its call.

"Why not?" he whispered to himself. "Why the hell shouldn't I?"

Delaney took her mouth.

It was more than taking. He was ravishing her mouth without desire, almost scornfully sure of himself. But he incited hunger to taste the forbidden, and Faith couldn't seem to fight him. . . .

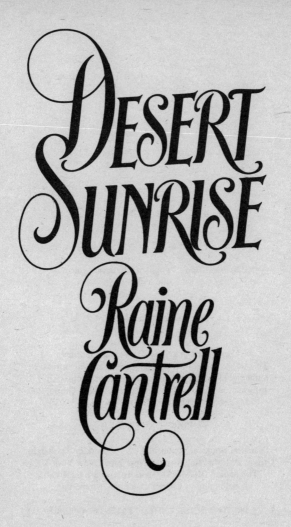

DESERT SUNRISE

Raine Cantrell

DIAMOND BOOKS, NEW YORK

DESERT SUNRISE

A Diamond Book / published by arrangement with
the author

PRINTING HISTORY
Diamond edition / May 1992

ISBN: 1-55773-702-9

Diamond Books are published by The Berkley Publishing
Group, 200 Madison Avenue, New York, New York 10016.
The name "DIAMOND" and its logo are trademarks
belonging to Charter Communications, Inc.

PRINTED IN THE UNITED STATES OF AMERICA

10 9 8 7 6 5 4 3 2 1

To my daughter,
Joelle,
who loves with an open heart

Acknowledgments

When a story haunts a writer, coming to live in heart and mind, a voice cannot be given without generous help and support.

I am most grateful to the following:

Arizona State Historical Society and library.

Jackie Blazok, who made her personal library, knowledge of the Apache, and love of turquoise available as needed and shared the Apache life-way, legends, and songs with this Anglo.

Marilyn Campbell, a timeless friend, who lived through the hours of my writing this book and remained a constant to hold me on course.

Joan Hammond, whose encouragement and faith never waver.

David G. Jackson III, Public Affairs Specialist with the Bureau of Land Management, State of Arizona, and Bob Munson, Architectural Historian of the Arizona State Historic Preservation office, for making me laugh and for the information needed for the journey.

Ken Ownings, Jr., for sharing his Arizona sources.

Evelyn Seranne, a new friend who showed me Prescott.

Jacki Whitford, who haunts the Smithsonian book sales for me.

Lastly, M., for being and believing.

A-co-'d to each one of you.

The Legend

SKYSTONE, THE PRECIOUS turquoise of Indian legends. A sacred stone, a talisman against evil, the stone of life-giving water and healing.

From the days of the Spanish invaders who desired turquoise and forced the Indians to mine it for them along with other precious metals, the stones never quite equaled the gem quality of the turquoise that the Indians wore for their own adornment and protection.

The use of turquoise was widespread among all the Indian tribes. They revered the stone in much the same manner as the *Inde'*, as they called themselves. But the Zuni Indians used another name that became theirs: *apachu* or "enemy." *Apaches de Nabaju* was once the name for all the invading Athapaskans. Today we call them Navajo and Apache. While there are roots of similarity in their ancient cultures, they have long been separate tribes.

Duklij is the Apache word for blue or green stone. The two colors are not differentiated in their language. The stone is a sacred substance. No matter what else the shaman (medicine man) may have lacked, he always tried to have a bit of the impure malachite known to the whites of the Southwest as turquoise.

Before the birth of a child or several days afterward, turquoise beads were fastened to the cradleboard as one of the protective amulets. A bit of turquoise tied to a bow or a gun made the weapon shoot accurately. The stone had the power to bring forth life-giving rain and to help find water in the desert. It could be found by the man who would go to the end of the rainbow after a storm and hunt for the stone in the damp earth. Small pieces of turquoise were tossed into a river before crossing to appease the spirits.

Duklij was the Apache shaman's badge of office; without it he could not perform his ceremonies to heal, to protect.

The land that became known to the Spanish as Pimeria Alta, the land of the upper Pima people, or Apacheria, the land of the Apache, is now called Arizona.

The Dragoon Mountains in the southeastern corner were once home to the Chiricahua Apache. These mountains may have held the secret location of a mine that yielded gem-quality turquoise.

But just as the burial place of the Apache chief Cochise went to the grave with the one white man he trusted, Indian agent Tom Jeffords, so was the mine's location lost.

Or was it?

Chapter One

FAITH BECKET HEARD the rumors that smart men in the Arizona Territory stepped aside for him.

She listened to the whispers about women who shivered in anticipation of drawing his attention.

She paid heed to those who boasted that he knew every Apache trick and water hole, for he had been raised with Taza and Naiche, the sons of Cochise.

She was cautioned by the claims that he rode the outlaw trail after his father died in Yuma Prison.

But foolhardy souls whose need was desperate sometimes ignored the whispers and the warnings.

Faith Becket was a woman in need and desperate.

Delaney Carmichael was the man.

He had the look of the land. Hard, unpredictable, and dangerous.

Overhead, the sun burned fiercely on the parched earth streets of Prescott. Faith smoothed the front of her gown before she approached where he stood alone, leaning against the corner wall of the mercantile. He was tall, wide-shouldered, with a lean, dark face. His high cheekbones were shadowed by the slant of his battered, flat-crowned hat.

Beyond a sparse move of his head, he did not acknowledge that he was aware of her. She fought the chill at the base of her spine and held her place. She had come to beg, even if innate pride made the act a bitter one.

"Mr. Carmichael—"

"No."

Faith looked up at his face and stared at his eyes. She realized that even the desert offered a promise of life. Delaney Carmichael's eyes were the same tawny shades as desert rock. But, just as the miracle gift of rain brought unexpected beauty to the land, so did the flash of amber and green in his eyes offer her the gift of hope.

He wouldn't look directly at her. She sensed an intensity of heat to his gaze that rivaled that of the sun until she blinked. The heat was gone. Still, she stared and felt as if she were looking into shadows, for his gaze seemed to hold the secrets of a man who had seen too much, and survived.

Faith's past almost overtook her own thoughts. She knew what it was to struggle to survive. It was part of the reason she stood there, refusing to be dismissed.

"For three weeks you've ignored my father's messages. Now you won't talk to me. Why?"

"Silence is an answer."

"Perhaps to you, Mr. Carmichael. I can't accept it."

Each word was starched, compelling Delaney to look at the young woman planted in front of him on the wooden sidewalk. There was no pleading in her voice. No flirtatious manner. He· shoe tips were worn and dusty, attesting to the long walk she had made into town. Her calico skirt was faded, and her hands, alight for a moment on barely discernible hips, were work-rough.

Sodbuster stock. Robert Becket's daughter. Delaney's decision was quick and brutal. Prideful, virginal, and trouble. The wind and sun had left their mark on her face, for all that she wore a bonnet, yet his gaze lingered. There was

a delicacy to her bone structure. Faith chose that moment
to look directly at him.

Sweet heaven! Delaney felt gut-punched. His lungs con-
stricted like the first time he had been forced to kill a man.
Her eyes were the color of skystone: bright turquoise with
stunning flashes of gold woven like matrix in them. Long
ago he had been promised that one day he would find the
mate to the skystone he wore on a rawhide thong around
his neck.

He had been a boy then. Now he was a man who did
not believe in promises. Anger rose inside him that he had
to check his involuntary move to touch the stone. It had
always felt cool, soothing in its place. Now a hot, almost
burning sensation spread out from where the stone touched
his skin. He took a deep shuddering breath and released it
to ease the tension that gripped his body.

The need remained to touch the skystone. A need strong
enough to send his blood pumping with a fevered surge.
Delaney had to exert himself to tamp it down. His gaze
cooled. She was a woman. Once need for a woman had
ordered his life and cost others theirs. But that, too, had
been long, long ago.

He noted, resented, and then buried the knowledge that
he had to force himself to breathe evenly, to look away from
her and her bewitching eyes.

Insulting. Rude. Arrogant. Faith spoke the words silently
to herself and gritted her teeth. She knew what he saw
when he looked at her. She was piqued to her feminine
core. There had been no time and less energy to devote to
primping. It would have served her no purpose if she had.
The long walk and stifling heat would have taken its toll,
had already done so. She could feel sweat collect and pool
down her back. Delaney Carmichael could go to blazes in
a basket if her appearance offended him!

"See ya found him, Miz Becket."

Faith half-turned, and shaded her eyes, before she smiled. "Oh, yes, Mr. Abbott, thank you."

Tolly Abbott lumbered across the street toward them, wiping his face with a bandanna. He was a thick-bodied man, full-bearded with an unkempt, windblown stand of gray whiskers.

"Del," he muttered as he joined them, resettling his hat firmly on his head.

Delaney acknowledged the greeting with a curt nod.

"Miz Becket's pa's mighty anxious to get south. Ya plan on takin' 'em?"

"We haven't had a chance to talk yet, Mr. Abbott," Faith answered, afraid that Delaney Carmichael would walk away.

"Ya ain't, huh? Sure enough hot, ma'am." Tolly directed the rest of his questions to Delaney. "Ain't ya got no sense? Why're ya standing out here? Take Miz Becket over to the café. Bet's got lemonade."

"Oh, no. I wouldn't—I mean, that would be an imposition on Mr. Carmichael. What I have to say won't take that long."

"Tole yore pa he's the best there is 'round here. Hell with a gun. Good man in a brawl, too. Knows every darn water hole an' seep 'tween here an' the border. Tracks near good as an 'Pache, too. Why, one time he got hisself cornered by three Ute up 'round Defiance an' he walked—"

"Tolly, ain't you got business down at your livery?"

"Sure, Del, sure. Jus' tryin' to help Miz Becket here an' her pa."

"Don't."

"Now, just one moment, you can't . . ." Faith nearly choked swallowing her words of protest. Delaney had not moved. But she shivered with the sudden impact that he was now somehow coiled, ready to walk or strike, she was not sure which, and yet, there was no visible sign that she could pin her feeling upon.

It was simply there. Like the man. Like the desert. Unpredictable. Dangerous. And hard. She would not forget again.

"Jassy's down to the livery, Tolly. Best you go see what he wants."

It was an order, nothing less. Faith knew it and so did Tolly.

"Ain't stablin' that mule of his, Del. Tole him so. Ain't gonna do it." He tipped the brim of his hat to Faith and with his lumbering stride left them.

"Are you always so rude? Tolly didn't mean any harm."

"Tolly never does. And if *rude* gets the job done, ma'am, well, I don't need to say more."

"Job done? Oh, I understand. Getting rid of me. How do you manage to get on, Mr. Carmichael, when you ignore people who offer you a decent job?"

"I ain't got a corral on that, ma'am. You're doing just fine ignoring the fact that I don't want to talk. Don't want a job."

If a thought could become a physical act, Faith knew she could be hanged for what she was thinking. But her need to hire this man did not stem from stubbornness; it was a matter of survival.

"Just listen to me. We can't stay in Prescott any longer. You may not realize how important it is for us to reach our land claim. We need time to scout the land, set up a proper irrigation system, and build a home. The Homestead law allows three years to show the improvements before we have to pay an additional dollar per acre fee. To some, that may not be a hardship, not if there's money enough to hire men to do the work. We can't hire help, but there's enough to pay you to get us there."

Delaney leaned back against the wall, crossed his arms over his chest, and slanted her a puzzled look from beneath his hat brim. "Cattlemen toss a cup of water over the land and call it irrigated."

"Fraud, Mr. Carmichael. Farmers are well aware of all the methods cattlemen employ to hold back land from them. We will do things legally. And we've already been warned about the cattlemen. No one is going to stop us from claiming the land we paid for."

Delaney stared above her head, dismissing the way she said *cattlemen,* like the word soured her mouth. He had no great love for them himself.

"Well?" she prompted.

"Ain't you heard? 'Pache are riding."

"From the talk in town they always are. *Haven't* you *heard* that the army issued a bulletin that assures all settlers coming into the territory that they will make every effort to patrol known trails?"

"Ma'am, for three hundred years men have been trying to run the Apache out of the territory. They ain't done it yet. Ain't about to. The army can't even keep them on the reservations. So take their bulletin and their assurances and use them to light your campfire. That's all they're good for."

"Obstacles, Mr. Carmichael, are meant to be overcome."

"The truth, Miz Becket, ain't to be denied."

Faith tapped her foot in annoyance. She was afraid that what he said was the truth and not to be denied. She had even tried to tell her father that approaching this man would be a wasted effort, but he had insisted. With her head bowed, she prayed for patience and then tried again.

"Didn't we offer you enough money?"

"No."

"Just no? Well, then, tell me how much money it takes to buy a man like you?"

With a quick, yet almost lazy shift of his body, Delaney half-turned and swept her back against the wall. Faith contained a cry as he towered over her. Beyond his brief touch on her shoulder, he made no other attempt to hold her, but she didn't move.

He studied her face with eyes that could track a man over desert sand and rock. Her chin, with a slight cleft, rose, but the rounded curve softened its most determined set. Her eyes met his directly, hot with pride. She had the kind of mouth that made a man look twice. Delaney was man enough to look his fill. The ready stance of her lithe body was set for battle. A grin, reckless and taunting, kicked up the corner of his mouth.

"Maybe money ain't my price, duchess."

The proposal was meant to shock her. Faith was quite sure of that. It worked. She was shocked, but not, she was just as certain, the way he had meant her to be. She was stunned to find herself angry that there was no desire in his eyes. For a moment under the blistering sun, she stared at the finely molded planes of his face. Reluctantly she turned her head to the side and stared out over the street. Her father called her wholesome, and she believed him, but that didn't give Delaney Carmichael the right to mock her.

"Everything they say about you is true, isn't it?"

Her tone condemned him like a preacher set against Satan. Delaney refused to acknowledge the hurt in her eyes. He stepped back and away from her to resume his leaning stance. He knew himself to be slow to rile, but the duchess grated his nerve ends.

Duchess. She was anything but in looks. Her manner now, that was another tale. His gaze shifted to the doorway across the street from them. He watched three men come out of the land office. More trouble. Miners, sodbusters, or cattlemen, it didn't matter to him what they were. They wanted land, and Delaney knew that the boundaries of the reservations would once again be pushed back. It had been nearly two years since John Clum had resigned as the Indian agent at San Carlos, the largest of the five Apache reservations. The fools in Washington couldn't see the worth of his demand to raise his salary and give him two additional companies of Indian police to run the reservation. The army, the merchants that supplied them, as well as the citizens of the territory refused to see merit in his plans. Or so they claimed. Delaney knew it was greed, pure and simple, that resulted in John leaving.

His gaze hardened as he watched the three men slap each other on the back before they walked down toward Whiskey Row. In two years the continued discovery of gold and silver at the edges of reservation land had the government nibbling at the boundaries to give the land away to whites. Along with that crime, goods that were to be sent to the reservations were diverted to the miners, and what was left for the Indians was inedible and insufficient.

There had been times when he actively disliked the strutting John Clum, but the man had been daring to give the San Carlos Apache a chance to speak their minds on the advisory council he started. Delaney knew how hard John had to fight to get the army to accept an Indian police force along with a court where Clum and an Apache sat in judgment. He could forgive John his personal ambition to make San Carlos succeed after he brought in four hundred and fifty rebellious Mimbreños from the Warm Springs agency in New Mexico along with renegade Chiricahua under Geronimo.

What he couldn't forgive Clum for was leaving the Apache that trusted him at the mercy of the army that wanted them wiped out from memory.

At the slight move Faith Becket made at his side, Delaney glanced at her but didn't say anything for a moment. He wasn't a man given to impulsive moves or to curiosity. He'd seen men die for either or both. Yet, before he could stop himself, he asked why her father had sent her to talk to him.

"Have we broken some unknown law out here?"

"Pardon?" he asked, puzzled.

"Talking to a woman, Mr. Carmichael. Does that break some male territorial law? Or does it offend you personally?"

"Didn't mean for you to think I don't like women, duchess. Like them well enough," he drawled, then grinned. "In their place. Now, why did your father send you?"

"His leg is broken," she replied quickly, unwilling to spar verbally over his thoughts on a woman's place.

"There's more," he prompted, swearing at himself for giving in to the urge to know and to keep her here a bit longer.

"He was jumped and beaten after he won heavily in what was to be a friendly card game. It happened the first night we arrived here. That's why he kept sending you messages to come and see him. If it wasn't for Tolly Abbott finding my father, I don't know what would have happened to him. We were lucky, too, that Dr. Holliday set his leg without charge, since he lost everything."

No pity asked for, none given. Delaney had to respect her. But he was annoyed with his reaction to her honey-rich voice. It made him feel . . . restless.

A razor edge of anger tainted his words. "Holliday ain't a doctor. He's a dentist. When he's sober, which ain't often, duchess. An' he's snake mean."

Faith shook her head in denial. The pale-skinned young man that she had met had been gracious and kind to her and her father, despite his sorrowful air. She remembered his soft, southern accent and the piercing blue of his eyes when he refused her offer to barter for his services.

Delaney wasn't going to waste his time arguing with her. He found himself wondering again at the foolishness of men who dragged their families into this barren land under the newly passed Desert Land Act to file their twenty-five-cent-an-acre claims on six hundred and forty acres of hell.

But then, hell was where he called home.

To check his forward move, Faith grabbed hold of his arm. "You can't just walk away. Give me a reason why you refuse to work for us."

Both their gazes lit on her hand. Faith could feel the sinewy strength of his arm beneath her fingertips. And the sudden warmth. She fought off the dark response that shivered through her.

"Give me a reason. Or name your price," Faith demanded. "But don't, don't keep me begging."

"Woman shouldn't ever beg a man. For anything."

"I never had to until now."

"Stubborn little—"

"All we have to call home is the land my father filed his claim on." Faith made a desperate attempt to regain her self-control. Suddenly she realized that she still gripped his arm, and she snatched her hand away as if burned. "I'm wasting your time and my own. But we'll get there with your help or without it."

"Prescott's got a sheriff. Might see the day when it'll get civilized."

"Our land is south of a new mining camp called Tombstone. You know that territory. Why won't you scout for us?"

"If your pa told you that's what he wanted to hire me for, he lied. He wants a gun."

The underlying bitterness in his voice surprised her. Before Faith thought what to answer him, she was distracted by two women who stepped out from the doorway of the mercantile. They started toward them, but the older woman spotted Delaney and with an abrupt about-face dragged the younger woman after her. For some unknown reason Faith was annoyed when the younger woman looked back several times and smiled at Delaney.

"Best be on your way, duchess."

She felt a stab of hurt for him. His slight move brought her attention to the weapon he wore as if it were a part of his body. All this time and she had most deliberately avoided looking at his gun. The gunbelt was worn, the buckle tarnished. The unadorned wood grip gleamed from a recent oiling where it rested in the plain leather holster. A restless shift of his body made the weapon cant out from his narrow flanked hip. Faith was struck by the thought that he was a man alone, with no one to care for him.

There was a threadbare look to his denim pants, and his blue shirt showed its wear and clumsy mending. His boots were scuffed and worn at the heels. She made note of each detail as her gaze tracked its way up the long length of his legs.

Faith knew she was staring, lingering overlong on the breadth of his shoulders, the sun-browned skin of his throat, and the intriguing set of his mouth. He was clean shaven, but she had a feeling that before dusk his slightly squarish chin would carry the dark stubble that matched his near-black hair.

"Finished?" he asked in a deep, almost predatory tone. "Woman looks over a man like she's buying a stud, an' he can't be blamed for taking it as an invite."

"No. I never meant that." Faith despaired to feel the heated flush that stole into her cheeks. Sweat trickled down her temples, and she had to wipe it away. "Is what Tolly said about you true? Do you know every seep and water hole from here to the border?"

"I know enough to survive."

"A man should have some other purpose in life besides surviving."

"Now, there's men who'll take exception to that. Surviving out here takes some purpose, and most folks make do by minding their own business."

"And by being very good with their guns, Mr.—"

"No mister. Delaney'll do. Folks hereabouts don't stand on ceremony, duchess."

"Thank you for those kind words of advice," she snapped, irritated with his continued drawled *duchess*.

"Warringer's got a barrel of clean water inside the doorway of the mercantile, if you want a drink before you leave."

"I know." His dismissal rankled. Faith almost turned on her heel and left him. She had to remind herself what was at stake. It was enough to stop her from doing exactly as he suggested.

Delaney hid a grin as he lifted his makings from his shirt pocket. She was stubborn, all right. A woman like this might make a go of it in the territory. If some Indian didn't lift her scalp. If some woman-hungry miners didn't get hold of her first. If the cattle kings let her live. If the trek across the mountains and desert didn't kill her.

"Mind?" he asked, already sprinkling his tobacco on the curved thin paper he held.

She shook her head, watching each of his deft moves. A quick lick of his tongue sealed the cigarette. Faith was caught staring at his mouth. For just a moment their gazes locked, and lightning scored her nerve ends. She looked down at his hands. His fingers were long and scarred, and surprisingly, his nails were pared and clean. The seven-hundred-and-fifty-mile journey west from Kansas had proved to her how little some men thought of cleanliness. Would those hands be gentle when touching a woman? she asked herself, and then dismissed her curiosity in the next moment. The heat and rawness of the territory were helping her to forget that a woman would not think such a thought about any man.

He struck the match against the wall, watched it flare, and raised it. Delaney inhaled and released the smoke, staring at its upward curl. "If you'd like," he said, tilting his hat brim forward, "I'll get a wagon from Tolly and ride you back to where you're camped." It was a reluctant offer at best. But it was the only one he was going to make her.

"That's kind of you." Faith prayed the flare of hope she felt was not revealed in the look she gave him. "And then will you talk to my father?"

They both glanced at the high-sided wagon rolling past them, its wheels screeching for want of grease.

"Can't rightly figure your pa sending you after me. Not after Tolly got done talking to him."

"Tolly wasn't the only one. Opie Burgess said some, and there were others who talked." She scored her lip with the edge of her teeth and hesitated. "Is it true that you not only track as well as an Apache, but that you—"

" . . . lived with them?" he finished for her, disgust evident in his voice. "Like I said, I know enough to get by."

She hadn't meant to ask or pry, but gossip had raised her curiosity, and now, having met him, she wanted to know more. Tolly Abbott had found a willing ear when he spoke to her father, and unashamedly, she had listened. There was the story of a man he had killed near Kingman who had called him a liar when Delaney claimed the horse the man rode was stolen from an Apache. A tinhorn had died for the poor judgment of calling him a cheat. But Tolly had a tale of Delaney taking a wounded miner out of the Galiuro Mountains and bringing him to Fort Thomas. "Good man to have on your side," had been Tolly's sage pronouncement, tacked on after each relished telling of Delaney's reputation.

"Guess hearing all that talk frightened you."

His uncanny perception of Faith's thoughts startled her. She hesitated once again. "Some," she answered honestly. "If you are as good as they say, why won't you work for us? Opie Burgess said you quit working for the railroad last month."

"Opie's an old gossip."

"Be that as it may. It's the truth. You're out of a job. I'm told that I am a fair cook. The children, if you are worried, will all mind." She couldn't resist touching the mended tear on his shirtsleeve with her fingertip. "I darn neatly, too."

"Those are mighty fine inducements. But how many days can you go without water? How many miles can you walk, duchess? You're heading down into country that men shed blood to tame and ain't finished with yet. They wrangled cows out of brush that'd tear your delicate white skin to shreds. They've fought and killed their share of men— white, Mex, and Indian alike—to keep what they claimed. Sodbusters moving in on miners and cattlemen are just gonna cause bloodshed."

"Stop it. I won't be frightened off by your talk."

"You should be. The desert's a mighty thirsty land, and it's got one law. Learn it and never, ever forget it, duchess. First come, first served. Be it water, land, or a woman."

Faith heard more than his warnings. She listened again to his refusal. She thought of her father's demand that she come here to convince this man to lead them through hostile territory. There were no clear-cut trails like the Oregon that would guide them. She knew how little money they had left. Faith knew the need that had driven them to this barren, godforsaken land. Bitterly she totaled the cost. Her mother's death along the way. The death of her own dreams.

For a long minute Faith stared at Delaney. Hard, unpredictable, and dangerous. He was all that and more.

"Nothing I say will change your mind?"

"My gun's not for hire." Delaney crushed his half-smoked cigarette under his boot.

"There are men in this town who hate you. They had plenty to say about you, too. They said you would kill a man for less than the price of a decent meal. I guess that's the real reason you're refusing. There's no killing to be done."

Faith stepped back and away from the chilling look he shot her. She angled her head high. "I have one last question for you. Do you know where I can find a man called Chelli?"

"Stay the hell away from him."

"You're not available. I don't have much time or choice." She pleated the calico skirt to hide her trembling hands. She had used up most of her courage to brave talking to him; now she would be forced to begin again. But she had told him the truth. There was no choice. They had to get away from Prescott and soon.

"Woman, what was wrong with the men where you came from? You don't belong—"

"There was nothing wrong with them," she stated, her body rigid with tension.

"Why the hell didn't you marry one of them and stay put?"

Delaney would never know the cost she paid to look up at him, or the price in pain for her to answer him.

"I did. The day we were wed, men rode out to our new home. *Cattlemen*, Mr. Carmichael. They didn't come to pay a social call. They didn't want us to farm the land my husband bought. He foolishly took exception to their methods of persuasion. I buried him on my wedding night."

There was more. He knew that, just as he knew he'd get his boots tangled with this piece of range calico if he gave in to the rush of compassion that sizzled inside him. No, he wasn't about to do it. But there was a welter of pain blazing in her eyes that a sweep of her short, burnished lashes hid quickly from him.

"If you can't or won't tell me where I can find this man Chelli," she announced in a brisk tone, fighting off her own demons, "I'll find someone who can."

"He'll rob you folks of whatever you've got and leave you somewhere to die. Well," he amended, his gaze sweeping her from head to toe, "maybe not you, duchess. You, he might sell south."

Her chin rose a notch. "Then consider us warned. And I'm not a helpless woman, Mr. Carmichael."

The regal tilt of her head, the strength of the conviction in her honey-rich voice that she was going south regardless of his advice, forced him to answer.

"Try down at the Prairie Dog on Whiskey Row."

Her curt nod seemed to dismiss him more than thank him as she turned with military precision and walked away from him.

He stared for a moment at the gentle sway of her hips, noted the soft drape of her skirt, and muttered, "At least the duchess had the sense to leave off stays and six petticoats." But she was heading in the wrong direction. Delaney almost called out to her, then shrugged. He'd let her wander about a bit, he needed some time. Damned if he knew why!

He stepped to the edge of the wooden walk and motioned to the man who had waited patiently hidden in the shadow of the alley.

Chapter Two

"GUESS I'LL TRAIL after her. Damn fool woman ain't got the good sense God gave a mule thinking she's gonna hire Chelli."

"One mule would go far to ease the hunger of many, *skeetzee*."

A few strands of gray threaded the dark hair of the Apache that had spoken. Delaney saw that the fine webbing of lines had deepened with age on a face that brought him a rush of boyhood memories. The frame of the once proud warrior was now gaunt. The Apache's statement and the visible signs of constant hunger were the result of life on a white man's reservation.

Delaney's gaze hardened as his eyes met those of Seanilzay by his side. "Is there trouble again? Since Clum left—"

"Always there is that, Del-a-ney. Anglos came to us with more pinole. Many were sick."

"Oh, Christ!" Delaney closed his eyes and felt his stomach roil. "Didn't anyone listen to the warnings after the last time?" He didn't expect an answer, nor did he get one. "What was it this time, broken glass or strychnine mixed with the ground corn and sugar?"

"The two. Does this matter?"

"Damn them! And yes, it matters." His hands fisted at his sides with the helplessness he felt. How could children be protected from this sort of viciousness? Pinole was a favorite treat of the Apache, and too many knew how they hungered for the sweet. By keeping the Indians on short rations, they were made vulnerable to attacks like this one, when white men came to the reservations under the guise of friendship. "What happened with the new inspector? I thought he would have enough evidence to get rid of Hart for fraud."

"Hammond took more of the western land. He claims it did not belong to us. There is a mine site that he sold to the son of Hayt."

"The son of the commissioner of Indian Affairs?"

"The same. He will not give up Hart to Anglo justice. Once more the cattle are too small or sick to eat. They no longer carry Hammond's special brand."

"Cursed gold! I hope to hell they find nothing."

"They knew there was gold before they took the land."

Delaney glanced skyward. "A few months ago Archie McIntosh's letter was published in the Phoenix *Herald*. I heard that General Fisk was going down to San Carlos to see for himself what was going on. He could get word to the secretary of the Interior. Schurz seems fair. When Jeffords urged Geronimo and Ponce to return from Mexico with Juh and Nolgee, he had to see for himself what was happening. Why didn't he do something?"

"He wants San Carlos back, but they do not listen."

"And Geronimo? He would not keep silent."

"They came to the reservation weary from fighting with the soldiers."

"Clum tried to show you how to work. Find a way to prove that the beef contractors tampered with the scales for weighing the cattle. Maybe someone from the Dutch

Reformed Church can get the bureau to listen. Or get McIntosh to go to the Board of Indian Commissioners. He saw for himself the graft and greed. Men like Hart and Hammond can't run the agency."

"Will you do as your father before you?"

Delaney looked away. "I don't know. But that isn't why you left the reservation and risked much to come here."

"The husband to Victorio's daughter was killed near Alma. Many think to leave San Carlos."

"Victorio knows no other path but revenge."

"He fights to give back what is stolen from all his people."

"Fighting isn't always the best answer," Delaney snapped, his gut curling at the thought of another outbreak.

"And the man Brodie, he searches still. He comes too close—"

"Then kill him," Delaney stated without emotion.

"That is for you to do. He took your *iszán* for his own. He stole your land."

"No. She was never my woman. Elise used me for him. And the land was never really mine for him to steal."

"Naiche will not raise his hand. He is weak, and there is a son."

Delaney's emotional detachment fled. "He's not mine." The words were grated from between his clenched teeth. But with these words the past burst from the darkest corner of his mind. Only for a moment and then, with a ruthless thrust, he shoved it back, deep into his memory's graveyard.

"There's more for you to tell me?" Delaney finally asked.

"It comes like the flow of sand upon the desert. The winter's cold without blankets or clothes. The food that comes too late to feed the belly of a hungry child. The Anglos that come in the dark to destroy the poor crops before our people can harvest them. And the hate like that of Elías who brought our enemies the Papago to kill us sweeps the land. Your iron rails grow in number, and soon more will come. They all want us dead."

"No one will forget Elías and the Camp Grant massacre. There was outrage on the part of whites. And it is good to remember that Eskiminzin still trusted Whitman even as he carried his daughter's body and returned to Camp Grant. And it saddens me as it does my brothers not to know the fate of the children that were taken by the Papago. But this was years past, and sometimes it is best to forget."

"My memory is long and as sad as my brother's. Crook and his hate of Whitman is not a memory to cast aside. There are many who remember that he sided with Elías as doing right to kill women and children when they were helpless without the protection of their braves."

Delaney was quiet. His memory alive now with the words Eskiminzin had spoken when he killed his white friend Charles McKinney: "Any coward can kill his enemy. It takes a brave man to kill his friend." This he had done to convince his people that there could never be friendship with the Anglos, after the cavalry detachment from Fort Apache rode through his new camp in Arivaipa Canyon and opened fire.

There was more that he remembered, but the darting shift of his friend's eyes reminded him of the danger to him if he was found here.

Delaney rolled another cigarette and lit it. He gazed at the empty street, smoking, and then asked, "Is Yancy still working for Brodie?"

"He rides for him. Sometimes he works for the Clantons."

"They still stealing cattle?"

"Brodie buys them, as do others. It is not good to ask questions of these *n'dé*."

"My *skeetzee* is right not to ask questions of these men."
Delaney impatiently crushed out his smoke.

"What of the *iszán* who asks you to bring her to our
lands?"

Delaney glanced at Seanilzay and grinned. "Does my
friend want her?"

"Her skin is too white. Her tongue sharp. For many suns
you have walked alone. This is not a good life-way for
a *n'dé*."

"It's good for this man. I like alone just fine."

"To see the eyes of this *iszán* is to remember."

"Oh, I have, Seanilzay. Believe me, I have."

"It is not good to forget all teachings in the time away
from us."

"I forgot nothing." For all that Delaney spoke softly,
there was an underlying harshness. "Tell Naiche that. Tell
him I have forgotten nothing. And tell my brother that I'm
coming home."

"It is time."

Delaney touched the stone hidden beneath his shirt. "Soon
I will repay my debt."

"May we live and see each other again." Seanilzay slipped
away on his soft moccasins.

Delaney wished his thoughts could slip away as softly.
As easily. Home. Home and Elise. Once he wove those
two words together as necessary to him as breathing. Elise,
his woman. Now Brodie's wife. Bitterness coated the inside
of his mouth. He wiped his lips with the back of his
hand and glanced down the street. His duchess was finally heading in the right direction not too far ahead. He
eyed his departed quarry for a long minute, deliberated
his sanity, then followed her. He was not about to question why the sight of her helped him keep the past buried.

The morning had bloomed cloudless and hot, as most of the days this late in spring. The clear skies and already burning sun promised another afternoon of hellish heat. If anyone moved, it was with slow deliberation. Delaney walked soft and easy for a big man. His duchess never once looked behind her to see him following.

Faith ignored most of the men who braved the heat and loitered in front of the assay office. She shivered to hear them talk about the good citizens of Silver City who were offering two hundred and fifty dollars for every Apache scalp taken. Her attention was caught by the news that the Tombstone Mining and Milling Company was building a ten-stamp mill on the banks of the San Pedro. While Faith was uncertain what a ten-stamp mill was, she felt hope that the area near their land claim was being populated. She smiled as Opie Burgess doffed his hat and stopped her.

"Miz Becket, how's your father doing?"

"Better, thank you. He's able to hobble about for a bit."

"Glad to hear it. You finally get to talk to Delaney?"

"I'm afraid he wasn't interested."

"Figured he would be. Can't understand why he quit working for the Santa Fe. They just got that land grant from Congress to finish laying track that the A and P started. Gonna see railroads running right through this territory. 'Course, the news don't sit pretty with the freighters. I tell you that Delaney worked as a swamper for a while back?"

"I don't remember, Mr. Burgess. But, please, you must excuse me. I have an errand that can't wait."

Faith hurried off, unaware that Delaney was closing the distance between them. He had heard the last of what Opie said, but he wasn't reassured by the news. He had worked stints with the railroad since '66, when the Atlantic and Pacific first made plans to build a line from Springfield across Arizona to San Diego. The line went broke in the panic of '73 and he had quit, hoping that would be the end of them taking more of the Indian lands. But the Atchison, Topeka & Santa Fe Railroad officials grabbed the opportunity to pick up the lucrative land grants that had been awarded to the A & P. It took them three years, but they managed to get Congress to appropriate a grant of twenty sections for every mile of track laid in the territories of Arizona and New Mexico. All to aid the booming growth in California.

Opie stopped him, just as Delaney feared he would. Delaney kept his eyes on his quarry's rigid spine as she walked more slowly. He was aware that across the street Bet Tampas paused in her daily sweeping in front of her café to watch his duchess's progress.

"Del, tell us what you think about the Southern Pacific figuring on beating the Santa Fe with its line."

"Ain't much to say, Opie. They're planning to build across Indian land."

"They only got as far as Fort Yuma. You worked on the Texas line from Marshall. They lost it all, didn't they?"

"Yeah. Same as the A and P in seventy-three." Delaney didn't know the men with Opie and so kept his thoughts to himself.

"You figure it's worth investing in them?" Opie asked, sensing that Delaney was distracted.

"If you hit a lucky strike and have money to throw away, it might be." But Delaney knew he lied. The government inducements offered to the railroads would earn profit. They offered them free rights-of-way, free use of timber and minerals to build the lines, and twenty sections of land for every mile of track laid. Along with this were the monies paid, sixteen thousand dollars if the track was laid across flat land, thirty-two thousand if laid across foothills, and forty-eight thousand dollars if laid in the mountainous country. It was a damn profitable venture when you added in the wheeling and dealing that involved the Arizona and New Mexico legislatures.

"I heard that Fred Harvey drove a shrewd bargain with the Santa Fe." At Delaney's questioning look, the man introduced himself. "Marcus Campbell."

"He's a cousin to John, our new territorial delegate to Congress," Opie explained.

Delaney nodded but did not offer his hand. He saw that his duchess's steps had slowed, and he wanted to leave.

"Do you know about Harvey opening another of his establishments like the one in Topeka?" Marcus asked.

"Know he got the Santa Fe to agree to give him all the profits while they foot the bill for his buildings, transportation, furnishings, and workers."

"That was privileged information."

"It sure was," Delaney answered and walked away.

Faith, unaware, turned the corner ahead of Delaney. She did not alter her stride on the uneven boards as she managed to open the ties of her bonnet to tuck a few stray damp curls beneath its back edge. She felt as limp as wet laundry after a rain and tried not to think about what she was going to be forced to do. Inwardly she cringed to hear the crude shouts and masculine laughter that came from the open doors of the saloons she passed.

Delaney caught the sun's bright gleam on her hair. The color reminded him of warm, golden brown honey. He licked his lips and wondered if there were remnants of the manners his mother had tried to instill in him before she died that kept him following the duchess.

One man bolted from an open doorway as she walked by and was about to step out after her when Delaney's left-hand shove sent the man flying back inside. A self-mocking smile played about his lips. He had never before been a guardian angel to anyone. But the duchess had to know that Whiskey Row and any of its saloons were not places for the likes of her.

Faith's thoughts paralleled his. She dreaded the act of walking into a saloon. Sparing a quick glance to newspapers stacked behind a grimed window, she wondered if Delaney Carmichael's name had ever graced a front page. If it had, she hoped it was with a wanted offer. More likely, he would have been hailed as hero for another killing. He claimed that Prescott was becoming civilized, and she supposed that since it was once again the territorial capital it could be considered as such, but it was a far cry from what she knew civilized to be.

She refused to allow thoughts of her past to intrude now. A mongrel dog growled at her as she stepped down to cross an alley. She glanced at the dog prowling among the garbage strewn about and raised her skirt to hurry along. Stepping up to the sidewalk, she nearly toppled a sign that advertised beds for two bits. Flustered, Faith could sympathize with the horses hitched before the hotel, twitching their tails in the growing heat.

The slide of sweat trickled down her back, and she could feel a growing pool of wetness under her arms and between her breasts. She longed for a bath, a real bath with hot water and softly scented milled soap. It was almost impossible to keep herself and her long hair clean. Water, as she had been forced to learn, was far too precious to waste on bathing.

Two men, singing off-key and stumbling, nearly pushed her off the sidewalk. Faith shuddered and hoped she wouldn't face more of the same when she found Chelli. It was better to think of how her younger brothers resisted the temptation to bathe once they learned they had to haul the water from a trickling stream. Pris was another matter. Her little sister ran off to the stream whenever she could. Sometimes she envied Pris her innocence, even as she swore she would protect it.

Thoughts of Pris directed her back to the problem at hand. The journey to come would be through desert a good part of the way, if the map her father had was accurate. Not only was time pressing to find someone that knew what he was doing to take them to their claim, but the constant flux of miners into Prescott created a danger for her. She had to find someone today so that they could leave the area quickly.

Lost in her musings, Faith tripped on a warped board and barely managed to keep her balance. Looking up, she saw the brightly painted sign announcing that she had reached her destination. In glaring red letters against a rough wood board was the name PRAIRIE DOG.

She squared her shoulders, took a deep fortifying breath, and released it. Cursing Delaney Carmichael to the deepest hole in the desert, she stepped inside before she lost her courage. And gagged.

The assault of odors nearly staggered her. Sweat, spilled liquor, smoke, manure, and others that were unidentifiable melded together, even as she felt relief from the sun's glare and heat in the adobe's cool, shadowed interior. A few quick breaths through her mouth helped to overcome the sudden roil of her stomach.

It took her those few moments to realize that men had stopped talking, drinking, and playing cards. They simply sat and stared. She took one hesitant step forward. An absolute silence grew until it was almost tangible.

She consigned Delaney Carmichael to hell for forcing her to come into this place. Faith refused to look at anyone directly. She directed her gaze to the hard-packed earth floor and then toward the long board set on two barrels that served as a bar. She wanted to turn tail and run. Although there had not been a sound, she looked behind her to make sure the doors were still open.

The sight of Delaney Carmichael leaning against the doorframe, his thumbs tucked behind his gunbelt, a cocky grin splitting his lips and a suspicious gleam of devilry alight in his eyes, made her stand her ground.

Inwardly fuming, she turned back. "I am looking for a man called Chelli," she announced in a firm voice. When that brought no immediate response, she took another step forward and added, "Would any of you know where I can find him?"

"Can't anybody do? I'm—"

"Shush yore mouth, Blucee. Can't ya see worth a damn? Finish yore think juice, boy, or you'll pile up grief for yoreself."

The young man addressed as Blucee, who had half-risen from his chair, sat down hard. Hard and fast. The battered-looking miner that had issued the warning leaned over the table they shared and gripped his arm.

"That's Carmichael with the little lady," he whispered a shade too loudly. "Guess workin' that claim done cost ya yore sight."

Faith's cheeks flamed hot. Her teeth scored her bottom lip and broke the skin. She counted to three, prayed, and then suddenly rounded on Delaney.

"You refused my offer. Don't you dare prevent me from hiring someone else."

"Or what, duchess?"

"Del? Del, that you?"

Faith spun around and swayed. At the far end of the room a woman paused in a curtained doorway.

"Chelli," she called out over her shoulder as she tied the ends of her wrapper, "look who's back." And to Delaney she explained, "He's got a faro game going with Holliday and Earp, so c'mon back. You know you're always welcome here, Del."

It wasn't the woman's smile but the husky invitation in her voice that set Faith steaming. "Just a moment, please. I need to talk to Chelli."

"Honey, Chelli's real good for anything a woman wants, but talking ain't it. Get yourself out of here so there's no trouble."

Faith clenched her hands at her sides. "You don't understand. I want to offer him a job. A decent paying job."

"Like I said, we don't want trouble."

"Edna Mae," a male voice called out from somewhere behind the curtain, "bring us another bottle. An' you tell whoever's givin' you a hard time that you got yourself a deputy sheriff back here name of Virgil Earp."

"It's a lady looking to talk to Chelli."

The mocking laughter that followed mortified Faith.

"Hey, Virg," Delaney yelled, "thought you were heading south to prospect."

"Waitin' on my brothers. Wyatt and James are comin' from Dodge with their families."

"Dodge?" Faith whispered almost to herself. Panic tremored through her body. For a moment she couldn't think, couldn't speak.

"Want a drink, Del?" Edna Mae asked, moving to stand behind the bar.

"Please, I need to talk to Chelli now," Faith said.

"Chelli! Get out here!"

Faith shot Delaney an exasperated look at his shouted command. But when she looked back, she couldn't deny it had gotten her results. A buckskin-clad man now stood in the curtained doorway.

"You have need of me, *amigo*?"

"When hell chills. No, it's the duchess here."

Faith swore that every man there could hear her teeth grate together. Delaney's brutal assessment of Chelli's character seemed to be born out by the sight of the man himself. Her gaze was quick and sharp. His clothes were dirty, and while he was almost as tall as Delaney, he was heavier in build. A jagged scar marred his left cheek. His hair was thick and black and curled at the temples from sweat. His smile widened as he leisurely inspected her, but there was no warmth to be found in his dark eyes. A chill began somewhere deep inside her and spread out to her skin. Faith wanted to run.

"Well, ask him, duchess."

"I will. Mr. Chelli, we need a guide south. My father is willing to pay whatever you ask, but he wants to leave immediately."

Chelli didn't answer. He pulled out a chair from under a snoring miner and dumped him on the floor. A light kick of his boot sent the body rolling toward the corner. The miner never woke. With a sweep of his hand Chelli cleared the tabletop of glasses and empty bottles.

"Please," he offered with a sweeping gesture, "sit."

Faith had no desire to step farther into the saloon. She most certainly didn't want to get any closer to Chelli, but she felt as if Delaney was silently goading her to do just that. I am not a helpless woman, she repeated to herself. I am going to walk over there, sit down, and discuss the terms with him.

She managed two steps forward. Chelli smiled.

Suddenly from behind her Delaney whispered, "Remember what I told you, duchess."

"You would not think to cheat an *amigo* from honest work?" Chelli asked, tossing the chair aside and starting toward them.

"The day you work *honest*, Chelli, I'll hang up my gun."

"A man could die for such words."

"Anytime, *amigo*, anytime," Delaney drawled. "Let's go, duchess." He knew Chelli was about to get ugly, and he grabbed her arm. "Edna Mae, save that drink for me, I'll be by later."

Faith glared at Delaney's hand on her arm and then up at his face. "Have it right now. I'm not going anywhere with you. I haven't finished my business here."

"You sure have."

Toe to toe they stood. Faith looking up, blue fire blazing from her eyes, and Delaney coolly gazing down at her face. Neither one was about to give an inch.

Fool, irritating woman, he thought. "Now, I'm a right accommodatin' man most times, calico. This ain't one of them."

His other arm snaked out, hooked her around the waist, and then he hauled her over his shoulder.

"Not a word," he warned her.

"Del!"

He glanced back at Chelli. The man had braced his weight on the balls of his feet, and his hands were splayed out from his sides.

"I've got my hands full at the moment; otherwise, I'd oblige you. You've heard of women changin' their minds, ain't you? This is one of those times."

To the sounds of whistles and catcalls, Faith left the Prairie Dog saloon.

And now that he had her, Delaney wondered what the hell he was going to do with her.

Chapter Three

"HANG TIGHT, DUCHESS."

Faith could do nothing else. It was a long way down to the ground.

Delaney glanced up and down the street. His scowl warned off the few men who shot curious looks their way until they drifted out of sight. He gazed at Tolly's livery sign and began to walk toward it, his steps soft and easy so he wouldn't jounce his burden.

He could feel the heat of her body. She didn't even weigh all that much. Not enough to cause a sweat to break out. He blamed the sun. Her silence had him imagining that she was furious with him. He spared a thought to trying to apologize but knew she would never believe him. *He* didn't believe he was sorry for what he did.

Faith braced herself with her hands resting gingerly above the sweat-damp shirt on the small of his back. His body was warm where it pressed against hers, and she inhaled the faint scent of lye soap from his clothes. She knew that Delaney was hard. Hardheaded. Hard-hearted. Now she knew how hard his body was.

Her jaw ached with her effort to remain silent. She was not going to cause another scene that would be spread as gossip. She couldn't have her name bandied about at all.

Concentrating on watching the little dust clouds that he raised with every step, Faith vowed her revenge. Somehow, big as he was, she would make him pay not only for this embarrassment of being carried like a sack of flour, but for costing her the chance to leave Prescott quickly.

A little voice warned her that if the rumors about him were all true, his retribution would be harsh and swift. Faith cast aside that warning to the dung heap.

The hard press of his wide shoulder against her stomach kept her breathing shallow. The only decent mark she gave him was for not making one suggestive comment. And if she were being generous, she would credit him for not attempting to do more than hold her securely.

The pungent odor of manure told her where they were before she spotted the bottom poles of the corral and saw a wagon tongue. She heard Tolly's greeting. Well, she amended, it started out to be a greeting, but it ended with Tolly sputtering.

She prayed that Tolly would take Delaney to task for what he was doing. He didn't seem to be afraid to speak his mind to Mr. Carmichael. God was not listening.

"Tolly, shut up," Delaney ordered. "Get me a wagon hitched. Miz Becket's finished her business in town. It's time for her to leave."

Faith squirmed against his hold, longing to be put down.

Delaney had to resist the urge to slide her down his body. Slowly. Very slowly and held tight.

They both took a step back from each other as he gently lowered her to stand.

"Wait here," he commanded, drawing a harsh breath. "I'll light a fire under Tolly."

Faith merely lifted her brow and ignored him while she shook out the hem of her gown.

"Don't be putting on airs and pretend you ain't glad I got you outta there."

Her head snapped up. She directed a level, almost feral gaze at him. "*Airs*, Mr. Carmichael? Is that what you think I'm putting on?"

"Whatever you're doing ain't pretty, duchess. I'd chance saying you're angry."

"I am many things," she answered softly as she carefully but most deliberately curled her small hands into fists. "But angry does not quite come close to what I am."

Delaney gazed at her with narrowed eyes, targeting her mouth with a glance that briefly revealed frank male hunger. He watched as she nervously stepped to the side.

"I'm not the one who's going to hurt you, but Chelli now—"

"I don't wish to discuss it." Faith looked behind him. Before she gave thought to what she was going to do, she closed the distance between them.

Delaney merely shrugged and looked toward the gaping barn doors. "Tolly, hurry it up."

"Oh, Mr. Carmichael," Faith called in a singsongy voice. His gaze snapped back to her.

The impact of her small fisted hand landing solidly in his gut took his breath. His eyes widened. Shock, surprise, and one staggered step back along with Faith's helpful shove sent him flying into the horse trough.

She planted her fists on her hips. "I warned you that I wasn't a helpless woman."

"Duchess," he growled, swiping at the dripping water on his face.

"Faith, Mr. Carmichael. My name is Faith Ann Becket—"

"Thought you were married, *Miz Becket*?"

"You're cruel. Cruel and rude and arrogant and—"

" . . . and you want me."

"Want . . . you . . ." she sputtered, unable to believe that he baldly stated that. There he sat, tucking his hands behind his head, ignoring his hat which had fallen off. She blinked several times. He seemed to be enjoying his position. His dripping boots and long legs hung over either side of the wooden trough and he dared, after that outrageous remark, to grin up at her!

"Don't get in a snit, duchess. Water's right precious. Didn't figure I needed another bath what with just having one yesterday, but it's sure cooling." His gaze raked the flags of color in her cheeks. "Sure is hot and get hotter."

"Drowning," Faith pronounced with all the disdain she could muster, "is too good for the likes of you. Tolly, Tolly!" she shouted, turning toward the barn. "Please hurry!"

"Keep yore skirt on, I'm comin'."

"Didn't figure you for a temper, calico."

"Well, you *figured* wrong."

Delaney slid forward and rose to his full height slowly. "Figure that you're a woman with grit, too."

"If that was a compliment, thank you. If it was not, I couldn't care less what you think of me."

Delaney opened his gunbelt and set it down easy on the ground. He ran his large hands down the length of his legs, squeezing the water out. Faith had not moved. He couldn't see her face with the bonnet's brim shielding it, but the curving line of her breast, her slender waist, and agitated toe-tap held his gaze for a long, long minute.

Twice he opened his mouth to speak, and twice he closed it. She was still an armful of trouble. A soft, womanly armful, but trouble just the same.

It wasn't his place to get involved. He had troubles of his own that needed his attentions. But damn, if she didn't manage to make him feel guilty. Irritated him, too, like a burr rubbing a saddle sore.

Who did she think she was hauling off and punching him?

With a grunt of disgust Delaney squeezed what water he could from his shirt without taking it off.

Here he went after her, protected her from a bastard like Chelli, and what thanks did he get? A soaking when he had already had a bath.

That was a woman for you. Do your best and get nothing but grief. Well, let some other damn fool man take her where she wanted to go. He'd got by just fine minding his own business.

Anyway, her tongue was sharp. How could he listen to it, mile after mile, having his back razored? He had made a promise to go home. So home was damn close to where they had filed their land claim. Wasn't his worry. He'd travel fast and light.

Faith glanced nervously at the tall shadow he cast. Edging forward, she presented her back toward him. She wished for the courage to look at his face. She had not bargained on dealing with an angry man. And every sense warned her Delaney was angry.

Well, he deserved it! She would never, not if she lived to be sixty, admit to him that she was glad that he had followed her. There had been something cold and greedy about Chelli that frightened her. If Delaney Carmichael's method of removing her from the saloon had been less than any lady could have wished for, she forgave him. It would stretch the limits of Christian charity, but she could do it.

Not that he would ever know. She could still feel the imprint of his hard body pressing hers. And that mocking remark burned in her memory! *"Maybe money ain't my price, duchess.*" Did he think she was a foolish woman who believed he would barter himself for her? She had never faced a man's desire. Not even—no, it was best to leave those thoughts of Martin buried. Just as he was.

"You know a man's mettle gets tested right early," he noted, willing her to turn around and look at him.

"So does a woman's, Mr. Carmichael," she replied with a catch in her voice, refusing to turn around.

"Figure that's a start."

"Start?" she repeated softly, clearing her throat.

Now, you'd think a smart woman would understand that he was trying to apologize, he thought. And if she was smart, she would face a man so he could do it properlike. He'd told her a woman shouldn't have to beg a man. Didn't she know that the same held true for him? Not only did the calico duchess have a tongue that wanted curbing badly, she needed a lesson in manners, too.

"Figure we got plenty to get straight between us. Like you remembering to call me Delaney."

She grabbed hold of her skirt with trembling hands, daring to hope, almost afraid that she was reading more into what he was trying to say. Fool man! How was she to know what he meant? Did he expect her to make it easy for him after what he had subjected her to?

"Since I won't be seeing you again, Mr. Carmichael, I can't see what difference it makes what I call you," she blurted out. "Seems to me that right now you'd better go light that fire under Tolly. He's taking a long time to hitch up a wagon."

Delaney glanced up at the open barn doors and then back at Faith. "Most likely he's standing right inside, listening to every word."

"And I suppose he'll be telling anyone who'll listen to him what happened?"

"Should be good for a few free drinks. Got to admit, it makes a fine tale." Delaney almost smiled but stopped himself. "Ain't many men could claim they put me down so easily." He ran his fingers through his hair and shook his head like a wet pup before he slicked it back. Shaking the excess water dripping from his pants and boots, he added, "I'd bet your name is gonna be whispered over every campfire from here to Tucson."

He wished the words unsaid. She hadn't made a sound, but her body went from soft to rigid before his eyes. Suddenly the thought of any man whispering her name sat like a lump of uncooked flour in his gut.

Faith's feeling almost echoed his. But her stomach roiled with nausea. She closed her eyes, prayed for guidance, and decided to ignore his remark. She couldn't drop a hint, couldn't let him know anything more about her now. Maybe there would be time later, maybe never.

"Seems to me," she said, her light tone forced as she mimicked his drawl, "that won't do me a bit of good. I still don't have what I came to town for."

"That ain't exactly true." Hell and damnation! Now he'd gone and done it. He pinned his gaze on her, his body tense.

Why was he agreeing to lead this woman and her family down hell's own path?

And damn her! She made him sweat, waiting for her to finally turn around. Her eyes met his, wide, bright, and glistening. He saw her lips move but heard only a faint murmur. Delaney was bewildered by the burning sensation that filled his chest. This time he had to touch his stone. There was no coolness, no soothing . . . just heat. And her eyes . . . Christ! If the sight of them didn't cost him his breath, her smile nearly rocked him back on his heels.

Faith Ann Becket was pretty. Pretty as the desert coming into bloom after the rain. But she was no fragile desert flower that would quickly fade and die. There was strength in her. A woman's strength that held a warm beauty all its own. Her smile made her face as radiant as the sunset that swept its red and gold colors to paint away the harshness of a land that only a man who loved it could see.

But Delaney had loved once. Betrayal was its cost. He had paid its demanded price.

He had thought that she didn't have the good sense God gave to a mule. With an ironic smile, he admitted to himself, that made them two of a kind.

"Guess you hired me."

"My father—"

"Oh, no, duchess. This is between you and me." He saw her smile fade and ignored her bewildered gaze. "We agree?"

Caught up in his sudden about-face, Faith looked away. She missed the intensity of his narrowed eyes and the bittersweet smile on his lips. But she nodded, afraid to question his terms.

"Dagnabbit!" Tolly yelled, lumbering out from the barn. "Took ya two long enough. Man's near to dyin' awaitin' on ya. Wagon's all hitched 'round back."

Delaney snatched up his hat and gunbelt. He shot Tolly a furious look and began walking toward him.

"Now, Del, afore ya go sayin' a word, I'll tell ya I figured ya'd help this little gal. Saddled yore horse an' tied him back of the wagon. Bet Tampas left yore saddlebags near the back door of the café so's ya won't lose time. Stuffed 'em full of yore clean shirts an' such."

"Tolly, someday you'll go too far. Someday," Delaney predicted, stalking closer to the old man who stood his ground, "you're gonna figure what a man's gonna do wrong. And when that someday comes, Tolly, I just hope to hell I'm around."

"Miz Becket, don't pay him no mind. Hie yoreself out back. Set a canteen under the seat so's ya have water. Don't be worryin' on where it come from. It's clean and new. Warringer put it on Del's bill. An' son," he added, looking up at a towering Delaney, "get to live as long as me afore ya get to believin' I can't figure the right measure of a man."

"You sonofabitchin' bastard! What else did you tell Delaney? You stood there talkin' to him long enough."

Powerful hands gripped the Indian's shoulders and lifted him until his feet dangled free of the ground.

"Talk, damn you."

"He knows what I was told to say."

"No more than that? And don't lie to me."

"No more." The Apache's head snapped back and forth from the furious shaking. "I told him no more," he repeated, kicking his feet uselessly.

The release was sudden, and the Indian landed in a crumpled heap on the ground. He kept his gaze lowered until he saw that the man had moved away and then he looked up at his tormentor. His hand rose slowly to wipe the trickle of blood from the corner of his mouth. He remained as he was, watching as the blond bearded man, nearly twice his width and two heads taller, reached into his saddlebag and brought forth two bottles.

He held them together in one ham-sized hand and with the other drew a true Arkansas toothpick from its sheath at his side.

"Brodie said to give you these. But if I find out that you lied to me, I'll come lookin' for you with this."

The dying rays of the sun caught the blade's sheen as Yancy Watts held it out from his body. He tossed the two bottles to the Apache cringing at his feet and laughed at the eager way he caught them.

Saddle leather creaked as Yancy settled his massive frame, and with a vicious yank of the reins he jerked his horse's head toward the south.

"You remember what I told you. Follow him. Make sure nothing happens to him. Brodie wants Delaney alive."

Robert Becket was a man with a secret.

Within minutes of meeting Faith's father, Delaney made that judgment. While the supper that Faith had made slowly disappeared, his gut feeling that something was wrong had not.

Instinct kept a man alive. If he had the sense to listen to it. Delaney had cause in the past to regret ignoring the warnings his own had sent out. He wouldn't be so foolish again.

It wasn't the evasive way Becket answered his questions about where they had come from. By itself, there wasn't anything unusual in that. Most men had some reason for leaving their homes and settling somewhere new. And Delaney knew the unwritten law was not to ask questions. But that was a law for men like himself. The drifters.

Farmers like Becket shouldn't have anything to hide.

Then Delaney added the way the children, as Faith called them, responded to his gentle probing. He swore they had been well schooled to reveal very little.

He sopped up the last bit of gravy with a golden-brown biscuit and decided that his duchess had been modest about her cooking. She was more than a fair hand at it. He had turned down her offer for a third helping of the jerked beef stew that had been flavored with wild onions from a nearby field that had gone to weeds. One adobe wall still stood, a reminder that people had once tried to tame this land. Delaney found himself wondering why the Becket family had camped so far out from town. True, this site was near a trickling stream, and the few cottonwoods offered shade while the standing adobe wall afforded shelter since they had two wagons on either end with a tarp stretched across. But the area was isolated.

With a satisfied sigh he set down his empty coffee cup along with his plate.

"You figure we can leave in a day or so seeing as how we agree on your fee?"

Delaney glanced across the fire at Robert Becket. The man sat with his back cushioned by a thickly folded quilt against the adobe wall, his splintered leg jutting straight out before him. He was near to fifty by Delaney's reckoning and bore little physical resemblance to Faith or her little sister, Pris. A thinning thatch of gray hair framed his gaunt, sharp-featured face.

"Think you're up to traveling?" Delaney asked, gazing off to the side of the fire so as not to impair his vision. Many a man had made the mistake of staring into his campfire, blinding him if he had to move fast in the shadows. By the time his vision adjusted itself to the dark, it was often too late.

"Can't wait here till my leg mends. Lost enough time as it is. Need to get down there and build us a home and get started with the planting. Take a good while to walk the land and find a site close to water."

"If there's water. The land'll support cattle, but farming, now . . . well, I can't say for sure how crops might do. You know you'll have miners to contend with since Schieffelin found float two years ago."

"Float? What's that?"

Delaney turned to face Keith, the oldest of Faith's brothers. She said he was fourteen, and Delaney figured he'd need a few years to fill out the promise of his lanky frame. It was the first question he had asked him since Delaney arrived late this afternoon. He was more than happy to hear Keith question him. It wasn't out of kindness or a wish to share his knowledge with the boy, but he needed to know the boy's strengths and weaknesses before they hit the trail.

"Float's surface rock that shows some color. Old Ed had been prospecting out of Fort Huachuca into the mountains for a year or two before he traced that float back to the outcrop of ore that assayed out to about two thousand dollars a ton. Now he's got the Graveyard, Lucky Cuss, Tough Nut, and Tombstone mines in his holdings."

"See, I told you, Pa, mining gold and silver can make a man richer than farming." Keith leaned forward, his eyes alight with excitement. "Tolly and Opie told us how that old desert rat found a streak of pure silver that almost blinded him. He was ribbed by the soldiers that the only thing he'd find in those hills was his tombstone. But Opie said that strike was so rich that when he pressed his last coin into the shiny streak, Ed could read 'In God We Trust' on the ledge. And he named that first strike Tombstone."

"They also tell you that there's near to two thousand moving in?" Delaney asked. "First came the prospectors like Ed and then the gamblers came, but right on their heels are the men with money to buy up claims and set up the stamp mills. A silver stampede is what they call it. And with them come the men running from the law. The land's not safe. 'Pache are giving them trouble since it's their land being carted off. You need to know what you're getting into."

"Now, don't be scaring the boy with talk of the Apache," Robert warned. "The army promised us they would see to it that the Indians are kept on the reservations. They said there wouldn't be any trouble."

"Well, they're right. There wouldn't be trouble if they kept their damn promises." He caught a pleading look from Faith and stopped himself from saying more.

Faith poured another cup of coffee for her father and then walked to Delaney. "There's a bit left if you'd like another cup, Mr. Carmichael."

"I'm just fine." Delaney thought about teasing her for calling him mister, but Faith shook her head in warning. A chill worked its way up his spine. How did she know what he was thinking? He watched her work around the fire, scraping off the supper plates, filling a basin with steaming water from the kettle, and found he was both soothed and unaccountably restless. When she lifted an empty bucket along with the coffeepot, he rose and crossed the clearing to her side.

"Let me take those. It's the least I can do after that fine supper."

Faith thanked him softly, conscious of her father's brooding look directed at them. "There's a small pool back up the stream a ways. Beyond that stand of willows," she called out as he was lost to the shadows.

"Faith, how much did you tell him about us?"

"Just that we needed him to guide us, Pa. I wouldn't think to say more."

"Keep that in mind, girl. I've seen the way you're looking at him. He's not a man like Martin."

"No, Pa, he's not a man like my husband was."

"I kinda like him," Keith said, gazing off to where Delaney disappeared.

"Me, too," piped a childish voice.

Faith smiled at Pris. She sat on a three-legged milking stool, hugging her rag doll. "Why do you like him, sweetie?"

"Oh, he said he loves peaches same as Joey and me. He even told me he could eat two whole cans all by hisself," she confided with eyes wide. "Won't he get a tummy ache like me?"

"There you go, Pris, asking stupid questions again," Keith said before Faith could answer her. "He's a man and you're just a dumb little girl."

"Keith, that's enough," Faith warned. She didn't bother to look to her father for support—he wouldn't give it—but at least this time he didn't stop her from giving Keith a reprimand. "Pris, Mr. Carmichael won't get a tummy ache 'cause he's a full-grown man and your stomach is quite a bit smaller. But someday, I promise, you'll be able to eat two cans of peaches and not get sick."

"I think you're right," Pris offered along with a shy smile that showed her dimples. "You know that Joey likes him, too."

"What makes you say that, sweetie?"

"Ask him. He'll tell you."

Faith crossed over to where Joey sat on the ground near the wagon wheel as far from his father as he could get. With a gentle touch Faith brushed aside the thick lock of light brown hair that constantly fell across his forehead.

"You've been very quiet tonight, Joey. But since everyone else is venturing their opinion, what do you think of Mr. Carmichael?"

"There you go babying him again, Faith. He's a boy, even if—"

"A boy, Pa. A little boy, not a man. Joey's real sensitive just like Ma was, and he sees things—"

"Sees? He'll never see! Stop dreaming like your ma. The boy ain't never gonna see anything again."

Faith closed her eyes and bit her lower lip for the third time this day. Unspoken by her father, but just as painful, were the words he no longer added: *because of you, Faith.* Joey's blindness was her fault.

"Don't be sad," Joey whispered, reaching out with his hand until he touched the cloth of her skirt, and found her hand with his. Clutching it tightly, he pulled her closer. "His voice is real nice, Faith. I think he liked it best when he was talking about the land. He made Pris laugh. But he don't know all about me, does he?"

"I didn't tell him yet. But I have a feeling that Mr. Carmichael is a man who sees and hears more than he lets on."

Joey squeezed her hand tighter. "You'll have to tell him, Faith. He'll be 'specting me to help with the stock and chores. He's got to know I ain't good for nothing but riding in the wagon."

"That's not true. You know Beula won't let anyone else milk her. There's lots you can do." Faith hugged him, taking as much comfort from his small arms holding her tight as she gave to him.

The sound of a man whistling warned her, and she stood straight quickly and turned. Delaney called out before he walked into the light cast by the fire. Faith smoothed her skirt, her eyes darting to his face, wondering how much, if anything, he had heard. His features revealed nothing.

Setting the full bucket near the fire, Delaney nodded toward Robert. "I'll bid you all good night. Morning'll give me time enough to check your supplies and wagons. And thank you again, Miz Becket, for that fine supper."

With no more than that he turned and left them. Faith found herself listening to the sound of him riding away. She

imagined him sitting tall in the saddle on the barrel-chested
bay mare that he claimed was part mustang and part blooded
stock gone wild and wished that he had stayed.

With an inward shrug for her foolish thought, she ignored
her father's scowl and set about getting Pris and Joey to bed
in one of the wagons. The other wagon held most of their
supplies. Privacy was sadly lacking, but Faith knew better
than to complain. Keith was already spreading his bedroll
near his father when she returned to the dying fire.

"Best get to sleep when you're done," Robert called out
as Faith washed and dried their supper plates. "I've got a
feeling that Delaney will be here at first light."

With a weary sigh Faith nodded.

"And you mind what I told you about him. Don't be
letting on more than he needs to know. Didn't fool me
none with his questions."

"Don't you think being secretive will make him aware
that something is wrong? He's not stupid, Pa. He'll figure
it out sooner or later that we're hiding something."

"Let him figure all he wants. Long as he don't know
about the reward, we're safe. You owe me, you owe us
all, girl. And don't be forgetting that. Think of your poor
ma, buried without a soul to care for her grave. And it's
all 'cause you wouldn't listen to me."

"I'm listening now, Pa. I'll mind what you said. He won't
find out the truth from me."

Finished at last, Faith slipped behind the wagon, but she
made no move to enter its canvas-shrouded body. She
stood alone, arms wrapped around her waist, without tears,
although pain encompassed her.

Off to the side a slight rustling noise in the brush made
her spin around, one hand clutching her throat.

"Who's there?" she managed to demand in a whisper,
frightened, yet certain that it was not a small animal.

She stepped back and then moved again, until her body pressed against the solid side of the wagon. She was sure someone was out there, watching her.

Long minutes passed. Her skin grew chilled. There were no other noises, no sound, not even the sigh of a breeze to disturb the silence.

Lost to time, Faith stood there. Finally she roused herself to crawl into the wagon. But sleep did not offer her a soothing escape. Memories crowded forth.

And the nightmare began again.

Chapter Four

FAITH WATCHED BLUE-GRAY light edge its way into the night sky, demanding retreat of its shadows to allow the sun to rise.

Morning. Hope. Her talisman that the coming day would end in a night of dreamless sleep. Kneeling beside the stream, she leaned over to fill her cupped hands from its trickle of sweet water. The cold silver shower against her face snapped her awake with a gasp. Even as she shivered when the cold shock of water slid down the bare skin above her camisole and soaked the cloth, her smile and laughter came for having stolen a few minutes for herself.

Within a thicket that grew to the stream's edge, a horse moved restively at the sudden sound of her laughter. Delaney bent his dark head and murmured softly. The bay mare quieted instantly. He made no move, no other sound to spoil the unguarded moment of watching Faith's innocent glory. And there was an innocence to her.

She moved with the sleek grace of a wild creature, and yet, within seconds her face held the look of a woman enraptured with her pleasure. She arched her head back to bare her throat to the droplets of water slowly released by her hands. He thought he heard the sigh that escaped her lips and couldn't help but wonder if the heat and slide of a man's lips would bring her the same pleasure.

The lush tumble of her hair appeared dark without the sun's gleam to fire its rich color. The sight presented him with a stirring contrast of dark against the pale sheen of her skin and the thin white cloth that clung wetly to her slender waist and rib cage. His gaze caressed the intimate curves of her breasts. His duchess's faded calico had hidden quite a bit. Delaney couldn't help but respond to the sight of her as she stood and pushed her hair back before lifting her face to the brightening sky. Sweet laughter, dark and light shadows, and nothing held back.

Would she come to a man the same way?

He reached for his stone and held it clasped within the heat of his hand. It wasn't a question he was going to have answered.

As if his move had somehow communicated an ending to her private moments, Faith hurried to slip her arms into the dangling sleeves of her gown. The thin cotton was immediately soaked. She was annoyed and fumbled to get the cloth buttons fastened. A few minutes later she had managed to secure her hair into a tightly pinned bun, filled the coffeepot, and was gone.

Delaney's eyes lost their heat as he urged his horse forward at a walk to cross the stream. He slid from the saddle with an unconscious fluid grace and flattened himself in the same spot that Faith had knelt. His belly curled with the imagined warmth she had left behind in the earth.

But his moves were quick, without any of the enjoyment Faith had displayed, as he slaked his thirst, then splashed cold water on his bare chest and arms.

The mare's warning nicker came too late. He was blinded and vulnerable the moment he tossed water on his face and started to rise.

The click of a gun hammer being cocked close to his ear told him how vulnerable he was.

The solid weight of a boot pressing down on the small of his back pointed out his blindness in letting the sight of Faith wipe out instinctive caution.

And the lingering sound of her sweet laughter in his mind had deafened him to anyone's approach.

Delaney responded to the silent order and lowered himself to the ground. The rough gravel and sand of the bank cut into his chest. The mare snorted and sidestepped uneasily but remained close to the prone man at her feet.

"Ah, the bay is well trained, *amigo*. But tell me, did you take the little farmer and train her as well last night?"

"Maybe," Delaney answered, turning his head so that his cheek rested on the damp earth. He couldn't see the tip of Chelli's boot, but he sensed that he was standing close to him.

"Edna Mae waited and waited for you to return to have your drink with her. It saddened me much to see such a fine woman disappointed. I promised her I would come to find you after I consoled her."

Delaney listened, not to the goad, but to the pebbles that scraped together when Chelli shifted his weight.

"You disappointed me, *amigo*. I had not thought you to be a selfish *hombre*. And the little one, she is like a new rose that would fetch a fine price for me in trade. It is hard for me to admit that I was wrong about you. Yet, I ask myself why you hid from her as I did? Was she not pleased with you?"

"You figure to stand there jawing about her, Chelli, or shoot me?"

"I have not made up my mind what to do with you. There are many who would pay me to see you dead. Maybe I should teach you what it means to cross me. I like you, *amigo*, even when you get in my way."

"It's nothing personal." Delaney inwardly gathered himself to move. He sensed the moment when Chelli made his decision.

His hand snaked out, and he grabbed Chelli's boot. Delaney had to twist his body tight, rolling hard against Chelli's legs, throwing the man off-balance. The Mexican's arm jerked high, and the shot went wide of its intended target. Delaney yanked on Chelli's belt, the wet gravel aiding him in bringing Chelli down.

Before Chelli could blink, Delaney straddled him. He obeyed the silent command of Delaney's hard grip on his wrist and released the gun. Chelli wasn't about to move, argue, or breathe deeply with the glittering knife blade pressed to his throat.

"I don't want to kill you, either, *amigo*. But you're snake bait if I catch you sniffing my back trail." There was no heat in Delaney's piercing gaze, which made the softness of his voice all the more chilling. With a deliberate move Delaney drew the tip of the blade across Chelli's throat. The line that appeared was as thin as thread. It was a measure of the fine control that he had exerted that not one drop of blood appeared. "For you to remember me, *amigo*."

"Stop it!" Faith shouted, holding her father's rifle on them. "Don't either one of you move."

From one breath to the next Delaney froze. Then, with a sudden, smooth, explosive turn, he lunged toward her. Gripping the knife, he used his forearm to knock the rifle barrel upward, and with his left hand he ripped the stock from her grasp.

Faith was stunned by the violence she witnessed, stunned by the violence that seeped from Delaney's body. She couldn't look at his face. His skin glistened with sweat, sleek bronze skin on the powerful muscles of his shoulders, arms, and washboard stomach. Her gaze slid down to the knife he held.

Chelli staggered to his feet, and Delaney stepped back to keep him in sight. "This loaded?" he asked her, bringing the rifle level with Chelli's gut.

"Yes," she managed to choke out.

Chelli raised his arms wide from his body and smiled. "It is over, for now." But when he leaned down to get his gun, Delaney stopped him.

"Leave it. I'll get it back to you later, *amigo.*"

"As you wish." He backed away, turned, ducked beneath an overhanging branch, and was gone.

Delaney's breath shuddered out from him. He tossed the rifle down and lashed out at Faith. "You ever dare aim a gun at my back, duchess, an' you'd better be ready to shoot first."

"No! I wouldn't have shot at you. I was frightened. We all were when we heard that shot." Faith stopped herself from saying more. Delaney turned his back toward her, his spine rigid with tension. She had to fight down the urge to go to him, to offer a woman's soothing touch, to brush the bits of dirt from the broad expanse of his bare shoulders, to somehow tell him she had been afraid for him.

His move toward his horse was dismissal, but Faith refused to leave. She envied the gentle strokes he offered his mare's outstretched nose before he grabbed his shirt that was slung over the saddle. Couldn't he see, didn't he know that she wanted to be held, too? A trembling started inside her, and shivers racked her body.

Delaney slid on his shirt and took his time buttoning it. He could feel her eyes boring into his back, could still see the shock in her gaze, and wanted to close his eyes to blot out the sight of her. Foolish thought. Impossible action. He wasn't going to make what she saw go away. He certainly had no intention of explaining or apologizing. She'd take him as he was.

"Go back to your camp, duchess."

"Stop calling me that ridiculous name!" Clasping her hands in a death grip, she managed to stop shaking. "Are you hurt?"

"No." He sheathed his knife with a deft move, picked up Chelli's gun, and hefted the near perfect balance of the Colt Frontier. The long-barreled revolver was a fairly new model, and Delaney estimated its cost before he emptied the chamber of bullets and put them along with the gun in his saddlebag. Not once had he looked at Faith.

"What should I tell my father? He'll want to know what happened."

"The truth. He'll appreciate it, even if you can't. He's getting his money's worth, duchess. I tried to tell you that."

"I've asked you, now I am demanding that you stop calling me duchess! I'm aware of what I look like, Mr. Carmichael, and it's far from being a duchess."

"Oh, it ain't your looks. It's the grand tilt of your nose."

Faith refused to spar with him. She knew she was plain, had been told as much most of her life. Even Martin had never called her pretty. It didn't matter a wit what this man thought of her. She wasn't interested in the hardheaded Delaney Carmichael! But against her better judgment, she knew she wanted to understand him.

"Why do you condemn my father for what he believes to be true? You can't deny that what happened with Chelli proves you're everything people say."

Delaney's shrug came in answer and annoyed her. She stared at his profile, noticing the slightly crooked slant of his nose. Broken most likely and more than once, she thought. His cheeks and chin were bristled with a near black stubble that matched the color of his hair. As if the direction of her thoughts had called his attention, he raked one hand through the straight, collar-length hair to push it back from his face. The first strong rays of sunlight picked out rainbow drops of water within its depth.

"What were you doing around here so early, Delaney?"

"Same as you."

"The same as . . . You were watching me?"

He wondered how she managed to sound prim, scandalized, and condemning at the same time. Not that he would bother to ask. With his back toward her he opened his buttoned fly, tucked in his shirt, and fastened his pants without apology. The sight of him wouldn't shock the duchess. She said she'd been married. And if she had nothing better to do than stand and gawk at him, well, he wasn't going to shy off behind some bushes.

Faith was gawking. She had seen the masculine gesture more times than she could count, but it was her father, her brothers, and Martin that had performed the task. Delaney made it . . . intimate. Faith hugged her arms around her waist to hold back the tiny curl of warmth that longed to unfold inside her.

Lifting his gunbelt from the saddle horn, he slid it around his hips and buckled it quickly. Delaney reset his gun in the holster. The narrow butt-base made it less handsome than either a Colt or a Remington model, but his Starr .44 was a highly efficient weapon since he could use it as a double-action gun by the use of one trigger, and a single-action by the use of another. The six-shot gun that Eben Starr made for the Union Army had become pretty common out here, but Delaney treasured it, since this one had belonged to his father.

With a smooth move he leaned forward and tied the thongs around his thigh, scanning the woods across from him. He grabbed hold of the reins and stood tall, sure that Chelli had gone.

"Seems to me, duchess, that you should be asking what Chelli was doing here before you start questioning me. Or doesn't it bother you that he was watching you?"

Faith felt her skin crawl at his low-voiced taunt. She had not spared a thought to what Chelli was doing here. The sight of Delaney, the savagery of him, had wiped everything but him from her mind.

"Yes, of course, it bothers me," she managed to say in a steady voice. "But you never answered me. Were you watching me, too?" Just saying it again should make her feel somehow violated, but Faith couldn't summon that feeling.

Delaney turned around to face her. "Sure you want to know?"

There was a remote set to his features that once again reminded her of the rumors about him. Faith took a few steps back. Hard, unpredictable, and dangerous. But she no longer had to depend on gossip. She had seen for herself the violence he was capable of.

"Well, duchess?" He took a step toward her. "You want a lie or the truth?"

Suddenly Faith didn't want to know. For a brief moment she met his direct gaze, then glanced down at the cynical set of his mouth. This time Faith was the one to turn her back.

"Don't forget your father's rifle. A good Springfield is worth its weight in gold in the territory."

Reluctantly Faith picked it up and held the weapon clutched to her body. She ignored the tremor that weakened her legs. But she wouldn't let him have the last word. "Will you still take us?"

Delaney was glad she wasn't looking at him. His slow appraisal of the proud set of her head down to the damp edge of her hem brought to mind his earlier sight of her. A slow heat built inside him. He thought about the kind of taking that would bring Faith to him with sweet laughter, dark and light shadows, and nothing held back. He licked his lips thoughtfully, almost as if he could taste the smooth, cool glide of silver drops from her skin. Absently Delaney rubbed his stone and remembered his own vow. He wasn't going to find out. But his lengthy silence had her glance over her shoulder at him. He couldn't meet the startling blue clarity of her eyes.

"I gave my word. It won't be me who breaks it. If you're having second thoughts, say so."

Faith was tempted to say yes. She didn't want him near her. What could she tell her father? He was upset knowing that Virgil Earp waited in Prescott for his two brothers and their wives to come from Kansas. They had to leave quickly, and that meant they went with Delaney.

"No second thoughts, Mr. Carmichael. There's coffee and biscuits waiting when you come."

"Faith, there'll be no trips alone to any water hole. You're a sight to tempt a saint, duchess, an' there ain't many of them where we're headin'." She turned, giving him a glimpse of her flushed cheeks. Delaney had no satisfaction. He stood alone, wishing he had never agreed to take them.

"We'll head southwest following Walker's Trail down the Peeples Valley," an exhausted Delaney explained to Robert once supper was over. He hunkered back on his heels at the man's side, drawing a crude map in the earth. "The first days will be rough going. From Date Creek," he said, pointing with a stick as Keith leaned over his shoulder, "we swing south across the Hassayampa and the Agua Fría through low desert and mountains. We'll stop in Wickenburg, then follow the Gilmer stage road to Phoenix.

Again we'll rest up a day there. Across the Salt River," Delaney stated, making an X, then a long curving line, "down along the Santa Cruz to Tucson. This is the San Pedro, and your land, near as I can tell, lies across from Tombstone." He tossed aside the stick, glancing at Robert, sure he still had questions.

"You figure it to be three, four hundred miles?"

"Never gave it no mind. If I was riding alone, I'd likely choose a different way. But this should be safe. Luck rides with us or not. We've got to figure delays for weather. And there's always some talk of stirrings going on one of the reservations. Then there's your leg. You may not be up to making five, maybe eight miles a day if the going is good. This here desert stretch will cost us time. We travel early, lay up a good part of the day, and then try to get in a mile or two before night falls."

"Why's that?" Keith settled himself on the ground closer to Delaney.

"The lay-up's to protect the mules and us from the sun. Can't be travelin' much at night 'cause a wrong step down a rabbit hole and you lose a mule."

"Your mare, too?"

"No. She's the best little night rider a man could want."

"With the extra water barrel and supplies you sent me into town for, we shouldn't have to worry much."

"I hope not, Keith."

Robert used both his hands to shift the position of his broken leg. "What about the Apache, Delaney?"

"I told you I can't give you a guarantee that we won't run into them. But I'll be scouting ahead most days, so I'll be the first to cut their sign."

"Ain't you scared of them?"

Before Delaney could answer Keith, Robert leaned forward. "Ain't a need for any of us to be scared. We got four new Springfield Trap Doors, boy."

"There'll be no killing, Becket."

Robert's mouth gaped open to argue, but he couldn't find the courage to say a word facing the chilling gaze Delaney directed at him.

Nodding his head, he settled himself back. "Fine. I'll leave them damn savages to you."

Delaney held back the defense that jumped to mind. He'd met men like Becket before this and would likely run into more. Nothing he said was going to change their views.

"Boy, better get yourself off to sleep. If Delaney is satisfied with the stock, supplies, and wagons, I am, too. Faith fixed up a right comfy spot in the wagon bed with feather ticks, and that'll do me fine."

Delaney knew she had. He had seen her do a woman's work and more this day. Much as he tried to spare Keith to help her, he needed to know the measure of the boy and kept him close helping him.

Standing, Delaney set his hat brim forward. "We're set. I'll be back at first light to help get the mules in their traces."

Faith glanced up at him from where she sat apart. It was the first time she had looked directly at him since this morning. She had expected him to bed down with them for the night. Was he going into town to see Edna Mae? The thought annoyed her. She had no right to question him. She had no right to what she was feeling. Faith set aside her mending away from the fire and stood up. She ignored the glaring warning in her father's eyes when Delaney walked by and murmured good night.

"Mr. Carmichael, please, wait a moment."

Delaney stopped at the back of the wagon and waited. Faith warned herself she had no right at all to this man. Then, why in heaven's name was she following him, likely bringing down her father's anger on her head? Away from the fire the night air held a chill that had her rubbing her arms. She closed out the sound of her father calling her back.

Standing in full view of Robert Becket and Keith, Delaney watched her graceful walk toward him. "What's wrong?"

"Nothing. I just wanted to thank you for being so kind to Joey and Pris. Joey especially. I know that Beula will slow us down, but Joey loves that cow, and he feels he's doing something to help by caring for her."

"No need to thank me. I like them both. Was Joey always blind?"

Faith closed her eyes. She should have been ready for this, but she wasn't.

"If it pains you, forget I asked. It's not important."

When Faith looked at him, he was leaning against a tree, deeper into the woods away from the wagons. She glanced back, hesitating, but her father didn't call her again, so she went to stand near Delaney, out of her father's sight.

"Our cabin wasn't finished, but we wanted to spend the night there. Martin and I didn't know that Joey had fallen asleep in the wagon until we were home. It was late and a ways from my parents' house. Martin carried him inside to the sofa in the parlor. Later, Joey . . . he saw my husband die." Faith twisted her hands together, trying to still the images in her mind. She wasn't really lying to Delaney. It was close to the truth. "When I finally got Joey to sleep, he seemed all right. But in the morning he couldn't see. The doctor wasn't sure what had caused it or if my brother will ever be able to see again."

"I shouldn't've asked." The words were cold and stilted. Delaney didn't know what else he could say. He knew what seeing a man killed could do to a child. Knew firsthand. Some carried visible scars, and others hid them. Delaney had both. He took his time building a smoke, lit it, and gazed skyward. Through the leafy branches the sky appeared clear, the moon just spreading its light to soften the night edges. But where they stood, it was deeply shadowed. He drew the smoke into his lungs and exhaled it slowly. He wasn't sure what the duchess wanted by coming after him. He didn't really care.

"Best I'd be gettin' on."

"What if Chelli comes back?"

"He won't."

"You sound sure." Faith wished he would take a drag of his cigarette. She wanted to see his face, and the trees effectively blocked the moonlight.

"I could tell you I'll make sure of it, or I could say I know he won't. Either way, you won't believe me."

"I want to. I should have told you that I thought someone was moving around behind the wagons last night."

"Why didn't you?"

"By morning it didn't matter. Then Chelli came."

Delaney reacted slowly to the underlying fear in her voice. He pinched off the lit end of his smoke, crushed it beneath his boot and put the cigarette in his pocket.

"What are you hiding, duchess?"

"Nothing. I'm not hiding anything."

Delaney let the lie pass. He lifted one leg to plant his boot against the trunk, cupped her chin, and urged her closer to the spread vee of his legs. "What makes you sure it wasn't me?"

"I just . . . know." This close she could smell him, the animal heat of his body, dark and potent. A strange, frightening excitement knotted her stomach and set her heart pounding. She couldn't admit to having covertly watched him all day while he worked around their campsite, greasing the wagon wheels, redistributing household goods and the supplies in the wagons and oiling the leather traces. He was a quiet man, soft-spoken, easy moving. No motion was wasted, no noise was jarring, no matter what he had been doing. She started to shake her head in denial, but the rub of his callused fingertips against her skin stopped her.

"I was afraid, Delaney. I called out, and I know you would have answered me to set my mind at ease."

"Maybe. Then again, maybe I want you to stay afraid of me." He released her chin only to brush his thumb over her cheek. A fire began to smolder in his belly. He could feel the length of her legs barely touching his and wondered if they'd be strong enough to lock around him, no matter how wild the ride. "Go back where it's safe for you, calico. I'll scout around before I leave."

"I'd feel safer if you stayed." It was as close as she dared come to pleading. Faith wasn't sure if he moved or she did, but the long hard shape of his thighs were now pressed against her. To keep her balance, she raised her hands to his chest and tried to keep some space between their bodies.

Delaney encircled her waist with his left hand. Her voice was hardly more than a whisper but firm with conviction. It bedeviled him that she seemed so sure of him. "Don't ever count on being safe with me, duchess. I'm a man, same as any other. I'll take what's offered and never look back."

Faith tried to pull away. His fingers bit into her waist holding her still. "I'm not offering you anything. And I don't want anything from you."

"Don't you?" He brushed her cheek with the back of his hand, and she jerked her head back as if he burned her. He couldn't stop himself from sliding his fingers into her hair to cup the back of her head, forcing her face up toward his. She was rigid against him, but he could feel her the length of his body, a feeling so strong and wrenching it flooded him with heat and made him grow hard.

"Tell me, calico, were you wondering all day what I saw this morning? How I felt? What I thought? Is that why I caught you sneaking looks at me six ways to Sunday when you thought I wasn't watching? Is that why you followed me tonight?"

"No. No, it wasn't like that at all."

"Then what was it like? You can feel what you're doing to me now, can't you?" His voice dropped to a murmur. "You've got eyes that could slide inside a man's guard and steal his soul if he's not careful, calico." He could feel the tremors that rode her body. Or were they his own? He didn't know, didn't care. With every word he had lowered his head until his mouth hovered over hers. He inhaled the scent of woodsmoke and a faint bit of something sweet from her hair along with the richer tease of a woman slowly becoming aroused.

"Duchess, I'll warn you, I'm not your kind of man."

Faith had been holding her breath, and it escaped in a rush. She could feel what she was doing to him. Just as she felt the power of his hands holding her. Her every tremble acted like a stroking caress from her body to his and back again. He was violent. Dangerous. She couldn't forget. He even warned her. But the warning disappeared, and the words seemed to drum excitement into the heated flow of her blood.

Delaney burned. Her breathing was suddenly labored as if she had run a long way. Every rise and fall of her breasts pushed them against his chest. He was tempted . . . so damn tempted.

Temptation curled its lure around Faith, too. She wanted his kiss. Wanted to taste the reckless slant of his mouth on hers. The desire was so powerful that she was shaking from it. But not like this. Delaney was angry, for all that he spoke softly. She pushed against the unyielding strength of his shoulders, certain it was anger and not desire that kept him holding her.

"Let me go. You don't really want me, Delaney. You've made your feelings plain enough."

"I have, haven't I?"

The fractional move he made against Faith stroked her in a long shuddering caress. His breath mingled with hers, and she parted her lips as if he had commanded it. The thud of his heartbeat matched her own. Slow. Heavy. Fierce. It had been so long since someone had held her. So long since Martin had died. Her lashes drifted down. She didn't want to think, or reason. Her warnings to herself were forgotten. A warmth unfurled inside her, spread slowly to every nerve ending, and Faith heeded its call.

"Why not?" he whispered to himself. "Why the hell shouldn't I?"

Delaney took her mouth.

It was more than taking. His lips seized and dominated her mouth to punish. His tongue thrust deep inside to overwhelm any resistance she could make.

Faith went stock still. He was ravishing her mouth without desire, almost scornfully sure of himself. But he incited hunger to taste the forbidden, and she couldn't seem to fight him.

His kiss changed subtly, his grip no longer hard, for his splayed fingers stroked her back as if he would pull her inside himself. His hand entangled in her hair tilted her head toward his shoulder, his knee thrust itself between her legs, rocking gently as he crushed her body to his.

She had never felt such a wild, exploding assault on her senses. The low, hungry sound he made before his tongue swept her mouth again, hot and fierce as if he couldn't get enough of her, made her cling to him, trembling helplessly.

His teeth held her lower lip captive, and she moaned to feel the lightning streaks that rushed to storm her skin, even as he guided her hip against the blatant ridge of his aroused flesh.

Faith curled her fingers into his shoulders, arching closer to the incredible heat of his body, his groan eliciting one of her own. He was hard: the only giving softness she found was in his lips, which urged her into a fever. A hot, wild mouth that tasted of tobacco and him. He was so dangerous. She knew that, for the night seemed to belong to him like the desire he called from her, dark, forbidding, and unknown.

Her breasts swelled, heavy with wanting. The force of his kiss bent her neck back, and her hands slid into his hair, drawing his head down, his tongue thrusting deeper, increasing the intensity of feeling that surrounded her until it was frightening.

His breathing became harder, faster, and there was nothing but hunger. She didn't know desire could burn this hot. She never knew she could want more of the shuddering press of their bodies, more of the kisses that devoured her mouth, more of the hard rocking thrust of his body, more of Delaney. She was empty, aching, and tormented by the need to be touched.

He could take her now. Delaney knew that. He wanted to. He wanted to know if she'd fit him so damn tight that he would be the one to go wild.

His prim, sodbuster duchess was soft and hot, coming to him with nothing held back. His lips ground hard against hers. He needed to drink her woman's passion to ease the raw ache in his soul. He lifted her closer, pressing her tighter, and her shoulder dug the skystone against his chest. His gut twisted with burning need. Needing a woman had brought betrayal.

Abruptly Delaney shoved her away from him.

She stood swaying like a delicate blade of grass caught in a sudden windstorm. Her eyes opened slowly, and she reached up to touch her swollen lips. She could still taste him, feel him. Bewildered, Faith couldn't speak, she could only stare at him.

"Stay away from me, duchess. You don't know me. You don't want to."

Faith recoiled from the savagery in his voice that effectively squelched any protest, any question that she thought to make.

The dark shadows swallowed him as if he'd never been there.

Chapter Five

DELANEY ABSENTLY SIPPED the last of the coffee that Keith had brought him. He glanced over to where Faith was burying the fire. She wore a shawl against the predawn chill while he had nothing to protect him from her frosty manner. It was what he wanted. She'd stay away from him after last night.

And he wouldn't tell her what he found that had made him uneasy. Someone had been around the wagons, someone who had waited and watched for hours. A man who had learned to be as still as prey in hiding or a predator in wait. A skill, Delaney knew, few white men could duplicate. But he wasn't going to tell Faith or her father. He was warned. It would be enough.

He moved to check that the false floor was secure over the additional supplies in the ten-foot-long light wagon. Whoever had built the box wagons knew what they were doing. The two-foot-high maple sides and four-foot-wide bodies were solid. The wheels of both wagons were iron-tired but had little iron reinforcement in other construction to keep the weight of the wagon down.

Yesterday he had made certain that none of the hickory bows circularly bent to support the canvas tops were warped. He could only hope that the hickory wagon tongues and the axles were as strong and sound as they appeared. These were the weakest parts of the wagon, subjected to abuse that caused the most common casualties.

Faith's voice, soft and low, reached him as she murmured something to a sleepy-eyed Pris. Delaney was tempted to move closer, to share their warmth, but he knew Faith would continue to ignore him, and so he let it be.

He bent to check the wheels. A few minor cracks didn't appear to be cause for worry. The extra water they hauled might be needed to swell the wheels since the desert dryness tended to shrink them. Hope was all he could offer that the choice wouldn't come between using water to swell the wheels or drinking it. He had seen the wrong choice made, where the water kept people alive but stranded when wheels cracked and the wagon couldn't be moved. But that was what Becket paid him for.

Each of the tallow buckets, hanging from the rear axles, were full to grease the dry axles as needed. He had stressed a warning to Keith that it would be his responsibility to keep them from squeaking. Noise in this territory traveled a far piece, and he wanted them to make as little of it as possible. No sense in calling attention to fully stocked wagons, a white woman and children, along with the damn cow. He still wasn't sure how he let Pris's pleading, Joey's shy smile, and Faith's unswerving belief convince him to take Beula with them. At least he won his point over taking off her bell.

Making the last round, Delaney went to the front of the wagon and paused to scratch a mule's ears. They were a smart choice for strong pulling in hard country. The jerk-line teams of eight mules to a wagon were sound. He had personally checked over each animal. He couldn't fault a one. Becket hadn't been stingy in giving himself and his family a fair chance to get to their land claim.

The largest pairs of mules, the wheelers, would help control the direction of the wagon, just as the wagon tongue did. Once again he looked at Faith. It would take strong arms to control the teams, and he wondered if she would be able to manage. Becket called out to him, and Delaney went around back of his wagon.

"We about ready? Feel like a mewling babe back here. Can't see a thing."

"Ain't much to see." Delaney couldn't help the sharp edge in his voice. Becket hadn't said one word to him about last night, but Delaney knew he'd said plenty to his daughter. Robert had Faith jumping to obey his commands for the past two hours. And he had a feeling it wasn't finished.

Keith climbed up to his seat, and Delaney shook out the few drops of coffee in his cup before he set it inside. Faith stood alone, helping Joey up to the center seat of the wagon she would drive. She was reaching for Pris to lift her up when Delaney reached her side.

Pris giggled as he swung her high, then set her next to her brother. But as soon as he turned and put his hands on Faith's waist, she shuddered violently.

"Don't touch me," she whispered. "I can manage fine without your help."

Delaney ignored her and lifted her up so she could stand on the narrow floorboard. She reached inside and got out a bonnet for Pris to shield her face from the coming sun, for the canvas top did not overlap the front.

"Where's yours?" he asked.

Faith lifted a man's floppy-brim felt hat, shot him a defiant look, and set it on her neatly pinned hair. She pulled on a pair of leather gloves that were too big for her hands and took her seat.

Delaney stifled an irrational surge of jealousy. They were a man's things, likely her husband's, and he had no right to what he was feeling. For a brief, charged moment they looked directly at each other, and Delaney thought he knew the feel of hell freezing. A remembered flash of the heat they shared between them last night came and went. Faith took up the reins and turned to stare straight ahead.

"Are we ready now, Mr. Del?" Joey asked, his voice excited, one hand clinging to Faith's skirt.

"We're ready, boy."

"And you think 'bout having peaches tonight," Pris added, smiling at Delaney. "Faith says when you think of something special coming at night, you don't feel all hurt and achy."

"I'll do that, little one. I'll keep remembering something special so I don't get all hurt and achy, either."

Faith was left wondering what he meant as he walked around back of their wagon to check that Beula's halter was secure and to mount his mare.

Ahead of them, keeping to a walk, Delaney led them out.

To the east of Delaney's party, on the bank of the Verde River above Fort McDowell, Seanilzay waited as Holos rose in the morning sky, making the Four Peaks, sacred mountains to the Yavapai, visible in the distance. His sharp eyes darted about as he closed out all sounds but for the steps of the man he awaited.

His stomach threatened to give away his hiding place, and he stilled its growling by sheer will. Alone and on foot he had come over the northern Bradshaws to follow a maze of canyons few men dared to travel.

Hunger was his one constant companion. It had been so since he had gone to live on the reservation, but he vowed it would soon end. He would have supplies and horses enough to take him far to the south to the Sierra Madres, where many of his brethren had escaped the *pindah* form of justice. Seanilzay spat to rid his mouth of the sour taste filling it at the thought of whites. His dream vision was to see the *pindahs* live on the hated reservations, which left no hope and stripped a man of his pride.

Once it was not so. Once the Apache had walked the land of their fathers with pride. Once they had taught their young the true ways of the people. Times before the Anglos. Times before lies and tricks.

Seanilzay knew he had lived too long in the shadow of whites, learning their ways and trying to understand their thoughts. For, try as he would, he could not rid himself of the feeling that he had betrayed Delaney and was about to do so again. Like his father before him, Delaney spoke no lies. Seanilzay knew the time was coming when Delaney would be forced to choose a path, no longer a man who could walk in both worlds. The whites would demand the choice from him.

Seanilzay, too, had chosen a path. He would not look back once this day's deed was done.

A mere breath of sound made him spin around. With a wary, narrowed gaze that betrayed nothing of his thoughts, he watched the approach of his enemy. He carefully noted the army major's silent body moves as he dismounted, and he let those moves speak to his senses. They told him more than Phillip Ross wanted him to know.

The major's skin had burned as red as the band that held Seanilzay's hair from his face. The long-limbed body moved stiffly, and Seanilzay smiled. The major believed himself to be as cunning as the coyote. He bragged of such. But the coyote brought bad luck to the Apache and made them sick. Seanilzay kept that in mind along with the warning that to touch its skin or smell its breath would bring him illness.

"Since you are here," the major said without greeting, "I assume you found Delaney. Where is he?"

"He rides south even now."

"You told him I had need of him?"

"He understands the army's desire to have all the Apache back on the reservation lands."

"Well, yes. We must protect them. It's the only way we can." With a folded index finger the major brushed the drooping ends of his blond mustache. "Did he agree to help me? And don't give me any of your lies. You were a scout long enough to know what'll happen to you."

"He knows there are others who speak all the Apache tongues that would help you."

"That isn't what I asked you. I want Delaney Carmichael because of his father. The Apache respect him, just as Cochise and Jeffords respected his father."

"He will be where you want him with the next moon's rising. Where are my horses and supplies?"

"You didn't bring Delaney to me, did you? You made me ride out here to meet you. Come back with me, and you'll get what you deserve for helping me."

"Snake tongue," Seanilzay spat, backing away from him.

"You useless savage!"

Seanilzay turned and ducked just as the major drew his pistol. The first shot passed harmlessly through the ends of his coarse black hair as he spun and rolled away. Coming up into a crouched stance, Seanilzay drew his knife for a throw. The major leaned his torso to one side, and the knife thudded into the tree trunk behind him. Taking careful aim, Phillip Ross fired two shots at the unarmed Apache. His gun did not waver as the first bullet caught Seanilzay's thigh. Without emotion he fired the second shot, swearing that it slammed into the downed Indian's shoulder and not his heart.

Holstering his gun, the major walked away.

*   *   *

Less than eight miles out of Prescott, Delaney chose a campsite near a small creek. He had wanted to push on, for it was barely late afternoon, but when he rode back to the wagons, Faith attempted to hide her exhaustion. He questioned her, she denied it, and so he called a halt.

Pris and Joey came into his arms readily to be swung down from the wagon seat. He ordered Keith to take them and gather firewood.

Standing patiently, he sighed heavily as he watched Faith. She was taking her time to remove her gloves and hat. He didn't understand his fierce attraction to her. Sweat had dampened her gown and plastered wisps of hair to her flushed cheeks and neck, making her look hot and tired. It had been a while since he had been with a woman, but that did not account for the taste of her that lingered on his lips.

She stood up and his gaze slid up the length of her long legs, remembering the feel of them pressed between his own last night. As his gaze rose, the fingers of his right hand curled as if he were cupping the soft weight of her small breast, and his left hand, fingers splayed, rubbed the hard length of his own thigh. The wide-eyed look of awareness she returned when his gaze snared hers didn't help him to remember his vow to keep away from her.

Irritated with the jolt of heat that spread through him, Delaney lifted his arms up to her. "Come on, duchess, I'll take you down easy."

Easy, she repeated to herself. Never. Everything about him was complicated and hard. She hesitated, glancing from his hands to his mouth. The same feeling of warmth flushing her inside that started with their explosive encounter last night filled her again. The very last thing she wanted was for him to touch her. She stared down at his dark, lean face, his wide shoulders and narrow waist, and stopped herself from looking lower. She did not want to see the long length of his powerful legs and remember how they felt trapping hers between them. But staring at his mouth made her lips and mouth go dry as if she could taste the wildness that had overtaken her with every savage kiss he had given her.

"No," she managed to whisper. "I'll get down myself." She turned, intending to climb down on the opposite side, when Delaney grabbed hold of her wrist and jerked her toward him. Thrown off-balance, Faith tumbled into his arms just as her father called out for her and Keith returned with Pris and Joey.

Her body was tense and trembling. She shot him a helpless look before he set her down and stepped away from her.

"Remember, your life could depend on obeying me, duchess."

Faith managed to steady herself and walk back to her father's wagon. She took Delaney's reminder to heart but wished she could make her willful body obey her own commands. Delaney was more masculine and threatening than any man she had ever met. Some instinct made her look back, and she found him standing where she had left him, watching her. With a quick shake of her head, she dismissed him and forced herself to listen to her father's complaints while she set about gathering what they needed for supper.

Trying to ignore the way her body ached and throbbed, she welcomed the chance to stretch her legs and feel the solid earth beneath her feet. She had forgotten how the long days of sitting and guiding the mules had left her exhausted.

Delaney had not forgotten why he stopped early tonight. Before Faith returned with a slab of bacon and beans already set to soak in a crock, he had the fire going, a kettle of water heating, and was filling the coffeepot from his store.

Faith whispered her thanks.

"Nothing to thank me for," he stated in a harsh voice. "You get dogged an' I'll be the one forced to drive that wagon."

Faith was too tired to answer him, but that didn't stop her from shooting him a cold, telling look.

Delaney ignored it. He knew he had to be the one to force distance between them. Snapping at her seemed the best way. He moved off to tend to his horse, only to find himself hiding a smile when he heard her mutterings, more colorful by the minute about men and mules. He had known few enough women who he could honestly say he enjoyed talking to, enjoyed being with, and liked. But his duchess, with her grit, tempted him to find out if there was more to her than a mouth and body that had him hard and ready with a look.

There was little talk until supper was done, and Delaney was the one to break the silence. "Keith, you take the first watch. I've got a spot picked out for you."

"There's no need," Robert said before Keith could answer. "We can't be that far from Prescott."

"You figure that makes it safe, Becket?"

"Well . . . well, yes, I do. Didn't see many Indians."

Delaney rolled himself a smoke. "Becket, Indians ain't the only thing to watch for. Below Yarnell there's mining camps. You ever been in one?"

"No. And I won't listen to tales that'll have us jumping out of our skins at the least little noise."

Lighting his cigarette with a twig from the fire, Delaney dragged deep and blew the smoke high. His gaze didn't leave Becket's face. "Keith stands watch. Now, and every night I say, or I go back to Prescott."

"Now, just hold on." Robert saw Delaney's shift to stand and stopped arguing. "Do as he says, Keith."

Delaney took his time getting Keith settled a ways up their back trail, explaining what he should be listening and watching for. When he returned to camp, Faith had already put Pris and Joey to sleep.

She had just filled a basin with warm water, intending to wash, but Delaney's appearance reminded her of how little privacy she had. Her father had insisted on sleeping in the wagon, and the children were bedded down in the other one.

Delaney saw her hesitation. He glanced at the basin she clutched, then up to her face. "Don't let me stop you, duchess." His voice was rough, and he turned his back toward her, hunkering down to poke at the fire. He swore softly under his breath, for he had hoped she would be asleep, too.

Faith fought down the temptation to dump the water on him. She walked back to the downed tailgate of the wagon where Pris and Joey slept. After setting the basin down next to a cloth and soap she'd set out earlier, Faith began to unbutton her gown.

The night was filled with soft rustlings, and Faith glanced around but without fear. Somehow knowing that Delaney was close by eased her mind from worry. She dipped the cloth into the water and lightly soaped it, scrubbing her face and neck before she slid the sleeves of her gown down her arms.

Delaney stared off at the forest, his keen hearing picking out the sounds of Faith's washing herself from those of the night moves caused by small animals and the slight breeze. The temperature was dropping. He couldn't help but glance toward the wagon, wondering what was covering her skin besides goose bumps.

He swore again, restless and trying to drag his thoughts away from where she tempted him. "Hurry up," he called out to her. "I want to get some shut-eye before I relieve Keith."

Faith had the cloth pressed to the valley between her breasts. She held it there, feeling the sudden increased pounding of her heart. His voice still sounded rough, but there was an added edge to it. What had she done to anger him now? With a temper-driven motion she slapped the cloth into the basin and jerked the sleeves of her gown in place. Holding the basin in one hand, she used the other to clutch her gown together and marched out to where he was kneeling by the fire.

Delaney rose and towered over her as she drew near him. Once again he eyed the basin where water was sloshing over the rim, adding to the dampness already causing her gown to cling to her breasts. It took an effort to raise his gaze up to her face, where color flagged her cheeks.

"Did you want help getting rid of that, duchess?" he drawled, holding her damning gaze steady with his own.

"Stop calling me duchess," she hissed. "Stop having fun at my expense. I know what I am, what I look like, and I don't need the likes of you reminding me at every turn." Without thinking, Faith released her hold on the front of her gown to clutch the basin with both hands before it spilled.

The hard glint in Delaney's eyes was hidden by his dark, blunt lashes. His nostrils flared. Her scent surrounded him. Every one of his senses sprang to life as desire slammed into his gut. His mind replayed every word she had just spoken. He shook his head and pushed his hat back, wondering what kind of a game she was playing with him. And finally he answered her.

"If you're looking for pretty words, duchess, I'm not the man for them."

"I'm not looking for anything."

"Sure you are. You're looking and asking right now, or you'd cover up what you're flaunting."

Faith glanced down and tilted the basin at the same time. Water spilled and splashed over Delaney's hips and thighs. The thin, wet cloth left nothing to her imagination, not even the fact that he was fully aroused. With a muffled cry Faith dragged her gaze upward.

"Some things, duchess, a man can't control. Don't expect me to apologize. And Faith," he warned, "that makes two."

Faith dropped the pan and backed away from him. In the dying firelight she saw the reckless slant of his lips and the dangerous, almost feral gleam of his eyes.

"You're as blind as Joey," he whispered, pressing the water from his pants. He cleared the distance between them in two long strides and caught her by the shoulders.

"Last warning," he grated from between clenched teeth. "I don't want to get my boots tangled with range calico like you. You'll want sweet words and promises, and I have none to give. I've wanted a lot of things in my life, but got damn few of them. I'll add you to the list." He shook her roughly, determined to make her understand that she had to stay away from him.

Faith heard him, but she felt a burst of heat inside when he touched her. Her lips parted, softening for the taste of his, and her lashes drifted down to hide her awareness.

Delaney leaned closer, his lips nearly brushing hers, but he pulled back. "Don't let feelings rule you, duchess. They can leave you wide open for hurt." He released her with a slight backward shove, knowing he was right. It was a lesson he had learned and never intended to forget.

Faith opened her eyes and saw him walk away. Again. *That's two, Delaney.*

Chapter Six

THE MORNING AIR was crisp when Faith saw Delaney ride out ahead of the wagons. Keith, impatient, called out for her to hurry up. The mules were balky and cantankerous in the mornings, and she was feeling a little of the same herself. She knew it would take her body a few days to adjust to muscles being strained, and the jolt and sway of the wagon. Plunking her hat on, Faith eyed the mules and climbed up, making sure that Pris and Joey were settled before she grabbed up the reins.

The children were quiet, allowing her time to think, although she managed to avoid the subject of Delaney until he rode back as the sun climbed high. "Half hour, no more," he ordered, riding past her.

Shooting a glaring look at Delaney's retreating back, she knew she was thankful they would stop for nooning.

Faith was wet. Sweat trickled down her face and onto her neck and bodice. Damp patches spread down from her underarms to her sides. Even her legs were coated with moisture. Her arms were sore, and her shoulders didn't bear thinking about at all. She longed to crawl into the back of the wagon and rest. More, she longed for a bath. What she did was to set the pole brake and watch as Pris, with Joey cautiously following, scrambled down from the wagon.

"What's to eat!" Keith yelled.

She didn't look at him, tempted to sit right where she was, but it was a moment's foolishness. Everyone was hungry, and she the one expected to provide for them.

Grumbling to herself, she stripped off her gloves and hat and climbed down. With both of her hands pressed to the small of her back, Faith bent forward, groaning, and then, very slowly leaned back in an arch to stretch out her sore muscles.

Arrested by the wanton sight she presented, Delaney paused in the act of dismounting. Her skin was flushed, her hair dark where sweat had dampened it, her eyes half-closed, and her head arched back. The soft noises she made rubbed his nerve ends. His gaze tracked the clean line of her profile, the smooth upthrusting curves of her breasts, and a waist that he could almost span with both of his hands.

She straightened up slowly, almost as if drawn up by her sudden awareness of him. For seconds her gaze locked with his.

Delaney stepped down and turned to fully face her. Tipping his hat back, his hands came to rest on his hips. His eyes narrowed and he deliberately glanced down. The skirt and petticoats she wore, clung to her legs and had caught in the veed joining of her thighs. Sweat broke out on his brow. With a choked sound he licked his bottom lip.

Faith watched him with a mixture of shock and sexual awareness. Heat shimmered through her body, her eyes widened, her lips parted as she exhaled a rush of air, and she could feel her breasts swell. Delaney was still staring at her, and she was forced to look down at herself. With a cry she plucked her skirt and petticoats free, nervously smoothing them down her legs. He moved toward her and she nearly tripped over her own feet trying to get out of his sight. She ran to bring fresh water to her father and set out their cold meal.

Delaney turned away and took a few deep breaths while he loosened the cinch on his barrel-chested mare. Mirage threw up her head and snorted. With a gentle touch he rubbed her forelock, then stroked down to her velvet nose, warning himself to ignore what just happened with Faith. The mare nudged his shoulder, wanting more of his petting, but this was not the female Delaney longed to stroke. A devil beset him, and he left Mirage nickering after him. With every step that took him up behind Faith, he repeated his own warning.

Reaching out for a cold, sour-milk biscuit, his arm brushed her shoulder. She jerked to the side, refusing to look up at him. If the sight of her had sent his blood rushing through his body, the touch, the scent of her, made his muscles clench with want and sent hunger prowling down to his bone marrow. That she could stand there, acting as if she were unaware of what she had done, was doing to him, setting him off so easily, made him forget and damn his own vow.

"Duchess," he leaned close to whisper, crowding her hips against the edge of the wagon's tailgate, "I've seen fifty-cent whores with smoother moves."

Faith swallowed a cry. She gripped the knife until her knuckles showed white. Temptation that had nothing to do with the passion he so effortlessly aroused in her gleamed in her eyes. His harsh words stung, but she held back a defense. Delaney Carmichael was not going to goad her into saying something foolish, then strip her hide over it!

"But then, I've never had to pay a woman," he remarked, knowing he was being a bastard and unable to stop himself. He did have the sense to keep a close watch on the knife she wielded.

Faith's teeth scored her lower lip. She licked her lip, her temper rising, hot and fast. So the devil wanted his due? "Somehow, Mr. Carmichael, that doesn't surprise me. But for fifty cents a look is all the likes of you is going to get." She slapped ham between the sliced biscuits and piled them together.

Delaney's hand hovered in front of her. Two silver quarter dollars plunked and rolled against the wood.

"Since I'm paying in advance, duchess, I'll pick the time and place to . . . look."

Tears smarted her eyes. Faith blinked them away. Hot color singed her cheeks. "You do that, Carmichael. And while you're waiting, fill the water barrels. It might cool you off." Gathering the biscuits up in a linen napkin, she called to Pris and Joey, wondering where the courage had come from to snap back in kind at him.

Delaney swallowed his laugh. He glanced down to see that the breeze had whipped her skirt hem in a tangle around his boots. With a thoughtful look he shook it free and went to sit with Keith.

"Del, we getting close to Rich Hill?"

Nodding, Delaney chewed slowly, still watching Faith.

"That's what I really want to do," Keith confessed, unaware that he did not have Delaney's full attention. "My pa don't understand the kind of riches a man could find for himself. He thinks breaking your back over a plow, and then standing to wait for rain or going hungry when your seed dies without coming up is all there is to life. I want more. A heck of a lot more!"

There was an edge to Keith's voice that forced Delaney to look at him. "You can't believe that mining ain't hard work?"

"No. I'm no fool. But the reward—the money you can have to spend—is all worth it."

"There was a saying that if you washed your face in the Hassayampa, you could pan gold dust from your whiskers, Keith. An' maybe that was true back in the fifties an' sixties. Up on Rich Hill, they said a man could kick up gold nuggets with the toe of his boot or dig them out with the tip of a knife. Almost every creek 'round here, Granite, Lynx, Big Bug, Turkey, and more than I remember, were sites for placer mines."

"Placer? That's all panning, no hard rock, and no digging?" Keith asked, his eyes intense.

"That's right. But the gold played out and the Cousin Jacks moved in an' the jackass prospectors moved on. Now the silver mines are the rich ones. Places like the Tip Top and Silver Peck in the Bradshaws and the McCracken and Signal further west. But it ain't easy picking. Man alone needs to be on watch. Goes to town to buy supplies and weigh in his poke at the assayer's office, an' he takes to worrying over who's watching to see where his claim is at. Ain't—"

"A man could get himself a partner," Keith cut in, taking a bite of his lunch.

Delaney nodded. "Sure he could. But more *partners* end up sole owners than you could count."

"You don't much like miners, do you, Del?"

He closed his eyes wanting to answer Keith honestly. Memory brought forth the sight of himself, sitting with Taza and Naiche while he struggled to understand the Apache words that taught him about Yusen and the abomination they believed it was to take gold from the body of Mother Earth. Much as he respected their right to their beliefs and their spirits, he had come to see for himself what the hunt and greed for gold had done to the land.

"Del?" Keith questioned, thinking there was something wrong.

"Sorry, boy." Delaney saw the flash of defiance in Keith's eyes. "No, that was wrong of me. You ain't a boy. But you've got growing years ahead of you. An' no, I don't much like miners." Delaney got up from the downed log they were sitting on, and before Keith could say anything, he left him.

When they were ready to pull out, Delaney tied his mare to the back of the wagon. Mirage didn't much care for the company of Beula, but the cow offered what almost passed for a wink from her soulful brown eyes as if to thank Delaney for a companion. Shaking off his fanciful thoughts, he strode around to the front of the wagon and climbed aboard, crowding the children and Faith.

"I'll drive," he said, taking the reins from her before she could move. "You take Pris and ride in back."

"Orders, Carmichael?"

He didn't turn to see her. "Yeah, duchess, orders."

Since she was getting her longed-for wish, Faith did not argue with him. She scrambled over the seat, taking Pris with her. How did Delaney know what she had been thinking about? Shrugging off a question she wasn't going to have answered, she coaxed Pris into one bunk built on the side of the wagon and settled herself in the other one. If she had not still been smarting over his taunting, she would have thanked him.

Delaney set himself back on the wagon's seat, spreading his legs wide so that his boots were braced on the edges of the lower front box. "Joey, come sit with me and guide these mules."

Joey turned toward the sound of his voice. "You're funning me. I can't see."

"There's lots of ways of seeing, boy. 'Sides, I've watched these mules. They're a good settled team." He held out his hand, hoping that Joey would sense how close to him it

was. Delaney made no move to help Joey find his way over
his leg to get settled on the seat between his legs. "You did
fine, boy. Real fine." Placing Joey's hands on the leather,
Delaney closed his own hands over them. "Now, we'll keep
these mules to a walk. One long pull on the jerk line will tell
them to go left and a few short jerks mean to turn right. The
leaders are real smart like I said, so you can shout 'gee' for
right and 'haw' for left, too. But an old skinner taught me
to let the mules pick their way. The leather will talk to you
all on its own. Now, yell 'stretch 'em out.' "

"Stretch 'em out!" Joey yelled, gripping the reins with
all his strength.

Delaney smiled and absently rubbed the boy's shoulder
to ease some of the excited tension from him.

Inside the wagon Faith listened to every word spoken by
Delaney. The rough edge that was always present when he
spoke to her was gone. His voice was soft, patient, and she
swore she heard him chuckle at something Joey whispered
that she couldn't hear.

The man, she decided, settling back against the pillow,
was as twisted as some of the trails he set them to follow. As
much as she longed to close her eyes and sleep, she found
herself straining to catch Delaney's words as he answered
Joey's questions.

"We're high in the Bradshaws. You can feel the sun on
your skin, and when it cools fast, the shadows come from
the tall stands of timber. Before long we'll ride where
there's low desert. It'll be hot during the day and chilled
down at night. We'll have buttes and mountains there, but
water might be harder to find."

"But Faith said you know where water is. How come?"

"I had good teachers, Joey. An' it's not all that hard
for any man to figure where water is if you learn the
land."

"The Apache taught you, didn't they? That's what pa says. He says you're like one of them."

Faith held her breath, and sat up, leaning forward to hear his answer.

Delaney hesitated. The hairs on the back of his neck rose, and he knew that Faith was awake. But he didn't want to try and explain to Joey or anyone else the beliefs of a people that he admired and called friends and who honored him with their trust.

"Well," Joey prompted, "ain't it true? 'Course, I don't think you act like no savage. You're real nice to me and Pris."

"Joey, even if I was Apache, that wouldn't change the way I am with you or your sister. An' for the ones I know, Apache love their children, same as white folks."

Joey's body was rigid. "They're turning. I can tell!" he whispered, frightened.

"Easy, boy. The leaders are just finding the best way. Lazy animals won't do a lick more work than they can get by with."

Even Faith had to smile. When Joey began to laugh, she offered a prayer of thanks for Delaney's caring and patience with her little brother. With a sigh she rested again on the pillow, her curiosity unappeased.

As if her thought had flown to Joey, within minutes he persisted with his earlier questions. "So where will you find water?"

"Tell you what. When we make camp tonight, I'll show you how to tell what kind of trees are growing. You feel the leaves, smell them, smell and touch the bark. Learn the scent of the land when water is near. You can always use animal tracks to lead you to *pozos* or *tinajas*."

"You need to be able to see these things, Del," Joey reminded him in a sullen voice.

"No. You can use the sense of smell to find anything, boy. An' there's nothing wrong with your hands. You can crawl and feel with your fingers to measure the size of a track. Figure if it's man or beast, though there's times when they're one an' the same."

"Huh?"

"Men, Joey. Sometimes they're worse than animals. But to get back. If you find an animal track, I'll show you some ways to tell what it is."

"You really know all that?"

Delaney's eyes darkened with memories. "Not all. No man, white or Indian, can lay claim to knowing all."

"What's a *pozo* and a tin . . . that other thing?"

"A *pozo* is a spring and *tinajas* are pools in the rocks. When the gully-washers come—that's a hard, driving rain, which floods the land," he quickly explained, before Joey interrupted him. "Well, the water collects in natural stone basins and can last for months. It ain't *agua fría*—an' that's Spanish for cold water, which you'll find in a spring—but when a man's thirsty an' his horse can't go on, you'll drink it."

"So, animals would know where water is or they'll die. Gee, Del, pa's wrong to call Indians ignorant savages. They know these things. A man has to be smart to figure all this out and then remember it."

"There's smart men and stupid men belonging to every tribe and all whites. You learn to take the measure of a man by the respect he earns from you, Joey, not by the color of his skin being darker or his beliefs being different from yours."

There were more, more questions from Joey, more answers from Delaney, and Faith listened, until the rocking of the wagon and the soothing deep tone of Delaney's voice lulled her to sleep.

The look Delaney shot over his shoulder into the shadowed interior of the wagon only confirmed what his senses had told him; Faith was sleeping. His chin brushed the edge of Joey's floppy hat as he turned back. The trail ahead was fairly clear, so Delaney reflected on why he acted the bastard with Faith.

So he didn't like the way wanting her had him twisting and turning on his bedroll at night. But he could blame her for trembling at his slightest touch. The heat was there, he wasn't denying it, and given half the chance, she wouldn't deny it, either. Maybe, he mused, that was the problem.

She was his for the taking. But the duchess wouldn't let it end there. While he wished it weren't so, he forced himself to accept that. It still didn't give him the right to treat her like a fifty-cent whore. An inner voice nagged him with all the reasons why he had to stay away from her.

His body had its own way of nagging. One that made him lift Joey up and over to sit beside him on the seat, so he could shift his legs and ease an ache that was becoming too familiar. Damn that skystone-eyed witch!

Faith woke with a start. Confused when she saw that daylight pierced the interior, she sat up, pushing aside her hair, which had come free while she slept. The wagon wasn't moving.

"What's wrong?" she asked, turning, but neither Joey nor Delaney were on the wagon's seat. She called their names softly so as not to waken Pris, but when no one answered, she came off the bunk and peered out of the front opening of the canvas.

They were stopped in a small clearing. A fire was already burning, and the big kettle she used for washing had been heating a while, for she could see heat rise from the water. The mules were no longer hitched to either wagon. But once again no one answered her when she called out.

Stifling a yawn, Faith climbed over the seat, looked around, burying her fear when a quiet sense of peace came to her. Gathering up her skirt and petticoats, she stepped down from the wagon just as Delaney, followed by Keith and Joey, came out of the woods carrying deadwood.

"Wait till you see the stream, Faith," Keith said, dumping his load of wood near the fire. "There's a pool deep enough to swim in."

She ignored her brothers and looked at Delaney. "Why?"

"Figure we could all use a bath," he returned, building another fire, smaller this time, and set a ways from the boiling kettle. "If you hurry, you'll have time to wash clothes. The water's sun-warm down below, and there's a few springs that have hot water. Don't know when we can stop again," he finished, taking his knife from its sheath to shave off dry bark before striking a match to the pile. The smoke curled up, and he added small twigs, while Keith broke the deadfall branches and handed them to him to feed the blaze. Standing, he turned to Faith but would not meet her direct gaze.

"Keith'll keep watch when you're ready to go down to the creek. Your father's fishing for supper."

"And Joey?" she asked, annoyed that he had made plans for everyone and expected them to be followed.

"He'll come with me." He looked at her then, saw the fear and questions in her eyes, and added, "Joey's safe with me."

Faith nodded. It was true. On some instinct level she trusted him with Joey when she could not trust him with herself. She spun around, hurrying to get the laundry and soap. She still wanted to ask him why he had done this, musing to herself that this might be his way of apologizing. Delaney reminded her enough times he did not apologize, so she shook off that thought as being foolish. With her

arms wrapped around bundled clothes, Faith came back to
the fire. She was going to have her longed-for bath. Nothing
could stop her smile.

Delaney placed his hand on Joey's shoulder, urging him
away from the fire. He glanced back to see Faith's smile
and found his guilt for being caustic rode a little lighter.
At the edge of the wood he took Joey's hand and set it
to grip the back of his gunbelt, before leading him into the
woods.

When he deemed they were far enough, and his own keen
senses gave him no warning of danger, Delaney stopped. "I
want you to breathe as deeply as you can, Joey, and listen.
We'll stand here, quiet for a bit. Then you tell me what
you hear and smell." He grinned to feel the excitement
that trembled through the boy's body. Delaney closed his
own eyes, took a deep breath, released it, and let his body
go still. With a skill he had learned from his childhood
Apache friends, he slowed his heartbeat. Within seconds
he had blanked his mind to all thoughts, and in whispers,
with delicate scents, the forest came alive for him.

He sensed the waiting stillness of the creatures as the man
scent was carried to them. Until the animals knew they were
not here as predators, they would remain quiet and hidden.
Delaney caught the far-off sound of water tumbling over
rocks from the creek south of where they stood. He stopped
himself from imagining Faith down there.

The soft cooing of a dove made Joey grip Delaney's belt
tighter. He quickly understood by the even breaths and lack
of tension in Delaney's body that he had nothing to fear. A
tiny rustling noise followed, and he turned his head toward
it, lifting his face to inhale. Joey tried and failed to place
the strong scent that he drew into his lungs.

Reaching behind him, Delaney took hold of Joey's wrist.
His steps, with the boy stumbling, were so quiet, that Joey

reached up with his other hand to touch Delaney's back. He smiled to feel a reassuring squeeze on his wrist. Joey vowed to try and be as quiet as the big man who was opening a new world to him. With Faith he didn't feel clumsy or unable to do for himself, but his pa never let him forget he was less than whole.

Stopping before a tall, massive, almost orange trunk of a ponderosa pine, Delaney used his knife to scrape a bit of bark and turned to Joey. Using his thumb, he touched the boy's cheek gently, then lifted the knife tip to his nose. Joey jerked back from the resinous scent, wrinkling his nose. He smiled when he came close again. "Vanilla?" he murmured.

"Good," Delaney answered, rubbing the small scar he had left in the soft, pale yellow wood. "It's from the tallest of the pines," he whispered, leaning close to Joey's ear. "Near ten times a man's size."

Once again he moved off, listening to the silence. He had to search a long ways to find what he was looking for, but he grinned when he did. Hunkering down, he urged Joey to kneel at his side. Placing a small cone into the boy's hand, he watched as Joey ran his fingers over and over the rough surface and then lifted it up to his nose.

"This is one of the most important trees that the Indians value, Joey. Piñon pine, not tall and stately like the ponderosa, but dwarf-size and twisted. Here, give me your hand so you can feel the shape of the trunk."

"It's sticky."

"Pitch, Joey. You get hurt, an' there's nothing better to close a wound. An old man I knew would heat this and mix it with his whiskey to rid himself of a cough. Makes a real fine glue and waterproofing for baskets so they can hold water. I'm gonna lift you up so you can feel the branches," he warned. "The curve of the log is good for building shelter, but what you hold could make the difference between going hungry or eating."

"A cone?" Joey felt himself back on the ground, and such was his trust in Delaney that he lifted the cone to his lips.

"Not so fast, boy. It's the brown seeds inside that you can eat. They taste like nuts." Once more, Delaney moved off, then stopped. "Reach your arm out to the right. Feel that bark. It's stringy, peels right off, and makes good tinder to start a fire. Junipers have berries, too. But only eat them when you're in need. They're kind of puckery-tasting, but the birds like them fine." Smiling, he watched as Joey stroked the bark and then began to finger it. In one corner of his mind Delaney cursed Robert Becket for making his son less than he could be. But Delaney did not hide from himself his own motive for teaching Joey. If something happened to him, Joey's knowledge could mean his life.

"Now, let's say you're ready to bed down. You could bundle up leaves, grasses, or pine needles to soften your place. But leaves and grasses flatten quick. Sometimes they're dry and rustle every time you breathe. Needles tend to pinch a man in the damnedest places. You grunt and tell someone where you are. Indians use this bark to weave a soft sleeping mat."

"That's woman's work, Del."

"Boy," he answered softly, unable to hide his laughter, "notions like that are gonna get you in a heap of trouble." Ruffling Joey's hair, he added, "Best not let your sister hear that kind of talk from you. She'll raise a ruckus for sure." And likely blame him, he thought.

The call of a wild turkey forced Delaney to be still. His eyes narrowed, scanning the forest. He placed his hand on Joey's shoulder, pressing to warn the boy to stay. When the call came again, Delaney left him.

Chapter Seven

FAITH HEARD THE echo of a shot and froze where she knelt on a flat rock by the edge of the stream. She lifted her head, searching the area across from her. She saw nothing but trees and shrubs growing close to the bank. Her thoughts flew to Joey and Delaney. Grasping the shirt she had been rinsing, she listened but heard nothing more. Just that single shot. Surely, if something had happened to Delaney, there would have been more shots fired.

Keith came bursting out of the tree line above her at a run, his rifle clutched in his hands. "You hear that? Pa, you think Del's got trouble?"

Faith glanced at her father. He offered Keith a surly look and shook his head. He had no liking for Carmichael, less in these two days that passed with Carmichael enforcing his way of doing things on all of them. Made a man feel less like one, Robert thought, tugging on his line, praying for another fish to go with the two it had taken him over an hour to catch. At this rate he'd be forced to eat something Delaney provided. It went against his grain, and his stomach rebelled in agreement.

Faith glanced from her father back to her brother. She motioned Keith to go back to camp. After another look around, she finished rinsing the shirts she had boiled and

scrubbed, then wrung them out before she spread them on
the low-hanging branches to dry. Woolen drawers belonging to Keith, Joey, and her father were still damp, as were
their heavy pants. She glanced up to see how much daylight she had left, knowing there was one last wash of her
belongings and Pris's.

Making her way back to camp, Faith felt edgy and shot
looks over her shoulder, but all was peaceful.

"You done yet, Faith?" Pris whined, squirming on the
milking stool where she sat feeding blades of grass to Beula.
"I wanna go swim. Keith said—"

"I promised we would," Faith snapped, cutting her off.
Wiping her forehead, she lifted a seasoned wood pole to
stir the boiling clothes. After a few minutes she raised a
piece of clothing high, letting the water drip before setting
it in her basket to carry back to the creek. "Get the soap
and our clean clothes, Pris. You'll come with me so we can
have our baths."

With Pris holding on to her skirt, Faith picked her way
through the trees, making sure she was far enough downstream out of sight of her father. She hurried to rinse the
clothes, impatient as Pris was to get into the water.

"Stay close to the bank, Pris. Delaney said there are
natural hot springs, and your hair needs washing."

"Oh, Faith, can't we just play and have fun."

Faith glanced to where Pris sat in shallow water, her
drawers muddy from a brief stint at digging along the bank.
She had to fight down the resentment that flared inside. Yes,
she longed to shout, I want to play, and rest, and not have
to worry about clothes, food, along with keeping you clean!
I'd like some time to myself, too! But while her voice had
an edge to it, she merely reminded Pris that they couldn't
linger long.

Even the short while she spent in the warm spring water,

washing Pris's hair, then her own, softened her mood. Once they were both dressed, Faith led the way back to camp. A teasing aroma made her hurry.

Her father was already back, resting against a wagon wheel. "There's fish to clean," he growled in greeting.

Keith, hunkered down near the smaller fire, looked up at her. "That shot we heard was Del shooting us a turkey." Faith saw for herself that Delaney was turning a make-shift spit where the turkey's skin was already starting to brown.

' "The fish, Faith," her father called out to remind her.

Before she moved, Delaney was up and across the clearing. He grabbed the string of fish and headed down to the stream. Faith walked closer to the fire, where Keith continued to turn the bird.

"Faith," Joey said, "I learned so much about trees and felt tracks of a white-tailed deer. Del showed me—"

"Wait, Joey. How did you know I was here, so close to you?" She stared at her little brother and wished that Delaney had stayed.

"Oh, I smelled you," Joey answered, wearing a smug smile as he sat a little straighter.

"Smelled me?" she repeated, glancing at Keith, who just shrugged. "But I just took a bath."

"That's why I could, Faith. I smell the soap you use."

Keith ducked his head to hide his grin. Flustered, Faith returned her brush and soap to the wagon. She took out a small sack of cornmeal and a bit of salt to use on the fish when Delaney came back, thinking that she would have to thank him for saving her the messy chore. Drawn back to the fire by curiosity, she first reminded her brothers about their baths.

"Oh, now that you're back, Delaney'll take us," Joey said. "And he let me keep all the feathers, Faith. 'Course, they're not as good as having eagle feathers, but Indian boys use these for their arrows. Del said if he has time, he'd make me a bow and some arrows."

The danger to Joey made her open her mouth to protest, but Delaney returned and she kept silent when he handed her the fish. "Thank you for cleaning them, Mr. Carmichael. I hope you'll like the way I fix them."

"Del won't eat them, Faith," Joey said.

She looked at Joey, hearing the pride and the confidence in his voice. A second later she cringed to hear her father muttering about the foolishness of getting a blind boy all het up over what he couldn't have. One look at the dark glint in Delaney's eyes, the muscle that twitched in his cheek and she knew she had to stop him from confronting her father.

"Joey, tell me what else you learned while I get these fish ready." She sat close to him so that they could keep their voices low. "Do you know why Delaney won't eat the fish?"

"If he's real, real hungry, he'd force himself to eat it, but the Apache don't much like it. They don't eat turkey, either, but Del likes that fine. He says the turkey eats too many bugs and worms and stuff like that so the Apache won't touch it. But it sure smells good, don't it?"

"It sure does." She leaned close to kiss his cheek and found herself snared by Delaney's dark gaze. Without a thought to what her eyes revealed, Faith smiled up at him. What he had given her brother was simply beyond measure of thanks.

"Faith," Joey said, drawing her attention by reaching out with his hand to touch her own. "This is the time of many leaves. We couldn't pick berries. They won't be ripe until the time of large leaves or . . . or . . ."

"Thick with fruit time," Delaney supplied. "You boys

want time for a swim, we'd best go now."

While they were gone, Faith finished supper preparations, sneaking looks at her father's brooding face. She didn't like the feeling that was creeping up on her, and when he finally spoke, she knew she had good reason.

"You're getting ideas about Carmichael, ain't you? I warned you, girl. Damn foolish. He's no better than—"

"Don't say it, Pa. You're the one who wanted him, not me. I tried to tell you to find someone else. But I don't understand how you can bad-mouth him when he's good to Joey."

"Good to the boy?" he sneered. "That what you call it? Filling his head with savage learning that ain't gonna do him a lick of good ain't no kindness, girl. Nothing will help him get back what he lost."

Faith turned the spit. She wasn't going to answer him. How could she? The guilt for Joey's blindness was her burden. Her fault. But when would her father begin to forgive her? The Lord knew that Joey never once blamed her. But then, she reminded herself, Joey knew the truth of what happened the night Martin was murdered. Shivering, she dragged her thoughts from the past.

To save Joey the chore, she milked the cow, frowning to see the pail half-full. Beula had to be bred and soon, or she'd go dry on them. The coffee was done, and she pulled the pot to the edge of the fire, just as the three of them returned. Faith found herself watching as Delaney stowed his gear in his saddlebag, her gaze warming to notice the taut play of his muscles beneath the doeskin-colored shirt he wore. She didn't have the courage to ask if he had washed his own clothes. But when he walked back toward the stream, she called out to him.

"Supper's ready."

"Be right back. Best I get your laundry before it's gone."

"Gone? There's hardly a breeze, Mr. Carmichael."

"Never know when someone might wander by and help themselves to whatever takes their fancy."

"Wait. I'll come with you." Faith ran to catch up with him. She did not want Delaney Carmichael near her unmentionables. The light was fading, so she stayed close on his heels.

At the bank he turned to her. "Duchess, go get your drawers and petticoats and what-have-yous while I gather these."

Blushing beet-red, Faith stamped her foot. How could he know! "Must you always find something to poke fun at when it comes to me?"

"Temper, duchess?" he queried in a rough voice. "Just understand that the last thing I want is to be alone with you. You've got yourself a mirror, don't you? Look in it, calico. Only do your looking through a man's eyes and not your own."

"You peevish—"

He rounded on her, forcing her to back away. "Your skin's peach-gold, and I've made no secret that I purely love the taste of peaches. Want more?"

"No. No, I don't want to hear more." But she lied, and she knew that Delaney was well aware of that.

"Ah, hell!" he muttered.

"Delaney?" But he ignored her, gathering up shirts and pants from the branches and bushes. Faith knew he would say no more. Pressing her palms against her cheeks, she turned away. *Peach-gold?* Did he really think her skin was that pretty? The thought of Delaney tasting her skin sent a tremor of heat through her body. Did men enjoy gentle kissing and touching? Would Delaney? He called out a warning for her to hurry in such a harsh voice that Faith set aside her musings.

Delaney Carmichael, she decided, had the disposition of a rattlesnake. Leave it to doze, and a body wouldn't know it was there. Step too close and you were likely to get bit. And only a fool would provoke a rattlesnake!

Faith was thankful the next few days passed without event. The trail they followed wound down through the trees along a steep switchback that would lead them to Peeples Valley. Keith asked questions, Joey asked his, and even Pris began to think of things to gain Delaney's attention. He answered them all as best he could, making their stops a bright spot to look forward to, when it was measured against the boring dullness of the days. This morning dawn had arrived in a crimson wash over the mountains to flush the stones with flame. Faith longed to share the beauty she found in the land with Delaney but never did. If she stopped to count, she didn't believe they had exchanged sixty words between them. It was a childish game that served to help her keep her distance from him. But the nights found her aching, restless, and going without needed sleep.

Each time she reminded herself to stop thinking about him, Delaney did something to bring himself to her attention. She couldn't help wonder if he did it deliberately.

He would ride by, ignore her, and take either Pris or Joey up before him on his horse and ride off. The children would come back filled with giggles and smiles that pleased her, for she often found herself smiling with them.

Keith now went out on his own to provide fresh game for supper, for Delaney had shown him new hunting skills. Her brother walked taller and spoke with a man's authority, which she sometimes found annoying.

There were no more challenges from her father, but she sensed he was building toward a showdown with Delaney about Keith's growing talk about mining. Delaney's manner toward her father remained somewhat puzzling. He would not confront him, but in his own quiet way he went about doing what he wanted, when he wanted, and how he wanted it done.

The nooning took place on a high point, and Keith eagerly questioned Delaney about the low desert and mountains that surrounded them. Faith heard bits and pieces, not really paying attention, until her father bellowed out Keith's name.

"Don't want to hear another word about mining from you, boy!" Robert yelled, hobbling toward Keith. "We're farm folk and don't you forget that."

"Don't be carrying on, Pa. I was just asking Del where Rich Hill was. Do you even know how much gold they found there? And now silver mines are making men rich."

"Rich? That all you ever think about, boy? Man owns his land, works and builds something solid to pass along to his sons. That's being rich." He glared at Faith. "It happens that way unless a man loses—"

"No! Pa, don't!" Faith cried out, running toward him, spilling the last of the milk from the tin jug she held. "Don't say it!"

"I'll have my say, girl, when I want."

"Then be glad that Ma never lived to hear such meanness from you!" she screamed and fled.

Delaney stopped Keith from going after her. He avoided looking at Becket, afraid of what he would do to the man. Without a second thought he went after Faith.

She was crying so hard she didn't hear him come up behind her. When he put his hand on her shoulder, Faith turned blindly and took shelter against him. For a moment Delaney deliberated over touching her, and then his arms came up to enfold her. He had no comforting words to offer, but Faith wouldn't have listened to him. She badly needed to cry, and he let her.

But now he knew for sure there were secrets the Beckets hid, secrets that had something to do with Faith and their coming to buy land in hell.

It was a long while before Faith lifted her head from where it rested on Delaney's chest. She brushed the last tears from her eyes, then touched the damp dark spot on his shirt but refused to look up at his face.

"I don't cry," she whispered, "not often."

"I know that," he murmured in return, unable to stop himself from stroking the clean line of her back down to her waist, then up again. "You're a strong woman, Faith, not the girl your father tries to make you."

"There are times when I'm tired of being strong, tired of—"

"Sure you are, duchess."

"Don't, please don't mock me now," she pleaded, trying to pull free from his arms.

Delaney held her for a moment more, then reluctantly he released her. He started to walk away but couldn't let her go on believing that he was mocking her.

"Faith, calling you duchess has nothin' to do with mockery."

She stared at the powerful set of his body, wishing he would face her, unable to ask him to do so. But that didn't stop one burning question from being voiced. "Del, why do you call me duchess? And don't be saying it has to do with the grand tilt of my nose. I won't believe that."

"Maybe calling you duchess reminds me to keep my distance," he answered.

The lack of emotion in his voice made Faith step closer. "But why, Delaney? I've never asked—"

"Don't say more," he grated, his body suddenly rigid.

"... you to keep your distance from me," she finished, ignoring his interruption.

"You should have," he shot back and walked away.

Faith had no choice but to follow him. Keith looked at her askance, but Faith ignored him, too. Her stern look kept Pris quiet, and Joey, sensing his older sister's anger, was silent.

In the days that followed, Faith knew the tension between herself and her father had to break, but she refused to be the one to begin. She sat on the swaying wagon seat, her mind replaying every word she had exchanged with Delaney, fighting a growing need to know more about him that gnawed at her.

They rode a narrow sandy trail up to Antelope Station, hemmed in by bitter barked greasewood and mesquite trees. Delaney continued his teaching of Joey, so Faith learned along with him that the mesquite trees sent roots deep into the earth in its search for water, but that finding the yellow-blossomed paloverde in a dry wash told a man that water was only a few feet from the surface.

They camped for nooning along the road where the stage ran, and Faith replenished a few of their supplies along with trading for fresh peas at Wilson and Timmerman's store. The scattered cabins were weathered, and most of the buildings were of adobe, clustered on the hills around them. While she was in the store, Delaney came in, and she overheard him talking with Mr. Wilson about Charles Stanton, the deputy county recorder.

"He's greedy, all right, and vicious," Delaney agreed. "Heard he's in league with the cutthroat Mexicans over in Weaverville."

"You heard that right enough. But he's more than that. Hires them to do his dirty work. Can't expect much else from a man that was forced to leave off studying to be a priest. Threw him out of the monastery, they did, on charges of immorality."

"Keep a watch," Delaney warned, then turned to Faith. "You near finished? We can cover some miles before dusk."

Rock wall corrals, stone houses, and saguaro cacti followed as they skirted the base of Rich Hill, and Delaney warned them all to keep their eyes open, for this was Weaverville. But Keith was too excited at being near the placer claims that had yielded almost a million dollars in gold. He fired questions at Delaney, asking where Antelope Creek was, and the peak just north of it, and was it true that a Mexican found the first nuggets before Peeples.

With an unaccustomed abruptness Delaney answered him, but Faith noticed that he rode close to the wagons with his rifle held across his lap until they were well past Octave. Keith, while obeying Delaney's orders to keep a watch out, persisted in wanting to know exactly where the Congress mine was located since it was the oldest producing mine in the territory.

And Robert Becket, riding behind his oldest son in the wagon, listened to every word that fed his growing rage.

Delaney pushed them to ride a little past dusk, until they were away from the occasional miner they saw, and made camp below Congress Junction. He hurried Faith through supper, smothered the fire, and then took one of the rifles to hand to her.

"You sleep with this tonight."

"Why? You've never suggested I take a rifle to bed with me before, Mr. Carmichael."

"There's gold. There's men who'll kill for it 'round here. You need more reason? I warned you to look at yourself. A woman like you makes a man remember gold ain't the only thing worth having."

Faith took the rifle, secretly pleased that Delaney once again made her believe she was pretty, desirable, and some-one he might want.

In the next moment she was swearing under her breath at him.

"Find your bush close by tonight, duchess: I don't want to come looking for you."

Fuming every step of the way, Faith, dragging Pris along with her, finally found a thick-trunked mesquite tree to afford them privacy while they relieved themselves. But she found it took a great deal of courage to walk back to camp to face Delaney.

Robert complained of an itch driving him crazy the next morning. Delaney offered him the choice of laying up for the day or going on. Robert chose to go on, but by midday, just within sight of an adobe mill on the Hassayampa River, he had to tell Keith to stop.

Delaney had started to ride back when an old miner hailed him.

"Del, you're a long way from Tucson."

"Henry, didn't think to see you here," he greeted him, dismounting and walking toward the man.

"I keep hoping that Mr. Phelps will do the right thing by me. All the money they gave me for the down payment is gone to fight this man and his New York interests that steal my mine."

Keith rushed to Delaney's side, elbowing him in the side to be introduced. "Henry Wickenburg, this is Keith Becket. A young man with a taste for gold mining."

Henry's eyes sparkled, and he pumped Keith's hand up and down several times, smiling to hear the eager questions pouring forth from the boy as he led him a ways toward his adobe house.

Delaney knew he wouldn't see much of either one of

them for a while. Henry had a tendency to talk someone's
ear clean off about his Vulture Mine and the smartest little
burro a man had ever owned. He couldn't blame Henry for
a bit of prideful bragging. If that burro had not wandered off
during the night, Henry would not have discovered surface
gold at the base of the mountain west of the river. His mistake, if Delaney could call it that, was to build an arrastra to
mill the crude ore while trying to work the mine at the same
time. It was impossible, so Henry sold his mining interest
but never got paid all he was promised.

By the time he walked back to the wagons, he could hear
Robert yelling at Faith.

"Thinking about sending that man clear 'round hell's half
acre," Delaney muttered to himself.

"I don't know what to do for you, Pa," Faith protested,
catching sight of Delaney coming near.

"What's the trouble?" he asked her, glancing into the
wagon to where Robert lay with his leg propped up and
a look of agony on his face.

"His leg is itching something fierce. I—"

"Becket, give me your hand," Delaney cut in. "Let's get
you outside an' strip off those bandages. Likely you need
breathing room."

Much as he hated having to depend upon Delaney to help
him, Robert stretched out his hand.

Faith snatched up the quilt from the wagon and spread it
on the ground while Delaney supported her father's weight.
Amid a great deal of groaning on her father's part, Delaney
settled Robert down. Faith eyed her father, believing that he
made more of his being uncomfortable than he really was.
She ignored his pleading look when Delaney took out his
knife and began to cut away the wrappings and climbed
into the wagon. After opening her mother's trunk, Faith
removed the top tray and searched below, where herbs and

other dried roots, leaves and seeds were stored. She glanced out to see that Delaney had the wooden splints off and was slowly unwinding the bandages from her father's leg.

Delaney would never deliberately hurt him, but Faith shook her head, knowing her father thought as much. Finding the little blue bundle she wanted, she lifted it free, one finger tracing over her mother's elegant copperplate handwriting that labeled this pokeweed. A tide of grief swept over her, one that she quickly buried. It wouldn't do to have her father see the sadness in her eyes. He'd use it against her.

She found the crock of lard and a clean bowl, then took them outside with her. Delaney had already filled a bucket with clean water, and she used it to wash the flakes of dry skin from the sickly pale thinness of her father's injured leg. She even managed a smile when Robert's groans turned to sighs of pleasure as she gently rubbed the leg dry and then spread a mixture of dried pokeweed root and lard over the skin to relieve the itching.

"You rest out here in the shade, Pa," she said, taking up the wrappings and bandages to put them to soak in the bucket. "I'll wash these and tear up fresh linen for you."

"Where's Pris and Joey?" Delaney demanded from behind her.

Faith spun around. "What? I haven't . . . oh, no! Where are they?"

Chapter Eight

"FAITH, WHAT—"

"Nothing, Pa. Don't worry. They can't be far. I'll find them and when I do—" She stopped herself from saying more, far from reassured. She hurried to Delaney's side, her look at him conveying the fear that took hold.

But he paid her no attention, busy studying the land. She found herself trying to follow his gaze, looking for a glimpse of bright cloth that would reveal where either child was. Shades of browns, rusts, and greens merged before her eyes as the earth, rocks, and bushes seemed to meld with the trees and man-size cactus into one empty, desolate view.

Delaney's gaze narrowed as he spotted three dark brown hawks perched for hunting on a sixty-foot-high saguaro. "Smart hunters," he murmured, knowing their prey had no chance to escape, for the hawks worked as a team to circle and flush it out to the open. But the sight drew him forward, and Faith to follow after him.

Delaney easily climbed a slope of sandstone rubble but turned when he heard Faith slide on the loose scree. She took hold of his hand, and he pulled her up beside him. About fifty feet away he spotted the children. "See them?" he asked, placing one hand on her shoulder to turn her.

Pris and Joey stood with their backs toward them in a small dry wash. Faith sighed with relief, but then she realized how still they were. Crying out softly, she grabbed Delaney's arm.

"What's wrong with them?" she demanded, sensing the lack of tension in his body, but absently dismissing it.

"Nothing." He stopped her from rushing down toward them. "Leave them be," he whispered. "There's a hummer on Joey's shoulder."

"A what?" Faith jerked free of his hold. "They could get hurt off by themselves. I know you've taught Joey a few things, but you can't forget that he's blind and Pris is just a little—"

"Duchess." Placing two fingers on her lips, he silenced her. "If there was danger to either one of them from a hummingbird, do you think I'd be standing here?"

Faith scanned his beard-stubbled face, looking deep into his eyes to find the truth. "No," she finally whispered.

Delaney held her gaze with his own. Dragging one finger across her bottom lip, he saw her eyes widen and felt the warmth of her breath sigh over his finger. Her breath rushed in and out, and he guessed at the sudden race of her heart by the pulse visible in the hollow of her throat. He drew a small sound of surprise and pleasure from her when he used his thumb to stroke her lip again, then caress her cheek. "So damn soft," he murmured, thinking about kissing her, deepening the kiss until hungry tongues slid and mated with the wild heat that flared between them.

"The children?" she managed to whisper, closing her eyes to savor the subtle caress.

Delaney allowed himself one more touch before he stepped away from her and gave a shrill whistle that made Faith open her eyes and look to see the children, Pris holding tight to Joey's hand, running toward them.

"Faith! Faith, did you see? It came right down on Joey's arm and then went on his shoulder. That little bird stood still in front of us with nothing to hold it at all!" Pris shouted, dragging Joey up to where they stood. "It flew backward, I swear it did, and I tried to make Joey see it! Over and over it went right in the air! Did you see? Did you?"

With a warning look Delaney stopped Faith from lacing into them. Tugging on Joey's red neckerchief, he smiled down into Pris's sparkling eyes. "The hummer thought Joey's bandanna was a bright red flower. He was looking for food."

"We weren't scared," Pris announced, slipping her hand into Delaney's.

"Seeing a hummer is going to bring us good luck, right, Del?" Joey asked.

"Well, more like good news, scout," Delaney answered, ruffling his hair. With a light touch Joey's fingers followed the length of his extended arm, and he moved to stand beside him. "But," Delaney continued in a soft, firm voice, "you two gave your sister a fright running off without telling anyone."

"Joey said we couldn't get lost. You taught him how to find his way."

Hunkering down so that their faces were close, Delaney smoothed back the tangle of Pris's hair. "Little one, I taught Joey and he learns well, but you don't worry folks that care about you. Ever." Standing, trying to keep a stern look on his face, Delaney took each child's hand into one of his. Mumblings of being sorry came from both of them.

From behind him Faith leaned close to whisper in his ear. "You constantly find a way to surprise me with your patience."

With a narrow-eyed gaze he glanced over his shoulder at her. He told himself he didn't want the closeness the soft warmth in her eyes invited. The only thing he did want was that smooth-moving body.

"Yeah, duchess," he answered gruffly, "I'm a right patient man."

Later that night Delaney stood alone in a quiet thicket of mesquite. The moonlight played over the shadowed black rocks, gilded them and the clumps of cactus.

There should have been peace for him; the sight of the desert stretching out forever usually soothed him.

But not tonight.

Delaney lifted the bottle of cheap whiskey and broke one of his own hard-and-fast rules: no drinking on the trail. He took a long, throat-clenching gulp. It was cheap, raw, and warm, filling his mouth before he swallowed. And he thought about finding himself a woman that was the same, but that wasn't going to cure what ailed him. The bottle wouldn't do it for him, either, he knew that, but it didn't stop him from taking another drink.

He was in a mood for trouble, and he knew it would come looking for him if he went into town. Just as he knew what would happen if he stayed near camp tonight.

His free hand rose to the skystone hanging in the open vee of his shirt. With his thumb and index finger he rubbed it over and over, thinking about the satin softness of Faith's mouth.

"Snakes in purgatory!" he muttered, corking the bottle. What the hell was he going to do about the duchess? He set the bottle down and rolled himself a smoke, cupping his hands around the lit match and quickly blowing it out.

"I'm friendly, Del."

"Jassy?" He spun and pinned the wizened old miner in place behind him. "You should know better than to sneak up on a man."

"Henry told me you were out here somewhere. Can't see all that good in the dark."

"Thought you were gonna stay in Prescott a while."

"Got lucky an' got a stake." Wrinkling his nose, the old man stepped closer. "That whiskey?"

Lifting the bottle, Delaney handed it over and relit his cigarette. He smoked, watching as Jassy helped himself to a few swallows, wiped his mouth with the back of his hand, and made a satisfied sound.

"Man can't walk worth two hoots in hell on one leg, Del."

"Help yourself to another. You come to find me for a bit of social time?"

"Tolly tole me what happened with Chelli. Figured you'd be interested to know that he rode outa town like his hoss was on fire."

"Where's he heading?"

"Him?" Jassy answered, taking another drink. "Figure he'd find hisself a *cumuripa*."

"And where's this rathole for Chelli?"

"Maybe south along the Gila. Don't know for sure. Met up with Silver Shumway afore I left, an' he was tellin' me that Chelli an' some renegades passed some woman over the prairie in Two Guns."

Delaney shot him a quick look but knew Jassy wouldn't lie to him. If he said Chelli and some renegades raped a woman, that is exactly what they did. Delaney dug into his pocket, pulled out a roll of bills, then peeled off a few.

"You add this to your stake, an' if you find more than iron filings, save some for me."

"Ain't a need, Del. You're always square with a man." Jassy wasn't given a choice; Delaney tucked the rolled bills into his shirt pocket. "I'm onto somethin' real good this time. If it ain't the real thing, may God knock my head off with sour apples. I made me a promise that I'm gwine find me a mother lode as shore as punkins ain't cauliflowers."

Laughing, Delaney pinched off the end of his smoke and squatted down to dig a small hole to bury it. He shared a drink with Jassy, thanked him, and walked back to camp.

He had warned Chelli what would happen to him if he sniffed his back trail. But the thought of Chelli touching Faith chilled him. He reached up for his skystone, felt its warmth, and let the cold rage subside. If the duchess wasn't for the likes of him, she sure as the hell-broth he drank wasn't for a loose-legged gully-raker like Chelli.

Faith stirred and turned over onto her back when she heard Keith come back to camp and crawl under his wagon to sleep. She dozed each night until she knew that Delaney was close by, keeping watch. Soothed by the thought that nothing could happen to any of them with him on guard, she fell into a dreamless sleep. The nightmares had stopped . . . was a half-formed thought.

Three nights later they were bedded down at the base of the White Tank Mountains. Delaney had been edgy all day. Faith sensed it, but when she asked, he shrugged off her question.

She was not sure what made her wake that night. It had been some time since Keith had come back. She listened but heard nothing to account for a feeling that something was wrong. Fear that Delaney could be hurt forced her up and out of the wagon.

Shivering in the night's chill, she listened once again. There was a tense silence in the air, and all was still. She started around the wagon when a hand clamped over her mouth.

Her response to the warmth and hard press of a man's body crowding her against the wagon wheel told Faith it was Delaney who held her before her mind realized it.

Her sleep-clouded mind instantly cleared. Something *was* wrong. She made no move to struggle. It would have been foolish when she felt the tension that gripped his powerful body. He eased his hold on her mouth so that she could breathe.

Shivers raced down her spine when he slid his hand up her arm, across the shoulder to cup her neck for a second before he drew her hair aside. Her stomach turned over and her legs trembled to feel his warm lips against her ear. Even then she barely heard the words he mouthed.

"Company's here."

All she could do was nod to show she understood that someone who shouldn't be there was prowling around the camp.

"Stay."

His command. Hers to obey. Before she drew another breath, he was gone without a sound.

Faith worried that her pristine nightgown acted as a beacon in the wan moonlight. She strained to hear where Delaney was moving, but all that came back to her was a brooding sense of quiet, an unease that made the animals restless for no apparent reason. There was a reason, she reminded herself. Delaney had given her the cause.

Someone was out there.

Reaching into the wagon, she pulled her quilt from the floor between the beds where Pris and Joey slept on, unaware. She glanced over at the wagon where her father slept, and below where Keith made his bed, but they weren't awake. After wrapping the quilt around her, she leaned the loaded rifle by her side and waited.

Delaney waited, too. He was concealed within a small thicket and knew there was a lone man out there. A man on foot who had learned the same waiting patience he had from the Indians, or was himself an Indian. There was no doubt to his conclusions. A white man got restless after long minutes had passed without sounds of pursuit. So Delaney remained still, listening to the night, as he had since he had been startled into awareness by the ancient sense of danger.

Overhead a nighthawk dived and veered off before attacking its prey. Delaney's head came up like a wolf's, and his nostrils flared, scenting dried blood, and with it a pungent herb. His unseen enemy was wounded and close to him. Shifting his stance, he had no worry of making a sound. The rawhide soles of his moccasins that he wore for night prowls allowed him to feel the smallest pebble. To dislodge a stone or twig could alert his enemy to his position.

Drawing his knife, he scanned the candle-shaped yuccas, the rock outcrops, every low-growing bush that could offer a hiding place to a man. Every breath he inhaled helped him to pin down the position from where the man scent came to him.

He couldn't help recall the nights when he was allowed to stay on the reservation with Taza, who with other boys taught him their hunting skills. He didn't know what made him think he would need all of those skills now, but instinct sounded an alarm he had to heed.

Delaney slipped from the thicket, his body braced for the attack that came from behind. A half-pivot helped him to avoid the downward thrust of a knife. Delaney jammed his elbow back, satisfied to hear a grunt and the rush of expelled air that followed. His hand fisted over the knife handle, and he spun to land a solid right to his assailant's jaw. The man went down in a crumbled heap.

He stood stock still for a moment. It was over too fast. Blood rushed through his warrior-honed body. For minutes he stood, scanning and listening, making sure that his senses had not failed him and that there was only this lone man.

A groan drew his attention. He hunkered down, still holding his knife, and using his free hand turned the man over. Wetness, warmth, and something sticky from whatever was on the man's shoulder now clung to his hand. Thought of the man's wound made Delaney careless. He leaned closer and found a blade at his throat.

"Shit! Better watch real careful with that. You're liable to cut someone."

"Del-a-ney?"

The hoarse whisper raked over Delaney's nerve ends. Even with the blade at his throat he swallowed.

"Seanilzay?"

"Come far. Find you."

"Why? What happened to you?" Delaney demanded.

Lowering the knife Seanilzay tried to sit up, but he was weak from loss of blood, the distance he had traveled, and the brief scuffle with Delaney. His fingers clenched like talons on his friend's arm. "Brave to speak with . . . blade at throat."

"As you are to attack a man so wounded. Talk will wait." Sliding his arm beneath Seanilzay's shoulders, Delaney raised him to sit. "Let me help you to stand. Camp is close."

"The pindahs—

"The whites do not matter. I make my own camp."

"Ah," Seanilzay whispered, "the woman."

To save Seanilzay's pride, Delaney offered no more than his support. He could feel his friend's weakness and knew Seanilzay had used up his reserves of strength.

In his concern for him Delaney had forgotten about Faith. When he came abreast of the wagon, she rushed toward him, stopping short when she saw the Indian.

"He's in no condition to scalp you, duchess. So save your scream."

"I can see that myself. And I wasn't going to scream." Drawing the quilt tighter, she glanced at the dark eyes of the Apache that watched her with unblinking steadiness. "What can I do to help?" she asked, directing her gaze to Delaney and catching him by surprise.

He wanted to refuse her offer, but Seanilzay's sagging weight forced him to answer. "If you've got a blanket to spare from your wagon, set it near where we made the fire. My bedroll's—"

"He's hurt and we shouldn't waste time talking, Delaney." She didn't stop to think but whipped off the quilt covering her and ran to smooth it out. Quickly, without waiting for Delaney to ask, she built up a fire, then left them to get water to heat.

"Rest easy," Delaney murmured to Seanilzay, using his knife to cut away the Indian's shirt.

"See to my leg. There is little feeling." Even these few words exhausted him, and Seanilzay closed his eyes.

Faith lit the lantern hanging on the side of the wagon. She murmured to Pris as she took a folded sheet from the top of the trunk. Hurrying back to the fire, she asked Delaney for his knife to tear the linen into strips.

"You don't need to help me."

"A man's wounded, Carmichael. I want to help, if you will let me."

He spared a quick glance at her. With the flames rising behind her, Faith's body was all shadows. But she moved and revealed clearly defined curves beneath the pale cloth of her nightgown.

"You might try covering up first," he muttered. Setting his knife down, he rose and towered over her. "Move. When you're done, stay with him."

For a startled moment their gazes clashed. Faith was embarrassed by her lack of modesty.

Seanilzay opened his eyes as she spun around. "You speak with a . . . rough tongue to the woman. Do not . . . forget . . ."

"I don't forget. But if you've got strength to talk, use it for something worth telling. Like naming who did this to you?"

"Still the young eagle who demands."

"You're as wily as the fox and as bloodthirsty as a weasel, Seanilzay. How many cornered you?"

"One," he whispered in a shame-filled voice, fighting to draw breath. "Only one *pindah*."

Only one white man. Knowing Seanilzay, Delaney figured the attacker had taken the Apache by surprise. He knelt beside him, gently probing both wounds. "Bullets out?" Seanilzay moved his hand. Delaney lowered his head to sniff, hoping there was no foul odor to indicate suppuration. "It is good that you used pitch to draw the swelling. I won't ask how far you've walked." Delaney knew that as a young man, Seanilzay could cover sixty or seventy miles in a day. But he was no longer young.

"Fort."

Delaney looked at him. "Whipple? Verde?" Seanilzay rolled his head from side to side. "McDowell?" Delaney was rewarded with a rapid blinking of the Apache's eyelids. Questions burned now, but he merely nodded.

Faith stepped back into the circle cast by the fire. She wore a faded calico gown, but her hair was loose and she held it aside as she tested the heat of the water. Picking up Delaney's knife, she sat on the other side of Seanilzay and, without a word, sliced into the linen.

Delaney rose and walked to where he had spread his bedroll. From his saddlebag he withdrew a small parfleche, the hide soft and supple to his hand. The strong thread that held it together was sinew, cut from the loin of the first deer he had slain. He opened it carefully so as not to spill his precious store of healing herbs and roots.

"No, Pa! No!"

In a reflex as natural as breathing, Delaney's gun was in his hand. Tucking the rawhide ties of the parfleche in his belt, he came up behind Becket and Keith but remained in the shadows. A cold rage settled in his gut when he saw that they were both holding their rifles on Seanilzay. Faith was kneeling beside him, facing her father.

"Get away from that filthy savage," Becket ordered.

"He's hurt, Pa. And you wouldn't be clean if you were wounded and had walked to find help."

"Move, Faith. Now."

"No. You can't hurt him. He's Delaney's friend."

"He's a stinking Apache, girl. Can't you see his dress? And those moccasins? Tolly said theirs had toes curled. You think I'm gonna give him the chance to rape you and slit our throats?" Becket's voice shook with fury. "Keith," he ordered, motioning with his rifle, "get her away from him."

Keith was about to obey and step to the side when he spotted Delaney, standing behind his father, his gun in hand.

"Pa," he warned, "look behind you."

Faith saw the burning heat of Delaney's gaze and raised her hand as if to plead with him, but she said nothing as her father turned around.

Becket eyed the gun, then looked at Delaney's face. "I don't care what—"

"Shut up, Becket. You're wrong, though. The Apache would never rape her. Her skin's too sickly and white. She could take all their luck if they touched her. Now, if your daughter was Apache, still a maid, he would be the one killed for daring to touch her. And if you weren't a blind bigot, you would see that he's in no shape to slit anyone's throat. Now, you got a choice, Becket. Lower that rifle or use it."

Faith bit back her cry. Delaney's face was cast by shadows as he stepped closer to the fire. But the lack of emotion in his eyes, in his voice, brought home to her that he meant what he said.

"Carmichael," Robert finally answered, "you're no better than this savage."

"Remember that, Becket." Delaney grinned, but there was no shared humor, no softening in his features. "Kill an Apache's friend, an' he'll follow you through hell to avenge it."

This time Faith could not hold back a soft cry. It was not for what Delaney threatened, but her catching sight for the first time of the knee-high moccasins he wore. They were the same as the Apache's. The rumors and whispers she had heard about him came rushing back to her. She knew they were all true. It wasn't only his own admission now, but his stance, the dangerous cold fire filling his eyes, and the warning screaming inside her that he would kill her father if he didn't lower that rifle.

There was no time to think, only to act. Coming to her feet, careful to keep her body between her father and the wounded man, Faith spoke.

"There's a man in need of help, lying here and losing blood. The water's boiling. I've torn linen for bandages, but I've never treated a gunshot wound."

Delaney, never taking his eyes from Becket's face, tossed the parfleche toward her. "Hang on to that. Well, Becket, you heard your daughter. I'm a patient man, but you're prodding my limit along about now. Set down the rifle or use it, Becket."

Chapter Nine

"SET IT DOWN, Pa," Faith implored, taking a step closer.

With a snort of disgust Becket lowered the rifle. He swayed where he stood until Keith rushed forward to offer his support. Hobbling back to the wagon, muttering, Becket shook off Keith's arm and stopped. Looking back to where Delaney still stood with his gun lowered but not holstered, he spat on the ground.

"You ain't heard the last of this, Carmichael. Remember, I'm the one who's paying you."

"Paying me don't mean owning me, Becket."

Keith felt a shiver of fear run down his spine. He took hold of his father and forcibly made him return to the wagon.

When they were out of sight and Keith back in his bedroll beneath the wagon, Delaney holstered his gun and returned to Seanilzay's side.

Faith stayed with Delaney, wiping sweat from the Apache's brow while Delaney cleaned his wounds in a gentle manner that surprised her. She replaced water in the basin as he needed it, avid curiosity making her eyes bright. Delaney's demeanor was forbidding, so she buried her questions about what herbs and plants he used or where he had gained such knowledge. Faith's respect increased as his skill and touch brought few groans of pain from the wounded Indian.

But when Delaney heated his knife blade and asked her to hold Seanilzay steady, her stomach churned. She had to turn her face away while he seared the skin to close the wounds. There was a sigh of relief from both Faith and the stoic patient as Delaney spread an ointment he made from grease, dried leaves, and crushed roots.

He left her for a few minutes, only to return and heat piñon pitch, which he smeared over linen strips and, in turn, wrapped them over and around the Apache's bare shoulder and chest. He burned the cotton shirt he had removed and replaced it with one of his own. The cut-off piece of legging went into the fire, sending up an acrid smoke. Once again he walked off into the woods, returning this time with branches thick as her wrist that he trimmed of leaves and bark. The leg was bandaged, and Delaney placed the branches around the leg, wrapping them together with still more linen to hold the leg stiff.

Using his own cup, he brewed a tea, then forced the Apache to drink it. Faith saw for herself how quickly it put the man to sleep.

With a neatness that she was coming to associate with Delaney, he cleaned and stored his belongings and then he came to her.

"We both owe you thanks for helping and for defying your father. Seanilzay will likely never say *a-co-'d* to you, but I will."

"Why?"

"It's simply the Apache way to show good will rather than say it."

"No. I want to know why you helped him."

"The Apache way makes it unthinkable not to help a family member in need."

"Seanilzay is your family?"

"Not in any way that you would understand." He raised his hand to her face, and with a gentle touch he stroked her cheek, her jaw, her throat. His grip tightened, not enough to hurt her, but just enough to let her feel his strength. He measured the beat of her throbbing pulse with his callused fingertips, feeling it become violent in seconds.

Like his own.

In the fading light her eyes had darkened so that the shimmer of gold flecks lay against the deeper, mysterious hue of shadowed turquoise. Delaney had to ignore the warming of his skystone against his skin just as it did each time he was near her.

"Go to sleep, Faith," he whispered in a voice roughened by the need surging in his blood. His gaze was shielded by short, blunt lashes at the pleading look in her eyes. Her mouth became a target. She had a mouth that he thought the most fragile one he'd ever seen on a woman. He wanted nothing more than to take her mouth, take her body with his own, until he couldn't reason why he should not.

"Delaney?"

"Go to bed," he repeated, dropping his hand, then sitting beside Seanilzay, he began honing his knife.

Faith went, not because he ordered her to, but for the dismissal that rippled through his body, more sensed than seen. She was reminded of that first day she had approached him, and without a move he appeared coiled, tense, and ready to strike. She had had a taste of Delaney's venom; only a fool would go back for more.

There was no sleep to be had for the rest of the night. She wished she understood what drove Delaney. There was a darkness inside him that seemed to cry out to her to heal it. She amazed herself that she knew he would never tell her what it was. To add to her sense of floundering in the dark, she was unable to tell anyone of her growing feelings for him. Every breath, every second that passed, filled her with loneliness.

She had no answers or any hope of getting them. The change in him tonight was one she couldn't ignore. He had called her by name, not the hated duchess. Even his touch on her face had been tender, almost a caress. Could a man like Delaney want someone like her?

Restless, she turned and twisted on her hard bed, tucking her hand beneath her cheek, surprised to find there were tears. Foolish woman, she admonished herself. Delaney did not want to get tangled up with her. He had made that plain enough.

Angry with herself, she brought forth from memory the stinging insult of his calling her a whore and his payment for a look.

If that memory did not cure her of foolish thoughts and daydreams about Delaney Carmichael, nothing else would.

The sun raised its curtain on a new day while she watched, spilling the soft brightness of pinks, golds, and blues across the sky. And she still thought about Delaney.

Birdsong sweetly pierced the chilled air, forcing her to reach for her shawl. The loud crack of a rifle shot close by sent her sitting upright. Listening intently, she was ready to grab the loaded rifle from the wagon's corner.

Hushing Pris and Joey as they woke, frightened, Faith released a sigh when the birds began to sing again. She pressed her hand over her breast to still the furious beat of her heart.

A shadowed silhouette stood before the back opening, and she saw that it was Keith, but before she could call out to him, he had moved away.

Pris crept into her lap, hugging her tight. "I was so scared. Papa said the Apache were going to come and slit our throats."

"No, honey, no," Faith murmured, rocking her. "Pa is wrong."

"Delaney won't let them," Joey offered bravely, but he found his way on the other side of Faith and hid his face against her shoulder. "B-but if I'm wrong, Faith, will they try to steal Beula?"

"I don't think so, Joey. And there was only one shot. If anyone was going to attack us, we would hear more." Even as she whispered this reassurance, Keith appeared near the back of the wagon.

"Delaney shot a deer. He's down by the river, dressing it out." Keith reached inside and ruffled Joey's hair. "Had you scared, scout?" His eyes met Faith's. "I was scared for a few minutes there myself. Best we get moving."

Faith helped the children to dress, and when they were outside, she hung a blanket across the open canvas for privacy. She heard her father's voice, but it was muffled. Keith yelled out that he had coffee on, and she hurried to dress, realizing that the lack of sleep had made her slow and clumsy. She had her shoe half-buttoned when she heard Delaney's voice raised in anger. The strong feeling that her father was not going to allow the matter of Seanilzay traveling with them rest made her leave off fastening her shoes, and with her hair falling to her waist, she climbed down from the wagon.

Hurrying to the fire, she saw Delaney kneeling by Seanilzay's side, her father and Keith both standing away from them. After pouring a cup of coffee for herself, she began to slice bacon, wondering if she should say something or let Delaney go on ignoring her. Her hands stilled as she overheard Seanilzay.

"Leave me," he whispered, gripping Delaney's arm. "I have told you what I have done. I am not worthy to claim your care."

Tugging his arm free, Delaney rose, trying to stem the anger that churned inside him. Before dawn Seanilzay had called to him, desperate to talk. He had listened to the confession of what amounted to betrayal, but the years and times between them were older, their good memories deeper, than the fresh cuts Seanilzay's words now made in him.

He tried to understand how hunger and the loss of pride had driven Seanilzay to make promises of help to Major Ross that he knew Delaney would never keep. But it was his promise to find Delaney for Adam Brodie, knowing what stood between them, that brought an unforgiving anger to consume him.

But how could he abandon Seanilzay, no matter that he pleaded for him to do just that?

He glanced over to where Becket stood with his son and knew he wasn't finished demanding that he leave Seanilzay behind, either.

"Well, Carmichael? I've waited long enough. You gonna leave him?"

"Becket," he warned, "you're piling up grief for yourself. The man is helpless. I can't leave him here alone."

Robert clamped his lips together, unable to stop the fury that was building over Delaney's refusal to leave the savage. Much as it galled him, he tried to reason with him once more.

"He'll slow us down. Even you can't deny that. You can't scout and hunt and then tend to him. My girl won't touch him if I say no."

"Girl?" Delaney asked with a sarcastic tone just as Faith rose and went to stand beside her father.

"This is men's talk, Faith." Grabbing hold of her arm, he shoved her away. "Go fix your hair proper." And to Delaney, "We got a standoff. I don't want him with us, and you won't leave him."

Delaney glared at him.

"Pa," Faith interrupted, rubbing her arm, "you can't speak for me. I'm not a little girl anymore."

"You'll do as you're told if you know what's good for you," Becket shouted.

Faith glanced at Delaney and saw him dig into his pant pocket and pull out money. Money her father had paid him.

"No!" she yelled, running to him. "Put it away. My father doesn't want you to leave us. And I will help you tend to Seanilzay until he's strong no matter what he says." She searched his features, hoping for a softening, for some sign that he relented. Delaney stood there, counting out bills. "Must I remind you, Mr. Carmichael, that the deal was made between us?"

"Quit prodding me."

"I'll prod or do whatever it takes to get you to keep your word," she snapped, incensed that he would be so stubborn. Ignoring her father's mutterings, Faith's gaze drifted from Delaney's face down to Seanilzay. She was surprised to see that the Apache's lean, hard face wore a smile. Faith took it to mean that he was offering her encouragement to argue with Delaney.

Stuffing a small fold of bills into his pocket, Delaney handed the rolled balance to Becket. "Take it. And don't bother to count it, it's all there."

He gave a sharp jerk to the front brim of his hat, shadowing his eyes, and turned to Faith. "Duchess, it's been a pleasure. Take care of Pris and Joey."

"Will you feel any guilt at all over our deaths, Mr. Carmichael?" she asked, dogging his steps.

"I'll be riding ahead and leaving sign. Follow it and nothing will happen to you."

"That's not good enough."

"Duchess, you keep biting on me, an' I'll bite back." He lifted his blanket and saddle, walking to where Mirage was staked.

"Go ahead," she whispered.

He spun around so fast she sucked in her breath and stepped back. "Women like you can make a man vicious."

Faith sighed with relief and didn't care that he knew it. "Listen to me," she pleaded, touching his arm. He went still, and her gaze followed his to where her hand rested.

"You like danger, duchess?"

"I don't know. Do I?" she asked with innate honesty.

Delaney didn't answer her. He couldn't. While the spirit of unrest burned in his blood, she was a complication to him.

Faith decided she had been far too bold and removed her hand. "I know my father is wrong about the Apache people. He's scaring the children with talk of them being stolen or of having their throats slit. If you stay, you can stop them from hearing these things. Delaney, we want to make a new life in this land. Will you bear the guilt of knowing that you could have taught Keith, Joey, and Pris to be understanding of the Indians' ways? Do you want them to learn from a man like my father?"

He searched her eyes and found the truth, but the darker shadows were there, too. "You don't much like your father, do you?"

"There are reasons. And don't ask me. I can't tell you."

"No one knows what the Apache will do with children. They might kill them right off, or take a cotton to them and raise them like one of their own with as much care and love. Mostly, it'll depend on a child's age, on how they react, on how fast the Apache have to move."

"You're telling me the truth," she murmured, wanting to know more and not knowing how to ask.

He saw the uncertainty in her eyes. Absently rubbing Mirage's neck, he said flatly, "You're owed that much from me. I've never seen a white child with any of the bands. That's not to say they're not there. Talk is that if they steal them, they run and hide in Mexico up in the Sierra Madres. Since the Mexican government refuses to allow the army to cross the border in pursuit, it's pointless to ponder. If you're still worried, there are men who work to take action to get permission for the soldiers to cross and search for them."

"Well, then," she returned, placing her hands on her hips, "if Pris or Joey are stolen, I'll know where to look for them." Faith waited. She reminded herself that he was hardheaded and hard-hearted. Delaney glanced aside. Her body swelled with temper. "Maybe Chelli would've been the better choice. I was warned of what he would do by a man I thought I respected, but you just proved how wrong I could be. I trust you."

"Stop kicking up hell's own noise, duchess." *She trusted him.* Delaney's mouth kicked up in a reckless grin. He found that fact to be as infuriating as it was tempting. "You're a real sassy-mouth. Ain't ever been called a coward before this—and never by a woman."

"I'll call you the devil's own if I have to. I'm asking you again," she said, reaching out with her hand to still the movement of his on the mare. "Don't leave us alone."

Delaney had heard that tone before. His mind shot back to the first time she had approached him. No begging, no flirting, just Faith and forthright demands. He already agreed with himself that neither one of them had the sense God gave a mule, and he couldn't deny the duchess had his respect for standing up to her father. He did owe her a debt for helping to care for Seanilzay. With a shrug he shook his hand free of her hold and lifted the blanket to Mirage's back. Smoothing it out, he finally answered her.

"Square it up with your father, Faith. We'll be pulling out in half an hour."

"Thank you, Delaney."

"Don't bother. I owe you." He looked at her, a grin creasing his lips. "Duchess, I like your hair loose. It goes with that sassy mouth."

Faith reached up to gather her hair away from her face. She wasn't sure what to say. But there was no way she could mistake the frankly male appreciation in Delaney's eyes.

"What about Seanilzay?" she asked, still flustered.

"I'll tend to his travel."

And Faith saw that he did. She envied Pris being able to stand and watch Delaney work. There was smooth, easy grace in every move. She caught glimpses of him cutting strips from the fresh deer hide. By the time she had doused the fire and returned from washing out the coffeepot, he was using the strips to tie crisscrossed saplings over Mirage's withers. The mare balked until Delaney soothed her with words Faith didn't understand. The vee-shape poles widened from the mare's hind legs, and Delaney tied more strips across them to form a web. Faith had to make sure the tops of the water barrels were secure, so she didn't have a chance then to ask him what he was making.

Once the children were up on the wagon seat, she walked over to him. Seanilzay was bound in what appeared to be an upright bed. Her quilt cushioned his body, and Delaney's blanket covered him.

"Will he be able to rest in this?" she asked.

"Snug and safe as a baby."

"Mirage doesn't seem to be pleased about pulling—"

"She's never had a travois on her, but I'll keep her to a walk."

"He'd be better off riding in the wagon," she said, taken aback by the scathing look he shot her. "I guess that was foolish to suggest."

"You said it, not me." He leaned down to whisper to Seanilzay, nodded at his answer, and stepped up into his saddle. Checking the rope that rested beneath his thigh, Delaney looked down at her. "About ready?"

Faith glanced around and saw that Keith had finished harnessing the mules and was up on his wagon. "Yes," she answered, gathering up her skirt and petticoats to run to her own place.

Slapping the floppy-brim hat on, Faith waited until Joey settled close by her side. His hand covered hers to help hold the reins. "Move out," he called without any reminder.

Delaney had intended to stay close and skirt the mountains, but the way would be a rough ride for Seanilzay. He led them out, closer to the Hassayampa, keeping them parallel with the river.

Mirage settled down after a few minutes of accustoming herself to her new burden, and Delaney allowed her to pick her way. His own thoughts wandered a bit. Major Ross had to pay for what he had done to Seanilzay. But he would have to wait until the Beckets were out of his way. Delaney could not have them involved. Yancy Watts and Brodie were buried in a sealed-off corner of his mind. There was a debt that needed settling with them, too, but that had been a long time in the making. He would wait. It wouldn't be hard on him. He kept telling the duchess how patient a man he was, didn't he?

* * *

Low spots in the rivers helped the crossings, but the days began to pass in a blur to Faith. She did not try to deny there was peace to be found in this land. The sight of towering pinnacles and buttes in the distance that arose from the desert floor was sometimes staggering. She would watch when she could, the shifting angles of the sun reflecting light and throwing shadows on the chiseled worn rocks. Red shales, yellow-gray limestone, brown sandstone, pink granite, and all the shades in between created a rainbow for anyone to gaze upon.

Seanilzay was rapidly regaining his strength. Her father, while tense and jumpy, had held his tongue about Seanilzay traveling with them. Faith only wished she could find a way to repay Delaney for the time and patience he offered Joey. She had to forcibly remind herself that her brother was blind, for Delaney had him working right along with him most days.

She was doing a bit of blooming herself and didn't think she was being vain to notice. The dark shadows from beneath her eyes were almost gone. Although it was hard work to break camp, drive the wagon, then stop to make camp each night, she was putting on weight and filling out her clothes again.

The only thing that preyed on her mind was Delaney's careful, deliberate avoidance of being alone with her. She did not believe anyone else had noticed how he would move away from the fire if she came near, or his calling to Joey to come help him with something when she stood close by.

It was not an action to take a man like Delaney to task over, and she knew that, too.

But knowing did not stop the wanting that filled her sleep with restless yearnings and dreams that made her wake, flushed and breathless.

Like tonight. She was drawn from the wagon by the low murmur of voices near the fire. Peering around the side, she saw it was Delaney and Seanilzay. A shaft of guilt speared her for standing there, straining to overhear what they said. She did not dare try to get closer, for she knew that Delaney would sense her presence.

"Our tongue has not the words to make you listen and to hear what I say. We will speak in your *pindah* tongue."

"I don't want to talk about my father. He's dead. You do not speak of the dead."

"I have done much against my people and my beliefs. This is one step I must take, and you must walk with me."

Delaney glanced at the fierce eyes that snared his gaze. He knew that Seanilzay was aware that he had not forgotten or forgiven what he had done. The deaths of his parents were a raw wound that had never healed. Now Seanilzay asked him to open that wound.

"Come, sit beside me. There is much to tell and little time for me."

Respect drove Delaney to sit beside him; friendship, time, and teachings forced him to listen.

"When Jeffords first brought your father to us, he called him an honest man. Your father desired to learn our ways and our speech. Many were willing to teach him and your mother. She was a good woman. Both of them had pure hearts and open thoughts. Your father sold us the beef he raised and did not cheat us. Your mother taught our children the *pindah* speech. They fought to get us blankets when we were cold. All this you must remember."

"I remember, Seanilzay. I remember the goodness in their hearts." Delaney rested his hands, palms down on his spread knees, his legs crossed at the ankles. He would not look at the Apache now. His thoughts carried him back in time, and he knew Seanilzay would remain silent until he was ready to listen again.

"You walk the path of the past, Del-a-ney. The time when the soldiers paid your father to speak for them. He earned little and would not tell their lies. When Jeffords left us, Brodie came to sell us his beef. He lied to all. His count was wrong. The beef poor. The live cattle sick. Your father knew this. He went to Brodie."

"Wait," Delaney cut in. "My father never told me."

"You were not here. You worked for the iron rail. Brodie was angry with your father. He made friends with many agents and the soldiers with his whiskey and money. They all knew that Brodie cheated us. They were the men who said your father lied. They did not stop the other soldiers who came to take your father to the white man's court. They did not tell what Brodie did. They helped him make the numbers that showed your father cheated us."

Delaney slowly turned to look at him. "You have proof that Brodie helped to falsify the records that the army used to convict my father and send him to prison?"

"I have nothing but my words to give."

Looking out into the dark, Delaney thought of the weeks his mother had faced alone because everyone claimed they could not find him. By the time he returned, it was too late. His father had died in prison, and his mother . . . no, he could not remember her fate.

"Brodie feared your father's truth. Some whisper that he had your father killed in prison."

"None spoke of this to me. Not one."

Seanilzay heard the deep, chilling tone. His fingers began to pluck at the blanket. "There were good reasons."

"Who among you knew of this? Who hid this truth from me?" His gaze targeted Seanilzay's, and he had his answer. The Apache closed his eyes. "Are you a man who can walk taller than Brodie? Shall I proclaim to all that your name is He Who Lies?" he grated from between clenched teeth. "Look at me! I gave all that you asked when you called my name."

"It is our way not to refuse such."

"I know that! I did it in friendship. I will call myself no friend of this Apache. May coyote take you to the underworld."

Stricken by his vile curse, Seanilzay followed his move to stand and tower above him. He had no strength to rise and meet the anger burning in Delaney's eyes.

"You must call me what pleases you," he responded with a simple dignity. "I will finish so that the anger that burns within you will force you to seek justice. Too long have you run. Brodie is your enemy. He will kill you as he killed your father. He will take the breath from you as he stole it from your mother when he searched your home for the journal your father kept."

"My . . ." Delaney swallowed painfully. He could not repeat the last words. Pain exploded inside him. Pain that was instantly swamped by a rage consuming him. "*Ahagahe!*" he cried, visibly shaking. Unable to trust himself not to lash out, he began to run until the night shadows claimed him.

"You no longer need to hide, Woman with Eyes of Sky," Seanilzay whispered in a weakened voice, gesturing with one hand for Faith to come forward.

"What did Delaney cry out?" she demanded.

"I have no word in your tongue. It is our word for a rage so great that no man will speak it until he has stood all that he can."

Despite her own anger with the old man, she felt sorry when she saw the tremor in his hands. "How long have you known that I was listening?"

"I made him speak in your tongue so you could hear."

Since she was searching the dark for a sign of where Delaney had disappeared to, it took a few moments for her to understand what he told her. "Then you lied to him to make sure that I heard." Her eyes seemed to glow from an inner fury. "Was everything you told him true?" Seanilzay nodded. She stopped herself from asking him more questions and walked to the edge of light cast by the fire.

"He will not come back soon."

"Then I'll go find him." Faith pulled her shawl tight, telling herself she was not afraid. Delaney needed someone, she was sure of that much.

"He will not speak to you," Seanilzay warned her. "Feed the fire, for my bones are chilled. Come sit, and together we wait. I will tell you of the man you hold within your heart."

Chapter Ten

RUN. THE DESERT land was his. He had hunted and walked and drank from its water. The land offered him shelter and freedom. The wind should have cooled his body, but such was his rage that he burned. Without breaking stride he stripped off his shirt and tossed it aside. Run. Like the prey. Like the hunter. It was the only thought, the only action he could allow himself.

He could race the wind. He could be a boy again, learning to run beneath the blazing sun, carrying a stone, whose weight needed both his hands to hold it. He could feel the taut stretch of his muscles, and hear for himself the beat of his feet against the earth. He demanded more speed from his body. His skin was sheened with sweat. He challenged the land to stop him, reckless in his flight, down dry washes, up their scree slopes, dodging the black shapes of rocks and cactus.

His lungs begged for air. He could remember the time before. He could not stop. He had to run his race and prove himself equal to the boys of Apache blood.

But there was no village in sight this night. There was no shaman waiting for him to come and take his turn to set his stone before him, lungs straining, throat burning, and waiting, waiting for the nod that would allow him to spit out the mouthful of water he had carried and dared not to swallow. There was no celebration.

Once again his chest heaved and his lungs cried out for air. His legs clenched with the agony of cramps. And still he ran. Pain lanced his side. Delaney ignored it.

There was a pain inside him that nothing physical happening to his body could touch. Grief welled. He tried to bury it. But this was a grief that had never been allowed its time of mourning. It welled up and spilled from his heart and mind until its need surpassed all others.

He staggered to a stop. Hunched over, dragging lungfuls of air into himself, a screaming began and poured forth into the night, a scream that rang in his own ears until the screaming and ringing melded, going on and on.

His belly contracted, driving him to his knees. Bile rose and he retched until there was nothing left. Sprawled in the dirt, he lay there.

. . . charred remains of a cabin. Not a leaf stirred, not one bird sang to welcome him home. From the clearing below he gazed at the hill where they buried his mother beneath the shade of the peach tree. No one could tell him why she had not escaped the fire.

He had been alone then, but now a new loneliness came to him. It overtook him suddenly before he was aware, and the tears fell. Once Cochise had told him there was no shame to cry when sadness came. His tears fell to the earth, and his hands gently raked the moisture in so that he could take comfort from knowing that Mother Earth shared his sorrow. A sorrow that went deep into the center of his soul.

"He took her breath." Seanilzay's words. They burned in his mind.

Delaney tried to raise himself; time and again he fell back against the warm earth. "Mother, lend me your strength," he whispered through parched lips. He managed to get to his knees, but when he attempted to stand, his legs gave out from under him.

His head fell forward, his hands rubbed his thighs, and slowly his hips sank to rest on his heels. Delaney raised one hand to touch his skystone. Of late there had been no soothing, no comfort from its touch; there was less now. It was cold.

Words from the past came to him, words that would begin the lightning ceremony, when White Painted Woman lay down and lightning flashed four times to act as a man to beget Child of the Water.

He gazed skyward, one hand clutching the stone, the other drawing free his knife. "White Painted Woman, I gave you to drink the salt of my tears." Lifting the skystone high, until he felt the rawhide dig into the back of his neck, he called out to the many spirits that guided the Apache, each with their special power to aid him. "Yusen, life-giver, White Painted Woman and Child of the Water, I call to you. Killer of Enemies and Mountain People, hear my song. I have protected the secret that has been entrusted to me."

Delaney held the stone with one hand and turned his knife so that the tip faced him. He took a deep breath and held it, bringing the blade nearer, until its point rested against his chest above the slowing beat of his heart. Drops of sweat fell from his brow onto the blade just as the tip bit his skin. He cut himself just deep enough for tiny drops of blood to well up.

"White Painted Woman," he whispered, watching as the first drops fell, "I give you my lifeblood." Again the knife bit his skin, forming an angled line to the center of his chest. "With every drop of my blood that falls, so will my enemy's." Gritting his teeth, he cut himself again, bringing the line down to his right side. "Lend me your great strength, Yusen. Give to me yours, White Painted Woman. Child of the Water and

Killer of Enemies, hear my need for the strength to vanquish my enemy that dared to spill the lifeblood of my father and my mother."

He set the knife aside, released the skystone to fall against his chest, and stretched his arms wide. "Thunder People, I call to you. Long ago you hunted for the *Inde'*. I ask you to give to me your great skills. Send to me your voice. Lightning, hear my cry. Send to me your power. You have tested me in my vision and not found me wanting. *Intchi-dijin*, the blackest of winds, raise your cry and call out for me to the Controller of Water. I beg to hear your voices."

With his arms outstretched he lowered himself until he lay prone on the earth, letting the blood seep into the soil of the land he loved.

The night became still.

Smoke spiraled from the fire. Faith was uneasy. "What can he be doing out there so long and alone, Seanilzay?" She gazed at the Apache, but his eyes were closed and his breathing uneven. "What's wrong?" she demanded, moving closer.

"Listen. Watch the sky."

Faith angled her head to one side. The flames of the fire began to dance, leaping higher, although she had not added any fresh wood. A breeze freshened, then grew stronger. "There is nothing but a wind coming up. I—" Her words were lost in the next moment. A howling rent the night.

Seanilzay took hold of her hand. "Do not be afraid."

She shivered when the sound came again. Her blood began to chill, for far off she heard the coyote's song. Her grip on the Indian's hand tightened. "Delaney! Please, let me go to him."

"Stay. He mourns his mother's passing. It is good to know he calls the spirits for help. He has not forgotten."

He held Faith's hand tight, refusing to let her go. "No. You must let One Like Lightning be as he must. Alone."

"One Like Lightning? Is that his Apache name?" Faith felt herself drawn to look skyward. Far to the west she saw flashes of forked light.

"You must never call him by this. It is a name we use to talk of him among our people. Never do we say this name to his face."

"I won't say it. I promise."

Seanilzay opened his eyes and looked at her. "Go to your wagon. The rain will come."

"No. The lightning is far off." But just then a rumble of thunder pealed. Faith started. Wild forked lightning lit the sky close to them. Seconds later thunder cried out in hammer blows.

"Lift up your face, Woman with Eyes of Sky. Taste the wind. Taste the tears he cried."

Faith couldn't stop herself from doing as he said. Within minutes drops of soft, warm rain fell on her face. The wind brought with it the dust, and she closed her eyes against its sting, but nothing would make her move to shelter. Delaney was out there, somewhere. Alone.

She did not know she had whispered the last aloud, until Seanilzay answered her.

"Now, he is not alone. He has called for our spirits. The wind has answered him. The thunder has come. The lightning shows him the way. The rain of life will turn. It will not fall as the soft rain of the woman. It will come as the hard and dark rain of the man. There is much strength and power in this man who you hide in your heart. He will be yours."

"Mine, Seanilzay?" she murmured through bloodless lips, trying to understand and believe all that the Apache had told her, yet frightened for Delaney, frightened, too, of what she was seeing for herself. "I wish it could be so."

Thunder growled like a beast; its deep voice shook the earth. Lightning spiked the black sky like snakes that writhed in agony. And the wind carried roiling clouds to pile them deep above them. Faith didn't understand why she felt so alive. Her tongue tasted the sweet rain, and she sipped it, feeling a soothing peace fill her.

Seanilzay watched and smiled. "Now you see."

Reluctantly Faith dragged her gaze from the eerie light that filled the sky while thunder belled over the land. "No, I do not see as you mean, but I do believe that some force is here, Seanilzay. Let me make your bed beneath the wagon before the rains come."

Once she helped Seanilzay, she hurried to the back of the wagon intending to seek her own bed. She was certain that Delaney would not return tonight. But the fierce, breathtaking power of the unfolding storm held her where she stood.

The clouds, dark, violent billows, coiled and rolled into massive thunderheads. Early summer thunderstorms had never frightened her, but she had never seen one with such potency.

Dust blew high and another warning rumble sounded close by. Flashes of lightning seemed to glow from the inside of the clouds. Thunder roared, as if to proclaim its might, and the wind rose with a rush to answer the challenge.

Birds flew, seeking shelter. Cottontails and other small animals ran in erratic directions. Swirls of dust appeared in the distance across the flats. The wildness filled her, and she did not want to think of Delaney and what the Apache told her. She could not believe any man had the power to call what she witnessed.

Again the lightning danced wickedly across the sky, again the thunder crashed until the ground on which she stood shook. She glanced back and then over to the other wagon, expecting to see her father or brother awake and watching as she was. She stood alone as the wind bent and twisted the mighty cactus. Crackling lightning revealed the greenish cast of the underside of clouds as the rain hit the earth in huge drops. But the storm played out its attack and retreat on the land before her, and she lifted her hand to touch the rain. The clouds surged away from her. Faster and faster the rain fell, disappearing into the thirsty land, and still she stood, watching as the storm unleashed its fury, until the black curtain of rain would let her see no more.

Faith awoke, stiff and sore, from where she spent the night sitting within the cramped space at the back of the wagon.

The light from the east brightened, and long shafts of color began to appear in the sky, lifting the land from shadows. The morning air was chill, but it would soon be gone in the heat of the coming day. She rubbed her eyes, seeing the grotesque shapes of the cacti silhouetted as a pale yellow glow was cast over the broken land. Yellow became lilac in the blink of her eye, then changed to rose, fanning out, even as she watched, to a pale orange, and then abruptly it was sunrise. The desert spread out before her in a broad, endless expanse of harsh browns and grays, warming as the sun began its climb.

She stretched and yawned, slipping down to stand beside the wagon. Faith rubbed her eyes, then looked out again at the land. She had listened and learned when Delaney spoke to them about the rains coming to transform the land into one of incredible beauty. When the rains were hard, flowers bloomed, what appeared dead burst forth life, all that was barren flushed full with the seeds of new birth.

She turned wildly, running a short way, and spinning around.

There was no beauty. No spark of new green to ease the stark browns, no flower edged with more than the morning dew, no rivulets of water sparkled under the first sun. Nothing, nowhere she looked showed signs that the skies had opened in a wild downpour. The land, to her eyes, appeared as lifeless this morning as it had when they made camp last night.

Had she dreamed? Or was this a nightmare?

No. She refused to believe that. She had heard the thunder. She felt the shaking of the earth she stood upon. She had tasted the gentle rain and felt it on her skin. Her eyes had witnessed the tormented dance of lightning across the sky.

Yet, even in her denial of what she now saw, she bent down to touch the earth. It was dry.

"No! It can't be." She ran back to her wagon. Crawling, she reached out to wake Seanilzay. He would tell her the truth.

But her hand closed over a bundled blanket, and as she drew the wool cloth toward her, Faith knew what she would find.

His bed was empty. As if the blanket burned her hands, she shoved it away and scrambled free from the wagon's underside. She forced herself to stand, a tremor starting inside until her body shook.

The storm had not frightened her, but fear found its way into her mind now. A mere whisper of a breeze brushed her face, and she lifted her eyes to the sky.

Believe what your heart tells you.

She closed her eyes. Where had the words come from? She didn't know. Didn't want to know. They were an offer of sanity to cling to.

A muttered swearing came from the other wagon, and Faith shook her head as if to clear it. Her father yelled for Keith to wake up and help him climb down from the wagon.

She slowly walked over to where the fire was blackened ash and touched the wood. It, too, was dry. She simply stared at it.

"Faith, you sick or something?" Keith asked, coming up behind her.

"No. Why?"

"You look funny standing there. And there's no fire, no coffee . . ." Shrugging, his voice trailed off. "Need help?"

A flash of surprise showed in her eyes. Keith never offered to help in the morning. "Yes, please. I didn't sleep well, the—"

"Yeah. I was kind of restless myself. Figure it might be 'cause we're getting close. Del said we're more than halfway."

Hiding her disappointment that he had not been kept awake by the storm, Faith set about her morning chores. She cast anxious glances toward the open land, hoping to see a sign of Seanilzay returning with Delaney. That is where the Apache had gone, she decided. There was nothing strange about his disappearing to find his friend. But they were nearly ready to break camp when Delaney returned, alone.

Faith searched his face as he strode up to the fire she had been smothering and poured himself the last cup of coffee. His eyes were dark, without a hint of the flashes of gold and green she had once believed showed the promise of life and offered hope. His cheeks were drawn, the facial bones prominent, and the thick growth of dark beard stubble only enhanced the masculine contours of his face.

He seemed to look right through her. Faith thought at first it was a trick of the light, but when she moved, his head angled as if he followed and watched her, but his eyes revealed no awareness that she was there. She had the presence not to cry out when she finally looked down at his bare chest and saw the wound that crossed from his heart to his side. A wedge of dark curling hair covered his chest, narrowing as it centered the washboard muscles of his torso. A blue stone, no bigger than a robin's egg, was suspended from rawhide and nestled against the dark mat of hair. She felt pulled toward the stone, pulled toward Delaney, in spite of his forbidding manner, only to stop herself when he turned his back toward her.

Faith raised her hand in a helpless gesture, unable to speak. She felt the wall of loneliness surrounding him and did not know how to break it. Turning, she saw that Pris, holding tight to Joey's hand, stood near the back of the wagon. Both children were quiet, their faces appearing to reflect the sadness she felt for Delaney. She glanced at Keith, but he shook his head, as if he, too, sensed the wall and would not broach it. Faith saw that her father, standing with the aid of a forked limb, stood back and away from him. No one tried to speak to him.

A roadrunner appeared, darting along, flipping its tail up and down before it ran off. She wanted to follow it. Faith took courage in hand and approached Delaney just as he spilled out the last of his coffee on the dying fire.

"Seanilzay is gone. He bedded down under the wagon, and when I went to wake him this morning, he wasn't there."

Delaney shrugged.

"Don't you care what happened to him? His wounds weren't healed. I thought he might have gone looking for you." She waited for him to answer, and waited in vain. She longed to ask where he had been. And the storm? No. She didn't want to question him about that. "I was . . . we were worried about you. Please, before we leave, let me tend to that cut."

He shook his head, refusing to turn around. Delaney closed his mind to the softness in her voice, to that special husky, almost breathless way she had of talking to him. He did not want her pity or her compassion.

Faith was undecided what to do. Once again she raised her hand to touch him, this time pulling it back when he suddenly spun around.

She had never seen such a bleak look in anyone's eyes. In a second it was gone from his. She forced herself to remember that Delaney was like the land, tough, hard, and dangerous. There was a stillness about him that stretched the moments of time, and she could not speak, could not move.

Believe what your heart tells you. Once again the words came to her, and this time she listened to them. Her heart was crying out to her that she could heal this man's wounds and ease the loss of all he held dear. She knew, without knowing how or why, that she could make him whole again.

If he let her near him. If she could break the wall that surrounded him.

"Delaney, please, I just want—"

"If you don't know what's good for you, I do. Stay the hell away from me."

"Your voice!" she cried out, tears blurring her eyes. Pain lanced her as he left. Every word had been uttered in a raw, raspy tone. But as much as she grieved for him, anger came.

She marched to the wagon and found the half-filled crock of honey. Bringing it to where he stood saddling his mare, she set it carefully on the saddle. "Use it. For all our sakes."

The glare in his eyes sent her scurrying. The small act used up her store of bravery, and she did as he ordered and stayed away from him. She really had no choice. He set a grueling pace that day, and the days that followed. Faith hardly saw him. He did not take his meals with them. She fretted over whether he ate at all, then called herself a fool for worrying. He had no more time to spend with Joey, less for Pris. Keith never attempted to talk to him, and only her father seemed pleased by the cold distance Delaney maintained.

Faith went back to calling him Mr. Carmichael when she had to speak to him, if she found him, if he stayed and listened.

They had little trouble crossing the Salt River, but when she braved his distant manner to ask if they could stop in Phoenix, he checked over their supplies and refused. It unsettled her to be left with the strong feeling that he couldn't wait to be rid of them.

Two days later they found a low spot to cross the Gila River and were stopped for nooning below a four-story-high mud-and-adobe ruin. Keith, too, braved Delaney's wrath and approached him about the ruins. Faith listened, not because she was curious, but for the satisfaction of hearing Delaney's voice return to normal. He answered Keith in the abrupt manner he had adopted, telling him it was the Casa Grande, the "big house," built by Indians who had farmed this area. She smiled to herself when he added a warning for Keith to be careful as he climbed up for a closer look.

Believing it was more than past time to mend the breach between them, Faith went to Delaney.

"I will need your help to fill my wash kettle."

"Why?"

"Since we plan to spend the night here, I intend to wash our clothes and bedding, Mr. Carmichael."

"No."

"Why?" she snapped, knowing it was foolish to argue with a man as thick-headed and hard-hearted as Delaney.

"Said so."

"Let me be sure I understand. You said we can't stop here for the night and that is that?"

"Lady, you can be the—"

"I know exactly what I can be, Mr. Carmichael. It is not important. We have a bargain between us, don't we? You either give me a good reason why we must move on, or we are," she stressed, with her hands on her hips, "staying. And what's more, Mr. Carmichael, you are staying with us." Faith stared him down, or up, depending on your view, she thought to herself, since he towered over her. But she did swear that for a moment, the corner of his mouth lifted as if he were going to smile.

Setting aside his personal demon, Delaney rubbed the back of his neck. Feisty little sodbuster! But her confrontation made him consider his actions toward her and her family these last days. He had to admit, under close scrutiny, he didn't measure high.

"Well?" she prodded, willing to stand there all day if necessary to get him to respond to her on some level, any level, even anger.

"There's reason enough," he admitted grudgingly. "Storms will be coming soon. I want us across the Santa Cruz before it floods, or we'll have the devil's own time."

"Thank you for a sensible reason, Mr. Carmichael," she stated in a prim manner. "Keith, come down. We can't be lingering here after all."

"There's more. We should hit the stage road to Tucson with luck in the next day or two. Travel will be easier." He finally looked at her and saw for himself that she was far from satisfied. He thought about walking away. The sudden realization that he had been doing that quite a bit lately made him stay. "We can rest up a day in Tucson."

"Your promise?"

"Yeah, my promise."

It was reluctantly given, and she knew it. Faith took no pleasure in having won the concession. She smiled, hoping he realized that it was for his talking to her and not for a sense of victory. "Thank you, Delaney."

"Sure."

"I'm glad your throat is better," she said quickly, to keep him with her. "I guess the honey did help. My mother said—" She stopped herself, for the bleak look was back in his eyes. "I'm sorry. I didn't mean to say anything that would hurt you."

Delaney glanced out over the land. "Seanilzay told you."

"Yes. I was with him the night you disappeared."

"Then you know it all."

Faith touched his arm, silently asking him to look at her. He didn't turn, but he didn't leave her. "I want you to know that I share your pain. My mother died on the trail. I can never see where we buried her, but I can keep the good memories and forget the bad."

"No one murdered your mother."

"No, but they killed my husband." She lowered her lashes and dropped her hand from his arm. She couldn't tell him that her father blamed her for her mother's death. She could not explain that without revealing her secret. This time she walked away.

But something had changed, for they made camp early that night, and Delaney gathered the mules to stake them, a chore that Keith usually tended to.

He stayed close by, and Faith, washing the supper dishes, wished he would call her duchess again, much as it annoyed her. She was filled with a restlessness she couldn't explain. When she looked up across the fire to where he was sitting, cleaning his gun, she wondered if Delaney remembered the kisses they shared. She wanted those kisses again, and all that came after. But he had made it plain that he wanted nothing to do with her.

Her gaze strayed to him again, this time to find he was watching her. Faith stilled. His gaze held hers with a tense look that was filled with hot promise. Her lips went dry. A shivery sensation began and built until heat spread inside her. She closed her eyes, imagining again the night his kisses had shown her a wild passion that they sparked off each other. She wanted it again. She wanted Delaney. When she opened her eyes, he was gone.

The easing of the tension in Delaney continued the next day. It was something Faith sensed, but she was surprised that both Joey and Pris found plenty to smile about as the day wore on. She had been forced to explain Delaney's anger had nothing to do with them but was for Seanilzay leaving before his wounds were healed. The children accepted it, but they had been careful to keep their distance from Delaney.

When they camped late the next afternoon, Delaney and Keith had to repair one of the wagon wheels. Faith walked a ways with the children, telling Joey what they saw, Pris chattering with an excitement that had been missing. Faith was the first one to see the dust clouds, and she called out to Pris, taking her hand, leading them back to the wagons.

"Delaney, there are riders coming."

He straightened and handed Keith the grease bucket. "Put it away and get your rifle. Stay close to the wagon. I'll ride out."

He tightened the cinch, then swung up on Mirage's back, seeing for himself the fine dust that rose under horses' hooves. The sun was high, pouring down in blistering streams. He could see the jerky fall of the hooves, telling how tired the horses were. Flashes of light made him shake his head. Brass. Army brass. Without waiting to see more, he turned Mirage and headed back.

Chapter Eleven

"DELANEY, WHO ARE they?" she asked as he rode back.

"Army patrol."

"Will they want to eat with us?" Faith had to turn and ask this of his back, for he went by, keeping Mirage at a walk.

"Reckon if you offer, they'll accept."

"Where are you going?" she called, running to catch up with him.

"Won't be far. Don't worry, duchess. They'll mind their pretty manners."

Grabbing hold of his stirrup, she forced him to stop. "I'm not worried as long as I know you're close." Looking up at him, Faith felt the same excitement she had the night of the storm. She licked her lips as if she could taste the sweet rain and saw Delaney's gaze target her mouth and narrow. The shadow of his beard intensified the male line of his jaw, but it was his mouth she stared at. His lips parted to show the edge of his teeth. Faith could feel the flow of her blood change, or so it seemed to her: It was slow, but flushing her from the inside out with heat.

"Why are you leaving?"

"Don't care for the company." He wanted to shake her hand free and ride. Only it wasn't Mirage he wanted under him.

"Delaney?"

The way she murmured his name with an aching note made him tighten his grip on the leather. His control was stretched hair-thin.

"You looking to burn me alive, duchess?"

"B-burn y-you?" Faith couldn't help but stutter. She was the one who felt burned. Slowly she shook her head. But she couldn't shake free of the hot, vital look of his eyes. "Stop. You take my breath," she whispered, feeling time and place spin away until there was nothing and no one near them.

Delaney hunched to the side, leaning closer to her. He targeted her mouth. "Is that an invite, duchess?" he murmured, cursing himself for the hard response of his body to being this close to her. "Is it?" he repeated, his voice deep, his eyes coming back to search hers. He wouldn't let her look away. He was tired of fighting against what he needed. Need that clawed at him. Need that wiped out thought of revenge.

Lightning arced between them. Faith had no other way to describe the feeling. She swayed and leaned against the warmth of Mirage. Without thought to what she was doing, her hand came to rest on his thigh. The scents of horse, leather, and Delaney melded together. She felt the muscles in his leg tighten. Her breath rushed in and out as if she had been running a long way. And Faith knew she had been doing just that from the day she first saw him. But she didn't want to run anymore. She opened her mouth to say something, anything, but no sound came.

Delaney stopped himself from closing the short distance between them and taking her mouth. But he wanted to. He wanted to taste the tip of her tongue that peeked over the edge of her teeth. His gaze skimmed down to her bared throat; the top three buttons of her gown were open. The shadowed cleft between her breasts made his muscles clench with the memory of Faith kneeling by the stream. He didn't need to close his eyes to see again the silver glide of water. He shifted restlessly in the saddle. A smart man would shake her free and move on.

He guessed he wasn't smart. The sight of her skin, soft, smooth, and peach-gold from the sun, tempted him to wonder how her breasts would feel under his open mouth. He knew without knowing how that she would want him gentle until the pleasure brought the wildness, then he could rake his teeth over sensitive flesh. He heard the change in her breathing, coming now as his own was, hard and fast. He looked into her eyes to see dark centers dilated, the blue darkening until the gold flecks brightened like lightning. Delaney felt his chest expand. His blood flowed to an insidious beat that caught every pulse point in his body.

"Burned alive," he whispered.

"Delaney?" Faith tightened her hold on his thigh and felt the incredible heat seep through the cloth of his pants to her palm.

"You know, don't you, duchess?" he asked, his voice deep and gritty.

"What?" She searched his face. There was a slight flush on his high cheekbones, and his eyes were narrowed, watching her so intently she couldn't look away.

"That's how it'll be with us."

Faith passed over her instant thought to deny it. Her lips seemed to swell even as he watched, and once more her breathing changed. She couldn't seem to drag enough air into her lungs. "Yes," she finally answered him. "That's how it will be. Burning. Dying and coming alive at once." She slid her hand down his leg and stepped back.

"But no promises."

Faith couldn't answer him. She closed her eyes and knew he urged Mirage off at a walk. She wanted to be alone, shaken by what just happened. Her father called out, and she turned to see him talking with the dismounting soldiers. Resentment flared inside her. She wanted them gone. She wanted to be with Delaney. But ingrained obedience made her paste a smile of welcome on her lips and move back to where they all stood.

Delaney pulled up, spinning Mirage on her hocks. He glanced back to see Faith walking toward the soldiers. He wanted her so badly, his insides knotted. Since the night Seanilzay told him about his mother's death, he had felt as if his strength of will had been undermined, for he couldn't hold the need for her at bay. He wanted her beneath him, with him inside her, riding her gently until she was all heat and softness, wild and needing, with her fingers clawing his back, like the desire clawing his gut.

He stopped his thoughts, aching now, and knowing that he would go on aching until he made love to her. *Love*? Where had that come from? He didn't want a permanent tangle with his calico duchess. He wanted that body moving like a willow, all grace and sway, that had soldiers scrambling to remove hats, crowding around to meet her.

She turned just then, and Delaney knew she saw him. Before he gave himself a chance to think, he rode back. A man had to be a fool from hell to leave her alone with men who outnumbered white women in the territory better than ten to one.

Delaney wasn't smiling to see the young private place his hands on Faith's shoulders to face her northeast. He stopped short of where they stood, listening to their talk, ready to step in.

"That's right, Miss Becket. The only battle fought in the territory was right there at Picacho Peak when two—or was it three?—well, they were detachments from Calloway's Cavalry troop that engaged the Confederate rear guard. 'Course, the name's kind of stupid, since *picacho* means 'peak.' "

"Peak Peak? How charming, Private Shellby." Faith slipped out from beneath his hands.

"Didn't you folks make camp near the water hole there? The sweetest-tasting water's—"

"I'm sure it is," Faith agreed, smiling as she turned and saw Delaney. She closed the short distance between them with the private dogging her heels. "This is Private Orrin Shellby. Mr. Delaney Carmichael."

The hand the private was about to extend was whipped back. Delaney had never moved his from his side.

Faith, bewildered, looked to Delaney for an explanation, but he merely shook his head.

"Mr. Becket didn't say you were with them, Carmichael."

"Maybe he didn't think it's important," Delaney answered.

Faith disliked the tone and the looks of the man that came up behind them with her father. She tried not to stare at the dull red scar that began where his left eyebrow should have been and continued up into his hair.

"It's important to me, Carmichael. Major Ross is looking for you. He sent word out over the trail weeks ago."

Delaney didn't answer him.

Faith saw that her father was listening to every word and making his own judgments. She did not like the sudden gleam in his eyes.

"Well, are you going to answer me, Carmichael?"

"Don't see a need to, Krome."

"That's Sergeant Krome to the likes of you."

Delaney glanced at the bright new stripes and back up to the sergeant's face. His lip curled and his eyes were hostile. "So you got them back."

"Damn . . . beg your pardon, ma'am. Sure I did. Your lies weren't good enough to keep them off me."

The sudden tension frightened Faith, and she stepped between them. "Since you and your men are going to share a meal with us, Sergeant, I would appreciate some help."

Krome glared at Delaney a moment more before he turned to her. "And we in turn appreciate the offer. Since our supply mules were stolen, we've had nothing but jerky."

"Stolen?" Robert asked, grabbing the sergeant's arm.

"Thieving Apache crept up on us while we were sleeping and ran them off. Can't trust the savages," he stated in a harsh voice, shooting an accusing look at Delaney.

"Funny, that's what the Apache say about you, Krome."

"Delaney, if you're still in a surly mood, maybe you'd best take yourself off," Becket warned. "Sergeant, about that thieving Apache—"

"Papa, you've been standing on that leg too long. You had best come sit down while I get food ready." Faith ignored her father's glaring look and took hold of his arm. "Private Shellby, would you be so kind as to help us?"

"Now, Faith—"

"You know I'm right. You'll be aching the rest of the day being bounced on that wagon seat." She pulled on his arm, forcing him to hobble along with her. Faith was sure he had been about to tell the sergeant about Seanilzay. She didn't know if he had been the one to steal their mules or not, nor did she care; some instinct said she was doing the right thing.

"Heard you quit the railroad, Carmichael," Krome said as soon as they were alone.

"You heard right." Delaney watched Faith for a few seconds and thought about what she had done. He was sure that the mules had ended up with Seanilzay. But how could she? There was no other reason that he could figure to explain what she did. And he owed her for it.

He started toward the wagon and found that Krome was following.

"You know, Carmichael, you could still be working for the army."

Delaney kept walking, ignoring him.

"Ross wants you back. Things are stirring up again. A man like you can name his price."

That stopped Delaney cold. He turned to look at Krome. His eyes were hard, cold, and filled with warning that more than matched his voice. "Working? Is that what they teach you sixteen-dollar-a-month boys to call lying?"

"No. You know that's not true."

"It's lying," Delaney taunted, shifting his stance.

"I'm not going to fight you, Carmichael. You know what the army policy is toward Indians. Keep the settlers and miners safe at all costs. People want this territory to grow so we can become a state with rights. The Indians won't stop their raiding and stealing and the murders. Even you won't deny that, not to my face, and still call yourself honest."

"I know the damn policy," Delaney grated, clenching his teeth. At his sides his hands fisted. "Wipe out the warriors, right? And it doesn't matter if the man is unarmed. Kill him anyway 'cause you need his land. You were—"

"You can't hold a grudge this long!"

"You were there that day. You stood by, *Sergeant* Krome," he stressed with scorn in every word, "and you watched the three soldiers under your command beat a man to death with their rifles. You did nothing when they gutted his wife 'cause she tried to stop them, and you sure as hell didn't lift a finger or say one word while they raped his two daughters."

"No! I wasn't there!"

Delaney opened his hands only to clench them tight. He ignored the troopers crowding around them.

"Carmichael, you can't hold that against me. I don't make policy."

"Maybe not," Delaney conceded, drawing deep breaths and releasing them, trying to hang on to his control when all he wanted was to feel the soft fleshy face before him break open from his fist. "But you take your pleasure in carrying it out, don't you?"

Krome wiped the sweat beading on his lips and chin. He was breathing too hard and making the mistake of letting Delaney goad him into a fight. He couldn't afford to lose face with his men, and it was too late to order them to back away.

"The only reason you keep the grudge alive is that you wanted a taste of that Injun gal your—"

"Don't finish it. They'll be your last words, you bastard." Delaney watched his eyes. He knew when Krome moved his hand toward his holstered gun. The troopers shifted back, widening the circle, and overhead a lone hawk circled over them. "Go on, do it, Krome. And while you're thinking about it, remember that she was fifteen. Her sister not yet twelve. She died in my arms not more than an hour after you and your men left them."

"You had your damn revenge!" Krome shouted, dropping his hand away from his gun. "You got my stripes and two months' pay. What the hell else did you want?"

Delaney's knife was suddenly in his hand. "I could skin you alive, Krome. Two months' pay to the girl who sits and rocks all day, and you think it was enough?" He watched the sweat pouring out of Krome to soak his blue uniform coated with red dust. Not one of the troopers moved to help him or stop Delaney. But even as Delaney stopped himself from using his knife, Faith broke through the crowd.

She had seen violence in Delaney's eyes before, she heard again the promise of it in his voice, yet she felt no fear of him, only for him. There was no doubt that what Delaney said was true. The darting, frantic look of the sergeant's eyes confirmed it.

The mood of the soldiers shifted abruptly. Faith's sweeping gaze saw the excitement flushing their faces, and the eager look in their eyes, anticipating a fight. She faced Delaney.

"The children heard it all."

He ignored the appeal in her voice. "Stay out of this, Faith."

She shrugged off a trooper's hand on her arm without looking at him. "Delaney, please—"

"If it happened to Pris, would you ask me to back off?"

For a long moment she held his eyes and saw for herself the torment dividing him. Slowly she shook her head and without another word pushed her way free and kept walking.

But Krome had watched, too. He knew the threat was over before Delaney slid his knife back into the sheath at his side. Bravado filled his gloating voice. "You're no damn better than the savages, Carmichael."

Delaney smiled but not with his eyes; they were cold enough to chill the sun. "You remember that, Krome. You remember that when you throw your saddle down at night, and you make sure to tell that to Ross."

"I'll tell him. And you watch yourself, too. Plenty of us have long memories, Carmichael. Bark from the same tree skins out the same," he taunted in turn, hitching up his belt.

Rage burned for the slur against his father. Delaney knew fighting Krome wouldn't solve a damn thing.

"For those of you who don't know, Carmichael's father was convicted of—"

Delaney's fist sent Krome's head snapping back. Blood spurted from his split lip. He crouched, fists raised, more than ready to take him on.

Rubbing his knuckles, Delaney spat in the dirt at Krome's feet. With rigid control he turned his back on him. Each of the soldiers directly blocking his way averted their eyes from his piercing gaze. Slowly then they opened a path for him.

Joey stood just beyond the circle. "Del?" he asked in a quavering voice, lifting his face and holding out his hand.

"I'm right here, scout." He took hold of Joey's hand and led him back to finish greasing the wagon axles.

Behind them, troopers found something that needed their immediate attention, leaving Krome standing beneath the sun alone.

The circling hawk flew off toward the mountains.

Faith finished frying up bacon and hurried to set biscuit dough in the hot grease to bake. She wanted the soldiers gone. Her father was of a different mind.

He seemed pleased to have the sergeant sit beside him. They didn't mention Delaney or what happened, but Faith was trying to listen to their conversation and distract Pris at the same time. Giving her sister a small piece of dough to play with, Faith groaned when she saw Private Shellby approach.

She refused his offer to help her, but he persisted in remaining and talking to her.

"I wanted to apologize for what happened, Miss Becket. Sergeant Krome is a good officer, but he hates Indians and any man who sides with them. He has good reason, you must understand," he explained earnestly. "That scar of his comes from almost being scalped. Our troop doesn't ride with an Apache scout when he leads. Now, losing our supplies means we return to Fort Lowell. Will you be planning on stopping in Tucson for a while?"

"Oh, yes," Pris answered before Faith could. "Delaney promised us we could."

"Then I hope I have the pleasure of seeing you there, Miss Becket."

"You're riding south?" Faith didn't look at him, but she glanced at her father. The feeling he had discovered their direction swept over her. She would bet anything that he would ask the sergeant if the patrol would escort them part of the way.

Shellby seemed to be of the same mind. "We could ride along with you. If you're afraid that there will be trouble between Sergeant Krome and Carmichael—"

"Do you know if what Delaney accused him of is true?" Faith gave up all pretense of stirring the pot of beans and looked at him.

The private found his scuffed red-dusted boots easier on his eye than the militant glare in Faith's.

"If you don't want to tell me, don't. Pris, go find Keith for me and tell Delaney and Joey that it's time to eat."

"I didn't mean to make you angry, Miss Becket."

"You didn't."

"I heard talk when I arrived at the fort about what happened. But it was just talk. I do know that Carmichael's father was convicted of fixing the weigh scales for the beef he sold to the army and the agents for the reservation Indians. He sold cattle that were sickly to them, too. He died a few weeks after he went to Yuma Prison."

Faith waited, silent, but hoping he would tell her more.

"There are some who don't believe that Ian Carmichael ever did a dishonest act in his life."

"And where were these men when he went to trial, Private Shellby?"

"I don't know."

Feeling that he was telling her the truth as he knew it, Faith smiled and offered him the first biscuit along with a plate of beans and bacon. Within moments the other soldiers crowded her.

"Oh, ma'am, that sure does smell good," one remarked.

"My gut's sure been letting me know it's empty all this while," another said.

One trooper, older than the rest, ate so fast that he was back just as Faith made up plates for her father and the sergeant. Keith took them over to the two men.

"More?" she asked.

"I could scoff iron filings an' horseshoe nails an' thank you kindly, ma'am, for a second helping."

"You're all welcome to what's left," she told him, after making up plates for Delaney and Joey. Not seeing them, she carried the plates around the wagons.

Delaney sat with his back against a wheel, holding Joey on his lap.

"I thought you two would like to eat here."

"Go away, Faith," Joey said, sniffing and wiping his nose on his sleeve.

"Smells real good, scout," Delaney said, shifting as Joey turned his face toward his shoulder. He cupped the boy's head with one hand, rubbing, and looked up at Faith.

"Why don't you leave the plates. Joey's not ready to eat now."

Faith set them down on the ground, then came to kneel at Delaney's side. She covered his hand with her own, so that they both stroked Joey's head. She knew he had been crying, but her questioning look merely had Delaney shake his head.

"Can you tell me what's wrong, Joey?" she asked softly, a warm feeling expanding inside to see him nestled in Delaney's arms. Whatever demons had plagued Delaney and kept him away from her brother, she knew they were gone.

"Make her go away, Del."

"Wouldn't be fair, scout. Your sister cares about you, or she wouldn't be asking what's wrong. But it's your decision if you want to tell her."

More sniffles followed. Faith glanced down at Delaney's skinned knuckles. She moved her hand to cover his.

"It was all true, wasn't it, Delaney?" Faith asked.

"Yeah." He leaned his head back against the spoke of the wheel, closing his eyes. "Her name was She Who Sings, and now she is silent."

"I guess there is more injustice done to the Indians than we know."

He shrugged and opened his eyes, staring straight ahead. "When I was a boy, I saw Cochise rope a man and drag him over rocks and cactus behind his horse. I've heard what the Apache and other tribes have done to whites, and I've come on a few places where the Apache left little to be buried. I know most white men don't try to understand their way of life or their beliefs."

"But what you're telling me proves that these Indians are cruel and vicious."

"Not cruel, Faith. They're hard and no more vicious than the whites. They have a lot of reason to hate and none to be tolerant of men who have lied and cheated them."

"Are they without compassion?" she asked, sitting down to resume stroking Joey's head.

"Most don't know what compassion is. They've never been given any. It's hard to explain. They don't understand why the white man plunders the earth for gold and silver. They are taught to live with the earth, not to destroy it."

"Can't there be compromise, Delaney? If you know them, can't you try to speak out for them?"

He looked at her then, seeing the earnest expression on her face, and he found himself smiling. "Why should you care?"

Startled, Faith lowered her head. Her hand stilled on Joey, and she realized he had fallen asleep. "I care because it matters so much to you."

"Faith," he whispered, raising her chin with one hand. "I'm trouble for you, duchess, in more ways than you know."

She covered his hand with hers, shaking her head. The hard, warm, resilient strength of his hand moved easily as she raised it to her lips and pressed a kiss in the center of his palm. She saw his nostrils flare and the darkening of his eyes at the same moment desire came to life in her. With a gentle touch her fingertips pressed his lips.

"You tried to warn me from the beginning. My heart doesn't seem to listen very well to your words." She gazed down at her sleeping brother. "My eyes see the gentleness in you no matter how much you try to hide it, Delaney. But I know you won't make promises. You can't. And if you did, well . . ." She stopped herself from saying more. She could not tell him of her past. She trusted Delaney, but the soft warmth in his eyes would quickly disappear if he knew the truth about the night Martin had died.

Joey stirred and Delaney shifted the boy's weight in his arms before coming to his feet in a tightly coordinated move.

"I'll put him in the wagon."

Faith started to rise when he looked back.

"Wait for me."

"Yes. I'll wait."

Chapter Twelve

FAITH WALKED TO the front of the wagon and looked beyond to see that Pris sat with her father and several of the troopers. Her little sister giggled at something one of the soldiers said, and Faith smiled, too. The sun was brassy overhead, and she knew they would rest here for a few more hours before pushing on. For once she felt no urge to hurry and clean up after their meal. The fire was a mere glow, the coffeepot and cooking kettle already pulled off to the side. Men lay about in the shade cast by the wagon, resting against their saddles. Since she was behind the second wagon, she didn't believe anyone would disturb them.

She sensed rather than heard Delaney behind her. With a nervous gesture she touched her hair, wishing she had time to brush it and smooth it into a coil. Turning, she saw that he carried a quilt. Her smile slipped, and when she glanced into the blaze of his eyes, she felt as if the lightning from the storm had pierced her, bursting like fire inside her. She took a short, sharp breath and watched him toss the quilt on the ground in the shade cast by the body of the wagon. He picked up the two abandoned plates of food and stood waiting, not saying a word, until she sat down before he handed her one and then joined her.

By day the desert stretched out, appearing more desolate than it ever did by moonlight. Faith ate without tasting the food, staring at the dun-colored earth that reflected the sun's hot glare. The land was broken by a few red rock outcrops, an occasional towering saguaro cactus, and a few clumps of thorny, low-growing ocotillo bushes.

After setting aside her half-finished plate, she smoothed her gown. "You love this land," she began without looking at him. "That love shows with every word you speak about it. Joey knows, so does Pris. You've taught them to see beauty and life where most people see nothing but barrenness."

"And you, Faith? Do you see its beauty, too?" Delaney lost his taste for food and leaned over to set his plate away from them. With his legs stretched out full length, he slouched down, tucking his arms behind his head, watching her.

"I've found a peace here that I've never known. And a special beauty that you reveal." She hesitated, drawing small circles with one finger on the quilt. "Sometimes it's hard to put feelings into words."

"Yeah," he found himself agreeing in a husky voice, each one of his hands gripping the forearm of the other so he couldn't reach out and pull her down to show her the feelings that had his body tense with a bold, surging rush.

Faith turned to him, and he saw within her eyes, those haunting turquoise-hued eyes, the same wanting that filled him. Her gaze fell to his mouth. There was hunger in her look, but Delaney knew as long as he didn't move, didn't act on what she was revealing to him, they were both safe.

He closed his eyes briefly, burying the temptation to kiss her until she melted with him in a hot passion that wouldn't leave either one of them with the strength left to lick their lips. He felt his body change at the thought of falling asleep with the sweet taste of Faith in his mouth, her body, soft and hot around him . . . Expelling a sharp breath, Delaney wrenched his thoughts to another track.

"There's a good chance the patrol will ride escort for you to Tucson."

Faith withdrew, raising her knees and wrapping her arms around them. She wasn't going to pretend she didn't understand what he was saying. "You want to leave us."

"Want? No. There are things I have to do, an' time's getting away from me."

"Because of what Seanilzay told you," she said, wishing she could tell him how she felt about him. Slowly nodding, she added, "Losing them both must have been very hard on you. There are times when I wish my mother was alive. My father wasn't bitter the way he is now."

"No matter how much you wish for it, you can't go back and change things."

"But that's what you're trying to do, Delaney," she pointed out.

"No. I'm going to make the man responsible for their deaths pay."

"And if you're hurt or lose your life, will the price be worth it?"

"I never thought about it that way. It's something I must do or I can't live with myself."

Somehow she knew that was going to be his answer. She wanted to argue with him, but it would be senseless to do so. Delaney would walk his own paths and find his own way.

"Don't care so much, duchess," he whispered, losing his own battle not to touch her. He slid one hand free to trace down the length of her spine with the flat of his palm. His thoughts and world narrowed down to the warmth of her body. "Faith, look at me." He murmured her name again, and when she turned, he shifted so he could brush her cheek with his fingertips. Her smile that invited his made him think he had never seen anyone as pretty as his duchess was at this moment.

"I wish I could keep your smile with me always. Nights when I'm alone, I'd want to take it out and be warmed better than a fire."

"Del?" She had to blink back the sting of sudden tears, remembering the first day she saw him and the feeling she had of his always being alone, with no one to care for him. Covering his hand with hers, she pressed it against her cheek. "I wish I could give you my smile to keep. I wish—"

His fingers moved to her jaw while his thumb dragged across her soft mouth in a savagely arousing motion. "And I wish I had your mouth." His thumb rubbed more insistently against her bottom lip, forcing it open, his gaze holding hers.

A quiver began inside, and Faith felt the fever that came with it. Her desire was there for him to feel and see. With a slight twist of her head, she freed her lips from his touch.

"I've never said no."

He levered himself up even as she leaned into him, tilting her head, offering her mouth. He brushed his lips lightly across hers, drinking in her quick, little breath. He never knew there could be such pleasure in so chaste a kiss and came back for more. Another butterfly touch, then another.

Sweet fire came with her sigh over his lips. With a hesitant, delicate touch, she returned his kiss. The soft, delicate touches weren't enough for either of them. Delaney settled his mouth over hers, tasting hot satin, and began to rock his lips with ever changing pressure until they had to separate to breathe, only to meet once more, clinging a little deeper, a little harder each time.

Faith reached up to cup his cheek, her hand as soft as the glide of his up and down her back. She felt bathed in heat, trembling from the exquisitely restrained kisses they shared.

Pleasure shimmered through Delaney to his bones. He had never kissed a woman like this, never knew there was passion and tenderness to be had from fragile tastings, and with this sweet surprise, he held himself still, wanting these moments to go on.

But his finely honed instincts never slept, and he heard the nearing murmur of voices. Lifting his mouth from hers, his quick move put plenty of distance between them just as Private Shellby rounded the wagon.

Faith still sat half-turned toward Delaney's prone body. She wasn't as quick to recover.

"Miss Becket, your father is looking for you."

When Delaney saw that Faith was incapable of answering, he came to his feet in a coordinated rush. "She just put her brother to sleep. The heat's gotten to her. I'll see what he wants."

Faith was trying to still her aroused senses when Delaney stepped past her.

"He doesn't want you, Carmichael," Shellby said. And with a knowing look, added, "Not many folks do."

That brought Faith to her feet. She didn't care if her lips were still damp and reddened from Delaney's kisses, she refused to hear one more slur made against him.

"You delivered your message, Private. There's no reason for you to remain. I happen to like Delaney Carmichael's company."

"You're talking to deaf ears, Faith. Don't waste your breath."

"Delaney, wait," she called.

Private Shellby glanced from her to Delaney's retreating back. "You're new to the territory and may not understand that most decent folks won't bother with him. He's got a bad reputation, Miss Becket. People here aren't any different than they are back East. They will judge you by the company you keep."

"I can't thank you for your advice, Private, although I suppose you mean well."

As Faith had expected, her father accepted the patrol's escort. She refused Private Shellby's offer to drive her wagon, angry with him for his unwanted attention and his attempts to slander Delaney. She kept Joey close by her side, backing away when he refused to tell her why he had been crying.

Keith set her mind at rest about Delaney leaving them since they rode with the troopers. Keith spotted him up ahead, and when they made camp that night, Delaney stayed close by.

With her father's encouragement talk turned to how well the army was faring against the Indians. Faith was shocked and disgusted to hear their tales of killings. Her senses were so attuned to Delaney that she could feel his mounting anger and tension as he forced himself to sit and listen without answering the goads or trying to defend the Apache.

The night grew cool, and soon the troopers began to seek their beds. The fire died down, and still Delaney sat, alone, she saw, as she came around the wagon. When she was not more than ten feet from him, he looked up.

"Go to sleep, duchess. It's been a long day for you."

She listened and, when she decided there was no rejection in his voice, came forward. "I want to be with you, not alone. Don't you know that, Del?"

"I know." He rose and looked off into the distance.

With his back toward the moon he was cast darkly against the land. Faith felt weak, drawn to him so that she was keenly aware of his intense physical presence, as if he had already touched her. She longed to ease the deep loneliness in him.

The feelings were all potent, and she knew now that she was coming to love a man who did not want her love.

Delaney's words confirmed it. "That wasn't really me this afternoon, duchess," he said in a soft voice that would not carry to the sleeping men.

"I won't believe that. You are gentle. You showed me how tender you can be with me. A woman doesn't find that in many men."

"You didn't?"

The time was long past for lies. Faith murmured, "No," and came to his side. She slipped her hand into his, entwining their fingers.

"Faith, why don't you talk about your husband?" The moment he spoke, he felt the tension that took hold of her. But he would not relent. He had to know. "Tell me."

"Martin shouldn't have died for what he believed in."

"That's not what I was asking, and you know it."

"Quit prodding me, Delaney. I don't want to talk about him. He's dead and so is the past. I want to forget."

"With me? You could be asking for something you can't handle, duchess."

She heard the underlying warning and looked up at him. "Yes," she agreed, "I could be. Show me the land you love, Delaney. I learn more about you each time you do." Her fingers tightened over his. He looked dark and fierce, capable of anything at this moment. Trembling a little, she felt her bravado slip and thought of what she wanted. She heard his teeth grind together. With her free hand she reached up to his jaw. "Do you want me to lie? I won't."

"I've been a long time between women, duchess."

"Will you ever stop warning me? Is there more? Tell me now, and I'll listen, but I still want you to show me what you love."

Such straightforward honesty was beyond him to deny. Delaney led her out to the desert. Gone were the sounds of the woodpecker shrieks or the rock squirrel whistles that warned of danger. There was a subtle change that Faith immediately felt, both tension and expectancy that she found hard to define. Her mood communicated itself to Delaney, for he gazed at her, squeezing her hand.

"This late in spring the cactus bloom, but night brings out the predators, so stay close," he whispered into her ear. Her sharp little intake of breath told him she was already aroused, and he grinned with the bittersweet thought; the feeling never left him. "We'll stay away from the water hole so the animals can drink."

"Is that why you never camp near water? I heard you argue with Sergeant Krome about it."

"That's why. Too many men camp close to the only water for miles. Animals scent them and won't drink. To deny the water needed for life is a cruelty to the Indian ways. Some animals can't move in the heat of the day and others can't move in the cold of the night, so there are only a few hours when the sun sets or just as it rises that they can hunt for water and food."

Delaney stopped, listening, and Faith with him. He lifted her hand toward a small outcrop of rocks. She strained to see what caught his attention, and for a moment a coyote was silhouetted in the moonlight before it leapt down and ran.

"Prey?" she whispered, standing on tiptoe to reach his ear. Delaney nodded and after a few minutes began to walk toward the rocks.

"The life circle, no different than for us. Sometimes it's brutal and intense, but without it there would be no life." He lifted his head as the cool breeze flowed down from the mountains, dropping the temperature. The light faded, and the stars began appearing. He knew Faith had stood

and watched this night after night before seeking her bed.
He knew because he stood alone and watched her. The air
took on an edge of chill, and he freed his hand from hers
to slide his arm around her shoulders and bring her closer
to his body.

Faith lifted her skirt hem free of a low-growing bush,
loving the deep, soothing sound of his voice as he told
her about the cactus used for survival as food and as water
for man and horse. When he stopped before close-growing
saguaro, he turned to her and placed his hands on her waist.
She gave a soft, startled cry when he lifted her high so she
could see the blossoms of the cactus.

"Touch one, Faith. It's soft as velvet. Doves love the sweet
nectar," he whispered, giving into temptation to brush his lips
across the undercurve of her breast. Her tremored response
made him repeat the motion.

"Delaney?" The warmth of his mouth and breath pierced
through the thin calico of her gown and the cotton of her
camisole to sear her skin. A violent trembling started inside
her. She barely managed to brace her hands on the broad,
resilient warmth of his shoulders. She inhaled the night
scents of the desert along with the smoky male scent that
was Delaney's, leaning her head down to rub her chin over
his thick, dark hair.

"I wish I could be as gentle as a dove and taste your
sweetness."

Faith raised her head, tilting it back down to look at his
raised face. His features were hard, set in a primitive cast. Her
breath caught when she gazed into his eyes. They seemed to
glitter with fire.

"When the bloom fades, the doves can't wait to feed
on the fruit." His lips brushed across her breast again,
sending every word and breath bone deep. He shifted his
hold, one arm locking around her waist, the other sliding

down to hold her buttocks. For a moment he hesitated, burying his impatience, stilling his hunger, before he raised her up to his lips.

"Del? Oh, please, Del, I—" Her voice broke. His hot mouth closed over one tightly drawn nipple. She felt as if flames had touched her through layers of cloth. Blood rushed to swell her breast, the feeling so exquisite that she moaned, arching her back, pushing her breast against his mouth.

It wasn't enough. She gripped his head, pulling him harder against her, wanting him with a fierce desperation that she couldn't begin to explain to herself. Whimpers came from her throat, and she twisted in his arms, needing more.

Desire clenched his gut, and Delaney forced himself to stop suckling her. "Sweet forbidden fruit," he breathed against the damp cloth clinging to the taut peaked crown, holding tight to her trembling body.

"N-not . . . forbidden," she managed to say, yearning to be touched again.

"I could feast on you until I know every soft bit of you." His eyes were savage with need, and his blood thundered through his body. "Do you want that?" The words were thick and guttural, but he couldn't speak any other way.

"Yes." Her gaze lowered to his mouth. "Yes, I want that, too. I . . ." He slowly slid her down his body, deliberately pressing her over the hardened flesh straining his buttoned fly, and both of them shuddered.

Damning right and wrong, Delaney took her mouth, need dictating to his body. The fierce urge to mate with her drove him wild.

His lips covered hers, and he pressed her slender body tight to his. He could feel the soft give of her breasts against his chest. Her tightly drawn nipples bit through his shirt to stab his skin. He shivered in reaction, losing control, unable to tell who trembled the most. Her arms held him, her fingers climbing up the back of his neck to tangle into his hair, every move too frantic with the storm that broke over them for touches to be gentle.

He caught a handful of her hair, pulling the pins out, angling her head back to his shoulder, and felt the glide and bite of her fingers grabbing hold of his arms. He slid his tongue deep inside her mouth, mating with hers, only to withdraw so that his teeth nipped her bottom lip. Delaney lifted his head a fraction, drawing needed breath, and looked down into her dazed eyes.

"More," she whispered, licking her lips, tasting him. She felt every tremor of her body stroke the heat of his. His eyes, in the moonlight, were bright with passion, and she needed to taste the reckless slant of his mouth, wanted it now, more than she wanted anything else. The wild beating of her heart matched his, making Faith glory in being the woman who kindled such desire in him.

His hand splayed over the slight curve of her hip to bring her closer to the blatant ridge of aroused flesh. She reached up to touch his mouth. "Kiss me," she demanded, rubbing her finger across his bottom lip. "Kiss me like you did the first time, and I felt I was caught up in a wild, hot storm, all fire and lightning and—"

The tip of his tongue stilled her. He bathed the curve of her lower lip, bringing a soft, exciting moan from her. "Soft." He licked her again. "Are you as soft and sweet and hot—"

"Del, please," she implored, trying to capture his mouth.

He drew his head back. He wanted to take her mouth fully, but watching her, seeing her flushed cheeks, fever-bright eyes and her lips glistening from the tiny licks of his tongue, sent ripples of emotion through his powerful body. He longed to give her what she asked for, what he wanted, too, all hot and wild, but he needed to pleasure her with the same depth of demand. Delaney tasted the curve of her mouth, drinking her breathless murmurs of his name over and over, feeling her sweet breath like a warm caress over his lips. Into his mind came the sight of her kneeling by the stream, silver drops gliding down her skin, and his own question of how she would come to a man.

He had his answer. Sweet smiles, dark and light shadows, and nothing held back.

He wanted her the same way. Against his chest the skystone warmed, and with every fleeting kiss that he brushed across her responsive lips, the stone grew hotter.

Faith followed the retreat of his mouth. She didn't want to be teased. She didn't want him kissing her cheeks or her temples. She turned her face, her teeth catching his bottom lip, and she held it captive so her tongue could bathe its softness. And remembered again, this was the only place that Delaney was soft. She felt the tightening of his fingers in her hair and released him with a satisfied smile.

"I've warned you time and again, duchess, if you bite me, I'll bite back." He dragged his mouth against hers in brief, searing kisses that aroused them both. His teeth raked over her bottom lip, the sweet sounds of need that she made driving him crazy. He couldn't stand to be without the taste of her filling him. Repeatedly he dipped his tongue into her mouth, and she caressed him with hers, tasting him in turn, trembling.

Her head tilted back even more, offering him her bare throat, and Delaney tested the smooth curve with kisses and gentle love bites that had her crying his name with husky sounds. Kneading her back and hips, he pressed her closer, then closer still, as if he wanted to draw her inside himself. The warm, hungry kisses she scattered wherever she could reach nearly sent him over the edge. The gentle rocking of her hips, cradling, then retreating from his violently aroused flesh brought his blood up in a rush that made him think he would explode if he couldn't bury himself inside her soon.

With a rough sound he claimed her mouth. Sanity intruded. He couldn't take her here, standing in the open, but he couldn't stop kissing her long enough to move. His fingers tightened on her waist, his thumbs brushing across the undersides of her breasts, and he felt the passion that fevered her, just as it spread through him.

He pulled his head back with a wrenching groan, tucking her head beneath his chin to put temptation aside while he fought to draw breath and still the wildness that shook him.

Faith cried in protest, feeling the world spin around her. She wanted the next touch, the next kiss that would send her into soft flames, with tongues of fire licking her everywhere his powerful body met with hers, proving she never knew how sensitive her skin could be. Showing her that she never knew herself at all.

"Be sure, Faith," he whispered after long moments had passed.

"I don't want to stop," she said raggedly. "I want you to love me." She raised her hands to the back of his neck, looking up at him, trembling with the desire he called from her. Her lips parted and her eyes met his. "I want you."

The blazing clarity of her eyes scored him to his soul. The hunger he had leashed flared up, shortening his breath, making his blood run heavily, hardening his body that was already rawhide taut.

"Burned alive," he groaned. His mouth was as hard and hungry, taking long, deep kisses that made her cling to him. His hand moved from her waist to close over her breast, and she offered him a low sound of pleasure, drawing tight to him.

Her body ached, her nipples burned and throbbed, and she needed his touch to assuage it. She didn't seem to have any strength of her own. Warmth coiled and unfurled in pulsing waves inside her, and she felt herself melt against him, twisting feverishly, needing something more, and unable to tell him.

Delaney jerked his head up and pressed her face against his shoulder. "Woman, you're burning me alive." The words were groaned, and he was shaking.

He looked around, weighing danger and distance, trying to clear his mind. He couldn't take her back to camp. He couldn't let her go. His gaze returned time and again to the outcrop of rocks, and without a word he clamped his hand over her wrist, striding toward them.

Chapter Thirteen

DRAGGED BEHIND HIM, Faith could hardly catch her breath. She wanted to ask him why he seemed angry, her senses bewildered by the cessation of pleasure. She ignored the low-growing bushes that caught at the hems of her gown and petticoats, but she stumbled, and he spun around, swinging her up into his arms.

She pressed frantic kisses on his neck, holding him tight. Sliding one hand into the opening of his shirt, she rubbed against the damp heat of his skin, tangling her fingers in the soft mat of his hair, uncaring of anything but the violent need that ripped through her body.

The first, exploring touch of Faith's tongue made Delaney miss a step. His breath stuck in his throat. Neither of them had had a chance for a bath, and he expected her to withdraw from the musky scent of his skin. He hadn't expected the purring sounds of pleasure to come with each hot foray of her mouth and tongue licking him. It took every bit of willpower not to take her where they were.

He circled the outcrop of rocks, fighting to ignore her touches and kisses, measuring the height through heavy-lidded eyes. They would offer concealment should anyone from camp decide to look their way. He kicked repeatedly around a flat protruding slab until he was satisfied it hid nothing dangerous to them.

Still holding her in his arms, he sat down and cupped her chin, dragging her lips across his flesh. "Look at me. No soft bed, duchess. Not even a quilt."

Faith couldn't answer him. Moonlight spilled over the dark thickness of his hair, his face, and shoulders. He was silvered and shadowed, lean and dark, locking her breath in her throat. There was no sound but their ragged breathing.

Unsure of what he wanted from her now, she raised her hands to the top button of her gown, her eyes holding his.

Delaney watched her, watched as the moon bathed the tiny bit of skin the first open button revealed. He saw how her fingers shook, and his own clenched not to hurry her, not to tear away the cloth that hid her from his eyes. Faith lowered her head, opening another button, and he gazed at the lightened sheen of her hair spilling over her neck and shoulders. He couldn't stop himself from reaching out to gather one long length of her hair.

"Stop, Faith. Open my shirt."

She lifted trembling fingers to do as he asked, her moves rough and jerky. The damp cloth fell away from his skin, but she stopped when she reached his belt buckle. Raising her head, she saw through the falling tangle of her hair that he was rubbing a lock of her hair over his skin. The need to see his face was intense. His eyes were closed. The dark, blunt lashes that shadowed his high cheekbones hid his gaze from her, but his lips were parted, and she could see that pleasure had flushed the one cheek that moonlight revealed. With a husky cry she united the ribbon that held her camisole closed.

But just as the need to see him was intense, so was the desire to touch him. With one finger she traced over the hard muscles that rippled beneath the hot skin of his stomach. He made a low, groaning sound, and she looked at his face. The sudden change made him appear wild, primitive, bringing in turn a tiny whimper of need from her.

Delaney lifted her hand to his mouth, biting the soft pad of flesh below her thumb and Faith shivered. Fire licked its way from that point being bathed by his tongue up her arm, and her body tautened.

Releasing her, he speared both hands through her hair, lifting her mouth to his, capturing her lips to take them deep in seconds with a mating that barely hinted of the wildness surging inside him.

He gave her his hunger with that kiss, and she returned its full measure to him with an explosion that rocked his body. His hands wouldn't be denied the pleasure of touching her. She was half-lying across his hard thighs, and he swept up her gown and petticoats until the night breeze whispered against her thinly clad legs. He kneaded her thigh, driving his tongue deeper into her mouth, the way he wanted to drive into the sleek hot softness waiting for his throbbing flesh.

Delaney tore his mouth free. "I can't wait anymore." One hard palm slid between her legs, cupping her, stroking her through the slit in cotton drawers, making her burn and him with her. Sweet cries ripped from her, and he stroked the sultry woman heat of her that he needed to touch as much as he needed water to live.

His body strained as he took as much of her softness as he could, wanting more, much more.

"Fire, Del," she whispered, tugging at his shirt, trying to touch his skin.

She melted around him. Her fingers awkwardly opened his belt buckle, and he had to let her go. He lifted her so she sat astride his lap, his belt whispering open, her fingers blindly unfastening metal buttons while her lips brushed like butterflies across his mouth.

She wanted him inside her so deep they couldn't tell where each one began and ended.

His lips drank the sweetness from her mouth, freely given, and he wanted to slide deep inside her, but he had no control left and he was afraid of hurting her. "Help me, Faith," he pleaded in a hoarse voice, pressing his lips to her shoulder.

"If you make me wait, I'll die."

"Faith, I . . ." His words were lost in an aching cry as her hands slid down to cup the hard, throbbing flesh between his legs. She freed him, caressing him, one fingertip catching up the tiny drop of moisture that escaped before it spilled against hot velvet and within her, tiny explosions built a tension that made her believe she really would die if she didn't have him soon.

He pushed the bunched cloth of her gown and petticoats up to her waist and gripped her hips, lifting her. She cried out, pleading want and need until he couldn't hear anything else. She was poised over his rigid flesh, all heat and open fire for him.

A moan built into a cry as Faith felt his hard flesh part her. She wanted him deep, fast and hard, but no matter how she twisted, how she implored, he took her by tiny increments. "Fire," she whispered, closing her eyes, her lips caressing his shoulder.

Passion's ancient dance demanded that he seek the hot, soft sheath waiting. He stopped himself from driving into her, knowing that once he was fully gloved inside her, he might never withdraw. He had never felt so much a man, listening to the pleasure he brought to her. Her cries of release went through him like sweet lightning, and he couldn't stop pressing deeper, then deeper still, for she was tight, and sleek, clinging to him, until time ceased. He felt her flesh pulse, tightening again, her fingers digging into his shoulders, and with a wrenching cry, he pulled her up and away, spilling in an endless release that shuddered through him, longing to share this with her.

What should have been the aftermath of pleasure so intense that she could not measure it turned into a bittersweet silent war for Faith.

"Why?" she begged him when she finally found her voice. "Damn you, Delaney! Tell me why?"

"Babies, Faith," he snapped with harsh, ragged-edged sounds. He held her still, ignoring her attempt to push him away. She made him feel raw, exposed, and vulnerable having to explain himself. "You were married, duchess. You know how babies happen."

Faith struggled to slide her hand between their bodies to touch her stomach. Her palm felt the warmth of her still-trembling body, but the back of her hand was seared by the fire that burned in his.

Delaney clenched his jaw until his teeth ground together. He could still feel how tightly she had gloved him. He was angry and felt himself somehow cheated by his own act, yet, he had held on to the last shreds of his control to protect her.

The desire to fight left her, and Faith rested her cheek against his shoulder, holding back the tears that stung her eyes.

He gathered her closer to him, rocking her gently. The storm of emotion between them seethed like the coil of clouds that covered the moon, leaving them bathed in darkness. He stroked her slender back, feeling the tremors that rippled over her body, burying his own frustration. Nothing had ever felt as good as being locked inside her, feeling her slowly come apart around him, his every pore drinking up the heat of her pleasure like the desert earth soaked up life-giving rain.

And he was still rigid, still hurting, still wanting her as if he had never had the smallest taste of heaven, only to lose it.

Hating the tension that gripped his body, Faith kissed the side of his neck. "I'm sorry," she whispered. "I know you were right. But I still ache, Del. I thought it would stop hurting so, but it didn't."

He closed his eyes, rubbing his forehead against her hair, his hands splayed over her back. "I told you we'd burn each other alive." He cupped the back of her head to stop her from moving. "Don't talk. Not one more word. I want you, and this time I won't think about right and wrong. I won't stop until I'm inside you so deep—"

"Yes!" she cried. "Yes. That's how it should be."

"Sweet mercy!" he swore, gripping her tight. "If I touch you again . . . No!" He lifted and turned her so she was half lying in his arms, kissing her into silence. Now that he knew what waited for him, it was agony not to touch, not to take her heat and softness and fire once more.

Faith arched her back, gripping his shoulders. She flung her head back as his mouth trailed fire down her throat to the thrusting curves of her breasts. Her fingers worked his hair, pressing him closer, even as he finished opening the last few buttons of her gown, spreading aside the cloth. The night air cooled her flesh as he lowered the sleeves and freed her arms.

Delaney lifted his head to look at her. The thin white cotton of her camisole strained across her breasts, the moon taking pity and coming out from its cloud cover to reveal the peach-gold of her skin. Her nipples were dark, swollen crests that begged for his mouth, and he lowered his head, brushing his lips from side to side between them. He bathed one crown, feeling her tense as he repeated the caress on its twin.

"Don't you like that?" he asked, waiting.

"Del, don't make this harder—"

"Harder, duchess?" he groaned in a bittersweet voice. "Nothing can get harder."

Faith felt an embarrassed flush that had nothing to do with passion seething inside. When his breath seeped through the damp cloth, she moaned. When his lips gently closed over one taut peak, she dug her fingers into the muscles of his arms. She felt herself drawn deeper into his mouth, and sweet pleasure burst inside her. He lifted her up even more, taking her soft flesh deeper still.

She couldn't believe anything felt this good, like a hot rain that brought her splendor and pain, running from her breast to her loin, where emptiness made her try to press her legs together. She tried to twist her body closer to him, but he eased his mouth from her.

"Soon. I promise," he uttered in a husky voice that was barely a thread of sound. His lips clamped on the other tightly beaded crown, suckling strongly so that she lost her breath and sanity.

With her lips on the side of his neck, she drank the fine patina of sweat that glistened on his skin, her teeth raking his flesh, her tongue instantly soothing. Her nostrils flared with every breath she drew of the hot, musky scent of his aroused body. She called his name in a voice raw with need.

She beckoned him. Sliding his hand up under the cloth of her petticoats and gown, he stroked the trembling length of her thigh, brushing lightly against the thin cotton drawers that covered her. He wished there was nothing between them. Nothing but flesh to flesh, heat to heat, hard to soft. His thumb pressed the crease of her leg, opening her leg wider before he found the slit in cotton that clung wetly, then gave way under his gentle strokes.

He felt her quivering response all the way down to his bones. Hunger, unlike any he had known, prowled his body, clawing at him, and he felt himself tremble in reaction. He eased one finger deeper, savoring the wild shivering he called from her, closing his eyes as the fire and the hot softness of her flesh tightened around him, wanting him, wanting more.

Faith's body arched as her hips lifted of their own volition, and she reveled in the wild rapture that shimmered through her with his every touch. She rocked against him, feeling him stretch her, returning the kisses and whispers that were as dark and potent as the flow of her blood. A coiling knot began to unravel inside her, and with a cry she melted against him.

"Burning, Del," she whispered, caressing his flesh as she drew her hand down his chest and closed it over the skystone. She felt the heat of the stone sear her palm, but she refused to let it go. She held nothing of herself back in the kisses they shared, reaching for his mouth every time he lifted it so they could breathe. She didn't know herself, for every move seemed dictated by the tension that tightened her body until she thought she would go mad.

The tiny, imploring whimpers she made sent him over the edge. He couldn't fight her and himself. Cotton tore under the urgent moves of his hand. He lifted and brought her over him once again. His body shuddered as hers did with his hard, fast entry. The unbearable ache became unbearable pleasure as she took him fully with a raw cry. Pressing her legs against his thighs, she drew him deeper, her hands clawing his back, her teeth scoring his skin. If he was wild, she was more so.

"Burning," he breathed. "Give me your mouth," he demanded, feeling the scald of heat they called from each other.

His tongue drove into her sweet mouth with the same harsh rhythms as he took her body. Ecstasy waited. Faith held him against the spinning world around her as he buried himself so deep inside her that she felt every pulse beat before her senses exploded without warning.

Her teeth bit into his lip to bury the scream that rose, and she had to tear her mouth free to sob his name as the force of his release ripped through her. With his head thrown back a guttural cry came from his throat, and she rolled her hips, holding him, knowing what it meant to burn, to die, and then come alive all at once.

They were bathed in sweat. His lips caressed her bare shoulder, and she stroked his damp hair. The night chill forced him finally to move, drawing up the sleeves of her gown, kissing her flesh before he closed a button, refusing to talk, refusing to look into her eyes. With a last kiss to the furious pulse beating in the hollow of her throat, he found his shirt and drew that over her shoulders.

"Did I hurt you?"

"No," she answered softly, knowing she lied. There was hurt, but not of her body. It was for longing to hear some word of caring from him. But he said there were to be no promises, and she had not really believed him, not then, but she did now.

Delaney helped her to stand. "I've got to take you back now, Faith." She nodded and turned away. He rose, buttoning his fly impatiently, torn over what more to say. He sensed what she wanted from him, but he couldn't say the words she wanted. He couldn't admit them to himself. "Come," he said, holding out his hand. Fingers entwined, they walked back.

As they neared the wagons, he drew her against him, pressing a gentle kiss against her lips before he released her. She took off his shirt and handed it to him without a word. Delaney stood, watching as she struggled to climb up into the wagon. Unable to stop himself from touching her once more, he hurried to lift her up, reluctantly releasing her once she was inside. Faith turned to him and, with tears glittering in her eyes, placed two fingers on his lips and then lifted them to hers.

"Don't cry." The words were wrenched from him, for he deeply regretted what had happened. He could never walk away from her now. The only hope he had to cling to was that Faith was unaware of his feelings.

Returning to his own bedroll cost him more strength of
will then he believed he had. Delaney wanted to hold her
all night. He dug out his makings and rolled a smoke, lit the
cigarette, and drew deeply. Faith left behind a soothing balm
that brought his soul deep peace after the intense passion they
shared. Faith, all heat and softness, holding nothing of herself
back. A woman for a man to love.

The wind rose, filling the night with murmurs and whispers that echoed his thoughts. And his skystone seemed to
beckon him to hold its shape, rubbing it, as he forced his mind
to remember the promise that came with the stone's giving.

But with this remembrance came another. One beyond his
finding a woman whose eyes would match the stone. The
duklij was a stone of healing, of protection.

Delaney knew he had to first heal the wounds left behind
by his parents' murders before he could keep his promise to
protect. Then, if he lived, he would claim the bond he had
made with Faith this night. Her sweet smiles and dark secrets
belonged to him.

If he lived. . . .

Young as the morning was, Faith saw the heat waves dance
and shimmer on the flat land, just as the heat had danced
and shimmered in her blood last night. She could barely see
where Delaney rode to the west of the party. Delaney. He had
shown her the path to ecstasy, but now she was filled with
despair. Last night she defied all she believed about herself.
This morning she was not being rational, or logical. She was
in love with a man who refused to share his love in return.

Memories rushed over her. She could still taste his kiss,
still feel the gentle tug of his mouth, and her body tensed as
if his hands were touching her again. She had loved Martin,
but the few times they had made love in the immediate

days before their wedding had not unleashed the passion she shared with Delaney last night. Faith tried to turn her thoughts aside. Restlessly she shifted her seat, wishing for a cooling rain.

The sun had risen hot and red. It grew steadily hotter as they rode across the barren land hour after hour. As they headed into the rising heat-haze, she thought the horizon seemed to disappear. Heat seeped into her, fresh sweat streaming from her skin. Trying to fill her lungs, she drew a deep breath just as the wind rose from the south and blasted all of them with more hot air. The animals' steps lagged. Sweat shone on the flanks of the mules and horses and ran down their faces in grimy streaks. Faith wiped her face with her sleeve and saw that many of the soldiers were doing the same.

"Here, Faith," Pris said, offering the canteen.

Faith took a sip and had to force herself to swallow it. The water was warm enough to be sickening.

Joey tried to drink but spat his out over the wagon's side.

"No, Joey. You've got to swallow it," Faith urged, wiping the gritty dust from her mouth with one hand. The effort to speak was costly. No one spoke. If it were not for the creak of saddle leather or the muffled jingle of the mules' harness, there would be no sounds to mark their passing.

"Hold up," a soldier croaked, pointing toward the east.

Faith squinted into the distance and saw a horseman riding out from a shadowed shelter of a giant sandstone. The mules needed no urging to stop. She let the reins fall from her hands and waited, unable to summon the strength needed to move. A quick look showed that her father and Keith didn't fare any better. They sat on their wagon, the soft, floppy brims of their felt hats pulled low to shade their faces, and were still as one soldier and the sergeant rode to meet the nearing horseman.

Faith couldn't tell if the man was a soldier, too. His clothing was covered with reddish dust. From the wild gesturing he made with his hands, she thought he was excited about his news.

Sergeant Krome seemed to be the same. He spurred his horse back toward the wagons and the rest of his patrol.

"Mr. Becket, we're leaving you. A band of Apache just ran off cattle from the Canoa ranch. If you'll spare us a few of your supplies, I'll see that you're repaid."

"Faith, you give the sergeant whatever he needs," Becket ordered.

Believing that once the soldiers were gone Delaney would ride closer spurred Faith with new energy. She wasn't sorry to see the last of them.

Private Shellby distributed the small amount of foodstuffs among the soldiers. When he was finished, he came to her side.

"I hope you'll allow me to call once you're settled, Miss Becket."

"No, that won't be possible," she answered without a moment's hesitation.

"It's Carmichael, isn't it?" Shellby asked, gathering his reins and stepping up into his saddle.

Faith looked up at him and smiled for the first time that day. "Yes," she whispered, relieved to reveal her feelings.

His expression became forbidding. "There's lots that can happen to a man out here."

Alarmed, Faith stepped closer. "Are you threatening—"

"No," he answered, tugging his hat brim forward. "Just reminding you of a fact, Miss Becket. The man has enemies. Don't forget that."

A light slap of his reins and the horse veered off at a walk around the wagon. Faith watched a moment more, then resumed her seat. With her father and Keith in the lead, she took up the leather and, without a word, urged the mules into a plodding walk.

A few hours later Delaney rode up to them. He didn't stop to talk to Faith but rode alongside Becket's wagon. Faith had to assume that it was by Delaney's order they changed direction to head for the buttes toward the west. She noticed the rising wind, longed for it to be cooler, but if anything, the air seemed heavier and hotter than before.

"Faith, I gotta go," Pris whispered at her side.

"A few minutes more, honey. Delaney seems to be directing us toward those buttes." She spared a glance down at Pris, reassuring her with a forced smile. Squirming in her seat, her little sister pressed her lips together and nodded.

Keith was already down, giving the mules water, when Faith pulled her wagon alongside his. "What's wrong?" she called out, coughing when she swallowed dust.

"Delaney thinks we're in for a blow," her father answered.

"Faith!" Pris whined.

"All right," she snapped, setting the brake. She reached out and lifted Pris over her lap so the little girl could climb down. "Joey, hold the reins until Keith comes. I've got to stay with Pris."

"Where are you going, Faith?" Keith yelled. "Get inside. I'll water the mules while you fill the canteens."

"Back in a minute!" she shouted against the rising rush of the wind. Those few seconds that she had turned to look at Keith and then forward cost her sight of Pris. "Pris? Pris, where are you?"

"Here," came a faint answer.

Faith ran toward straggly bushes at the base of the butte. Another strong gust buffeted her, tearing off her hat. Her skirt and petticoats lifted and twisted, and she tried holding them down as she chased after her hat. Within seconds dust swirled up and around her, stinging her eyes so she couldn't see.

"Pris!" she shouted again, choking when she took in another mouthful of dust. Blindly Faith spun around. She couldn't find the wagons. She froze. Her hat was forgotten. Pris didn't answer her. She tried to calm herself, but panic had a foothold inside her. If she couldn't see the wagons, how would Pris find her way back?

Stinging dust made her eyes water. She lifted her skirt to shield her face, and Delaney loomed up in front of her.

He shoved the hat on her head, grabbing her hand to hold it in place. Tearing off the bandanna that covered his lower face, he yelled, "Get back to the wagons!"

"Pris," she whispered.

"Where?"

Faith couldn't speak, she had no moisture left in her mouth. Shaking her head, she tried to turn, but Delaney cupped her cheek.

"I'll find her."

"No," she croaked. "Me . . . too."

Delaney wasn't going to argue. He grabbed hold of her waist and lifted her over his shoulder. If he wasn't so worried about where Pris was, he would have smiled to remember carrying her like this once before. But Faith was struggling against his hold, and he staggered, barely recovering his balance. He dumped her unceremoniously inside the wagon.

"Stuff the cracks and stay here."

If there had been moisture left in her body, Faith would have cried. "Find her, Del."

He nodded and said something, but the words were torn and carried off by the wind. Faith stared out at the red dust clouds that covered everything in sight, even his retreating body.

"Please, let him find her quickly," she prayed.

"Faith, I'm scared."

She dropped the canvas over the opening. Joey was huddled on his bed, a quilt drawn up and around him so that only his eyes showed. Faith rushed to sit beside him and hold him tight.

"Don't be afraid. The storm will be over soon, and Del will find Pris. He won't let anything happen to her."

But even as she reassured him, the wagon rocked as the force of the wind increased. Faith gave him a tight squeeze, then hurried to push what blankets she could to seal the wagon. The heat was stifling, and she drank greedily from the canteen, uncaring for the warmth of the water. It was wet, and that was all that mattered. Dust still lashed her skin inside the wagon. Returning to Joey's side, she held him as they lay with the quilt covering them.

Faith was desperate to know what was happening outside and just as desperate to shut out the wailing sound that rose but never abated.

She wanted to believe that Delaney had found Pris and was sheltering her someplace until the storm ended. She had to repeat this belief like a litany as time dragged on and on and only the wind screamed out for her.

It took Faith a while to realize that what she was listening to was silence. The storm was over. Joey slept, and she eased herself from his side. Dust filled the air inside the wagon, filled her lungs with every breath she drew. Tearing aside the canvas, Faith stared out at the land blanketed in quiet dusk.

"Faith?" her father called out, limping up to the wagon. "Delaney's come back." He raised his hand in a helpless gesture.

Faith could only mouth Pris's name.

Robert shook his head. But Delaney rushed forward to break Faith's fall as she fainted.

Chapter Fourteen

FAITH CAME TO. Her father was kneeling by her side, bathing her face with a cloth. She pushed his hand away, forcing herself to sit up. But when she opened her mouth to speak, all she could make was a croaking sound.

"Here, drink," Robert ordered, holding a cup of water to her lips.

The water was sweet and cold. As soon as she drained the cup, she asked for more.

Keith already had a fire going against the encroaching dark, and Joey sat close to him across from her. Faith did not see Delaney.

"Del's back out looking for Pris," Keith said before she asked. "Don't worry, he'll find her." He poked at the fire and then looked back, meeting her gaze with a pleading look. "He will, won't he, Faith?"

"If anyone can, Delaney will." But she couldn't meet his gaze any longer, hearing the lack of conviction in her own voice. She accepted another cup of water from her father and finished that, too, then struggled to stand.

"Why don't you rest, Faith?" Robert asked.

"No. I want to help find Pris."

"Delaney said for us to stay here. Please," he added, and then, with unaccustomed gentleness, took hold of her hand. "We need you here with us."

Before she could respond to her father, Faith heard the sound of horses. Keith grabbed his rifle, and Robert stepped in front of Faith to shield her.

"Becket," Delaney called out. "I've got Pris."

Faith ran forward only to stop herself when she saw the men with Delaney. Pris was seated before one of them. It wasn't until they came closer to the light cast by the fire that she realized they were Indian for all that their clothes were those of white men.

After swinging down from the saddle, Delaney stepped close and lifted Pris into his arms. In a whisper he spoke to Faith as he handed the little girl over. "They found her and kept her safe. Make them welcome."

Hiding her fear, Faith obeyed him. "Please, share our fire and our food." When none of the three Indians moved, she looked at Delaney. "Do they understand—"

"They understand you just fine, Faith. These men are Pima, not Apache. That should please your father no end. Dressed like white men, speak like white men and civilized by the nuns of Saint Joseph's."

"I heard that, Carmichael," Becket said, hurrying to stand in front of them. "I do thank them for finding my little girl and bringing her back." Becket saw that they were dressed like white men, but for their long dark hair and braided earlocks. He forced himself to look away and touched Pris's head. "You all right?"

She nodded, tightening the grip she had on Faith's neck.

Faith murmured softly and walked back to the wagon with her little sister. She heard Delaney's guttural voice and answers that came from one of the Indians.

"Keith," she called, setting Pris inside the wagon and taking up a bucket. "Fill this wherever Pa found that cold water. I want to bathe the dust off Pris and make sure for myself that she's all right."

"Pa didn't find the water. Del did."

"Just hurry, Keith." After climbing into the wagon, Faith used a quilt to cover Pris and made her hold it while she undressed her. "You'll feel better once we get you clean, honey."

"I was scared. I couldn't see you. You didn't answer me when I called. And I tried to come back, Faith. I really tried, only I couldn't find you."

"I know," she answered Pris, rummaging for clean clothes in the chest. "I tried to find you, too. Delaney—"

"And then I saw them. But they didn't hurt me. We all laid down with the horses and got covered up. It was so hard to breathe. They gave me their water and then Delaney found us."

"Here you are," Keith said, handing in the bucket.

"Start supper, Keith. It's the least we can do. And never mind what Pa says. You make sure they eat."

Keith nodded and spun around only to crash into Delaney.

"Take it easy, Keith." Delaney looked up to see Faith watching them. "Pris all right?"

"Yes . . . and you?" Her gaze met his.

"Hungry." He resettled his hat and walked away, leaving Faith with her mouth half-open. She heard Pris call her but for a moment didn't move, didn't answer her. She could not shake the feeling that Delaney wasn't talking about food.

Delaney sat at Joey's side. "You come through this in one piece, scout?"

"Faith stayed with me," he answered, as if that explained everything to Delaney.

And in a way Delaney believed that it did. He glanced at the three Pima sitting across from him, looked over at Becket who stared at the ground, nervously rubbing his hands down his pant legs, and squeezed Joey's shoulder. "I'm gonna help Keith, scout." And as he worked, he couldn't keep his mind from coming back to Joey's statement about Faith. She was strong. He discounted her fainting when she heard that he had not found Pris, and thought instead of her reaction to the fierce-looking Pima. No vapors, no need for more than his simple reassurance that she had nothing to fear. Each day reaffirmed his belief that she would last in this land. But he had been a fool to tell her he was hungry. Faith had to know he wasn't talking about food. Not when he heard Keith swearing as he sliced the last slab of dust-coated bacon.

"Wash and dry it," Delaney ordered, knowing all their food stores were likely in the same condition. He used his coffee, tightly wrapped against such an occurrence, and set the pot at the edge of the fire just as Faith and Pris rejoined them.

"I'm afraid we have little food, but we will share what we have with you," Faith said, looking directly at the Indians.

It took courage for her to stand there and receive their measuring stares in return.

"The woman is *s-ké-g*," the oldest of the three said.

Delaney smiled. He made his own leisurely perusal of Faith's body. The dust was gone, brushed from her hair, and shaken from her gown, he guessed. Her skin had a golden tint, with only a bit of flushed color on her cheeks. His gaze snagged hers and held it for a second too long before he lowered it to her mouth. He wondered if she remembered his claiming every secret her mouth had for his own. His breath caught in his chest before he could release it. Her breasts rose and fell with the same shuddering breath. His body was strung tight recalling the feel and taste of her. Once more he lifted his gaze to meet hers. His smile became a reckless tantalizing grin.

The sight snapped Faith into awareness that they were not alone, and she was infuriated when he kept looking at her. "What am I?" she demanded. "What did they say about me?"

"Sure you want to know, duchess?"

"Yes." But she wasn't. Not at all.

"Beautiful," he answered, his voice suddenly husky, his eyes glittering with a possessive look.

There were grunts of agreement that Faith refused to acknowledge. She was flustered and didn't know if she should trust Delaney's translation. Pleating the side of her skirt in a nervous gesture, she thought to ask Delaney if it was true when he spoke.

"Yeah. Not all white men's words rest easy on the Indian tongue."

"Oh." Faith smiled, unsure of what to say. No one had ever called her beautiful. Once again she found the Pima giving her measuring looks. And once more the oldest turned to Delaney, directing his question to him as she knelt to fry the bacon.

"The girl child is yours and this woman?"

"No," Delaney answered quickly, this time turning from Faith's look. He didn't want to remember her pressing her hand over her belly. But the thought drew him, just as he knew he had to see her eyes. Faith foiled his intent. She kept her head bent, busying with laying strips of bacon in the pan.

"The woman is yours?"

Delaney shook his head. "The man is her father, and the two young males are the brothers of this woman." He watched their eyes now and smiled. He knew what was

coming. When the youngest of the Pima stared too long
and hard at the rifle that Keith had carelessly left near the
fire, Delaney leaned over and picked it up. "The woman isn't
mine, but the gun is."

Dissatisfied grunts met this, but Faith frowned to hear a
warning in Delaney's voice. She found that anger wormed
its way inside her to hear him deny that she was his, only
to chide herself. *No promises.* And last night hadn't changed
his feelings about her. She glanced over at her father, in vain,
it appeared. He was still standing, staring at the ground. She
wasn't even sure if he was listening.

"Keith, open a fresh sack of flour," she ordered. "Maybe
there's one the dust didn't get into." She ignored his scowl
as he moved off and wished she had gone herself. Faith was
uncomfortable with the way the three Indians watched her
every move.

Pris spoke from where she stood behind her. "I don't know
what to call you. You didn't tell me your names."

"Pris! That's rude," Faith admonished, only to find herself
on the receiving end of a cutting gesture from the older
Indian. She was not mistaken about his move; she had used
the same one toward the children.

"Come, little one. The women of the robes give to us the
names of white men." He waited until Pris stood in front of
him and, pointing to his chest, said, "I am called Joseph."

Holding out her small hand, Pris smiled. "Thank you for
keeping me safe, Joseph."

"They have named me Henry," the Indian on his right
said.

Pris repeated her thanks to him. Faith watched as
her sister moved to the last one, who said his name
was Eli. She started as Pris shyly pecked his cheek
and then ran to hide behind Faith's skirt. She realized
that Henry and Eli couldn't be much older than Keith.

Her brother returned with the flour. "It's the best I could find."

Taking the bowl, she warned Keith not to let the bacon burn, seeing for herself the hunger the Indians' faces revealed, wishing the soldiers had not taken food supplies.

Delaney rose from his place, holding onto the rifle. "I'll get some jerky."

Faith could only stare at his retreating back. It was not the first time that he seemed to know what she was thinking and act before she said a word. Keith dished up the crisp bacon, and she set the dough in the grease to bake. When Delaney came back, Faith asked him to get the two tins of peaches she had been saving. His smile was warm, and she treasured it as he did what she asked.

Every crumb disappeared. Faith scoured her pans with sand once supper was finished and listened to the murmur of Delaney's voice while he spoke their language to the Pima. She resented the way her father had begrudged them every mouthful of food and wished they had not noticed. How could he behave this way toward them after they had returned Pris to them unharmed? She could only guess that he kept silent because of the warning looks Delaney directed at him.

Both Pris and Joey were sleepy, and Keith offered to put them to bed, leaving Faith to wonder if she should leave the fire. Glancing up to find that the one called Joseph still watched her, she made her decision. She rose, still holding her pan.

"The woman is *s-kawk.*"

Delaney didn't even look at Faith. He sipped from his cup, then carefully set it down, away from his body. "Yeah. She is strong."

"S-doa?" Joseph demanded.

"Healthy?" Delaney asked and, when the Indian nodded, answered with a shrug. "Guess so."

"Must you talk about me as if I were stone?" Faith snapped at Delaney, incensed by his grin.

He was tempted to tell her how far from being stone she was, stopping himself at the last moment. Ignoring her was his only choice.

"The father made no *iagta*," Henry stated.

That forced Delaney to sit up and look at Robert. "Becket, they want you to make them an offering in thanks for your youngest daughter."

"That why they're paying all this attention to my Faith? These sav—" He stopped and glared across the fire at the Indians. "They can't be thinking of having Faith?"

Delaney cooled his anger and spared a blessing for whatever wisdom Robert had that stopped him from calling the Pima savages. With a smooth coordinated rush he came to his feet and walked over to Robert.

"You've got to offer them some token worthy of your child's life."

"No."

"Becket, you—"

"I won't offer them a damn thing. I won't deal with them. You talked me into letting that Apache travel with us. Don't think I was fooled for a minute. I know he's the one that stole those army mules. Now you think you're gonna bully me into giving something else away?"

Delaney forced his hands to remain at his sides. He wanted to shake the old man. "Did you tell Krome about Seanilzay?"

Robert couldn't meet his eyes. "No."

"And what is this something else?" Delaney demanded, his voice low and grating.

Becket looked up at his face. His hate glared out from his eyes. "You've taken my pride. You've got my boy, Keith, looking up to you for everything. And my girl . . ." Once more Robert stopped himself from saying what he wanted. He wasn't going to confront Delaney about Faith. Not with her listening to every word. He was afraid that she would side with Delaney again, and he would lose her. Spitting to the side, he turned to walk away, surprised when Delaney's hand gripped his arm and stopped him.

"You don't understand. I've got no time to explain it all. But you've got to offer them something. I can't. She is not my child. If Pris was, I wouldn't own anything more precious to me than her life."

Pulling his arm free and rubbing it, Robert refused to answer him.

"Would you risk all our lives over some trinket?" Delaney demanded. "What kind of a man are you, Becket? I warned you once before—"

"You want me to give them something, Carmichael? All right. I'll get something they won't forget."

Delaney turned, speaking rapidly to the Pima as his long strides took him to stand in front of Joseph. The older Indian rose, as did Eli behind him. Their voices angry.

Faith watched but glanced back to see what her father would bring them. It was her cry that alerted Delaney. He fell silent and looked over his shoulder.

"You stupid fool," he whispered.

Becket stood with his rifle pointed at the Indians. "You tell them to leave. I fed them, Carmichael. That's payment enough."

Turning slowly, Delaney shielded Joseph with his own body. "This is the wrong move, Becket. We're on their lands." But even as he spoke softly, Becket cocked the rifle.

"It's mine to make. I'm tired of taking orders from you when I figure you're wrong, Carmichael. Time's come for you to earn your keep. I want them away from here."

Faith moved closer to Delaney and added her pleas to his. Her father's accusing look made her step back.

Becket glared first at Delaney and then at his daughter. The sight of the two of them standing together, blocking his view of Joseph and Eli, infuriated him. Henry chose that moment to come to his feet in a rush. The move appeared threatening to Becket and he acted.

Two shots erupted from the rifle, thudding into the young Indian's body. For a moment they all watched as he staggered back and then fell.

From the wagon came Pris's scream and Joey's cry. Faith tried to run only to have her arm grabbed by Eli.

With a lethal quickness Delaney leapt for Becket, ripping the rifle from his hands. Hooking his foot behind Becket's leg, Delaney delivered a blow to his gut with the rifle stock that sent Becket sprawling. He saw Keith, armed as well, and ordered him back, all the while working the lever, ejecting the shells until the rifle was empty. Cursing, he threw it off into the dark.

"Do you know what you've done?" he grated from between clenched teeth. It was as stupid a question as Becket's move, and Delaney knew it.

"Henry's dead!" Faith cried out from behind him.

Closing his eyes, Delaney swore to himself. When he opened them, Becket was clutching his belly, trying to stand. He had no chance to utter a word; Faith's cry was abruptly cut off, and he spun around. Joseph held a knife to her throat. Eli had already gathered their horses.

"Damn you, Carmichael, do something!" Becket yelled. "Keith," he demanded, "use that rifle. Stop them!"

"Use it and your sister's dead," Delaney warned. "Get back to the children and keep them quiet," he ordered in a soft, chilling voice without turning around. He hoped that what Becket accused him of doing with Keith was true. That the boy would obey him and not his father. He forced himself to meet Faith's terrified gaze and willed her to accept his silent entreaty for her not to struggle. Delaney knew that blade at her throat was honed finer then a razor.

Eli used sharp, guttural commands to still the plunging tugs the horses made on their rope halters and quiet their frantic neighs as they scented Henry's blood. He managed to lift Henry's body over the back of one horse and with a smooth leap mounted another. Joseph backed to the third horse, dragging Faith with him.

"You can't let them take her!" Becket screamed in fury.

"Move and I'll kill you, Becket," Delaney promised, filled with an impotent rage. He didn't dare do what Becket wanted. He would cost Faith her life. And for a heart-stopping moment he thought it was all over as Joseph tried to mount and not lose his hold on Faith. Delaney measured the distance and knew he could never reach her in time.

"Go quietly, duchess," he whispered. "I'm right behind you."

With a scream of challenge Joseph threw Faith facedown over his horse and swung up behind her. The horse's dark hide gleamed as his front hooves rose, pawing the air only to come down and pound the earth. Delaney didn't wait for them to leave. He ran for Mirage.

Chapter Fifteen

THE DARKNESS SWALLOWED Delaney's quarry. Sand muffled the unshod hooves of the Indians' horses. They were riding southwest toward valleys and mountains he barely remembered. The moon hid behind a dense blanket of clouds, limiting his vision. He gave Mirage free rein without slackening her stride, allowing the mare to pick her own way as they began to leave the desert behind.

Delaney swore when Mirage's hoof hit a hidden stone. To his ears the sound was far too loud as he once more guided her around the base of a rising stretch of mountains.

He judged the lapse of time and knew that Faith's arms and legs would be numb, her body aching from the position she was in. He whispered to Mirage, urging her to hurry, fear worming its way inside him that he would not find her.

Faith drew a deep breath and tried to push herself off the horse when Joseph pulled up. Despite the feeling in her arms and hands that a thousand needles were piercing them, she slid down, swearing when her legs collapsed beneath her. The fierce grip Joseph took on the back of her gown tore the cloth as he hauled her back over the horse, pinning her with a broad hand splayed across her waist.

Faith shivered. "Let me go," she pleaded, chilled to the bone from the coldness of the night. "You know he's coming after you." She tried to move, feeling every ache and bruise, swinging her arms wildly to rid herself of the numbness. A rippling tension passed from horse to man. She lifted her head and heard the sound again. A hoof struck stone. Delaney was close! With a sob she struggled, trying to wiggle backward, desperate to delay them.

She barely heard their soft murmurs. Eli rode off, and suddenly she was moving again, climbing this time. Bushes scratched her hands, and her hair tangled only to be torn free as Joseph pressed his horse for speed.

A coyote howled in the distance. Faith couldn't lift her head to see and knew fear was racking her body. Her scalp was on fire, and she tried to shut out the pain and think only of Delaney riding after them.

A rush of cold air forced her eyes open. Her lips formed a scream that never came. They were stopped at the edge of a trail, and she was looking down at a sheer drop that had no bottom.

The horse shied, and Joseph whispered. Holding her breath, Faith watched the first tentative step the horse made. Again Joseph murmured something, and Faith sensed the animal's fear along with her own. The sweat and heat of the horse's hide soaked the front of her gown, but the warmth was welcome. Another few steps and her breaths were shallow, for she couldn't tear her eyes from the hooves that touched the rock ledge, knowing their lives hung in the balance.

It all became too much. She didn't want to see the abyss below. She didn't want to watch for the misstep that could plunge them over the edge. Very gently she rested her cheek against the trembling muscles of the horse's side, closed her eyes, and let the pounding thud of her heart fill her ears.

Time ceased to be. Faith couldn't summon the strength to pray.

The faint smell of pines roused her. The horse snorted and picked up its pace. Faith thought they were on level ground, but the darkness made sight impossible. The pine scent grew stronger, the dense foliage thicker, and another faint sound came to her ears, like water rushing over rock. She lost track of the twists and turns the horse made under Joseph's guidance. She tried to shake off the stupor that held her tightly in its grip. Hoping to distract Joseph, she pleaded with him to let her go, gathering her strength to make another attempt at escape.

She swore at herself for not realizing that the Indian was no longer holding her. Faith knew it would not be easy. Her moves had to be quick, and she repeated them to herself, until she was sure she could manage. The best chance she had was to slide, roll away, and hide.

If Delaney was following close behind, it would gain him time. If Joseph stopped to look for her. She refused to allow the thought of failure to enter her mind.

The horse started up a small incline, and Faith buried her pain. With a heave she came backward off the horse, falling before she could tuck her body tight. There was an agony exploding inside her body. She managed one full body roll before she tried to crawl. Faith had no reserves of strength. She lay sprawled, unable to catch her breath.

Joseph's foot nudged her side. Faith clawed the earth. Her eyes filled with tears when he grabbed hold of her hair and lifted her head.

Rearing up and snorting, his horse demanded his attention, and Faith's chin hit the ground when he freed her. She was beyond caring what he did to her. Nothing could make her move. Not even the challenge Joseph called out when Delaney appeared moments later. Scraping her cheek against the earth, Faith turned her head and could barely make out his shadow sliding from Mirage's back.

She didn't know if he saw her. He was absolutely still. A whisper of sound added to her feeling that Joseph had moved slightly away from her.

"I lied to you," Delaney murmured. "The woman is mine." Joseph didn't answer him. Delaney unbuckled his gunbelt and looped it over the saddle horn. Without taking his eyes from the Indian's still figure, he began to unbutton his shirt. "I will fight to keep what I claim." Throwing the shirt over the saddle, he used one hand to flip open the saddlebag and reached inside for his moccasins. "You are a man of honor, Joseph, not to leap on your enemy when he is vulnerable."

"That way brings shame to a warrior."

Delaney whispered his agreement and lowered himself to sit and remove his boots, never losing eye contact with the Indian. He slid his supple moccasins on, deftly tying the knee-high boots in place, and came to his feet in one smooth, graceful move. Blood coursed through his body with every breath, every heartbeat, until it flowed with a lethal intensity that he had learned from the Apache warriors.

Joseph drew his knife from its sheath.

Delaney followed suit. "Before we begin, know this. I am sorry for Henry's death. And I do not wish to kill you."

"The boy was my brother. First blood will not be enough."

Delaney nodded. He knew his strengths and his weaknesses, but the outcome was always uncertain. Joseph outweighed him by a good twenty to thirty pounds. Delaney was far too aware that a slip, a wrong move, a too-late twist of the body ended a man's life. He had to try and protect Faith.

"I will accept a fight to the death. But let the woman take my horse and go."

A savage cry filled the night. Joseph leapt over Faith's prone body, ending all talk.

Faith forced herself to crawl out of the way. Feeling was slowly returned to her limbs, and if she believed herself in agony before, she thought she was in hell now. Her body screamed demands to stop moving, sending a wave of blackness in warning of what would happen if she didn't stop. But the choice was not hers. She was too close to them. The thought that Delaney might trip over her and be hurt sent a fresh surge of energy into her. Huddled against a tree trunk, she could not drag her gaze away from the flash of knives. A thin trickle of light filtered down through the trees, and she strained to see their crouching figures.

The soft rustle of their moccasins finding purchase on the earth was the only sound Faith heard. No curses, no taunting passed their lips, but after a few minutes their breathing grew harsh as they darted and twisted their bodies to avoid the other's knife. She was too frightened to utter a cry, too frightened for Delaney to think of what would happen to her if he lost.

But Delaney thought about it and knew he had to block thoughts of Faith from his mind. Joseph was a worthy adversary. Delaney knew the Indian's pride and code would not allow him to accept a wound. He needed all his skill, all his wits, to dodge the Indian's slashing blade. With every moment Delaney knew he couldn't let Joseph live, or Joseph would hunt him until he was dead. The clearing was small. Delaney knew Joseph was backing him toward a stand of saplings that would limit his own knife thrusts.

Joseph, like him, held his gaze to Delaney's. A man's eyes would give away his moves before he made them. There was a chance to distract the Indian, and Delaney had to take it, allowing him to attack rather than defend.

He lowered his gaze for a fraction of a second, throwing

his knife from his right hand to his left. Joseph followed the move with his eyes, giving Delaney the advantage he sought. With a quick twist of his body Delaney leapt and pivoted, his knife slicing Joseph's arm. His ploy to use a border shift that rarely worked with a gun left Joseph with him at his back. Regret flashed and died. There was no time left. Joseph was turning, and Delaney knew if he didn't move, he would die. With a brutal thrust he sank his knife deep into the Indian's lower back, missing the spine. Delaney clamped his free hand over Joseph's mouth to cut off his cry. No force was going to free his knife quickly, not buried to the hilt. Delaney raised his knee and pushed the man's body forward, ripping the knife out at the same time. The Indian sagged to his knees, and Delaney ended his life with a clean cut.

"Get his horse," he ordered Faith without turning. When she didn't answer him, he repeated his order and heard a soft sob. "Don't quit on me, duchess. Eli went for help. Mount up and make a run for it."

"I can't move," she whispered, closing her eyes to shut out the sight of what she had witnessed.

Delaney ran to her and lifted her to stand. Shaking her, he demanded, "I didn't kill him so we'd get caught." He ignored the trembling of her body and shoved her ahead of him. Mirage backed away when she smelled the blood on his body. He whispered softly, and she stilled. Lifting Faith astride the saddle, he placed the reins in her hands, forcing her fingers to close over the leather. "Ride like hell. Let Mirage pick her way, but don't let her stop."

"What about you?"

"Hell, duchess, I ain't no hero. I'll be dusting your trail so close you'll feel me up your skirt tail." With a slap on Mirage's rump, he sent her off, running to get Joseph's horse, praying that Eli hadn't had time to find his way back to their reservation and block the trail.

Curbing his feeling of urgency, Delaney had to soothe the Indian's horse, who shied from the unfamiliar smell of a strange man. Swinging up onto the horse's back, he spared a brief thought to having killed Joseph. Pride would not let the Indian be satisfied with less than his death. There really was no choice. But he touched his skystone as he passed the body, whispering words of the man's bravery to the night sky.

He caught up with Faith at the start of the trail that followed the narrow ledge.

"I can't do this, Delaney. I can't ride—"

"Hush, duchess. No talking." He knew there had to be another way out of the valley, but time was against them. The clouds had thinned, allowing the moonlight to spill over the rock walls. Dismounting, Delaney came to her side and lifted her down. She clung to him, and for a moment he held her tight, wishing he could lie and reassure her. But they were a long way from being safe.

A glance at the ledge reaffirmed his judgment that they had to go out single file, and if she wouldn't or couldn't ride, the horses had to be led. With the shivers racking her body, Delaney didn't believe she had any reserves to call upon.

And he had no time to be gentle.

"If you won't move to save your own neck, duchess, then do it for Pris and Joey. Eli's gathering men right now to ride down on them. Our only chance is to get there first."

"I told you I can't."

Delaney pushed her away. "I ain't got time to pamper you. I'm getting the hell out," he stated in a cold, flat voice. He took hold of the Indian horse's rope, knowing that Mirage would follow.

"You'd leave me here?" Disbelief colored her voice. Faith saw him move off onto the ledge. "You unfeeling bastard!"

Delaney kept walking.

Mirage's rump was almost out of sight, and Faith stood

there with her arms wrapped around her waist. She could not walk that ledge. But she couldn't stay there alone.

She lifted one hand and touched the rock face, her fingers finding the small crevices. If she pressed against the wall, she wouldn't need to look down and see death waiting. Splaying her fingers wide, she took one hesitant step. How could Delaney leave her? How could she think she loved him?

Anger burned inside her, forcing her to forget the cold, the danger, and her fear. Her cheek was pressed against the rock as she felt with one foot for safe purchase, found it, and took another step. She would show that arrogant man who had as much feeling as the rock she kicked out of her way that she didn't need him. With each handhold her fingers found, she became more sure, breathing easier as she rounded the slight curve in the ledge. It couldn't be much farther. She hoped it wasn't. And she hoped that Delaney waited at the end for her.

Small stones fell with a clatter into the canyon below. Faith stilled. Tears poured down her face. She was not going to make it. Her fingers froze like claws, and she began to shake.

"Just a few steps more, duchess. You're almost here," Delaney whispered, stepping out onto the ledge to ease one hand into his own.

"Don't touch me. I don't want your help. I don't need you."

He heard the defeat and the terror in her voice and had to close his eyes, refusing to let them sway him. But he refused to release her hand.

"Take the steps. Prove you don't need my help."

"I hate you," she whispered.

"I know, duchess, I know."

But she took the last few steps to safety.

Delaney jerked her against him and took her mouth for a

quick, brutal kiss, only to tear his lips away seconds later. "You're more woman than you know." Before she had a chance to utter a sound, he swung her up on Mirage. "We're gonna make hell's own ride, duchess. Hang on tight."

Keith anxiously peered into the dark as he made another patrol around the wagons. He had all in readiness just as Delaney ordered. The sky was paling when he heard his father call out to him. Keith wanted to ignore him. He couldn't understand what had made his father shoot the Indian boy. And he didn't want to ask. Somehow he knew he had to make his own choice about where he stood and would stand. It troubled him that his decision would likely put him against his father.

"Any sign of them?" Robert asked as Keith returned to the back of the wagons.

"No."

"Maybe he won't find her."

"Delaney will. And he'll come back for us, too."

"Don't be so sure, Keith. Carmichael's a—"

"He's a man that would never shoot—"

"You'd dare judge me?" Becket bellowed, incensed that Keith glared at him. "You didn't see the way those savages were looking at your sister. Who knows what Carmichael was telling them? I did what I had to do to protect all of us."

"You killed an unarmed boy! He wasn't much older than me."

Robert backhanded Keith across the mouth. "I'm your father. Don't forget it, boy. You'll not accuse me, and you don't sit in judgment of me! Carmichael's not going to set you against me when you're still a boy not a man."

Keith tightened his grip on his rifle until his fingers ached. "You're wrong about me. I'm not a boy." He stared at his father as if he were seeing him for the first time—and he didn't like what he saw. Wiping the blood from his split lip, he spat off to the side, knowing his decision had been made for him. Before he could put it into words, he heard Delaney's warning shout.

Keith ran past his father and grabbed the canteen from the wagon Faith usually drove. Pris's and Joey's faces were barely visible in the paling light of dawn as they huddled near the opening behind the seat.

"Did he bring Faith back?" Joey asked with a tremor in his voice.

"He's got her. Del wouldn't come back without her," Keith answered as he waited for the slowing horses, trying to keep his own fear at bay. Faith was slumped over the horse's neck as Delaney drew rein on the one he was riding, and Mirage, blowing heavily, walked the last few feet.

Delaney was down and lifting Faith before Keith moved. The wild tangle of her hair fell over his arm and shoulder. Delaney lost any regret he had that he had killed Joseph when he saw the bruises darkening her cheek and chin.

"Is she all right?" Becket demanded as he joined them.

"Keith, give her some water and then get up on the wagon and I'll hand her up to you. She's done in." Delaney saw that her eyes were open, and he longed to soothe her with soft kisses and even softer words, but there was no time.

She sipped from the canteen Keith held to her lips and met her father's anxious gaze for a moment. She didn't want to talk to him, much less look at him.

Delaney shifted her weight and handed her up to Keith. "Get her inside. You fill the water barrels?"

"Just like you said. Move out of the way," Keith ordered the children as he helped Faith inside. "You two take care of her and let her rest."

"What happened back there?" Becket asked.

"They split up. Eli's likely gone back to the reservation,

and Joseph is dead." He wiped the sweat from Mirage's hide with his spare shirt, knowing he was pushing his mare to ask her to carry him on another hard ride. "We've got a four-, maybe five-hour lead on them." He took the canteen from Keith, sipped sparingly, and then poured water into his hat for the mare. "Fill it again and mine, Keith."

"We'll head for Tucson," Becket said.

"No. They'll expect us to ride directly south—and they'll be waiting." Delaney nodded as Keith hooked the canteen over Mirage's saddle and climbed up on the wagon. He moved toward his horse, but Becket grabbed hold of his arm.

"Hold up. I've a right to decide where it's best for my family."

"While we stand here jawing, Becket, you're costing us time. I want to see them safe, too. So let me do what you hired me for."

Leading Mirage, Delaney went to the back of the wagon. Drawing his knife, he sliced through the rope that held Beula to the wagon. "You're on your own, brown eyes."

"You can't leave our cow!"

"Becket, we're gonna ride for our lives. She can't keep up," he explained impatiently, scanning the land with a narrowed gaze. "Would you rather see her breaking a leg and being shot?" Swinging up onto his mare, Delaney ordered Keith to move out.

"We're heading east, Becket, before the Pima gather enough men to run against us in relays."

"You're always so damn sure," Robert said resentfully.

"I'd better be. If I'm not, we'll all be dead, and it won't matter who's right."

Delaney took the lead. Mirage settled into a smooth, ground-eating stride that allowed Delaney to turn his attention to the land coming to life under the rising sun. It was almost an hour later when he spotted the smoke and counted two from the west and an answering one from the far south. He slowed and walked Mirage to cool her, letting Keith catch up with him.

"There's a shallow gully ahead," Delaney told him as he walked abreast of the wagon. "Take them down real easy. Sand's loose and treacherous." He took note of the tension that marked the boy's face. "You're doing real good. How's Faith?"

"Sleeping." But his lips formed a grin for Delaney's praise, and he moved ahead.

Delaney waited for Becket, annoyed that he was steadily falling behind. "What's wrong?" he asked, lifting his hat to wipe the sweat off his brow before he resettled it with the brim slanted forward.

"I'm not killing my mules on your say-so!"

"Don't. Look behind you, Becket. Count the smokes. There's four now. A few minutes ago there were only three. And there'll be more. Choose. The mules or your life." With a flick of the reins Mirage turned, and Delaney rode after the other wagon.

Another hour should see them in the forested canyons and mountains where Delaney knew of a hidden valley whose entrance was almost impossible to find unless a man knew it was there. The valley had thick grass and sweet water, but it was more than a place to recover. It was in the Apache's territory. Delaney drove his mare now, finding the easiest path for the wagons to follow. The Pima would give long and serious thought to entering their enemy's land to find him.

The hairs on the back of his neck rippled with warning. Delaney slowly lifted his head, searching the rim of the canyon's mouth before he went farther.

A press of his knees brought Mirage to a standstill. His right hand hovered over his gun in an involuntary reflex.

He studied the four mounted silhouettes that appeared above him. For long minutes he watched and waited, knowing he was an open target.

Tension ebbed from his body. Pushing his hat back, Delaney raised his arm and smiled.

Chapter Sixteen

A LONE HORSEMAN disappeared as the three waited above, watching Delaney. A few minutes later the man rode out from the deep shadows cast by the canyon's walls.

"Mahtzo," Delaney called in greeting as the Apache neared. Briefly he explained what had happened and their need to rest for a few days.

Nodding, Mahtzo said, "At the end of the third sun I will come for you. Look no more, Del-a-ney, we will watch."

"It is good to be home," Delaney answered, waiting until he rode off before he signaled Keith to follow him.

Four hours later he reached the small hanging valley that opened over an enormous canyon. Tired as Delaney was, he stepped down and unsaddled Mirage, slipping the split-ear bridle from her head and allowing her to run free in the thick green wild grasses of the meadow. Slinging the saddle over his shoulder, he walked slowly, feeling the peace this place held renew his mind, body, and spirit. The dam he had built across the stream now had a fair-sized pond backed up behind it, fed from the spill of cold, sweet water from the limestone ledge at the far side. A stand of young cottonwoods shaded half the pond, but even here, in this hidden valley, he chose to camp away from the water.

Dust-streaked and exhausted, no one had energy to talk as the mules were staked out and a cold supper put together. Faith spoke once to ask if the pond was safe to bathe in, and receiving Delaney's assurance that it was, although cold, she took herself off. Now, as twilight fell, there was a soft, hushed silence in the valley, and Keith joined Delaney near the dying fire.

Not wanting to push Keith, Delaney waited, but he sensed that the boy was troubled.

"This place would make a good home," Keith began.

"I thought so once."

Keith shifted, restless, and lifted a piece of deadfall, stripping off its dried bark to feed the fire. "You've been lots of places, haven't you?"

"Some men are born restless, Keith; some move on 'cause they're searching an' ain't sure what they're looking for." Delaney thought about his own moving around and knew his time of running was nearly done. He caught Keith sneaking looks at him and wondered what troubled the boy that he couldn't say. "There's about enough for two cups in that coffeepot. I'd welcome another cup."

"You don't have to stay awake on account of me. I've got some thinking to do."

"So do I, Keith, so do I. Pour the coffee, and we'll sit quiet or talk."

They sipped from their cups, and Keith added another log to the fire. "When does a man know it's time to stop running?"

"Depends on the man," Delaney answered, shaking off the tiredness when he heard an underlying fear in Keith's voice. "Depends, too, on what a man is running from."

With a cautious look around Keith moved closer to where Delaney sat. "We didn't up and leave Kansas just to find us a new home and land to farm. We had to get away."

"Think a bit more before you tell me anything, Keith," Delaney said. "If it's not—"

"I thought we were friends?" he cut in.

"We are."

"And friends trust each other, don't they?"

"Well, sure. I didn't mean that you couldn't trust me. I was trying to caution you about telling me things your father didn't want me to know."

"He don't matter now. I've watched what he's done to my sister, and I don't like it. He thinks I'm still a boy. I'm not. I'll make my own decisions about what's right and wrong. And I need to tell you. I need to talk to someone about what happened back home."

"All this because of what your father did?"

"Yeah, Del. He had no right to kill that Indian boy."

Delaney studied Keith's face and saw for himself the need in the boy's eyes. He realized he was more exhausted than he knew. Although his instinct that the Beckets were hiding something was true, he was now uncertain he wanted to know what it was. With a quick shake of his head Delaney swallowed more coffee. He was going to listen to what Keith had to say.

As if he sensed Delaney's willingness, Keith leaned close. "There's a reward back home for Faith."

Tension rippled over Delaney's body, and he was thankful it was just dark enough to hide it. He had no reserves left to control it. A hundred questions flooded his mind, but he stopped himself from asking Keith even one of them. But his duchess was wanted?

"You don't believe me, but I swear to you it's true."

"I believe you, Keith. Just give me a minute to swallow that."

"You don't sound surprised. Did you know about us before you agreed to ride for us?"

"No. I didn't know. I'll admit that I suspected all of you were hiding something, but I didn't have reason to think of one of you being wanted."

"Well, what I said is true. Can't figure you sometimes, Del. You didn't ask what she's wanted for." Keith shot him a puzzled look.

"If you told me this much, you'll get to the rest. Don't see a point in asking when you'll say it in your time and way. And you need to know, Keith, this stays between us. I'm no damn bounty hunter."

"Wouldn't trust you if I thought that. Anyway, there is a reward for her. The cattlemen's association thinks she's the one that killed two of them the night they murdered her husband." In a softer whisper Keith continued.

"We had a good time at their wedding, Faith and Martin's. That was his name. He was a big, easy-speaking man, but my ma said he had himself a thick stubborn streak on account of his folks coming from Missouri."

Delaney couldn't help but grin when Keith flashed him a smile. He'd heard that saying before. With a quick look he noted the time and the covering darkness that was descending on the valley and found himself worrying about Faith. She'd been gone a long while.

Keith spoke again with a serious note in his voice. "The cattlemen didn't want Martin to farm the land he bought. All the while he built their cabin, they came around, warning him what would happen. Martin didn't believe them. He never told Faith about it. The night they got married and went home, the men were waiting for them. Martin tried to talk to them, but one of the men threw a rope around Faith and started to drag her behind his horse. Martin ran after her, and they shot him." Keith stopped, squeezing his eyes shut. He knew he had to tell the rest, but his chest felt tight, and tears burned behind his eyelids. His shoulders sagged, and he lowered his head, ashamed to let Delaney see his weakness.

Delaney saw each protective move, and he remembered his own grief, his own tears. He came to his feet, unable to find words to comfort Keith. Lifting the boy to stand, ignoring his attempt to pull away and hide the wetness on his cheeks, Delaney slung one arm over his shaking shoulders and led him away from the fire.

"Once there was a man who I loved like a father. He told me there was no shame in a man's tears. I didn't believe him, Keith, and you may not believe me now, but I give those words back to you."

Blindly Keith turned to him, sobbing as Delaney held him, whispering broken words that slowly finished the terror of that night.

"They were going to kill Faith," Keith repeated over and over. "They couldn't let her live to tell what they had done. No one was there to help Faith but Joey." Keith pulled free of Delaney's arms and turned away, furiously wiping his eyes. "Joey grabbed Martin's loaded shotgun. He said he couldn't see the men, but he fired the gun. All he tried to do was help my sister. He didn't know . . . Joey just didn't understand what he was doing."

All the bits and pieces that Faith had told him came to Delaney in a rush. Joey had been there, witness to her husband's murder. Joey, waking up blind in the morning. And Faith, taking the blame and being made to pay by her father.

Delaney placed one hand on Keith's shoulder, urging him to turn. "Tell me why you wanted me to know. You've held this bottled up inside you a long time, Keith. Why now?"

" 'Cause I hate him! I can't respect him and listen to him anymore. He's made her pay for this. He made Ma pay for it. He's the one that made us leave. Faith wanted to tell what those cattlemen did. But he said no one was going to believe her. He didn't want her getting free of him."

"Easy, Keith. I'm not your enemy. He is your father, and if you don't like his way, you'll have to find your own. But have you tried to talk to him—"

"He won't listen to me. He thinks I'm a boy. I told you I'm not." With a defiant stance he again wiped his eyes. "I want to leave him. I'll make my own way."

"What about Pris and Joey? They still need you. And Faith. Your sister will likely take the brunt of your father's anger if you take off."

"I can't be worrying about them."

"Then don't call yourself a man, Keith, if you can turn your back on those who need you." The words were cruel, and Delaney knew it, but Keith needed some harsh talk to make him stop and think before he acted. "You figure to leave them behind?"

Keith walked a few steps and stood with his head thrown back, staring up at the night sky.

Delaney let him be a few minutes and rolled himself a smoke. He leaned down to strike the match against a stone, and when he straightened, he found that Keith was watching him.

"What should I do, Del?"

"I'm not the man to be asking. You had a rough two days an' might want to sleep on this."

"I might," Keith conceded grudgingly.

"We can talk again if you'd like. I'll admit I'm not thinking too clear myself right now."

"Yeah. I'd like that, Del."

He walked back with Delaney, bid him good night, and took his bedroll a ways from the wagons.

Delaney glanced at his own bedroll set near the fire, and as tired as he was, he knew he wouldn't sleep now. He finished his smoke, his mind filled with what Keith had told him. He glanced at the wagon, wondering if Faith was sleeping. A moment later he knew that even if she was not, he wouldn't go near her. Things had happened too fast between them. There had been no time to talk then, less afterward. To himself, he admitted he wasn't sure he wanted to confront his feelings for her. Not now, when he had so much of his own past to resolve.

Restless, he began to walk. A loving woman like Faith deserved more than he had given her. His thoughts drifted back to what Keith had said about Joey's blindness. Delaney puzzled over its cause. Had the boy's mind closed out the sight of his shooting a man by refusing to allow him to see? Or had something gone wrong with the shotgun when he fired, causing a blinding flash that made Joey lose his sight?

He recalled Faith telling him the doctor could find no damage to the boy's eyes. That ruled out the second reason Joey could not see and left Delaney thinking about the first.

He found himself nearing the pond and stopped, gazing at the moonlit surface. His head was crowded with too many thoughts, too many decisions to make. Suddenly Delaney was tired of it all. A cold-water bath and sleep was what he needed. Morning and decisions that couldn't be put off would come soon enough.

He rounded the pond to the limestone ledge on its far side.

From within the stand of cottonwoods Faith watched Delaney. She had taken her bath but found herself unable to return to the wagon. There was something about the peacefulness of this place that lured her to stay. When Delaney stripped off his shirt and the moonlight gilded his skin, she knew she should leave or call out to him.

She did nothing.

He placed his gunbelt on top of his shirt and sat to remove his moccasins, then neatly place them to one side. In a graceful move he came to his feet and quickly shucked off his pants.

Faith's breath caught in her throat. Delaney's body was beautiful. He stretched his arms wide to the sky, and she stared, filled with a sense of doing the forbidden. Unwanted memories of Martin and the few times before their wedding that they had made love rushed into her mind. She had never seen Martin undressed. Their couplings had been hurried, awkward gropings with little time or chance to remove their clothing. Each time she had been left feeling restless, unsure of what was wrong and unable to ask anyone, least of all Martin. He had been too pleased. Now, with a guilty start, she realized she had never had a desire to see Martin fully unclothed. And she had no need to ask anyone what she had been cheated of when they made love. Delaney had showed her the beauty of shared passion.

She wanted him. He was smooth-muscled strength and raw masculinity in every move of his straight-limbed body. Faith rubbed her hands against her thighs, remembering the feel of his muscular shoulders and arms. She longed to touch him again. The breeze lifted a leaf that brushed her cheek, and she closed her eyes briefly, imagining her cheek brushing the soft mat of hair that fanned across his chest and narrowed into a line down the center of his body before it spread outward to cup the potent maleness that sprang free.

He untied a narrow band from around his hips and she saw him hold the small bag attached to it for a moment before he set it down. His legs were long and powerful as he walked to the water's edge. Faith was struck anew by the sight of him; he was overwhelmingly male, a pagan in this ancient place, as wicked, untamed, and dangerous as the land he loved. Her body's response intensified in a wild, warm rush, and her blood began to beat to an insidious rhythm. Water rippled out when he entered it. Moonlight cast his face in shadow, then light, teasing her with the intriguing cast of his features.

Her want became hunger.

The water was hip-deep as he made his way to the silver spill falling from the ledge. Images flooded her mind. She envied the lacy tendrils of water that caressed his body when she yearned to do the same.

She wished for the courage to join him.

He turned toward her. Faith was sure he saw her within the protective shelter of the trees. She could feel the burning intensity of his eyes. Water spilled from the ledge above him, making his long dark hair a sleek, wet helmet before it ran down his face and body. He didn't move or speak.

Was he angry that she was here? Faith neither knew nor cared. She was drawn to move away from the protection of the trees and walked slowly to the edge of the pond. There she waited.

Delaney stared at her. He tossed his head and stepped aside, out of the water's flow. She was every dream that came to tantalize him. The moonlight silvered the honey-rich color of her hair, which fell in a tumbled mass over her shoulders. That same light coming from behind her revealed the shadowed outline of her legs beneath her gown. It was all she wore. The chill of the water on his body disappeared with the flood of heat that sight of her brought to him.

Ducking beneath the water, Delaney grabbed two handfuls of sand. He rose and shook his head to clear the water from his eyes, and without taking his gaze from her, began to scrub his arms, shoulders, and chest. His moves were slow, deliberate, stretching out the seconds that brought a visible change in her breathing. Still, he didn't speak to her. But he was remembering, and memory of Faith, soft, soft skin and sweet cries, made his body tighten. Exhaustion fled.

As if his thoughts had been carried to her, he saw her lips part, her eyes grow hungry and dark, and her breasts rise and fall with unsteady breaths.

He didn't want to linger. He ducked beneath the water to rinse the sand and dust from his body, then came toward her, only to stop when water lapped above his thighs.

"If we were Apache, and I dared to watch you bathe, I would lose my life."

"But we're not Apache," she whispered, willing him to come to her. "And you didn't watch me," she added with a breathless catch in her voice.

"What are you doing here, Faith?"

She watched him raise his hands to his hips, standing where he was. Faith lifted her gaze to his lips. He was not smiling. "I didn't mean to spy on you," she offered in her own defense. "I was there," she explained, gesturing toward the trees, "when you came. I meant to say something and warn you I was here." Nervously she licked her bottom lip. "I . . . couldn't."

"Why?" he asked in a soft, relentless voice.

Her gaze locked to his. "I didn't want to," she admitted.

"I thought you hated me, duchess."

"Please, Del—"

"No. You said you hated me."

She looked away from him. "I did. Back there. I really didn't understand why you lashed out at me. But it was the only way, wasn't it?"

Her admission that she didn't hate him made tension ebb from his body. "You weren't the only one who hated me. I hated myself for having to hurt you after all you'd been through." He lowered his head, staring into the dark depth of the water, suddenly wanting her understanding. "You know I had to kill him, Faith."

"Yes, I know. Now," she added, unable to keep the regret from her voice.

"Sometimes a man doesn't have time to decide if there's another way. And I had to protect you." With one hand he stirred the surface of the water, following the ripples that spread out and away from him. As his exhaustion had fled, so had his caution. He warned himself to listen to what he was admitting to her, then, to carefully think before he said another word.

Faith looked back at him. There was a lonely air about him, a solitary man struggling to survive, and she ached to comfort him. But just as he had shown her strength and beauty in what she believed to be barren desert, she needed to return its measure to him. She didn't want Delaney to blame himself. She wanted to give him her love, and that desire made her bold.

"Are you planning on hiding in the water, Delaney?"

His head jerked up, and his gaze snagged hers. For a moment he felt strange, almost defenseless, as if she had seen into his mind and his heart and knew the secrets they held. It was a feeling that had little to do with his naked state and everything to do with the emotions that were getting tangled with the lovely woman watching him. He wanted her, and that forced him to strip pretense away.

"Do you want me to come out?" he asked in a husky voice.

"Yes," she answered without coyness, without hesitation. Raising her arms to him, the gesture both pleading and one of welcome to her warrior, Faith waited for him to come to her.

She took his hand, a whisper of laughter escaping at the renewed shock of icy water against her heated skin.

"I'm wet," he said, the corner of his mouth lifting in an off-centered grin at his own foolishness.

"It doesn't matter, Delaney. Nothing does but us." With both hands she smoothed the water down his chest, caressing the sleek, potent warmth of his skin. She leaned close and pressed a kiss over his heart.

Gently Delaney brushed her hair back from her face, his gaze lingering on the thick curls that entwined over his damp fingers. His thumbs met beneath the soft skin of her chin, and he slowly tilted her head back. The air around them stilled as he gazed into her eyes, searching them before he spoke.

"There's so much giving inside you, Faith, that you make a man want to take and take, then offer all he is in return." He pressed his forehead to hers, then licked the drops of water that fell from his hair to her skin. "I haven't touched you, and you already want. Do you know what that does to a man, to know that a woman, his woman, is helpless to stop the need that burns when he looks at her? And when I touch you," he whispered, sighing the words over her parted lips, "I know that you'll come to me with nothing of yourself held back." He dipped his head, the bruise on her chin needing a feather-light kiss before he pulled back. "Is there anything that you would deny me?"

She closed her eyes against the blaze of his, afraid he would know the words she longed to say. But Delaney was not ready to hear about love, so she answered him in kind.

"No. I can't deny you, if you need and want me. Not if you care."

One hand untangled itself from her hair, drifting down, dampening the cloth of her gown. With the backs of his fingers he brushed lightly over one taut nipple in a blatant, deliberate caress.

She trembled in reaction, unable to hide from him. But his grin was now a male smile that was reflected in his eyes.

"With a little coaxing you'd give yourself to me whether I cared or not."

"Would that please you, Delaney? I would." She was beyond denial. But she was not prepared for the pain her own admission cost her.

Delaney repeated the caress to her other breast and let his hands fall to his sides. The smile disappeared.

"But I do care. I care more than I want to, more than I ever intended. When I first saw you, I thought you were all starched pride, a virgin, and trouble. I swore I wasn't getting my boots tangled up with range calico like you. But there's no more pride in you than a woman has a right to. And—"

" . . . and I wasn't a virgin, Delaney," she whispered, afraid of what he was leading up to. Faith decided to use some of that pride she had a right to and stepped back. With a blatant gaze she made a quick sweep of his body, finding that pride was no substitute for the brazen act she intended. He was too potent, too male, and fully aroused. She stared down at his feet. "Since you're not wearing boots, you don't need to worry about getting them tangled with the calico I wear."

"Faith, look at me." He slid his hands into her hair. "That sassy mouth's gonna get you in trouble." He smiled, drawing her head up so she was forced to meet his gaze. The light, teasing scent that was all woman, only hers, sank deep inside him, and his body tightened in a heated rush. "You're trouble for me, Faith. More trouble than you know. You steal into my thoughts. You—"

"I need you to kiss me, Del," she softly demanded, for passion was now a fever in her blood, and need for him to ease it her only thought.

He nipped her lower lip, soothing it with his tongue, but once again lifted his head away.

"Del," she moaned, locking her arms around his neck, shivering as the lingering dampness of his body soaked her gown. For a moment her gaze was pleading. "You told me once a woman should never have to beg a man for anything.

Did you lie to me?" she asked, scattering tiny kisses over his bearded jaw. "Is that why you're teasing me?" She closed her eyes, took a deep shuddering breath, and released it. Her lashes lifted reluctantly, her gaze searching his, finding his eyes dark, intense, almost fierce. "Do you want me to beg?"

The question kindled something explosive inside him. "No. God, no, Faith," he groaned. His mouth crushed hers, and he delved into the pleasure of kissing her for long, endless minutes.

The feel of him this close, the touch of his hands gliding over her heated body made her tremble. She couldn't hide her need from him. The shape of her mouth molded to his, opening to the slow stroke of his tongue inside until the taste of him filled her, blended with her own, and became one taste.

When he felt her trembling, he drew her closer, his touch gentle from her nape down her slender back to the slight flare of her hips. He repeated the same caress a second time, less gentle, deliberately arousing her and himself, pressing their bodies tighter. The stroke of his tongue became heavier, deeper, and he was kneading her flesh against his, forcing her swelling breasts to his chest, forcing her hips to cradle his.

Wildfire. Burning out of control. He lifted his head, breaking the kiss, his breathing labored. His lips whispered over her hair, brushing her eyes closed, for the desire that blazed in them sparked his own. His mouth followed a random path over her cheek, nudging her hair away from her ear, and Delaney gently captured the soft flesh of her earlobe with his teeth. There had been no time to know the shape of her delicate ear, but his mouth learned it now, and his mind was filled with soft, sweet sighs from her lips.

Faith felt his chest dragging against her breasts with every move, his long powerful legs pressing against hers. For every touch that his mouth offered her skin, she returned its measure until her legs felt weak.

His tongue trailed fire across her jaw, and she lifted her face, giving him whatever he wanted of herself. The string of tiny love bites he offered the taut arch of her neck made her cry out, her hands holding tight to his arms. Restless need filled her.

"Please, Del . . . don't . . . stop," she whispered, her voice broken, feeling totally vulnerable to him.

"I can't. I won't." Need was in her eyes, and she looked just as she had once claimed, that she would die if he didn't make love to her. And that same need clamored in his blood, in every taut nerve of his body. "I want you too much," he murmured between kisses that covered her face. "I wanted to love you with nothing between us, Faith." Even as he spoke, he began unbuttoning her gown, stopping when it was open to her waist. He couldn't control his labored breathing and stepped back, his eyes all that touched her. "Show me how beautiful you are, Faith," he demanded in a passion-rich voice, as dark with hidden promise as the night.

"Am I beautiful to you?" she asked, suddenly feeling shy.

Delaney's gaze lifted to hers, and he let the desire show. "You are woman, the most lovely of all gifts given to man."

She thought of making love to Delaney without anything between them, feeling his skin against her own everywhere they touched. And she longed to be beautiful for him. With a hand that tremored she slid the gown from one shoulder, following his gaze to see the cloth caught on her nipple.

"Beautiful," he whispered again, need no longer a sweet song but a fierce demand. "I remembered the taste of you on my lips and deep in my mouth. I want you like that again, all soft heat and fire, burning for me, coming apart for me. And you want that again, don't you?"

Faith couldn't answer him. She didn't know that a man felt this way, that any man, that Delaney could say these words to her. With a small move the cloth fell and bared one breast. She held his gaze with her own, needing his silent reassurance, needing to see a new, hotter blaze kindle in his eyes. Sliding the sleeves down her arms, she felt her gown pool loosely around her hips.

"Nothing between us, Faith. Nothing but burning, dying, and coming alive."

She pushed the gown over her hips and stood proud in her nudity, letting her lover look as she did at the one whose joining would make her complete. Passion tautened his features. Her own body, under the caress of his eyes, felt tight, and hot, filled with a building tension.

Hiding nothing of her feelings, Faith went to him.

Chapter Seventeen

DELANEY TOOK HER hand and led her away from the pond to where the moon pooled its light on a cove of walled rock with a thick carpet of moss at its base.

The scent of the moss was rich and pungent mingling with their own aroused scents. Desire throbbed in his body. Delaney turned to her and saw a strange new fear in her eyes.

"Why? I won't hurt you, Faith."

"I know. But I look at you and see power, a male strength—"

"That I would never use against you. Come to me."

She went into his arms, lifting her face for his kiss, knowing that she could not tell him that his gaze whispered of a possession his lips would never speak. What she craved to hear he withheld, even as his tender kiss built quickly into one that was wild and deep with passion's promise.

Faith found herself needing to cling to his strength, feeling out of control, shaking with want. As if she had spoken to him, he drew her tight to his body, his mouth demanding now, his palms cupping the sides of her breasts, his thumbs sliding between their flesh to rub the taut peaks. She felt the world tilt and swirl as he lifted her into his arms before lowering her to nature's softest bed.

He broke the kiss, slowly levering his chest over her bare breasts, feeling the bite of her nipples into his skin. She raised her arms at his whispered urging, looping them over his neck, her fingers tunneling through his thick, damp hair, drawing him closer. Her eyes were dark, and he felt a new need to pay homage to the woman's gift she gave so freely to him.

He kissed the bruise on her cheek, murmuring words that he knew she could not understand. Dark words, Apache words, and softer, sweeter words of Spanish that eased his guilt for not speaking the few words she wanted to hear. Each gentle touch his lips first made to her eyes, her mouth, her skin, praised her woman's softness and strength and told of her special beauty to him.

Delaney learned new tastes from her. The skin of her throat was warm like cream, her lower lip throbbed and swelled within the heat of his mouth. And she trembled. He knew the fire that waited. Tiny kisses weren't enough, he discovered, lingering to lick the hollow of her throat, measuring the blood that quickened her pulse until it beat as wild as his.

His hunger grew with every kiss, every new taste of her that he found with his tongue. He wanted to be gentle, tender, and loving, but the tiny sounds she made, the very restless moves of her body made other demands for him to heed.

Faith listened to his whispering, to the husky tone that grew deeper, and longed to know what he was saying. Nothing could make her ask. This was a pleasure too intense, a spell of tenderness he wove that she could not break.

His body shifted, leaving her bathed by the cool night air. His kisses were still gentle, shaping the curve of her breast, and she lifted her arms to free him, stilling the words of longing she wanted to murmur. There was a tension in his body that spoke of his fierce restraint, but his potent maleness pressed her thigh, and she arched her body to his, unable to stop this silent entreaty.

Delaney crushed the soft moss within his hands, touching her only with his lips. They had called fire from each other once and soon would do it again. He could feel its heat build within him, and he fought its pull. He refused to tell her he loved her no matter how his heart sang those very words. Love was a promise to Faith, and promise meant life together for all days to come. He had no such certainty to offer her.

The lithe, feminine twist of her body almost made him lose control. His tongue dipped into the tiny indentation of her navel, and he smiled against her skin when she stilled, then shivered. He rubbed his bearded cheek against the soft skin of her belly, whispering his breath over the lush curls that had to wait while he pressed kisses to the sleek length of her thigh. Her knee rose when more of the warmth of his body left hers. She turned to him, her hands feverishly seeking to touch him, and he slid out of her reach, one finger tracing the shape of her ankle up to her knee.

The fire had built inside her, burning every sense, and she had to see him. Bracing herself on one elbow, Faith found him watching her.

She leaned over and caressed his shoulder, smiling when he trembled. Hadn't she always known what her touch could do to him? Wasn't this rightness of loving him always with her?

"Come to me," she murmured, trailing her fingers down his chest, gently rubbing the hard pebbled tip she found nestled in his hair. Her gaze held his as a fleeting butterfly-light breeze caressed them. "I want you inside me."

She entwined his fingers with hers, bringing his hand to her mouth, gently biting him. Her gaze never wavered from his, and she wondered if her smile matched the wicked slant that shaped his mouth. She turned his hand, kissing the fleshy pad at the base of his thumb, remembering how he had made her insides tighten. With delicate cat licks she bathed his skin, then softly sank her teeth into him.

"Faith . . ."

"I want you."

His body covered hers, his lips barely touching her mouth as he pulled their joined hands to the side of her head.

"If you want me inside you . . . open your mouth." He drank her cry, feeling as if he had fallen over the edge of a precipice. His tongue penetrated her deeply, in thrusts that lifted her up against him. He groaned, savoring the hunger of her kiss, giving her more of his body's weight. His hands slid under her bare back, the move tearing the velvet moss, releasing more of its rich scent as pleasure filled him and he devoured her mouth.

Faith struggled to free her hand from his, needing nothing so much as to touch him. He wouldn't let her go. She fed and tasted from their kiss as deeply as he, loving the feel of his aroused body pressing hers to the earth. Her every breath was filled with the scent of Delaney.

Fire swept her body. Passion called, demanding a joining just as he tore his mouth from hers.

"Yes, love, yes," he whispered, seeing the need in the dark fevered look of her eyes. His body was rigid with desire, his hips thrusting against hers, and he nipped her lower lip roughly, possessively. "I want you," he breathed into her mouth. "Want you and want you." Her answer was a cry, the wild tossing of her head and the uncontrollable shaking of her body moving beneath his, desperate now for fulfillment.

"Soon. I promise you that." He wanted to bury himself in her softness, lose himself in the heat of her, but he dragged his lips down to the taut peaks that begged for his mouth. He drank her scent and taste until it was deep inside him, a part of him that he could never forget.

Hot breath and delicate licks had flames blazing in her body. Faith was crying, twisting up to his mouth, and hurting with need.

She clutched his shoulders, forcing him to stop. "Love me. I . . . can't . . . oh, Del . . ." She urged him inside her, wanting to hold him, wanting the Delaney who was lonely, the man who was gentle, and vulnerable, the man who would not say he loved her, but whispered such words with kisses and touch.

She stilled when he claimed her. Delaney closed his eyes. The endless loneliness that always waited disappeared. Her legs clamped around him, holding him deep, offering him love, hope, and the eternal giving of woman.

"Look at me, Del." *You'll always have my love,* her eyes told him.

And he whispered in his heart, *I love you, my woman, I love you.*

Passion would not wait. In sharp, powerful waves it ripped through Faith, its force relentless. A fragile cry escaped her lips.

She shuddered everywhere, inside, where he wanted to savor the heat of her that tightly gloved him, outside, where his lips drank the mist that sheened her skin. He couldn't be still.

There was no time for gentle arousal, for slow deep strokes that would bring them together. Faith was wild, her fingers biting into his, her teeth raking his shoulder.

Fever rose in him in a vicious, merciless need.

And Faith was there, urging him deeper with the rough thrust of his body.

Faith, tangling her legs around his, crying out his name in plea and demand.

Faith, smoldering and burning, bursting into flame, and taking his mouth with the hunger that ripped through him.

Faith, who whimpered and tore her mouth free, cupping his cheeks and watching him as passion ignited.

Watching him as he watched her. Feeling as he felt the tension come to a racking point. Pleasure beckoned him over the edge. He was shattered and helpless, knowing that she still watched him.

But it didn't matter now. Nothing mattered. He burned and took her with him. Dying. Endless flame and life.

Faith closed her eyes. He was truly hers. She was shattered and renewed. She loved him. Loved only him.

There was agony in his eyes when he looked at her and heard her whisper her love. Delaney silenced her. With kisses, with a fierce gentle loving, and then once more with fire. He loved her until even the heat of their joined bodies could not keep the chill of the night away.

He reluctantly left her, quickly returning with his bedroll, cradling her against him until the stars began to fade and she slept. His own eyes finally closed, and he felt himself drift off into sleep only to wake with a start.

Between the night noises he heard her cry out, broken words and whispers before the silent tears. She quieted when he drew her back into his arms, murmuring softly, wishing it had been Faith and not Keith who told her secret.

All his own thoughts of women and betrayal and their cost came rushing back to him. He regretted his thought that Faith would betray him as Elise had done. This woman he held trusted him and would betray herself rather than one she loved.

For this night she was his woman, his to hold and to protect, his to love. He stroked her cheek and waited for the tension to leave her, listening to her breaths become deeper, even, now that sleep reclaimed her.

He placed a kiss on her lips and made plans to give her a gift for the one she had given him this night. A gift that would chase her nightmares and allow her to be free of guilt. A gift that would not equal what she had given him, but the only one he could give her from his heart.

When the morning sun broke the night's grip, Faith woke to find Delaney gone.

Tears streamed down her cheeks. Around her was the scent of him, and she turned her head, only to find tiny daisy flowers scattered over the moss that had made their bed.

She reached out to touch one delicate lavender-tipped petal, almost afraid that she was dreaming and it would disappear like Delaney.

The flower was real. She lifted one and brought it to her lips, giving the kiss that she had thought to place on Delaney's mouth when he woke. The complete joy she had found in his arms would not be tainted by sadness. He had loved her. They had been one. The flowers were not for good-bye. They were a promise of his return. They had to be.

Faith lifted her gaze to look above her and froze. There on the edge of the rock wall lay a huge mountain cat. Delaney had warned all of them that mountain lions and jaguars often hunted this land. She hadn't even realized she was holding her breath until she released it. Tension seeped from her when the cat made no move to lunge at her.

The glossy coat was tawny in color, small dark spots marking its rounded head, larger ones appearing on its neck, then changing shape at the cat's sides to squarish black marks circled by a deeper yellow with a dark spot in its center. A jaguar, she decided, noting its torn ear. The cat was over eight feet long, and she couldn't guess its weight.

Time disappeared. She forced herself to meet the cat's unblinking gaze. Golden eyes seemed to hold her own. Faith was struck by the strange feeling that other than its size, this hunting cat was no more dangerous to her than the orange tabby she had been forced to leave behind in Kansas.

The feeling was strengthened when the cat yawned, presenting her with its pointed teeth. Lowering its head to rest on the crossed paws, the eyes seemed to close but gave the impression that they watched everything.

With a great deal of caution Faith sat up, and when no sound, no move was made by the cat, she slowly rose and stood. Backing away, her eyes never leaving the cat, Faith put distance between them before she turned to run.

Drawn for one more look, she did. The cat was gone.

The turn of the sun had already cast its late-afternoon shadows when Delaney returned. Robert was the first one to see him ride in from the mouth of the valley. He had been angry to find Delaney gone without a word to anyone, anger that grew to impotent rage when he saw the soft glow in his older daughter's eyes. He knew Faith had been with him.

He stole furtive glances at Delaney, envying him the ease of riding his mare like he was an extension of the horse, envying Delaney his freedom. Shaking his head, he finished cleaning the last of the mule's hooves, then tucked the hooked pick into his pocket. He had enough to worry about without envying the man that was the source of his new and very deep concern.

Had Faith, in her foolishness, made Delaney privy to their secret? That soft glow in her eyes had triggered memories of her mother looking much the same when Robert first married her.

The knowledge forced him to realize again that his Faith was a woman, married and widowed. She had a right to marry again, likely would. He knew that, but on some level he couldn't begin to name or fully understand, he hated the thought that Delaney was the man she chose.

There was fear mixed in with his anger. Delaney was not a man that Robert could ask his intentions toward Faith.

He was certainly not a man Robert could question in any way. So he was left to watch Delaney approach the wagon, then lean down to speak to Keith, forced to stand helpless while Delaney rode Mirage toward the pond.

Did he know about them? The question burned in Robert's mind. And if he did, what would a man like Delaney, a man who owned a horse and his guns and little else, do with the information Faith may have given him?

Robert stood, staring after Delaney's retreating figure, knowing that in this territory fifty dollars could buy a man's death. The five-hundred-dollar reward posted on them would be a fortune to someone like Delaney Carmichael.

He became aware again of the solitude of the valley. He was sure he could find the way out without Delaney. If this was a hidden place that few men knew about, and Delaney was left behind, they would be free of him and their secret safe.

A moving shadow forced Robert to lift his gaze. There on the far rim sat two mounted Apache. His shoulders sagged in defeat. There would be no leaving Delaney behind. He would have to take his chances and deal with Delaney in his own way, in his own time.

His thought was echoed by Delaney as he walked Mirage toward the pond. Becket's looks made him realize that he would have to deal with the man, about Faith and Keith, and Becket's need to use a gun to solve his problems. If he was allowed to keep on with no one taking Becket to account for his actions, he could lose his life and cost his children theirs.

The sight of Faith standing with her back toward him chased thoughts about Becket from his mind. Slanting shafts of sunlight filtered through the cottonwood leaves wove gold strands into her honey-brown hair. It was loosely tied back with a ribbon, and he remembered its scent and feel against his skin. He slid down from Mirage's back, dropping the reins, and started to walk toward Faith.

"It's Delaney!" Pris shouted from where she stood in the pond. Splashing water she yelled again. "He's come back, Faith!"

She spun around, dropping the linen she held, her eyes riveted to his. They faced each other tensely for long moments, then Faith dragged in a slow breath and released it. His eyes were shadowed by the forward slant of his hat brim, but Faith saw the flexing of the smooth muscles in his cheek. The commanding life-force of him, so resolutely masculine, urged her toward him. She wondered at her own weakness.

"I knew you would come back, Del," she whispered, stopping in front of him. Her gaze followed his to where two wilted daisies were inserted into the buttonhole above her breasts.

"I hoped they pleased you," Delaney said softly, wanting to sweep her into his arms, aware that Pris had come out of the water and was watching them.

Faith had no such worry. She took the two steps that separated them and rested her cheek against the smooth leather vest he wore, inhaling the dust, the scent of leather, and a faint musky smell that held an irresistible appeal for her.

"No questions, Faith?"

"You'll only tell me what you want to anyway." She rubbed her cheek against him, longing to feel his arms around her, longing to know what he was thinking, feeling, and yes, she admitted to herself, what had driven him to leave her.

Cupping her chin with one hand, Delaney lifted her face to his. The stunning depths of her turquoise eyes hid nothing from him. Love waited for him, all he had to do was claim it. His thumb brushed the slight swell of her bottom lip, and he had to close his eyes, fighting not to remember the wild, sweet abandon of their lovemaking.

"You tempt me to turn my back on all I know, all I must do, Faith."

The regret was in his voice, but when he opened his eyes, she saw what he could not hide for a brief moment. A hope there would be a way.

"I don't understand all that makes you the man you are, Delaney. But I have never thought of myself as a woman who would trap a man by any means she could. I won't lie to you or to myself. You know that I love you," she whispered, watching the color of his eyes deepen, taking it as a sign that he was withdrawing from her. "If you don't want my love, then go. Is that what you want? To hear me say it? I can't hold a man like you. No one can."

Lifting her hand, she touched his chest and found the shape of the skystone beneath his shirt. "Seanilzay told me that when you were given this stone, you made promises and received others in return. You need to keep your word before you can have what this will bring you."

"And still you ask for nothing from me?" Her touch sent heat sizzling like lightning through him. He wanted to press her hand and hold it there, but Faith moved away from him.

"What I want from you, Delaney, is not a thing to be asked for. It is a gift, freely given, with nothing expected in return." She started to walk toward where Pris stood, water dripping from her pantelets, silently staring at them.

"Faith," Delaney called softly, "I do have something to give you. Freedom, in a way. If I'm right," he added, walking to her side when she stopped but didn't turn. "I want to take Joey with me to see someone that might help him."

"No one can, Delaney," she said more harshly than she had intended. "I should tell you the truth about Joey's blindness. After last n-night . . ." Her voice faltered, and she stopped for a moment. Looking away from Pris and the pond, closing off the sight of Delaney bathing there, Faith gazed at the light shades of pink and rose that colored the creviced granite walls rising from the valley. But she couldn't hide or close off the need to give this last secret to Delaney after she had trusted him with all else.

He wanted to stop her from telling him what he already knew had to be the truth. Keith would not lie to him. Yet, there was a need, a selfish need, which came from some deep last corner of resistance that refused to believe Faith was a woman totally without lies. Even as he admitted this to himself, he cursed another woman who had taught him that love came wrapped in betrayal and lies. Faith was not Elise. He knew it in every corner of his heart. And could only blame the nearness of home that stirred memories he had once believed buried.

Faith began to speak then, refusing to look at him as she told him what happened in detail the night that her husband was killed and she helpless to prevent it. He did not touch her, didn't say a word to stop her when she stammered out a picture of Joey, struggling with the weight of the shotgun, shooting the man whose rope had her sprawled in the dust between the cattlemen's horses.

" . . . Joey fired a second time and wounded a man who later died. I never understood why they rode off and didn't kill us. But that is what happened, and I was grateful they had spared our lives. And Joey, well, he refused to talk about it." Faith wrapped her arms around her waist, wanting to tell him the rest. "There is a five-hundred-dollar reward for me as a murderer. That is the reason we came here and why I can't use my married name." The last was a mere whisper. She was braced for his rejection.

"That explains why your father was in a hurry and willing to camp out each night." She barely moved her head, agreeing with his statement. Her total honesty filled him with guilt that he had doubted her. Coming up behind her, Delaney cupped her shoulders and drew her to lean against his chest. "Let me try to help your brother, Faith," he whispered against her hair. "Take this as a gift from my heart and the only one I can offer to you now. Will you give me Joey?"

"Is that all you want from me?"

Her voice tore into him, a blend of defeat, sadness, regret, and other dark emotions. They lashed at him, memory echoing her voice filled with a passionate declaration of love, her sweet teasing laughter, the soft whisper of her joy. Ruthlessly he buried them and silently answered her question: *Give me every smile, every tear, all of your fears, and all of your joys.*

He tightened his grip on her to keep her from turning around to look at him. He couldn't bear to see the love she had for him in her eyes, knowing that it would weaken his resolve.

"I guess your silence is an answer, Delaney. What do you want to do with my brother?" She pulled away from him.

Delaney let her go. He sighed deeply, aching to hold her, to kiss her, realizing that if he touched her again, he wouldn't let her go at all. He turned aside. "I want to take Joey to a shaman."

"Shaman?" she repeated. "Is he an Apache doctor?"

"In a way." He lost his own small battle and gazed at her, reaching out to brush his hand against her cheek, but she jerked her head back. Delaney's hand fell to his side. "A shaman is a medicine man, but there isn't just one. Some have a power to heal and others do not. There are those who claim they can read omens, and others who can bring rain. It's hard to explain to you how their beliefs and lifeway are entwined. And," he found himself admitting, "some things are not my right to tell you."

"Total trust, Delaney? That's what you are asking of me."

"Yes. Will you trust me with Joey?"

Faith knew her answer before he finished speaking. "Take him. I'll tell my father."

"No. I don't need to hide behind your skirts."

Her smile was sad. Shaking her head, she said, "I never thought that you would. I need to do this for me, not you, Delaney. It's time I stopped running." She gathered her courage and added, "Maybe the day isn't far off when you'll do the same."

Her words cut him to the quick. He had no defense, because she was right. He had been running.

Faith's smile faded.

"When I get back with Joey, we'll leave for Tombstone."

"Fine. I'll make sure we're ready."

"Faith," he said as she moved away, stopping her. "I want you to know that no harm will come to Joey. This man, this shaman I want to take him to, has a gift for healing and intense spirituality. Some call him the Dreamer of Dreams. I just know that if there is anything to be done to help Joey see, I must take him with me."

Her searching gaze studied him for long minutes. "Is that where you were the night you disappeared into the desert? Were you with a shaman who could heal you?" She wanted to ask him more, she wanted his trust, she needed to know what had happened that night.

He turned away from the intensity of her look. "You ask what I cannot tell you."

"No, Delaney, you're wrong. I have my answer. Stay with Pris, I'll get Joey."

Delaney knew he had never wanted Faith as much as he did at that moment. Wanted her with thoughts of all the days to come, wanted her beside him, wanted her to rid him of the loneliness that made him ache.

But he wanted revenge with an equal force. And revenge

won, tipping the scale with the knowledge that the past could rise and come between them unless it was buried.

He waited, and watched Pris swim, knowing that Faith was right about needing to confront her father.

Robert was too shocked to be angry when Faith told him about Joey. She did not yell, but fury vibrated in her voice.

"You've punished us all long enough, Pa. If there's a chance for Joey to see, you'll stand aside. I never wanted to run, to lie and feel hunted and guilty. But I listened to you. No more."

"Joey is my son, Faith—"

" . . . and I'm your daughter. Refuse me this, and I'll leave you."

"For the likes of Carmichael?" he asked, his eyes filled with scorn.

"No, Pa," she answered in a gentle tone that was nonetheless firm. "Not for anyone but myself. I can't live like this. I can't live with you if you're going to fill our days with your bitterness. If you can't put aside your feelings for the chance to help your son, then you're not a man I want to claim as my father. Delaney won't let anything happen to Joey."

"He's a killer, Faith," he reminded her, unwilling to admit that she had shaken him.

"So are you!" she snapped, going to the back of the wagon to lift Joey down. "You heard it all, didn't you, Joey?"

"Pa's real mad."

"I'll talk to him, Joey. Do you want to go with Delaney? I know you were angry with him for letting Beula go."

"But he told me why. I miss her, but I didn't want to see her dead. Maybe someone nice found her."

"Maybe."

She saw that Delaney was coming toward them, carrying Pris wrapped in a blanket. Mirage followed at his heels.

"Del?" Joey said, turning to him as he neared.

"Right here, scout. You coming with me?"

"Yes," Joey answered, extending his hand.

"We'll leave for Tombstone tomorrow, Faith."

"I'll be waiting," she said, watching them ride off.

Chapter Eighteen

THE NIGHT BLANKETED the land, and a full moon rose to embrace the earth as the air grew still.

Delaney lit the fire he had built. "It is time," he said to Joey, rising from where he had sat at the boy's side. "You do all that I told you, and remember there is nothing to be afraid of no matter what happens. I'll be close by even if I don't speak to you."

"I'll remember," Joey answered, drawing closer to the fire that was beginning to share its warmth with him. He held the small amount of sacred pollen that Delaney had given him in one hand, and in the other, a lightning-struck twig. He knew when Delaney moved away from him but sensed he had not gone far. At his side, Joey knew where each of his gifts were placed and recounted to himself the order that he must present them. First the bag of smoking tobacco, then a black-handled knife, a black silk handkerchief, and last a soft deerskin. With his acute hearing he listened to the rustle of cloth as if someone had joined them and was settling himself on the ground across the fire from where he sat.

Joey felt a flutter in his stomach and knew he was afraid. He thought of each of the steps that Delaney had patiently explained to him and hoped that he would not fail and make Delaney ashamed.

"Listen and feel, little one," a deep voice intoned. "Beneath you is the earth. If you are always good to her, she will let you feel her heart beating. Lift your head high, and you will hear the wind who whispers into the minds of men of all it touches. Open your mind and your heart, and become one with them, a child of the land.

"Let them take your fears and your secrets. The earth will bury them for you, for men know of no measure to hold her. Give your fears and secrets to the wind, and it will be as your brother and carry them far, far from you. Trust what your heart speaks to you. You will never hear lies."

Joey tried not to grip the pollen and twig that he held, struggling to understand what was wanted from him. A long silence followed before he smelled a scented smoke from the fire.

"Come to me, little one."

Every move that Joey made spoke of his hesitation and fear. Within his dark world he held trust as the dearest of his possessions. He didn't know when Delaney spoke to him that he would not easily give over that trust to a stranger.

He stood up and felt the warmth of the fire slightly in front of him and to his right. Its heat was his guide. The first step was the hardest for him to take. He didn't know what waited for him. Joey had to fight the need to call out and hear Delaney answer him. He remembered Delaney's promise and knew he would not lie. It gave him the courage he needed to make his way around the fire. Sensing another's presence, he stopped and waited.

Firm hands on his shoulders made him tense. He wanted to run. But the hands only guided him to step to the right. Joey took his bearing from the fire again, it was directly behind him now. He knew he was breathing too fast, but now he was excited by what he must do.

"In the name of all children, in the name of Yusen, in the name of White Painted Woman and in the name of Child of the Water, I ask you to help me."

He was proud that he spoke each word without the trembling that he felt inside himself. Kneeling down, he used his left hand still holding the twig to find the toe of the moccasin. There was temptation to examine the shape of the soft hide, but he didn't give in to it. He opened his right hand and, with one finger of his left hand, dipped it into the pollen.

"I give you this twig of lightning-struck wood, for I have come to ask you for light," Joey said. To show his respect and his faith, he marked the foot near his hand with a cross of pollen. With two fingers he took small pinches of pollen and sprinkled them toward the man's body. He kept just a little to make a cross on the other moccasin.

Joey found it hard to stand and find his way back around the fire to where he had his other gifts. By touch he found the bag of smoking tobacco and with firmer steps returned to where the shaman waited. Feeling the heat of the fire, Joey placed the bag on the ground.

"I accept your gift."

Joey smiled. Within moments he inhaled a stronger smoke from the fire behind him. The scent was different than the one before. He knew the shaman would smoke some of his tobacco and that he must wait until he did. He used the time to remember what Delaney had said about the sacred pollen. A symbol of life and renewal, was what he called it. Tobacco smoke wafted past him, and Joey knew it would be blown to the four directions. All things were done in fours. His gifts and the words that came.

"May it be well."

Joey had to wait until the words were repeated four times. He did not linger when the last sound faded. He returned and found the knife, brought it around, made his request for help again, and waited for his gift to be accepted. With each step, each acceptance, he became more sure of himself. Until the last gift. It seemed as if the time would not come that the prayer for aid would be said.

"The boy has come in search of help. I want to give it to him. There is an evil inside him that will not let the boy see. He is searching for the light. All your Power must go into the life of this boy."

Joey did not move but lifted his face. He knew the man had stood, for his tobacco-scented breath drifted down to him. He was no longer afraid. All was happening just as Delaney had told him. He felt the light touch of pollen on the back of his neck, an even lighter touch on each of his shoulders. He held his breath, fighting not to squeeze his eyes closed, as pollen was brushed across each of his eyelids.

"I accept your *yeel*, little one."

"I am happy in my heart that my gifts are pleasing to you," Joey answered. He smiled to feel the soft brush of the eagle feather over his face. Delaney had warned him not to laugh even if it tickled him. This was a hard part, Joey thought, sensing the man moving, knowing that he would pass the eagle feather over and around his body to take away the evil. Joey shifted from one foot to the other, growing restless with the need to talk. He pressed his lips tight, knowing it wasn't time.

The song began. Joey did not understand the words, for they were sung in Apache. Each song would call for power from their spirits. The tone of the voice changed, now low and deep, now crying out. Joey inched his fingers up to his pocket. He had his turquoise with an eagle feather through a hole that Delaney had made. Only men and boys were to give these to the shaman.

Silence came. Joey handed over his curing symbols.

Allowing himself to be guided, he was led away from the fire. The air was cooler, but he knew the ground remained level. Urged to sit, Joey did and felt a cup pressed to his lips. He didn't like the smell of it but took a sip. The taste was bitter, but he drank what he was offered.

"Your heart is open, little one?"

"My heart is open."

"Your mind is open to let the evil free?"

"My mind is open." Joey said the words, but he felt funny. His voice didn't sound right. He licked his lips and found his mouth was dry. Something touched his forehead, and he wrinkled his nose, trying to smell and sense what it was. He heard the chanting begin again, softer this time, and found that he was rocking his body back and forth. But he was yawning. He felt so sleepy. Delaney had said nothing about falling asleep. He tried to fight it, but his head kept falling forward, and he jerked himself back.

"Del? Where are you? I feel funny." He thought the chanting stopped. He wasn't sure. Everything seemed to be going around and around. Was that Delaney holding him? He lifted his hand—or tried to—but he couldn't touch anything. Joey cried out.

"Remember, little one. Open heart and open mind. Just remember what happened that night."

"I can't. It hurts, Del."

But he had been sleepy that night, too. They had so much food to eat, and everyone was happy. There was music and dancing. Mama laughing. Papa lifting him high. Running and playing. It was late and he went to the wagon to rest. Martin kissed Faith. They didn't see him in the wagon bed. He felt the sway of the wagon and knew they were going home. Faith would not be mad when she found him there. And he liked Martin.

*But Faith scolded him before she tucked him into bed. She
had kissed him on the cheek and wished him sweet dreams.
Why were they yelling? He pulled the quilt over his head
and buried his face in the pillow. Faith was screaming. She
shouldn't be screaming.*

" . . . Faith was happy. But she kept screaming. I had to
help her. They were hurting her. Hurting Martin. Help her!
Del, help her! Don't let them hurt Faith!"

Joey's terrified scream pierced the night. He soon quieted
with gentle strokes and rocking and soft murmurs. But he did
not speak again.

Faith was waiting, just as she had said, when Delaney
returned with Joey in the half-light before dawn. She had
never seen her little brother's face filled with such peace as
it wore while he slept in Delaney's arms. But though Joey
slept at rest, Delaney's face was drawn, lines of exhaustion
clearly marked for her to see.

"Joey'll sleep most of the day," Delaney told her, handing
the boy down to her waiting arms. He was grateful that
she accepted this without questions. After dismounting, he
stripped the saddle from Mirage, used tufts of grass to give
his mare a quick rubdown, then set her free.

Faith returned and poured him coffee, then sat beside him.
"Are you hungry?"

Delaney shot her a curious look. "That's all? Just if I'm
hungry?"

"Delaney," she said with a sigh, "if you want to tell me
what happened, you will. If you don't want to say, there's
nothing I can do to make you."

The rumbling in his stomach answered her question. She
shook her head and rose to dish out the jerky stew she had left
simmering in the kettle. Balancing two biscuits on top of the
plate, she brought it to him.

Resuming her seat, Faith watched the dawn spread its painted lights across the sky. Birdsong broke the silence, and she felt a contentment that she did not want to end.

"I wish we didn't have to leave here," she said after a few minutes.

Delaney stopped eating to look at her. She sat in profile to him, but it was the longing in her voice that caught his attention. "You mean that, don't you?"

"There is a feeling of time being stopped here. It is hard to explain, but I have a sense of being safe. You'll think me foolish, but that's how I feel."

Setting the plate aside, satisfied that his fast had been broken, Delaney reached over and lifted her hand to his lips. He kissed her palm and then rubbed the backs of her fingers over his bearded cheek.

"I don't think you're foolish. I feel the same way."

"But we still leave today?"

She withdrew her hand from his, and Delaney let the moment pass. "Yeah. We leave today." Sipping his coffee, Delaney knew he had to tell her that he would leave them in Tombstone. But when he spoke, what he intended wasn't what he said.

"I don't know if Joey wants to see, Faith. That's all that keeps him blind. He talked a little about that night, but not his part in it. I can't offer you any hope."

"About Joey?" *About us?* she wanted to add and didn't.

"Yeah, Joey." He couldn't add *and us*. It was a desperate feeling he had. If he didn't say the words aloud, she would somehow know that he wanted her to wait. If he lived. . . .

Delaney finished sopping up the last of the gravy with a piece of biscuit, then poured another cup of coffee. Restless now, he cast about for something to say to keep her with him a bit longer.

"I wish I could have taken you to Tucson, Faith."

"Why?" she asked with a directness she knew made him uncomfortable.

"It's more civilized. Contention, Millville, and Tombstone are raw mining camps. It was just a thought."

Faith tossed her own promise aside. She turned and faced him. "Just once, Delaney Carmichael, say what you're thinking!"

Those eyes that stunned him on first sight seemed to pierce his skin and see inside him. Delaney lifted his skystone free from his open shirt and held it up before her.

"Look at the stone, Faith. It matches your eyes. There was a promise made to me when I was given this to wear, and I gave one in return. Until I keep that promise, I have no others to make or give. Is that plain enough, duchess?"

Faith memorized his face. She had the feeling that time was slipping away, too quickly, and she longed to stop it.

"Answer one question for me, Delaney. If you were free to make a promise to me, would you?" He stared at her in silence for a long minute, his face giving no hint to his thoughts. Only the desire in his eyes gave him away. She scrambled to her feet and started to walk away.

"Faith," he whispered, stopping her. "I swear on all that I hold sacred in this life, if I could, I'd make one to you."

Silent tears of thanksgiving fell from her eyes, and she stood with her head bowed, willing him to hold her again, kiss her once more, and tell her that he loved her.

But she stood alone and sounds of the others stirring warned her that the time was past for him to come to her. Delaney had demons to put to rest. She loved him enough to set him free. She loved him enough to wait for a whole man to come to her with nothing held back. She had given him no less; she knew she would accept no less in return.

*   *   *

They camped outside of Contention City that night at Robert's request. Faith was surprised that her father spoke first to Delaney before they both agreed not to go to the mill town.

There was a raw wood shanty beside a pole corral, but one look inside the cabin and Faith chose to sleep near the wagons. The low-ceilinged room was hot and laden with the odors of bacon grease, sweat, and manure.

When Joey did not immediately drift back to sleep, Faith hid her disappointment that he couldn't see. She had faced down her father to let Joey go with Delaney to an Apache shaman, wanting to believe as Delaney seemed to, that her brother's sight could be restored.

She hated the way her father smugly told her it had been a waste of time, and that Delaney was a vicious man to cruelly raise Joey's hope for sight. Refusing to believe that of Delaney, she nevertheless kept her disappointment to herself, worried about how Joey would feel. Strangely, her little brother was the one who offered her comfort.

Tomorrow would see them near the end of their long journey. Everyone seemed on edge tonight but Joey. When Faith helped him get ready for bed, he hugged her extra hard. She stroked the back of his head, holding him as long as he wanted. He finally let her go, and she leaned over to tuck his blanket around him.

"Sweet dreams," she whispered.

"You said that to me the other time."

"What other time, Joey?" Faith settled herself on the edge of the narrow bed in the wagon.

"The night Martin died."

"Yes." She answered without thought, then realized what he said. Hope filled her. Delaney had not failed if Joey was at least willing to talk about what happened. She waited for him to say something more. When he didn't, she found her own curiosity surface. "Who was with you and Delaney last night?"

"I don't know," he sleepily murmured, tucking one hand beneath his cheek. "Del. I remember him talking and holding me."

"Just Delaney?" she prompted.

"Hmmm . . . guess so."

Brushing aside his hair, Faith leaned close to whisper, "You know that Delaney never meant to be cruel and raise your hope to see."

"I know that. Del wouldn't ever hurt me. It's not time. I've got to want to see hard enough to get all the bad things out."

"Oh, Joey, I pray that you do." Faith left him with little satisfaction and her curiosity piqued.

It remained that way as they rode out in an early morning mist to follow the San Pedro River to Tombstone.

The raw mining camp was in the desert on a flat mesa surrounded by rolling plains and hemmed in by the Dragoon and Whetstone mountains. Faith reminded herself that she had been warned by Delaney of what they would find, but nothing he had said prepared her for a dust-blown town of tents and shanties. The main street swarmed with men. Some were building. Others seemed to be prospectors by their dress. Still other men loitered about. Faith cast a glance at Delaney, who rode close to the wagon. He was grinning.

"Don't say I told you so," she warned him, then smiled. She began coughing on the dust the mules kicked up, and she thought Delaney said something about dry being better than wet.

"What?" she asked him, her eyes smarting.

"Mud, duchess. When it's wet here, the mud'll be up to the wheels, and you'll have the devil's own time."

Burros brayed and Faith had a hard time controlling the mules. She was embarrassed to see the men—for the most part, unshaved and likely unwashed, judging by the state of their clothes—begin to turn and stare at her.

"Can't blame them, duchess. Ain't many white women here. But not for long. The silver'll bring them and gamblers."

Faith kept her gaze focused straight ahead, unwilling to attract anyone's attention.

Delaney chuckled at her prim look.

"That's Private Shellby, ain't it, Del?" Keith yelled back from his wagon seat.

Following to where Keith was pointing, Delaney saw it was the private. He was standing on a few rough boards, holding the reins of several army horses. There was no sign to indicate what the building behind him was. Del's lips tightened when he saw the smile that creased Shellby's mouth as he recognized Faith.

Shellby waved them down, and Robert pulled up, giving Faith no choice but to follow suit.

"We heard you had trouble, Mr. Becket. Glad to see you made it here safely."

"Well, it was no thanks to you leaving us," Becket said in a gruff voice. He was anxious to move along. The sooner he was camped, the quicker he would be rid of Delaney.

"Carmichael!" the private yelled, waving him over, annoyed when Delaney remained beside Faith's wagon. "Major Ross is here, and he's looking for you."

Delaney offered no sign that he heard him, turning instead to Faith. "Your father has his map to your land claim and—"

"You're leaving us? Now?"

"You knew I would." It was his mistake to look at her. "Don't make this harder," he pleaded, stopping himself.

"You said those same words before. Remember, Del?" She was sorry the moment she spoke. His eyes darkened, and his face had a look of anguish. But for a moment he held his gaze to hers, and she saw that he did remember a desert night and burning alive. "I'm sorry," she whispered, forcing herself to look anywhere but at him.

"You hear me, Carmichael?" Shellby shouted.

With a hard cutting gaze Delaney pinned the private where he stood. "I heard you and so did all of Tombstone. Tell Ross I ain't interested in anything he has to say." Delaney reached into his shirt pocket and took out a roll of bills and leaned over to place them in Faith's lap. "Give that to your father. It's all there, the money he paid me. You'll need it for supplies and such to get started."

"He won't take it."

"Then you use it for a scout and Pris. Shellby'll make sure you get an escort if you want one." He urged Mirage closer to the wagon and said quick good-byes to the children.

Faith couldn't stop herself from leaning over to touch his arm.

Delaney burned. He thought about taking her mouth in sight of everyone, and knew if he gave in, he would mark her in everyone's mind forever as his. And if he didn't come back, she would be forced to live with that.

It tore his insides to pull away from her.

She heard him whisper words she didn't understand but recalled from the night he made love to her. Mirage moved off at a walk, and words crowded her mind, all the things she meant to say and never did. She had to bite her lip to keep silent. Joey's hand entwined with hers, and Faith held it tight, knowing there had been pain in her life, as much pain as she had thought she could stand, but nothing like this.

This was pain that spread and, with it, emptiness that seemed to drain her very lifeblood. She couldn't see him.

Tears filled her eyes, and she heard shouting, blinking and focusing, because it was Pris who yelled.

"They're gonna shoot him!"

Shellby was running with his gun drawn. Soldiers poured out of the building where he had been standing. Faith heard him demand that Delaney stop. She heard the shots, dropped the reins, and nearly fell trying to get down from the wagon.

"Delaney!" she screamed, running toward him. He was still mounted on his mare, but three soldiers blocked his way. Shellby was behind him. Faith heard a new voice firing commands and turned. Her hand flew to her mouth to stifle her cry. Seanilzay, bound in rope, was being pushed forward in the street toward Delaney. She wanted Delaney to run, knowing that he wouldn't, sensing danger for him.

Delaney saw Ross approach him, shoving a stumbling Seanilzay in front of him, but his senses alerted him to Faith being near. He wanted her gone, out of harm's way, but the major claimed his attention.

"We've been waiting here for you," Ross said by way of greeting.

Delaney's face was carved granite, his voice as hard and as cold as that stone under a desert night. "You've wasted your time, Ross. You've got nothing I want, and it would take that for me to deal with you."

"Your friend's life," Ross said, pushing Seanilzay closer.

Delaney was forced to look at Seanilzay, knowing that he had denied the Apache his friendship. But it was forgotten when he met Seanilzay's dark, unblinking gaze. Seanilzay was the one who turned away.

"He means nothing to me," Delaney said, risking a bluff. He heard Faith gasp behind him, and once again wished her gone. The spirits were not listening to him. Neither was Ross.

"I know different. And I do have something you want. Come inside with me, Carmichael."

It was an order, nothing else. Delaney saw that Ross was already turning, preparing to walk back inside the building. He waited until the major was nearly to the door. "Ross, you don't hear good. The answer is no."

The major executed a sharp turn, glaring at Delaney.

"Popejoy," he intoned in a chilling voice to one of the privates blocking Delaney's way.

"Sir!"

"Shoot the Apache. He's a prisoner trying to escape."

"Sir?" the young man queried, glancing at his fellow soldiers.

"You heard my order," Ross stated loud enough for all to hear. He resented the crowd they had drawn, resented the cool stare that Carmichael returned to him, but he had his orders and he would carry them out any way he had to.

Faith broke the tension. She ran past Shellby and stood in front of Seanilzay. "I won't let them kill you."

The Apache flicked a glance at her and then returned to looking up at Delaney. It was to him that he spoke. "If you tell their lies for them, your heart will never know peace."

"I gave you an order, Popejoy!"

"Del? You can't let them kill him!" Faith couldn't believe he remained still, uncaring of the people around them, the heat, the dust, letting Seanilzay's life be taken. She stared at each of the soldiers in turn, finally turning to her father. "Please, help him."

"You can't interfere in army business, Faith."

"*You* can't do it, Pa. But you don't speak for me. Is there a man here who will try to stop them?" she yelled to the tightening crowd of miners.

Ross shouted again for the private to come forward. The man reluctantly moved, stopping beside Seanilzay. His hand holding the gun was shaking so badly he had to brace it with his other hand.

Delaney felt no pity for the private as he glared into his eyes. "Pull that trigger, soldier," he warned softly, almost too softly to be heard, "and I'll show you how the Apache avenge a friend's death." He watched the sweat pop out on the private's face but refused to feel anything for him. There was a tense silence that added to the heat and the thickness of the air. A tension that grew until the gun wavered in the soldier's hands.

There was no satisfaction for Delaney when the boy's shoulders sagged and his head lowered before his hands fell to his sides.

"I can't do it," Popejoy whispered.

Delaney had to stop himself from telling him that damn few men could kill in cold blood, but Faith stepped closer, touching his knee. Love shone from the brilliant blue of her eyes.

"Thank you, Del," she murmured.

He had to ignore her and focus on Ross, who moved to the edge of the boarded walk. "You're a bastard, Major. Now that you made your play, tell me what you want."

Ross hesitated. He thought about shooting the Apache himself. He certainly had no qualms. But there was a warning in Carmichael's merciless eyes that he had to heed.

"Inside, Carmichael."

"Right here," Delaney shot back. "This time I want witnesses to hear what you have to say."

Hate spilled from the major's eyes, but his smile was chilling. "I do have something besides the Apache's life that you want."

Instinct sent up an alarm inside Delaney. It was more than the gloating tone of the major's voice; it was in his eyes. He had won.

"What the hell have you got?"

"You've always wanted to clear your father's name, haven't you, Carmichael?"

Delaney didn't move, didn't speak; he couldn't. He had to concentrate on forcing the rage that boiled inside him to subside.

Ross waited and then shrugged. "Well, if you're not interested . . ." Deliberately he stopped and turned back to the doorway.

Delaney knew he would do it. Ross would go inside and leave him to beg. He swallowed pride and gall. "You pushed enough, Ross, spit it out."

The major took a moment to savor bringing him to heel. A moment longer for Delaney to sweat and wait, just as he had been made to do. A few seconds while he turned and faced him. "It seems that your father kept a journal, and I know where it is."

Chapter Nineteen

"A JOURNAL?" DELANEY repeated, slicing an accusing look at Seanilzay. The Apache's dark eyes revealed nothing of his thoughts. Delaney's tension communicated itself to Mirage. The mare pawed the dust, tossing her head, but for once Delaney didn't seem to care.

Seanilzay had sworn that Brodie killed his mother to possess this journal. How did Ross get hold of it? He felt as if a trap had been baited and closed around him. Ross knew he would kill to have a means to clear his father's name. Betrayal and lies. Reason was deserting him. He could trust no one but himself. He met Faith's unwavering gaze and for an insane moment wondered if she had been a part of this. She backed away a few steps as if she had sensed his thought. Shaking his head, Delaney shuddered. Faith loved him, and he believed her. He had to. But he could not give away more than he already had to the major.

"Cut Seanilzay free, Ross, or we don't talk."

"That's not how it works, Carmichael. I give the orders. I have what you want. You don't get it until—" Ross could not believe what he was seeing. Delaney had drawn his knife and was leaning down to slice through the Apache's bonds.

"Stop him!" Ross ordered, but no one moved. There was a murderous fury that promised death to any man who moved in Delaney's eyes. For a second Ross recoiled from that look. "I can have you arrested for interfering with army—"

"Try it, Major."

It was the absence of emotion in Delaney's voice that stopped Ross from answering.

Seanilzay stood rubbing his arms, and Faith offered him her hand. "You must be thirsty. Come to the wagon with me."

"You have a good heart, Woman with Eyes of Sky. I stay."

"Go back to your wagon, Faith," Delaney said, stepping down from his saddle. He handed the reins to Seanilzay. "If I find out that you have betrayed me—"

"No. This I did not do."

Delaney stared into his eyes and slowly nodded. "Wait." Looking at no one, he walked to where Ross waited and followed him inside.

Seanilzay scanned the crowd of men that were beginning to move away. He offered no sign that he noticed the blond bearded man who stood a head taller than the men around him. He marked Yancy Watts, watching without seeming to, as the man lumbered across the dust-laden street and mounted his horse. The man would ride north to find Brodie and tell what he heard. There could be no stopping what was meant to happen now.

At his side Faith whispered, "Who is he, Seanilzay?" She, too, had taken note of the man, not for his height or hefty build, but for the hate that came from his eyes toward Delaney's back.

"Go to your little ones," Seanilzay said. "Wait for him. When all is done as it should be, he will have need of you."

"Will you stay with him?" Faith asked, needing the added reassurance that Delaney would not be alone. "I don't trust Major Ross. There is something about him—"

"Yes, he is a man of lies. I will stay."

Something in his voice made Faith hesitate. "Was he the one who shot you?"

"This does not—"

"I'm not a child to be sheltered, Seanilzay. If you don't want to tell me, say so." Her voice was sharper than she had intended, but Faith was angry with the helplessness she felt toward Delaney. Instinct warned her to do as he said, to go to her wagon and leave here. All the love she felt for him made her want to stay and find out what the major wanted from him.

In the end her father made the decision easier for her. "Faith," he called from his seat on the wagon, then waiting until she was near to ask, "I know we need supplies, but could you manage another night without them?"

"If we had to, yes."

"Private Shellby said our claim isn't all that far. We won't need anyone to show us, and I want to go, Faith." In a surprising gesture he reached down with one hand and touched her cheek. "It's for the best that we leave now."

His look of compassion went a long way toward healing the breach between them. Faith nodded. He was right, and it was what Delaney had asked her to do. With a last quick look at the doorway Delaney had disappeared into, she climbed up on her wagon, disdaining the help Private Shellby offered.

Delaney stood well back from the grimed window, watching the wagons pull out. Before the dust had settled, he turned to where the major sat. The room was furnished with a roughly made wood table, a bench, and the chair Ross occupied. He walked to the back wall, where a ragged curtain hung and ripped it aside. A few scattered packing crates littered the empty room. In the dusky light Delaney saw that the back door was boarded over.

"What did you expect to find, Carmichael?"

"You're lucky I didn't find a damn thing, Ross." Leaning against the back wall, where his view of the door and window were unobscured, Delaney waited for the major to begin.

"General Wilcox wants you to find Juh and Geronimo and convince them to come in."

"That's it, no promises, no lies."

"You know what to promise them," Ross snapped.

"What I know, Ross," Delaney drawled, pinning a narrow-eyed gaze on him, "is that you believe war is needed, the kind of unrelenting war that will slay every man, woman, and child and leave their bodies rotting."

"I follow orders."

"Orders, Major? You were ordered to find me? You were ordered to use any means at hand to force me to tell your lies? And then, Major," Delaney continued in a soft, relentless voice, "you were ordered to kill Seanilzay? I have it all right, don't I? You were just carrying out orders?"

Ross grated his teeth together. His body was rigid, and his eyes held impotent fury to withhold an answer to this man's mockery.

"Why didn't you ask Clum or Jeffords?"

"They both want San Carlos back," Ross replied, trying to understand what he was trying to find out.

"Yeah, that's true enough. An' McIntosh is still feeling raw 'bout the army printing his letter in the paper. All three of them would want something from you, right? Something you couldn't promise them, couldn't deliver if you did. But me, now, ah, there's a horse of a different color. For me you found a journal I didn't know about that could clear my father's name. A name the army smeared in filth. But that's all past, right, Major? You're doing the right thing now."

"That's it, Carmichael."

"I don't believe you, Ross. You're a lying sonofabitch." Delaney came away from the wall, and with even strides he quartered the room. Ross was hanging on to his temper, and that worried Delaney. He knew Ross; there had to be something more to this that he had missed.

The chair scraped back as Ross stood up. "I've no time to waste. Either you will do it or won't."

"Sit down, Major. We're not done. I want to know more about this missing journal. Where was it found? How did you get hold of it?"

"None of this is important, Carmichael. The fact is that I know where it is."

"Where it is? You don't have it?" Delaney demanded, stopping his pacing and glaring at Ross. "Real convenient how it showed up when you needed it."

Ross shrugged. "Sometimes things happen that way."

"Tell me, Major, you set for a promotion if I pull this off?"

"What the devil does that matter!"

"Oh, it matters. It matters a great deal to me. See, I think you're less than horse dung, soldier boy."

"That's enough!" He saw that Delaney started for the door, and all his plans were going to go with him. Ross swallowed bile. "Carmichael, wait. You've insulted me, and I've taken all I can. Just because I wear a uniform, that doesn't make me less a man. But what is needed here is a spirit of cooperation to benefit all."

Delaney turned and studied him. Whatever Ross was after, it was damn important to him, more important than a promotion. At least he knew he was on the right track. He nodded after he saw sweat break over the major's brow and saw the man sit. Walking to the table, Delaney kicked the bench over toward the wall, then sat with his back protected, facing the major.

"The Apache respect you, Carmichael. All the army is asking is that you talk them into coming back to the reservations.

Victorio is leaving a bloody trail across northern Chihuahua.
Juh and Geronimo are capturing wagon trains and if you had
seen the torture inflicted on those teamsters you wouldn't be
so ready to defend the Apache. It's got to stop. The army has
made mistakes, no one is denying this. But we cannot rectify
the past unless they come forth in a show of good faith and
allow us the chance."

He was good, Delaney thought, just the right note of sin-
cerity in the voice, an earnest plea in the eyes, and the words
all rang true. But Delaney had a problem in believing that
Ross knew what a show of good faith was. That he regretted
his mistakes, Delaney accepted as fact. The major wasn't
going to rest until Seanilzay was dead.

"Look," Ross said, "all you need to do is talk to them. Tell
them that General Wilcox will listen to their grievances. He's
under orders from Washington to put a stop to this any way
that he can, Carmichael. Soldiers will die along with civil-
ians, but so will more of the Apache."

"And if I agree, when do I get the journal?"

"When you come back."

"Not good enough, Ross. I want to see it. Just to make sure
it's real."

"I can't do what you're asking. You'll have to trust me."

"Major, I'd sooner trust the devil. No journal, no deal."
But Delaney didn't move. He sat and waited, reading the
desperation in Ross's eyes. He was being set up, but he
couldn't figure for what. Delaney knew his own thoughts
were clouded by the temptation of possessing his father's
journal and clearing his name. But this was one time he
wasn't able to bury it.

"I can't give you the whole journal, Carmichael, but
would seeing one page satisfy you that it does exist?
You would recognize your father's handwriting, wouldn't
you?"

If Delaney had ever believed that his self-control had been tested before this moment, he knew he had been wrong. He urged every fiber of his being to sit quietly and merely nod his acceptance when he longed to sink his fists into Ross.

"Wait here and I'll get it. Once you've seen it, you can leave."

"After I see what you have, I'll let you know what I decide." Delaney watched him walk outside, his mind churning with questions. If what Seanilzay told him was true and Brodie had the journal, where did Ross fit in? And if his mother had been killed, why was the journal hidden all this time and not destroyed? He was missing a piece that would tie this together beyond his certainty that the army intended to use him.

Minutes later the major returned carrying his map case. He placed it on the table and opened it, withdrawing a small folded piece of paper, which he then held out to Delaney.

There was no betraying tremble in his hand when Delaney leaned over to take it. He unfolded the paper, one edge torn, and knew at a glance it was his father's writing. The light was poor, so he rose and stood near the doorway to read the few lines.

I was there this time. I saw the scales and weights. The cattle are fat, glossy-coated, and worth top dollar.

Tuesday, 16th of May. G. sent word for me to come. Of the fifty head purchased only fifteen were delivered and these sickly. The scales were tampered with again. Now I have a name to bring up on charges

A water stain blotted out the rest of the page. But it was enough for Delaney to understand that his father had tried to document each incident of theft. And if he succeeded, he had died for it.

"Satisfied, Carmichael?"

"More than you know," Delaney answered, refolding the paper and tucking it in his shirt pocket.

"Then I'll tell you what terms you are to bring to the Apache."

For the next hour Delaney listened and offered no advice no matter how wrong he thought some of the terms suggested were. Ross and men like him, he decided, never tried to understand that crowding the different bands of Apache on one reservation couldn't work. Their beliefs and needs were not the same. In addition the army refused to guarantee there would be no more taking of reservation lands to satisfy miners. But then, he countered his own thought, knowing that President Grant himself had stolen over five hundred acres with his order that reduced the reservation's boundaries to allow miners into the area.

Finally Ross sat back in the chair, pointing to his map. "You know this area, and that's all the help I can give you." He circled the lower southeastern corner of the territorial map. "They've got to be hungry. That should make them at least willing to listen."

"Hunger usually does, Ross."

"I have two packhorses loaded with supplies for you to take to them. Shellby will accompany you."

"No. I go alone. One spare horse for me. Get rid of the army saddle."

Ross opened his mouth to argue and closed it. "All right, Carmichael."

When Delaney went outside, Seanilzay was still waiting.

"You will do as he asks," the Apache stated.

"Do you know where they are?" Delaney countered.

"The places are few where it is safe to hide. You know them all."

"I'll go alone, Seanilzay. But you'll ride out with me. I want you to keep watch over the Beckets. I don't trust Ross. They have claimed land south of here, near the river."

"What of Brodie?"

"He's waited this long, he'll keep until I get back. The bastard has my father's journal. I just can't figure where Ross fits in with Brodie."

"Does he know that Brodie searches for gold?"

"Could be. It still doesn't explain why Ross is so anxious to use me to talk for the army. He knows my own feelings."

"If you spoke lies believing them true, *skeetzee*, he would be rid of you."

"But I know General Wilcox. Ross did not lie about him. Perhaps the days alone will give me the answers I seek." Delaney looked up and saw Popejoy leading a big raw-boned bay and a hammerhead roan toward him. He left Seanilzay holding Mirage while he looked over the horses.

"The major said these were the best he has."

Delaney didn't answer him. He ran his hands over each of the horses, checked their eyes, teeth, and limbs, and listened to their breathing before he stepped back.

"Load the supplies on the roan. I'll ride the bay. And I'll need a horse for Seanilzay."

"The major didn't say—"

"Ask him," Delaney snapped, moving to strip the gear from Mirage and saddle the bay. "Go with him, Seanilzay, and find a good mount. We have hard riding ahead."

Before the afternoon shadows had deepened, Delaney and Seanilzay rode out of Tombstone. Delaney looked back once. Popejoy still stood, watching them. Keeping the horses to a walk, Delaney gazed at the hundreds of tents and shanties that surrounded Tombstone. The area was treeless, offering little cover. An hour later Delaney motioned for Seanilzay to ride ahead, leading the roan and Mirage. He topped a small rise and slid from his saddle to scan his back trail. A lone horseman could be seen in the far distance, heading in his direction. Delaney knew that Ross would have him followed, but he wasn't going to try to lose the man now.

By the time he caught up with Seanilzay, he knew he would head north up to the Dragoons, where Cochise once had his stronghold. This was the lesson the army never learned. They continued to try and fight a mountain-bred people in their own mountains.

Down in a dry wash they stopped. "We part company here, Seanilzay. You can double back and head south. Tell . . ." Delaney stopped, wondering what he could tell Faith. He wanted to see her; mere moments later he admitted to himself he needed to see her again. He reached into his shirt and withdrew the skystone, then, without giving himself time to think, he removed his hat and slipped the rawhide over his head.

"Give this to her for me."

Seanilzay took it and carefully wrapped the rawhide thong around the stone before he tucked it into his cloth belt. "May we live to see each other again."

"May it be so," Delaney answered, taking the lead rope and reins from him.

Riding alone in the forested base of the Dragoons, Delaney felt a sense of homecoming. To the east was the valley where his home had been. He felt a longing to see the place again but knew that would wait, just as facing Brodie would.

He made a cold camp, secured the horses in a gully a good distance away, and set out on foot to find the man tracking him. Delaney figured the man was a good two hours or so behind him. He was wrong. The distance had been closed to less than an hour. If he had not stumbled near the man's horse, Delaney wouldn't have found his cold camp. And not a sign of the man. This gave him pause. He quieted the horse when he returned to him, finding the brand by touch on the flank, and discovered that it wasn't army issue. The slash was an older, deeper scar, the letter D unevenly shaped. Altered crop that he could find.

Dropping to his knees, Delaney felt the ground, hoping for a clear footprint. Luck wasn't with him. Obviously the man who tracked him knew to wipe them clean with a sweep of a branch, for that was all he discovered.

Covering up his own trail, he made his way back to his camp. If Ross had someone following him, he might expect a signal when Delaney found the Apache. The major could be planning to be close enough with the hopes of capturing Juh and Geronimo. It made sense to Delaney. Ross would be free of any promises made to the Apache. They would go back as prisoners.

Delaney thought about leading his shadow out into the desert, where he knew he could lose the man, but the move would cost him time. He continued on as if he were unaware that he was being trailed. For the next two days Delaney made no effort to conceal his tracks, yet he sensed another, unseen presence followed him. The third night he trapped a rabbit and built a fire, knowing the scent of roasting meat would carry. If there were Apache close by, they would leave him a sign, and if the man following him was hungry, he might be drawn to seek Delaney out.

Only embers remained. Hidden in a rock basin high above, Delaney waited. Exhaustion threatened to overtake him, and he fought to keep his eyes open. Out of the night sounds he heard a throaty rumble. His hand slipped to his knife, hunter senses alerted. Down below, a golden-eyed jaguar prowled his camp. Delaney crouched, ready to defend himself if the big cat caught his scent. He watched the powerful muscled animal sniff at the rabbit remains, but to his surprise the cat turned away to settle himself on Delaney's bedroll.

Through the darkness Delaney felt the piercing gaze of that golden-eyed cat find him. For minutes time ceased. He knew the cat had seen him. A warrior and a survivor, Delaney thought, seeing the torn ear. And just as suddenly he knew the cat meant him no harm. Not instinct, not a thing that was sensed, but a deep abiding knowledge that he had nothing to fear.

He left the cat to watch, and he slept. In the morning the big cat was gone. So was the rabbit skin.

Delaney headed southwest across a valley whose water was tainted with sulphur. There was a clear spring, which few white men knew about, and it was there that he refilled his canteens, once again taking the time to climb high enough to check his back trail. This time he saw no sign that he was followed.

Keeping clear of the mining camps, Fort Bowie, and a few scattered ranches, Delaney switched horses every few hours, pushing himself and the animals harder now that he rode through the Chiricahua Mountains and Apache reservation lands. Another two days and he would be near the Guadalupes. If he did not find Geronimo and Juh camped with their band, he would head south into Mexico.

The sun was high in the heavens, throwing its blistering heat on anything that moved. Delaney wiped sweat from his brow, time and again, the water in his canteen sickeningly warm. The horses, too, were in need of water, but he knew he had a few hours' grace to find it for them. He dismounted and led the horses up a torturous mountain trail, realizing how deep into Mescalero Apache country he was.

Mirage snorted, drawing his attention, and he turned to see her ears pricked up.

"Man or water," Delaney muttered to himself. Ahead was a wide-mouthed canyon, and he welcomed the shadows cast by its sloping sides that abruptly steepled into a sheer rock wall about forty feet high. Behind him the horses crowded close, and he knew there was water. Shading his eyes, he found the small trickle running down the western face of the canyon's wall. He set the horses free after pulling out his rifle. The grass was sparse, but they needed the rest. Water for him had to wait. The canyon was a boxed dead end.

Delaney sat with his head thrown back, searching the rim of the canyon. Satisfied for the moment that he was safe, he allowed his thoughts to turn to Faith. He hoped that Seanilzay had managed to give her his skystone. She had to know the promise it held for him to return to her.

Heat waves shimmered in front of him. Delaney licked his parched lips, his gaze returning to the trickle of water. He rose and stretched, feeling his clothes rub the grit against his skin. After riding for six days, the thought of being clean held a great deal of appeal. Delaney had to forget it. The risk wasn't worth it. But there was a time when he'd given no thought to how many days he rode and slept in the same clothes.

"Guess I've spent more time bein' civilized than I knew," he whispered, walking over to the water. The horses were cropping the grass when he knelt down and pressed his face against the rock, letting the water run over his skin to cool him before he drank.

The small stone basin didn't have enough water to fill his canteens. He was uncomfortable remaining in a box canyon, but he couldn't go on without fresh water. He quickly hobbled the bay and the roan, leaving Mirage free, knowing she would not wander off. After flinging down his saddle, he stretched out, never intending to fall asleep.

When he woke, the sky was overcast. He sat up, swearing to see the horses gone. And with them his canteens.

Was a trap waiting at the canyon mouth?

He wasn't going to find out. Delaney regretted leaving behind his saddle, but beyond filling his pockets with bullets for his gun and rifle, he took nothing else with him. Another drink at the replenished basin, and he set off to find a way up and over the walls.

Behind boulders on the east face of the canyon, Delaney eyed a narrow chimney that was barely the width of a man's body. Up near the rim he could see a hollow. He glanced back once, weighing his chances, and decided the climb was his best shot to get out.

Stripping off his pants belt, he looped it around his rifle and slung this over his shoulder. Sweat dampened his palms, and he rubbed earth against them to give him purchase on the slippery rock face.

It wasn't so much a climb as it was inching his body up the chimney. Sweat poured down his face and smarted in his eyes. He could feel it trickling down his back. No matter how he tried to control his breathing, he was gasping about halfway up, his muscles aching from the strain.

The chimney had deceived him. It widened. Delaney looked up. He still had over twenty feet to go. The gap was almost four feet wide now and his palms were once again slippery.

The thought crossed his mind that he didn't know what or who waited up there on the rim. But it wasn't as if he had a choice; he had to go on.

His hand slipped at the same time his right foot did. He couldn't stop his body's slide for a few feet. For an agonizing moment he couldn't move. Fear gripped him and held on to to him until he lost track of how long he remained braced between two rock walls before he tried again.

Cooler air was welcomed, and he drew it in deeply, feeling renewed by knowing he was closer to the top. His body was racked by the strain on his muscles as the spread in the chimney widened a few more inches. Delaney ignored the scrapes on his palms. The pain was easy to bury; the blood that made him pray with every inch he moved was not.

When he felt his fingers curl over the rock edge, he rested a few minutes before he made the final heave that saw him up and over. He rolled onto his back and lay there, panting, gazing up at a dusk-laden sky.

And while he lay helpless, they surrounded him.

Chapter Twenty

EVERY LIMB TREMBLED. Delaney had no control over them. He counted six rifles pointed at him and closed his eyes. They were Apache, but there wasn't a face that he recognized. He longed for enough breath to speak, but even that was to be denied him.

Not one of the Indians spoke or made a move.

It took Delaney time to understand that they weren't going to kill him.

In the fast fading light Delaney studied his captors, swearing to himself when he saw their style of breechclouts and moccasins. These were *Netdahee*, the killer warriors, each chosen because he was the fiercest fighter, dedicated to wiping out the Apache's enemies.

The rifle beneath his back was damn painful, and Delaney slowly began to sit up. When no one made a move to stop him, he lifted the belt holding his rifle over his head and set it down beside him.

Breathing a little easier, he began to speak, telling them who he was and why he had come. Delaney watched the circle around him break, and he rose, lifting the rifle with him. He was given no response, but with three of them on each side already moving out at a fast trot, he knew he had to go with them.

The air was sweet and cooling to his body. They circled the rim of the canyon, then began to climb down the tumbled boulders near its entrance. Four more warriors were waiting there with horses, including Delaney's.

"Del-a-ney," one of the warriors said, coming forward.

"Perico?" Delaney answered, relief flooding his body, for this was one of Geronimo's family. He smiled to hear the rapid orders that followed, telling of his friendship to the people, demanding the return of his horses to him.

"The packhorse is filled with little foodstuffs, but it is a gift, Perico. When I am done with the bay, I will turn him free."

"What you bring will be welcomed." He mounted and motioned for the others to leave, waiting until Delaney came up beside him. "I will take you."

"Before we ride off, I want you to know I was followed."

"No more."

It was not until they reached the camp, hidden deep in the mountains within a cave high enough for the horses to be ridden inside, that Delaney noticed the brand on Perico's horse. The deep slash and uneven letter were the same ones he had touched. Whoever had been following him was dead.

Torches lit the huge cavern where most of the band was gathered. He dismounted and saw his horse led away into one of the many tunnels that branched out from there. This was only one of such places where caches of dried foodstuffs, blankets, and weapons could be stored and left behind if the band was discovered and had to leave quickly, allowing their travel to be light and fast.

He scanned the crowd while Perico went to where the men were seated. Chee-hash-kish, Geronimo's young wife and mother to his son and daughter, was the only woman he knew. Naiche was not here, but then, Delaney never expected him. He saw that his gifts were accepted, the women quick to unload the sacks of flour, beans, and coffee.

Perico returned to his side. "You will have food, then you will talk."

Seated before a fire, Delaney ate roasted yucca stems, not a favorite food of the Apache, but one used when other sources were scarce. Dried chokeberries mixed with the dried, then soaked crown of mescal and a few piñon nuts along with a sweet gruel made from mesquite beans satisfied his hunger.

Gourds of "gray water" were passed around, and Delaney drank his share. The weak beer called tiswin was made from corn and in sufficient quantity could make a man drunk. Since what he sipped was not sour, it told him the band had been here for over two weeks, for tiswin took that long to make and would spoil after two days.

He shared his smoking tobacco with all who wanted it and rolled himself a smoke. The women had drawn themselves and the children off to one side with their cooking pots so that they could eat. It was time for talk.

"Many of you here know that I speak no lies to the Chiricahua. I come with word from General Wilcox that he wishes all of you to return to the reservation. The army knows there are problems to be worked out. There are good men who try, but if you run, they become helpless as the child who needs his mother before he walks.

"These men fear that the raids and killing will bring more soldiers. If there is no peace, there must be war. Victorio's way leads to death."

"Th-they t-treat us like d-dogs," Juh stuttered.

Delaney looked at the stockily built Indian with a soft deep voice. "There will always be *pindahs* who look at the color of your skin and see you as less than them. I cannot change the way these men feel and think. In this I can only say my words. Peace will help the Apache survive as a people."

"Th-the re-reservations w-will k-kill us all." At a gesture from Geronimo he fell silent.

"The wrongs they have done to all are many," Geronimo said, his snapping black eyes alive with an unrelenting hate.

There was no answer that Delaney could give the man who held the Power. Apaches did not seek a vision quest as did other tribes, but if they were of the chosen, the Power was given to them in sleep. He had witnessed Geronimo's uncanny knowledge of what was happening in places too far from him to know by any other means to question him.

"It is good that you do not seek to cover this truth."

"I have come with an open heart and an open mind. The major who called me for this is one I do not trust. His words are lies. He wishes you gone from this southern area, and I add my belief that it is to open the land to miners and farmers."

"Always they come for our lands. It is not a thing to be owned."

"But it is the white man's way."

"This is so. Wil-cox gave us flour when we were hungry. He wanted to make us the prisoners of the army so he could get us food. For a little time we were fed." He measured Delaney with a shrewd look, and all waited until he spoke again. "Ross waited many days to find you. All knew that he searched for you. Why is this? There are others who speak to us."

Delaney's rueful smile quickly faded. "I gave much thought to this myself. I was followed, which led me to believe that Ross hoped to discover where you are hidden and bring soldiers to capture you."

"I told you he is no more," Perico said and rose. He walked to where a saddle and bags were laying up against the stone wall. From the pile he withdrew a gun and came around the circle of men to show it to Delaney.

Reaching out for the Colt, Delaney remembered hefting its near-perfect balance once before. It was Chelli's gun.

"You knew the man," Geronimo stated.

"He was not a friend, but yes, I knew him." But why, he asked himself, had Chelli been following him for Ross? Or had he? If not Ross, then who? Brodie? Why? He shook his head trying to make sense of this. Handing the gun back to Perico, he gazed around the circle, suddenly feeling as if they all knew the answers and were waiting for him to find them.

Finally Geronimo broke the silence. "If you come to us with your truth as your father did before you, we listen and believe what you say. If you come to us with lies so cunning that we believe them true, there will be no trust for you again."

"And a wise man is needed to tell the truth from the lies."

Nodding, then smiling, Geronimo agreed with Delaney.

"Ross could not be the fool and believe that you would meekly follow me back like sheep."

"It is what they believe of us, that we are like women and sheep. Others have gone before us to do this. They learn to farm the land and go hungry when the rains do not come or the crops are beaten to the ground by the soldiers' horses. They set our enemies to spy on us. They send us to land that is too cold for our people and for us to farm.

"We need men like Howard, who kept his word with us and treated us like brothers."

Delaney wished right along with Geronimo that General Howard had been left in charge. He had dealt fairly with the Apache. Cochise knew he had respected them. Howard had gained the Chiricahua band title to their homeland, which caused dissatisfaction with the Warm Springs bands when their request was disallowed.

"We have always wanted peace to live our ways. When he who was before Naiche left this world, it was his wish that we keep our word."

Again Delaney could only nod in agreement. He knew that Geronimo could not say Cochise's name for fear of calling his ghost. But he remembered how Cochise's son, Taza, had been raised to lead, only to die when he toured Washington, and Naiche had taken leadership with Geronimo at his side.

His thought drew him back in time to remember that Skinya, one of Cochise's leading warriors, refused Taza as leader, refused the peace, and with his brother Pionsenay went on the warpath, killing the station keeper at Sulphur Springs and two other white men.

"Yes, I see you remember how all were thought to be as a few."

"The cry went out," Delaney said softly, "to slay all the Chiricahua. But when Naiche shot he who caused this, you fled—"

"Only to go to Warm Springs to our friends on the Alamosa. Clum did not wish to see me live. Every deed he placed on me. Soon all *pindahs* spoke the same of me. They want my death. I will not belong to the soldiers. Taza trusted them, and they poisoned him. They took away our homeland.

"Can I forget the heated irons that Clum put on me? Or that he gave me a bed of straw like an animal to sleep? He lied then, too. They sent word that Ponce was raiding far from where he was held prisoner. How can this be? One man in two places? This was a time when I believed my life lost."

"The smallpox was with us," Perico added, taking up the talk. "Many died. The soldiers did not want Clum to make order for us. When they took him away as agent, there was no one to trust. When they lied about your father and we spoke up for him, they chased us."

"When Hart came, he set me free," Geronimo said. "The smallpox spread. The yellow fever came. There was no food and no clothing for the people. All we asked is that we could go back to our lands. This was refused. I will not go back to San Carlos. They asked my word and promised that all would change. They would give us food. They gave us nothing."

Delaney closed his eyes for a moment before he glanced around the circle again. There were nods of assent. He knew and could not mention the death of Geronimo's nephew after a scolding from Geronimo that made the decision for them to leave the reservation.

"You must tell me all that you want. I will bring the words to General Wilcox. I will see that either Jeffords or McIntosh come again with his offer."

They spoke long into the night, and in the morning Delaney left them with a warning from Perico.

"The man called Brodie searches for gold. If you wish to bring peace, kill him. He goes too near the place."

"This I have already sworn to do, Perico. He has killed my father and my mother. He dishonored my name. His death will be at my hand."

"When your heart is troubled, come to us. Go now and may we live to see each other again."

Three *Netdahee* warriors rode with him as far as the San Bernardino Valley, and there they left Delaney to continue his journey back to Tombstone.

Since he was riding up from the southwest, Delaney knew a sudden longing to see Faith before he made his report to Ross. The major wasn't going to be pleased with what he had to tell him, but one way or another he'd give up that journal.

As he rode those solitary hours, he reflected on all that he had learned of Brodie's activities, from dealing in prime cattle brought up from Mexico after being stolen in Texas, with the blame laid on Geronimo's head or another renegade band, to his attempts to find what he believed to be a hidden gold mine in the Dragoons.

Once Delaney allowed his thoughts to dwell on Brodie, other memories of the past surfaced. He knew where Brodie had first gotten the idea that a gold mine was located in the mountains, and it was Delaney's fault. He couldn't blame Elise for telling Brodie about the mine, after Delaney's pride had caused him to boast of knowing a secret place. He had been nineteen the first time he met Elise in Tucson. Love had hit him like a lightning bolt after she smiled at him. He knew he wanted to marry her before he ever held her in his arms to dance. And needing to impress her, he realized later he had made the mistake of telling her the little he did about the secret place that the stone he wore came from.

"A place of riches," he murmured aloud now, using the same words he had told her. For him it was just such a place. But Elise believed he had been talking about gold. She haunted him, teased him, and withheld kisses, but he was too blind to understand how greed for wealth drove her.

Delaney remembered thinking she was too young to marry. He took his first job with the railroad and was gone over a year. Adam Brodie's family had settled in the area, and he began courting Elise. Until Delaney came back. Elise had sworn to him that he was the one she loved, the only man she would marry as soon as he had enough money to give them a good start.

Fool that he was, he believed her. He would take any work that paid well, sending every penny he could spare to Elise. But within that year he heard rumors that forced him home again. Elise silenced his questions with kisses that drove the boy he was crazy, and let the man he was now reflect upon the calculated motives that drove her. He had left her after a bitter fight when she insisted he go after the gold mine hidden in the Dragoons. He had been too afraid of losing her to tell her the truth. There was no gold, there never had been any. The place was sacred to the Apache, who took bits of precious skystone for their own ceremonial uses. The Indians abhorred the taking of gold and silver from the earth.

He had to stop himself from remembering more and set about making a cold camp, but it seemed that once the grave had been opened on the past, it would not close.

On the sigh of the wind he heard the whisper of Elise's sultry voice calling him, begging him to do what she asked so that they could marry. He seemed removed from himself as he felt again the guilt when they first became lovers and his need to make enough money to satisfy her.

Lies and betrayal. She had married Adam and taken every penny of the money she had been saving for their home to use for a trip to San Francisco.

With his hand cradling his head, Delaney stared up at the night sky and watched the stars appear. For every bitter memory that he recalled of Elise, he found that Faith's image came to dispel them. He slept with the whisper of her name on his lips and woke with a driving need to see her and hold her.

It was late afternoon the next day that Delaney rode near the north-flowing San Pedro River. Cottonwoods and willows dotted the broad meadows and hawks glided overhead. The faint smoke from a campfire wafted on the breeze, and Delaney followed it toward the riverbank.

"I'm friendly and coming in," he called out.

Keith ran out from the clearing where the wagons were, whooping and hollering, Pris and Joey close behind him.

Delaney caught up the little ones before him feeling warmed by their welcome. Keith walked at his horse's side into their camp. From a ways down the bank the sound of an ax biting wood could be heard, but before he could ask, Keith said their father was cutting trees for their cabin.

Delaney came out of the saddle first, then lifted Pris, who covered his bearded cheeks with kisses and gave him an extra tight hug before she let him release her.

"I have a secret to tell," Joey whispered in his ear when Delaney held him in his arms. Still holding the boy, Delaney walked away, the strong sense of homecoming needing only Faith to complete it.

"So what's this secret, scout?"

"You promise not to tell anyone, not even Faith?"

"I promise, Joey. There's nothing wrong, is there?"

"I don't know. Yesterday I was trying to track a deer like you showed me, Del. I was doing real good, too. But I got this funny feeling, and all the trees seemed to go around and around. Just like that night," he added, searching Delaney's features with his hand. Pressing his fingers over Delaney's mouth, Joey spoke in a hushed voice. "I had to sit down and . . . and for a few seconds I thought I saw the trees. Not real clear. And it went away. But I hoped that maybe all the good medicine worked and I would be able to see again."

"Joey," Delaney murmured, hugging him close, blinking to keep the tears from his eyes. "You only have to want to see, want it with all your heart."

"I'm scared, Del. Scared it might not happen no matter how much I want it to."

Cradling Joey's head against his shoulder, Delaney tried to find the words he needed, and he saw Faith coming up the path from the river. "Love," he whispered, walking toward her. And the words came easy. "Just love the world as you once saw it, Joey. Remember only the good things, the pretty things. Like a smile that would rival a desert sunrise, or eyes of blue so beautiful there are no words to describe them."

He shifted Joey's weight to one side and opened his arm to hold Faith close, burying his face against her hair and closing his eyes to savor the scent of her.

"You were talking about Faith, weren't you, Del?" Joey asked, lifting his head and smiling. "She missed you," he confided, then added, "I did, too." Tilting his head to one side, he asked, "Are you gonna kiss her?"

"Think I should, scout?" But he was already lowering Joey to stand on his own when Faith took the decision from him.

She cradled his cheeks and drew his mouth down to hers, putting every bit of love, every moment of longing into her kiss. Faith willed him in her heart and mind to believe in her, to believe in the love she had for him.

Hearing the words no longer seemed important. She had the look in his eyes as she came toward him to cherish now. Delaney had whispered the word *love*, and that is what she saw in his gaze: love, untarnished by the past, glittering with a promise of the future.

With reluctance their lips parted before passion's need was unleashed. Delaney rested his forehead against hers, mingling his breath with hers, touching the tip of his nose to meet Faith's.

For a moment they were alone in the world, and Faith used one fingertip to trace the smile of incredible tenderness on his lips. She felt the loneliness that dwelled deep inside him yield and give way to the powerful emotion that bonded them.

"I love you," she whispered, breathing the words against the softened line of his mouth, whispering the same with her eyes.

And he drank that love and her kiss like a fertile rain spreading its balm on a parched desert land, for Faith was all that gave life to him.

Reality intruded with Joey's whispered warning that his father was coming, and Delaney eased his lips from hers but kept her cradled to his side with one arm around her waist.

Resentment flared in Becket's eyes when he saw that Delaney had returned, but it disappeared when he looked at his daughter held at Delaney's side. Faith's joy glowed in her eyes, and he knew no matter what objection he could voice against Delaney, she was beyond listening to him.

"You back to stay?" he asked Delaney.

"No. I stopped here first before I find Ross." Faith tensed, and he pressed his hand in warning for her to be silent. "I wanted to make sure all of you were settled and without trouble."

"That's all?" Becket shot back, setting his ax against a tree and coming toward them. "Keith, take Pris and Joey downstream. What I've got to say isn't for them or you to hear."

"Pa—"

"Hush up, Faith," Robert warned, waiting until Keith obeyed him before he spoke. "Carmichael, I'm building a home for my family here. I can't say I like you, but if you figure on coming around here for my daughter, you'd best speak up now and plainly set my mind to rest. If you don't, I'm warning you, I'll raise my gun and run you off."

"No! Pa, I won't let you—"

"He's right, Faith," Delaney said, cutting her off. With his grip on her waist he propelled her in front of him and gazed down at her. "I want to marry you, Faith, but there's something I must do before—"

"Brodie?" she whispered, clutching hold of the skystone she had worn since Seanilzay brought it to her.

He gazed back to where Becket stood waiting. "Is that plain enough for you? If I come back, I want your daughter for my wife. If she'll have me," he added, looking again at Faith.

"Yes," she answered but had to close her eyes to hide the fear that suddenly gripped her. She felt Delaney's hand cover hers, and the heat of the stone build against her palm. His lips brushed her mouth, and she opened her eyes. "Is there nothing I can say that will change your mind?"

"Brodie violates a trust that I was given. I can't let him live, Faith. I can't let the deaths of my parents go unpunished. For me there is no choice."

"Then go with my love," she whispered, releasing the stone and, with her step back, asking him to release her. She slid the rawhide thong over her head. "I want you to wear this. Seanilzay told me there is a promise you must remember and someday tell me. But I want to add one of my own."

She took off his hat and dropped it. Holding the rawhide wide with both hands, she lifted it over his head, then settled the stone beneath his shirt. Her fingertips lingered to touch his warm skin and caress the pulse beating in the hollow of his throat.

Faith lifted her face and gazed into his eyes. "If love can deny nothing to love, I promise to deny you nothing. If love lives by love, as I believe, then I need you to live to love me, for I know that we already are one in heart and spirit."

Chapter Twenty-One

Ross DIDN'T HAVE the journal.

Delaney heard the major's words ringing in his ears. He pinned Ross with an icy stare, then looked away toward the grimed window of the same room where they had met before. Coolly he contemplated killing Ross. He thought of the encampment of additional soldiers he had passed on his way into Tombstone and knew his chances were less than slim to leave here if he killed the major.

Ross hid his disappointment that Delaney said nothing. He had gloated over his own cleverness in using Carmichael to find out where Geronimo and Juh were hiding. But he wanted more. He wanted Delaney broken for forcing the woman he loved into a marriage that could only end with the death of her husband. Ross knew he had no compunctions about killing a man, but he drew the line at killing his cousin, Adam Brodie. He could barely contain his need to share this with Elise. One small payback for what Delaney had done to her. But he had to stop thinking about Elise and finish with Carmichael.

"You understand that the only thing I needed from you, Carmichael, was the location of where Geronimo and Juh were hiding. By tonight I'll have that information. There are detachments of soldiers coming from Lowell and Huachuca to join the force I've already assembled." Ross knew he had captured Delaney's attention, for he turned around to face him. Topping off the glass of whiskey on the table, Ross gestured with the bottle to the empty glass as if asking Delaney if he wanted a drink.

"I'd sooner drink with a rattler, Major. Come to think of it, there ain't all that much difference between you."

Ross shrugged it off. "Suit yourself. Within the week I'll have that renegade band back where they belong on San Carlos."

"And a promotion to boot?" Delaney asked, savoring his own knowledge that Ross would have nothing.

"I would expect there to be one. But I must admit that you've accepted the news about the journal rather calmly. Not at all what I—"

"Thought about it, did you?" Delaney interrupted. "Well, you gloat about your plans and your promotion, Major. You're gonna come up as empty as me." He headed for the door, smiling because Ross was choking on the whiskey he had swallowed.

"Hold it, Carmichael! I'm not through with you yet."

Delaney stopped in the doorway and faced him. "Major?"

"I'll win! I had you followed, Carmichael. Once the Apaches find out how you betrayed them, they'll kill you." Ross waited for the fear, he wanted that desperate panicked look a man wore when he was cornered. He needed to see Carmichael beg.

Delaney's lip curled, and all the scorn he felt was directed at Ross. "You've a long wait ahead of you, Major, if you're hoping that Chelli's coming back."

"What!" Ross shoved his chair back and stood up, pushing the table aside and knocking over the bottle and glass.

Delaney gazed at the liquor spilling into the warped floor-boards, then lifted his gaze back up to Ross's face.

"Chelli's dead."

The major's roaring demands that he return followed Delaney down the street. He ignored them just as he ignored the curious men that stopped whatever they were doing to watch him walk by.

There was a lone tent set up at the end of the street, and here Delaney stopped. A look inside showed him serious gamblers and the hardcases who weren't wearing their guns for show. He stepped inside, needing a drink to wash the bitterness from his mouth. A plank set on two barrels served for a bar, whiskey the only drink offered. Delaney motioned for the barkeep to leave the bottle.

By the time he paid for it and turned around, the murmur of voices had dropped, then lifted, as men looked away from his sweeping gaze and went back to their card games.

Delaney headed for the lone table in the far corner, the only empty one set deep in the shadows cast by the lanterns hanging overhead from the tent poles. He had no desire to draw attention to himself. There was serious thinking to be done.

No matter how he tried to direct his thoughts, possessing the journal to clear his father's name and killing Brodie were all he could think about. And Faith.

The whiskey was raw belly-wash, made and bottled the same day, but he downed his first glass quickly, trying to block the image of Faith from his mind. She wouldn't leave him. He couldn't rid himself of the feeling that he was somehow defiling her and her bright hope of love with all the filth that trapped him from the past.

When the bottle was half-empty, Delaney admitted to himself that the power Faith wielded was stronger than his will. He would reclaim the journal by whatever means he had to use and be rid of Brodie, for that was a debt of honor he could not forget, but he swore that Brodie would not die an easy death.

He had set himself a hard road to ride, the only one he could. His decision made, he rose and started to walk out.

"You leavin' the bottle, mister?" a man called out.

"Paid for, take it," Delaney answered without turning, only to be stopped as he neared the open flap of the tent.

"Sit in for a game?"

Delaney glanced at the pale long-fingered hands fanning a deck of cards across the wood tabletop. He sized the man up as a tinhorn and shook his head. "You can't match the stakes I'm playing for."

"Name it. I've had a good night," he answered, indicating the pile of poke bags that would lure some fool into losing his hard-earned silver.

Before he could stop him, Delaney's hand covered the spread of cards. The gambler swallowed when he realized how intently this stranger was staring at the backs of his deck. A quick look around showed that whatever this man had in mind, no one would see, for his back blocked the table from view. His fears were realized when four cards were pulled from those spread on the table.

One by one Delaney flipped over the cards. "Aces and eights."

The gambler started to sweat. The cards, a pair of aces and a pair of eights, were the dead man's hand since Jack McCall shot Wild Bill Hickok through the back of the head during a poker game three years ago.

"Listen up, stranger, I've given you no call—"

"No. You haven't. I'm just showing you what stakes I'm playing for, mister."

He didn't watch the man leave, but the tinhorn quickly gathered his cards and winnings. He'd call it a night. But he couldn't help looking at the deck, wondering how in the hell the man had spotted his markings. They were the best;

he'd paid John Bull, the best of the knaves, a small fortune for them.

Harper Poe could not leave without knowing who the man was that spotted his marked cards. He asked the barkeep first if the stranger had been a "king," the best of the best, gamblers like Dick Clark, Doc Holliday, and Luke Short. No one knew. No one cared. Poe did. He lit out for Globe that very night.

Delaney rode in the opposite direction, camping near a dry wash, waiting for morning.

Brodie would be warned by Ross, Delaney figured, but that couldn't be helped. He wasn't going to wait any longer.

And he knew he would have to face Elise again. But she no longer had the power to hurt him. No one but Faith had that.

Before the last morning star had faded from the sky, Delaney was awakened by Seanilzay.

They talked of what happened with the major as coffee brewed. Seanilzay set aside a small bit of the cooling ash, and they drank their coffee in silence.

"In the days when I first knew I had the Power, I was afraid to use it. In your mind the path is set that you must take, Del-a-ney. You think you know your enemy."

Delaney lowered the cup from his lips and stared at the Apache. Tension began to tighten his body, and he knew what he would be asked to do.

Seanilzay nodded. "Yes. You know." He scooped up a bit of the cooled ash and held it out to Delaney in the palm of his hand.

There was only so far a man could run before he had to stop and face what he ran from, and what he was. Delaney set the cup aside and with one finger made a cross of ashes on his left hand. Holding it up to the morning star, he waited for the sign of where his enemy was. Such a simple act, he thought, gazing upward, praying silently to have his need answered.

"Look to the north, Del-a-ney. See where your enemy hides."

And Delaney looked to the north to where a flash of lightning appeared in the sky. "I have done as you asked. The way north is where Brodie's ranch is, no surprise, just confirmation of my enemy."

"Brodie alone is not your enemy, Del-a-ney. The woman is more deadly than the sting of the scorpion. The days you were gone from here, I watched as you asked that all was well with the family of Woman with Eyes of Sky. They had no need of me. I followed Ross. He rode north to see the woman of Brodie. This Elise is faithless. She has no honor for her husband."

"Elise and Ross—lovers?"

"She, too, is your enemy. It is she who has the journal."

"So that's how Ross got hold of a page. I thought he was involved with Brodie's hunt for gold. It made sense to think the major was greedy and wanted the Apache gone from these lands so they could claim them."

"Yes. Yes," Seanilzay repeated, nodding. "Now you begin to see. This Elise wants Ross to kill Brodie. Only this did I hear."

"And the journal? She still has it?"

"Ross wanted her to burn it. I do not believe she would do this. When you asked me why I did not speak of all this, I could not tell you. I was not ready to see the end of my days. Elise cursed me and said that I would die if I told what I knew."

"What are you saying, Seanilzay? Elise couldn't hurt you."

"She was there the day your mother went from us. She stole the book before Brodie came. I was there to bring venison to your mother and saw Elise run from the cabin.

It was easy to follow her. When I saw that she held your father's book, I asked why she stole from your home. She said that Brodie would come there for the book. She took it to keep it safe for you. I said I would bring this journal to you, and she refused. Elise said I would be named the thief. She was going to tell the *pindahs* that I stole from your home."

"Elise knew that Brodie was going to kill my mother?" Delaney shuddered. His mother had loved Elise, and no matter how Elise betrayed him, he didn't want to believe she did nothing to prevent his mother's death.

"I do not know if Elise knew what Brodie planned."

"Why did you wait until now to tell me all this?"

"You loved this woman. You claimed her as your own before Brodie came. All knew of this. Your father and mother were not of our blood, but we cared for them as one of us. We saw the boy grow to a man who followed the peace of our ways even as he learned those of a warrior. Your heart was as true as any Apache."

Seanilzay met the piercing intensity of Delaney's gaze and with a saddened voice continued. "What peace would I bring to one such as you if I spoke these words when your grief was new and wild? You would have sought your enemies' deaths then as you must do now, this is true. But the Power you hold would have died and been no more. All that makes you the man that you are would not have come to pass. The loss, ah, Del-a-ney, the loss would have been great to all. Fear for my own life, worthless as it has become, held me silent as well. On this woman Elise's word the *pindahs* would have killed me if she told her lies."

Delaney knew this was the truth. Elise had only to hint that Seanilzay was near the cabin the day his mother died, and they would have hunted and killed him. Elise. Lies. And a deeper betrayal. A tense silence remained between them until Delaney could stop remembering, could still the raging grief inside him.

When he rose to saddle Mirage, Seanilzay asked, "Will you let me come with you?"

"No. I go alone."

"We should sing to make you strong before you face your enemies, Del-a-ney."

"You sing for me, my friend, there is no time left, for this has waited too long."

Seanilzay watched him ride away. He, too, rode off, but toward the southwest, where he could send smoke safely. He would not let Delaney ride alone against his enemies. The *Netdahee* would come.

His Power would will it so.

Brodie's ranch lay out in open country, but the small adobe house that Delaney remembered was now a sprawling mass of buildings. Cottonwoods grew close to offer shade to the Spanish tile roofs, and a low wall surrounded the house, with a wooden gate the only entrance. From the high vantage point that Delaney had, he looked down into the empty courtyard. The squeak of the windlass came from somewhere behind the house, telling him that someone was drawing water from the well.

His gaze was drawn toward the two-story tower that stood cornered to the house. The wide arches were open on four sides and revealed that no one manned it. Brodie must be very secure, he thought. A few workers tended the fields where water from several streams ran into irrigation ditches. Delaney could barely make out the scattered herd of cattle far off in the distance.

Leaving Mirage tethered, he made his way down to the wall, keeping low until he reached the side where the trees were the thickest. Climbing the nearest one, he smiled to see a pair of narrow paned doors open. He waited, listening and watching, before he came down on the other side of the wall and made it inside.

The doors leading out of the room and into the house were closed. Delaney once again listened before he eased one open. Archways graced the wide hall, and Delaney saw the main *sala* was across from him. The massive furniture of another showed him the dining room. Farther down the hall were closed doors, bedrooms, he assumed. He glanced into the room behind him and realized from the delicate line of the chairs and settee that he had come into the house through Elise's sitting room.

Would she keep the journal here? A low-voiced argument came from down the hall, forcing him to step back inside and close the door. From the Mexican dialect he heard something about the fiesta being planned for later this week.

He set about searching the room, without any hope of finding the journal this easily, and he wasn't disappointed not to discover it. A child's cry and a scolding voice sent him back to the door. It was Elise's voice he heard demanding that someone called Nita come take the boy.

Every sense warned him that she stood beyond that closed door. He heard the patter of bare feet, the soft, liquid soothing of a young girl's voice, the whining tone of the boy. Elise's son. He could have been their own. Standing slightly to the side of the door, he stared at the brass handle, almost willing it to turn.

He smiled to hear her call out that she was not to be disturbed.

And watched the door open.

He knew she didn't see him standing off to the side as she swept into the room, slamming the door closed. He watched her head for the side table where a decanter and glass rested on a tray. After pouring a drink, she tossed it down as neatly as any man, then refilled the glass for another.

He hadn't given much thought to what he would do when he saw her again. So her name whispering from his lips was as much of a shock to him as it was to her.

Elise spun around and didn't move. He watched her eyes widen, and he moved to lock the door, pocketing the key before he came toward her. There was fear in the doe-brown color of her eyes.

"No greeting, Elise? Aren't you glad to see me? Surely you're at least shocked? Surprised? Or maybe you were warned I was coming?"

"I . . . I can't believe you're back, Del."

Soft. Sultry. Her voice washed over him, bringing with it unwanted memories. He didn't even want to look at her. Angel's face. Angel's body. Host to a whore. Delaney almost smiled to see the darting, trapped-animal look of her eyes. Her breathing, which changed to a rapid pant, drew his gaze down until he took his fill of that body of hers. Such a lush, exciting body that had always been able to make him forget that beyond sex they had nothing.

Elise had used her body to get whatever she wanted. Facing her again, Delaney suddenly realized that he had been aware of her cunning and female tricks but had kept silent for the sake of his own pride.

"Del?" She moistened her lips with the tip of her kittenlike tongue and took a step back.

"Afraid, Elise? Why? Did you think I'd come back to kill you?"

"No. No, of course not. Why would you kill me? I've done nothing," she declared. "It was—" She paused and with a pleading gesture reached out to him, tears trembling on the sweeping tips of her lashes, which were the color of newly minted gold. "I've prayed and prayed that you would come back to me, Del. I've needed you so much."

"Tired of Brodie already? Can't understand that, Elise. He's given you more than I ever could. Even a son. The boy is Adam's, isn't he?" he asked in a soft, drawled voice.

Her eyes flashed him a furious look before she bowed her head, one finger dabbing her eyes. "I will forgive you for saying that to me. I know how much I hurt you, Del, but you loved me. I know you did. I really do understand why you're behaving this way, so cold and distant." When he didn't respond, she looked at him. "I thought you came back because you heard that Adam keeps me a prisoner in this house. I want to leave here, Del. Please, please say you'll help me."

"A prisoner, Elise? I didn't see any armed guards outside. No one tried to stop me from coming into the house." With a sweeping look that barely hid his disgust, Delaney took in the finery of her gown, the glitter of the gems on her ears, the pearls that graced the combs holding back the silky sheen of golden blond hair, and he suffered the memory of knowing what lay beneath was rotten.

He couldn't stand being in the same room with her another moment. She was a whore in the ugliest sense.

"Del, you can't forget. I won't let you!" she cried out softly, running to him. She clasped his head with both hands and ground her mouth to his in a counterfeit act of passion.

There was no gentleness in the way Delaney pulled her hands away and shoved her aside.

"Bastard!" she hissed, her eyes glittering with hate, the mask finally ripped away. But she was truly afraid of him now. There was no mercy to be found in the eyes that once looked on her with desire. "Don't hurt me, Del. I beg that of you."

"I'd have to touch you to hurt you, Elise. Even I haven't the stomach to do that." Delaney could barely stop himself from wiping the taste of her from his mouth.

Fear seeped out of her as she realized that he meant what he said. He was not going to hurt her. "One scream from me and you're dead," she stated, tilting her head to the side.

"One sound from your mouth, and I'll slit your lying throat."

"But you just said—"

"I can use a knife without having to touch you, Elise. All I want is the journal and to know why you stole it." He saw her stiffen and wondered if being confronted with the fact that he didn't want her, didn't intend to punish her, had thrown off her natural cunning. He smiled, but there was no warmth in him. "From the first time I saw you, Elise, I left myself wide open for you to use me. Lust is a weapon that you use well. You used it on me, Adam, and now Ross, but I don't care."

"You know about Ross?"

"That really frightens you, doesn't it? I know about Ross, about Adam killing my parents, but it's you," he said, stalking closer to her until she was forced against the wall with nowhere to turn, "that I came back for." It would be so easy to kill her. He could smell the cloying scent of her body melding with fear that he would do just that. A few seconds, that would be all he needed. The fragile bones in her neck were no match for the strength of his hands. Elise would break as easily as a slender reed.

He raised his hands and stared down at them, looking up in the next instant to snag her gaze. "Yes," he whispered, "I'm thinking about it."

"Don't hurt me, please, Del. I'll tell you. I swear I didn't know what Adam planned to do that day. He wanted the journal so he couldn't be implicated. I overheard him talking with his men. One of them had a friend who was in Yuma with your father. He's the one who told Brodie about the journal. Your mother didn't even know about it. I only went there to save it from

Adam. I knew you would want it, but you never came to me."

"So you stole the book for me and threatened to blame Seanilzay?" Without touching her, Delaney leaned forward and pressed his hands against the wall on either side of her head. "No more lies, Elise," he warned in an icy tone.

Her body sagged against the wall. "All right. I took the journal to keep Adam from leaving me as he threatened. As long as I had it, Adam was helpless. He knew that I would make sure you would get the journal if anything happened to me and that he'd be the one brought up on charges of fixing the scales and selling sick cattle to the Indian agent."

"And Brodie had my father killed in prison?"

"Yes."

"He set fire to the cabin and left my mother to burn to death?"

"Yes," she answered, her voice a bare thread of sound.

"Where is the journal, Elise?"

She looked up at his face, hoping to find a sign that he had softened, but there was nothing in his eyes, not even hate.

"I buried the journal beneath the peach tree on your land."

Delaney spun around, stepping away from her, and heard the soft rustle of her skirt as she moved back to the table. He wanted a drink to wash away the bile from his mouth, but he couldn't touch a thing that she owned.

"Where is Adam now?"

"Will you kill him, Del?"

Her words were a throaty whisper edged with excitement. A chill shivered down his spine, and he found himself having to turn around and face her. There was a light flush on her cheeks. Her eyes were dilated, darkening even as he watched. Her lips parted and Delaney recognized the look. Elise was aroused by the mere thought of his killing her husband.

For a moment he felt trapped, unable to move or to speak as she came to stand in front of him. Sipping her drink, she lowered the glass, tilting her head to the side, then smiling. "Will you kill him?" she repeated.

"Where is he?" His voice sounded strange to his own ears. Delaney wanted to move away from her, but something held sway over him.

Elise arched her head back, staring at him through half-lidded eyes, trailing the fingers of her free hand down the slender column of her bare throat. Using only one finger, she traced the lace edge of her gown over skin that was as white and smooth as cream. Her laugh was soft, knowing, and so, so taunting.

"You once loved to kiss me here, Del. And bite me. . . . Remember how excited you could make me?"

"I remember bedding an animal in heat."

"So rough. So damn impatient," she went on in a dreamy voice. "We could share that all again. Here. Now."

"Where's Adam?"

"He can wait, Del. I don't want to."

"Find another stud, Elise." The force of her slap stung his cheek, but it served its purpose; she stepped away from him.

"If I tell you where he is, will you come back?"

"Tell me."

She finished her drink and glanced at him. "Adam set up a base camp on the mountain. He's sure that this time he has found the mine. You could have had everything—me, the gold, all of it. You'll end up with nothing, a loser."

"There's no gold. There never was. And the only thing Adam'll find up there is his death."

"And you," she stated in a brittle voice, unable to bear the scorn in his eyes, "will make sure of that, won't you?"

"If you wanted Adam dead, why didn't you kill him, Elise? Or have Ross do it for you. You've always known how to make a man do exactly what you wanted."

"Not quite. And never you, Delaney. Ross would not kill him, not even for me. You see," she said, smiling again, "Adam is his cousin. He was willing to help Adam to get rid of you, but at heart he's a coward. More of one than Adam ever was."

"Then you're well matched this time, Elise."

"Perhaps." She let him reach the courtyard doors and knew she couldn't see him leave without another try. "Wait, Del, please. I made a terrible mistake that I'll always regret. I was too young and thought I needed all that Adam could give me. I should have loved you. You were the only man I ever wanted."

"You didn't make any mistakes, Elise. You don't know how to love. But then, a whore never does."

Delaney was over the wall when the sound of glass breaking was followed by a woman's scream. From his vantage point above the house, he watched men scrambling to saddle the horses milling in the corral. Minutes later they rode out.

He would have little chance of catching Adam by surprise now. He should have expected Elise to make sure that she protected herself on the chance that Brodie was the one who lived.

Lies and betrayal. He couldn't wait to be done with them.

Chapter Twenty-Two

STILL GUARDED BY the Apache, the trails Delaney followed wove through the Dragoon Mountains. As he rode, he kept remembering the two young Apache boys who had shown him all their secret places.

Memories pulled at him, even as he sensed unseen Indians watching his progress to their sacred lands.

Delaney stopped at Burnout Springs to wash himself and drink, knowing it would the last water he would take until he came out of the mountains.

Taza. Naiche. Their names came with images into Delaney's mind. They had shown him this spring. Tall, heavily built Taza, always smiling, his face nearly an exact replica of his grandfather, Mangas Coloradas. And Naiche, handsome, slender, his manner reserved like his father, Cochise. He heard the echo of their boyish, long-ago laughter and remembered their games. For here is where they had played together and later talked, learning each other's beliefs.

But even in play the Apache brothers had taught him their skills. Taza helped him make his first bow and arrows. They had raced their horses, run together for long distances, and Delaney smiled to recall the day Taza had come to show off the tips of his moccasins marked with the blood of his first kill. Delaney had been jealous. Taza gifted him with a pair of moccasins, then asked his father if Delaney could learn with them.

Delaney roused himself and stripped off his shirt, splashing the cool water over his upper body. When the water stilled, he flattened himself on the ground and drank, then waited until he could see his reflection in the water. The skystone ground into the skin of his chest.

He stood up quickly, fighting the images that came one after the other, time slipping away against his will, slipping back to the day Taza had challenged him to find his trail up the mountain on rocks that held no print.

Pride wouldn't let him refuse. Naiche had waited below, here at the spring with their horses, sure that his brother would win. He had taunted Delaney with pride in an older brother's skill, that Delaney would never find him.

Naiche had been right. Delaney never found Taza. He had discovered the cave and, curious, explored it. Once he had found the torches and lit one, Delaney followed the tunnel that led to the cavern, with other tunnels opening from it. The walls were greenish in one place, blue stone marked with white in another. Trickles of water echoed from deeper in the mountain.

Delaney knew the sharp, wedge-shaped adz that he found was ancient in design. What he didn't understand was why stone fragments littered the floor where he stood and whispers seemed to come to him. He had been holding the adz by its grooved handle when Taza found him.

"What is this place?" he had asked the Apache boy.

Taza had not answered but drew his knife, and Delaney knew that Taza would try to kill him.

"Tell me what I have done!" he had cried out, fighting, knowing his skills were no match.

He closed his eyes now, remembering the boy's fear as he lay beneath his friend's body, the cold blade against his throat, the unbelievable relief that Taza was pulled off him, the helplessness of not being able to move until Cochise had helped him to stand.

He had learned the secrets that day, and to Cochise he had sworn never to tell what he knew. The skystone had been both a gift and a constant reminder that the Apache shamans had great power.

Delaney cast aside the memories. He looked up at the mountain. He had promised to keep the secret safe then; now there was another to hold from all men.

Unsaddling Mirage, he turned her loose and piled his gear together. A handful of dirt rubbed along his rifle barrel made sure that the sun would reveal no glint of metal and give his presence away.

Filling his pockets with shells for the rifle, he slipped on his shirt and once again used his pants belt to make a sling for the rifle.

Now he was ready to make the climb that would bring him to a spot overlooking the place he believed Brodie would have chosen for a camp.

There were few sweet-water springs close by, and white men tended to camp near them, regardless of the animals and the Indians that would go thirsty.

Within minutes of his working his way among the boulders, Delaney felt the heat of the sun, the air growing close, almost stifling.

Nearly two hours later he was high enough to look out over the land. In the distance he saw heat waves dancing and thought of the many men who lost their lives believing in the mirage of water the heat caused when it shimmered against the sand.

Delaney had to cross an open crest, and here he hesitated, surveying the land around him and below him. He caught the faint whiff of tobacco smoke and dropped to the ground, flattening himself, not daring to breathe. Lying so still, he listened and heard a stone rattle, then one fell. There was the clink of metal on stone. A spur, he thought, forced to wait. Brodie must have had word that he was coming up here for him and already sent out men to search.

"Any sign of him?" a man yelled from below.

"Nothing. He'd need to be a goat to climb these rocks."

Delaney grinned. The man who answered was no more than fifteen yards to the right of where he lay. With a wave of his rifle to the man below, he moved off. Delaney eased himself backward until he was sure they couldn't see him, and then stood up.

Because they were watching for him, Delaney chose a different route, the climb harder, as the sun was intense and the rocks retained the heat. But with each minute that passed, each minute that brought him closer to his quarry, he found added strength. Ragged chasms that he was forced to jump, narrow ledges barely the width of his foot, nothing stopped him from what he needed to do.

There were places where he had to turn away and find another path. Rocks had broken, walls had been scoured by the years, wind, and rain to become slick and smooth, allowing him no handholds.

With patience and determination, he found his way up. Mountain goat was right, he repeated to himself, wiping the sweat from his brow. Even the neckerchief he had tied around his forehead was drenched, and he squeezed it dry to keep the sweat from dripping into his eyes and blinding him.

He looked down at the twenty-foot drop that ended with a wide jutting ledge. Below it was Brodie's camp.

Delaney settled himself behind a boulder, counting four men. There was no sign of Brodie. If there were only two others searching for him, it added up to six men, but Delaney had a feeling there were more. He could expect no help from the Apache. If one of them killed a white man on Indian land, the army would sweep down on them.

And this wasn't their fight. It was his.

Up the trail came a man making no effort to hide. Delaney directed his gaze down the path behind the man and was rewarded to see a flash of sun on metal. So, Brodie had another man watching below. Seven.

But all he wanted was Brodie in his rifle sight. He heard the murmur of men's voices, but not the one he most longed to hear. It was only now that he gave thought to the possibility that Elise had lied to him and that Brodie wasn't there at all.

There was only one way to find out. Cradling his rifle against his cheek, Delaney drew a bead on a rock ahead of one man standing in the open with his back toward him and fired.

The man dropped, rolled, and disappeared in a crouching run beneath the ledge. His shouted warning was lost in the second shot Delaney fired. No one shot back. Delaney fired two more shots to make sure they stayed back of the ledge.

When the shot echoes died, Delaney yelled, "Brodie! You're the only one I want. Come out or I'll pick them off one by one."

"Go to hell, Carmichael!"

Delaney grinned. Brodie was here. But he had no time to gloat over this, for a volley of shots sent bullets whizzing up his way from far below the camp. Delaney edged back from the rim, unwilling to have a stray bullet hit him. From here he saw five more men concealed in the rocks below spread out in a half-moon with their rifles aimed at him.

Twelve men plus Brodie. Not the best odds he could have wished for, but it didn't matter. No one was going to cheat him of killing Brodie.

A steady barrage of fire began from those five men, forcing Delaney to stay low and withhold return shots. He wormed his way back and to the side, lifting his rifle and sighting to the far right. Waiting, holding his breath, he aimed for the man who tended to raise his head with each shot that he fired.

With a gentle squeeze of the trigger Delaney fired.

There was a choked cry, and another man yelled, "Yancy's dead! Brodie! You hear me!"

The firing from the four remaining men intensified. Delaney sighted the next man on the right, a man who was cautious to stay down, for all that Delaney could see was the tip of the rifle barrel poking up each time he shot. The damn fool was shooting blind!

Suddenly he realized that the other three guns had been silenced. Even as the knowledge came to him, the man he was sighting stopped shooting.

"Del-a-ney!" Seanilzay shouted. "I have come with the *Netdahee*."

Delaney watched and saw a *Netdahee* warrior stand and hold one of Brodie's men before him with a knife at his throat. If Delaney could see, the same scene was visible to Brodie and the men below with him. There was silence, then another warrior stood with his hostage, and lastly, the other two.

"Seanilzay, Brodie is the only one I want!" Delaney yelled in Apache. "Don't let them kill the men," he continued in the native tongue. "There are troubles enough for the people. If these men die by Apache hands, the army will come out in force."

"These men have no honor!" Seanilzay declared. "You

know they will not allow you to fight one alone." He felt strong making his declaration in his own tongue, knowing that Brodie and his men would not understand. "I could not let you come to this place alone. For all that has passed, for all that I have withheld from you, the *Netdahee* are my gift. They stand ready to fight at your side."

"Brodie," Delaney called down to him, "will you let these four men die for you?" Delaney no sooner finished speaking than a whisper of sound made him roll and aim his rifle.

Up over the rim, coming from the same path he had used, were *Netdahee* warriors. Only one spoke to Delaney.

"This is our place. It is not for you to fight alone."

"To kill all these men and have their blood spill on this place will mark it forever. I would not have it so."

"Then it is for us to guard your back."

At his gesture the warriors came forward, one by one, silently making the drop to the ledge below. Delaney counted fifteen. He crawled to the edge and saw them look toward Seanilzay, who stood with his hand raised. As he lowered it, the warriors went over the ledge as if they were one. A man's cry was cut off, and Delaney knew how the men below must feel facing the fiercest of the elite Apache warriors.

Angry murmurs rose from the men with Brodie when Delaney again demanded that he come out. A shot ricocheted off the ceiling of the overhang, and Brodie landed in a sprawl on his back out in the open. The *Netdahee* did not make a move to touch him.

Delaney rose, pointing his rifle at his enemy. His hand clenched, holding the barrel steady. His finger locked on the trigger. One gentle squeeze. That was all he had to do. Delaney felt himself shake as he pit the force of his will against the strength of his need to shoot Brodie. He could not let him die this easily.

"Get up," Delaney ordered, watching him closely. Brodie was nearly his height, but heavier built, none of his weight coming from fat.

Adam Brodie came to his feet slowly and pushed back the high-crowned black hat he wore. Shading his eyes, he looked up. The sun came from behind Delaney so that he appeared an armed menace. Lowering his hand, Adam fisted it at his side and waited.

"On your left is a way up here, Brodie. Take it."

Adam looked behind him and saw the Apache warriors with their hostages coming toward him. In front of him were more of the savages, and within the overhang his men turned their backs on him. Even money, he suddenly realized, could not buy loyalty. There was no choice but to do what Delaney ordered. After stripping off his vest and tossing aside his hat, Brodie smoothed the short black leather gloves he always wore and started for the boulders that would bring him up on the rim with Delaney.

"Take all their guns, Seanilzay," Delaney called out. "As long as they don't make a move to interfere, let them live." He stepped back from the edge and waited for Brodie.

Sweat glistened on Adam's face as he pulled himself up and over the last rock. He stood panting, his green eyes feral as they watched Delaney step closer, then stop.

"Drop the gunbelt, Brodie. And take out the knife you sheath in your left boot."

"You'll never get away with this, Carmichael. Those men down there aren't going to keep quiet. Ross knows about you, too. He'll make sure every one of these Apache hang."

"Only if someone lives to tell of it. If I ask, the *Netdahee* will slit their throats."

"You just said that they would live!"

"You gettin' a conscience now, Brodie, about other men's lives? Just do what I told you. Nice and slow, unbuckle the

belt and throw your weapons over the side to Seanilzay."
Delaney grinned to see the impotent fury in Brodie's eyes.
The man's short, dark hair was already plastered to the shape
of his head under the unrelenting force of the sun pouring
down. But he finally did as Delaney ordered.

"Now what? Do you think you could kill an unarmed man,
Carmichael?"

The taunt didn't matter; it was his coolly superior look that
Delaney hated. "Unarmed man? The same way you had my
father killed? He was garroted. I've never tried strangling a
man with my hands. Or did you mean unarmed the way you
killed my mother? Yeah. I could easily kill an unarmed man
like you, Brodie."

"I didn't—"

"Shut the hell up! The lies are finished." Delaney threw
his rifle down to Seanilzay, then slowly unbuckled his own
gunbelt and withdrew his knife. The knife he tossed down
into the rocks on the other side. And he had to smile to see
the way Brodie watched where it fell. "Just in case one of us
makes it down that far." He lifted the gun from the holster
and tossed the belt down below. "Step back from the edge,
Brodie. I don't want you to fall and cheat me." Delaney
waited for him to move, patient now that he had his enemy
within reach.

"What the hell are you going to do?" Brodie demanded,
eyeing the gun Delaney held.

"This was my father's gun. It might be fitting to kill you
with it since you destroyed his name and took his life."

"Listen to me, Carmichael. I'll make it all up to you. I
know there's gold here. We found nuggets in the stream. I'll
write out a claim to you for half. I'll—"

"And Elise? Would you give her back to me,
too?"

"If you want that bitch, take her."

"And your son, Brodie? Would you give him up as well so that you could live?"

"Yes. Christ! Yes. Anything. Anything you want."

"Will you get on your knees and beg me for your life?"

Brodie didn't wait for him to finish. He went down on his knees. "I'll beg you," he whispered but found no mercy in Delaney's eyes.

"It's not enough," Delaney answered very softly. "Not even your life is enough payment for what you've taken from me. But it is the only thing you have that I want."

A furious red flush colored Brodie's face. Awkwardly he came to his feet, his gaze pinned to the gun.

Delaney caressed the double triggers. Six shots. He wouldn't have to touch Brodie at all. But all within him that was Apache taught and bred cried out for a slower death. He looked up and found Brodie staring at the gun.

"Go on, make a try for it," Delaney goaded, knowing how much of a coward the man was, knowing, too, that he was a dirty fighter. Delaney made his decision; he placed the gun down and stepped away from it.

But Brodie didn't make a try for the gun, he ran for Delaney, lunging at him, his fist sliding harmlessly off the shoulder Delaney turned to him. His bootheel slipped, and he went down on one knee, crying out.

Delaney yanked Brodie's hands off his body. One kick and he knew that he could send Brodie to his death. He backed away, unable to let this man die that quickly, that cleanly.

Brodie crouched, wiping his mouth with the back of his gloved hand, spitting off to the side.

Watching Brodie's frantic, darting eyes, Delaney knew he was searching for another way down. Since he stood near where Brodie had climbed up, he knew Brodie wouldn't try to come at him again.

"You could try for the gun," Delaney taunted.

Brodie shot a look over his shoulder. There was no easy path. He feinted to his left, then made a flying leap for the gun, but Delaney kicked it out of his reach. Brodie rolled, his foot shot out, catching Delaney mid-thigh. He came to his feet and made another dive for the gun.

Delaney landed on top of him, gripping his wrist just as Brodie clutched the gun handle. Brodie's heavier build had him at a disadvantage. Delaney couldn't hold him down. They rolled over. Then over once again. Brodie's arms were extended over the edge of the rock as Delaney straddled him and made a grab for his wrists. The gun went off.

Brodie slammed his forearm against the side of Delaney's head, but he couldn't shake him off. He landed another blow, breaking open the skin on Delaney's cheek and, with a forceful shove, rolled them over again. This time Brodie was on top. His powerful legs pinned Delaney's. He tore at Delaney's hold on his wrist, ripping the sleeve of his shirt, but the leather gloves were slippery from the sweat and blood, and he couldn't get control of the gun.

Jabbing his left fist into Brodie's side, Delaney heard his grunt of pain, but he couldn't dislodge him. His knuckles were scraped raw as he tried to keep a grip on Brodie's wrist so he couldn't point the gun at his head.

Delaney twisted, his moves hampered, his blows lacking power since both his arm and Brodie's were outstretched from their bodies as they fought for possession of the weapon. His face was on fire from the punches Brodie landed, and his back was sliced by the rock beneath him. The gun went off again. Brodie ripped at his fingers, and another shot was fired.

Using the heel of his hand, Delaney pushed against the man's jaw, shoving his head back. With his elbow braced for some leverage, Delaney managed to lift Brodie's hand holding the gun into the air. Delaney felt as if the muscles of his arm were being torn as he stretched until his finger closed over Brodie's on the triggers. The last three shots went off one after the other until the gun was empty.

Bracing his heels, Delaney shoved Brodie off him. He barely avoided the gun that Brodie flung at his head.

With quick, easy grace Delaney was up in a crouch when Brodie charged him. Brodie slammed his fist into Delaney's midsection, knocking the breath from him. An uppercut rocked Delaney's head. Grabbing hold of Delaney's shirt and twisting it tight for seconds, Brodie landed another solid blow to his belly.

Delaney hooked his left foot around Brodie's leg and shoved him off-balance. Ignoring the pain in his hands, he rained blows on Brodie's head and gut, taking, in turn, the man's heavier punches on his body.

The moccasins allowed Delaney better purchase on the rock's surface. The hearing in his left ear was gone from the repeated blows he had taken. Breath was nearly impossible to draw.

Backing away, breathing in gulping heaves, Brodie came at him again, lowering his head. Delaney was dangerously close to the edge of the rim. He caught Brodie's broad shoulders, bringing his knee up at the same time, and had the satisfaction of seeing the stunned surprise in his eyes.

With blood running from his mouth, Brodie bellowed a cry of sheer rage. Delaney braced himself for another attack. But Brodie spun around and leapt to the boulders below. He had found the way that Delaney and the *Netdahee* had come up. And left Delaney no choice but to go after him.

The first jump down forced Delaney to clutch his side. From the sharp, searing pain he knew one of his ribs was broken. Drawing short, shallow breaths, knowing how fast Brodie could get down, Delaney drew on inner strength and made another four-foot leap to a flat-topped boulder just as Brodie appeared above him.

There was no time to dodge Brodie's booted foot. It caught Delaney's shoulder, throwing him off-balance. He slipped and slid down the side of the rock, pain ripping through him just as his skin was torn and abraded. Again, Brodie did not follow up his attack but continued his climb down.

Delaney had to drag himself to stand. No force was going to stop him from going after Brodie.

Brodie spied the glint of the knife blade in a rock crevice. He shot a look behind him. Delaney was still coming, but he was holding his side. Brodie grabbed at the blade. The handle was wedged tight. His gloved hand was sliced, yet he made another try, knowing that unless he killed Delaney, he would never leave the mountain alive.

Sweat dripped and stung his eyes. He rocked the blade back and forth, feeling it give. Come on. Come on, he repeated silently, desperate to have the weapon. He heard the raspy labor of Delaney's breathing.

Swearing and then cursing, he disregarded the sharpness of the blade and closed his fingers over it to yank it free.

With a yell he turned, taking Delaney's punch to his battered jaw.

"Bastard!" Brodie cried, spitting blood.

A vicious swipe with the knife sliced across Delaney's stomach, only the quick flex of his body saving him from a deeper wound. One eye was closing, and he saw Brodie through a blurred haze. Delaney's body was screaming in protest as he forced it to move. He knew he had to end the fight now.

He lunged at Brodie, using both his hands to force the arm and weapon back against the rock. Delaney hung on, lifting and slamming Brodie's arm against the stone, taking blows to his body that he no longer felt. He heard the bone snap and the knife fell from lifeless fingers, but Brodie still had enough strength left to pound Delaney to his knees.

Delaney saw his raised leg. Saw the black leather of his boots and knew that kick was coming toward his head. He wanted to move. Had to. But his body and mind seemed pulled in opposite directions. The kick never came.

Delaney managed to stand, weaving back and forth, not understanding the look of frozen terror on Brodie's face. He shook his head, trying to clear it, trying to hear, and finally turned.

Nine feet of growling, spitting jaguar was poised above them.

Delaney wiped the sweat from his eyes. From behind, Brodie's kick hit the small of his back, sending him to his knees. Delaney tensed. He couldn't move fast enough to avoid the cat's claws ripping his skin. He looked up, but the cat leapt over him. A tawny stretch of spotted grace and sheer power met his vision as he staggered to his feet and watched the animal bound from boulder to boulder, cutting off Brodie's escape.

Half-crawling, Delaney made his way down. Brodie had trapped himself against a smooth rock wall that led out to a ledge barely inches in width. The big cat prowled back and forth, its tail whipping with agitation, a series of deep, raspy, coughing grunts coming from its throat.

Hanging on to a rock for support, Delaney lost his breath when the cat stilled and turned to look at him.

And Delaney saw the torn ear.

He kept going.

Brodie screamed his name.

Delaney didn't look back.

Halfway down the mountain Delaney heard the cry. It was high and shrill. A death cry. Within his mind a voice called: *See me.* Unable to disobey, Delaney looked back.

High on the rim, with the sun glowing like fire behind it, the cat appeared black. Except for the eyes. Even with the distance between them, Delaney felt the power of those golden eyes.

He touched his skystone and through swollen lips whispered, "I see. Your place is safe, for another will watch. It is forbidden that I speak your name. But I have kept your secret safe as I once promised. I give to you my thanks for letting me go with hands untouched by his death."

Go to your iszán. For I, too, have kept my promise.

Chapter Twenty-Three

FAITH WOKE LONG before sunrise. Lying still in the dark, she was filled with a special serenity. Nestled within the warmth of her husband's arms, she listened to the slow, deep beat of Delaney's heart. Four months had brought her more love and happiness than she had ever known.

The shadows cast by the days until Delaney had healed and she could bear to be apart from him were being chased by the unfolding love they had for each other, a love that grew stronger with every new day.

And there were the new, brighter memories they gifted to the other to replace the dark corners of the past.

Soon, she knew, she would add a different richness to their lives. Just as she knew that Delaney was awake.

He didn't move, didn't make a sound, the beat of his heart remained the same, but with the bonding that love alone gave, she sensed him gazing down at her.

With a sleepy murmur she lifted her face, waiting for his morning kiss. As with each of the mornings that had passed since the day they had been married by a minister to please her father, by their own simple, soul-sworn vows beneath the sun, Delaney's kiss came to her in tender promise.

The gentle touch and whispered accolades from her lover's lips brought the scent of sleep-warm bodies to a heated intensity. Radiance spread through Faith as she silently returned the praise with kisses and hands that paid equal loving homage.

A light rain began to fall in the gray hours as the sounds of their loving woke the day. He gave to her the gift of life, and she believed they both stole a small piece of heaven.

Smoothing back the damp hair from Faith's face, Delaney knew again the deep abiding peace that only she could bring to him. Always, there was a need inside him to share all that was beauty with her.

"Woman of my heart, come see the beginning of the day with me," he whispered.

"Yes, a beginning," she murmured in return, thinking of what she would tell him.

In the shadowed light she watched him dress, drawn to the lean, hard power of his body. Faith thought again of the man she had first seen who had the look of the land, hard, unpredictable, and dangerous. She remembered the barren air about him much as the desert had appeared barren until a closer look had showed her its life.

She knew there were those who said Delaney Carmichael had not changed. Faith smiled. She knew different. It was there in the softened look of his eyes, in the teasing grin that kicked up the corner of his lips, in every touch, every kiss, every moment he was with her. Delaney was no longer lonely; the darkness could not remain where love shed its light.

Faith raised her arms to her love, and her smile deepened as he wrapped her in the quilt before he lifted her and held her close to his warmth.

The single large room of their cabin held the chill of morning air at bay, but as Delaney carried her outside, she freed one hand to catch the warm gentle rain.

A well-worn path led up the grassy slope, and at its top spreading a canopy of branches were a pair of peach trees. Here Delaney set her down, cradling her back against his chest.

"Watch the sun rise from here, love," he said, pressing his lips to her cheek and taking her scent inside him.

The first pale light seeped over the horizon. The star of morning faded. Everything was still around them. Faith gazed at the desert spread before them, the shadows lifting so slowly as the first sound of life came to them.

A cactus wren sent the rapid-fire beat of its song from its perch on a saguaro. The doves cooed. Quail chattered and the woodpecker swooped noisily. The coyotes and foxes made their last prowl before seeking their dens, and the deer came to water at the seep below where they stood.

High over the distant peaks the sun began its break. Pale gold light deepened, tinting the sky with its rainbow colors, painting all life with a special beauty. Faith watched a mother raccoon lead her young to water, and beneath the quilt her hand moved to cover her belly.

Life. Its gift had no measure. Her gaze roved the spread of green, the night-blooming flowers already closing their petals as others opened theirs to the sun.

The rain ceased, leaving behind a jeweled dew. Gifts and life. An endless cycle.

"There was one time," Delaney whispered to her, "that you asked me to someday tell you of the promise I was given with my skystone." He cupped her cheek, turning her face so that he could look into the stunning color of her eyes. But it was not the color he saw; it was her love.

"You are the promise I was given. A woman without lies. A woman who gives joy with her smile, love with an open heart, and whose inner strength is the power that feeds mine." His thumb shaped her lips with a light caress.

"All that I am is yours, Faith."

The brilliant sparkle of her tears clung to the tips of her lashes and rivaled any dew that graced a flower. Delaney leaned down so his lips could drink the joy of them.

Faith wanted to speak then, needed to tell him what she believed, but his kiss sighed and breathed over her lips. He lifted her into his arms once again and carried her down the slope, down to the home they had made for each other.

Seanilzay was waiting there.

For a long moment the Apache studied the two of them. "It is good that you have told her, Del-a-ney."

Delaney set Faith to stand, his arm around her shoulders. "The time had come for the words to be said. She is the woman of my heart. And you have stayed away for many weeks, Seanilzay."

"There was much I was called to do. I bring you news that will spread the joy of your hearts." From his cloth belt Seanilzay withdrew a folded paper and handed it to Faith.

She opened it and saw her father's cramped writing. After glancing at the opening words she began to read aloud.

" 'Joey's sight is improving, sometimes lasting all day. He and Pris miss you. I have made an offer of marriage to the widow I wrote you about. Now it is time for us to make peace, Faith. I hope you will give us your blessing. Keith is willing to wait until we are married before he leaves to try his luck at mining.' " Faith gazed up at Delaney. "Two weeks from now they plan to be married. Will you go with me?"

"Will it make you happy, Faith?"

"Yes. And I want to—"

"Wait," Seanilzay said, placing his hand on hers.

Sensing there was more to his reason for visiting them than bringing her this letter, Faith waited.

"We'll go to the wedding," Delaney said, "but let's go

inside now." He still had his arm around Faith and turned toward the house only to stop when Seanilzay spoke.

"There is no time for me. The end is nearing. I am of a glad heart to see that you have shared the beginning of the day and rejoiced in the rain. The people rejoice, too, when the land is filled with life. I could not wait longer to bring you my gift."

"Del?" Faith asked, gazing at her husband. "What does he mean, the end is near?" But Delaney's attention was all for Seanilzay, and she watched the Apache, too. Seanilzay untied the canvas that shrouded a bulky pack on his horse. Why hadn't she noticed how thin and frail he had become?

Carrying his bundle, Seanilzay once again stood in front of them. "My gift. I have waited long to give this to you. Your woman's tears have ended the barren drought of your life with the spirit of the new life she carries. May your son live to be strong."

"But, Seanilzay, I just . . ." Faith couldn't say more. How could he know what she had only realized herself this morning? And beyond that, telling her there would be a son?

Delaney knelt and unwrapped the gift. The cradleboard was finely made, decorated with bags of sacred pollen, lightning-riven wood and skystones. There was reverence in the gaze that he bestowed on his wife.

"There's to be a child?"

Faith could barely nod. How could love grow and expand in seconds, paling all that came before? She did not know. But looking down into the eyes of the man who knelt before her, she was blessed with sharing his joy. Touching the skystone that hung from the cradleboard, she placed her fingertips on his lips. "A son like you. This is my promise."

Seanilzay rode away, out into the desert sunrise. A new day. A new life. The beginning, even as it was the end of the life-way of his people.

Author's Note

SEVERAL YEARS AGO the New York jewelers Tiffany & Company purchased land around the Gleeson area in southeastern Arizona to mine turquoise.

They found turquoise, but not enough of the gem-quality stones to make their operation worthwhile to continue and so abandoned their plans.

There are people who still search for the burial place of the legendary Apache chief, Cochise.

One day the mountains may give up their secrets and reveal each of these two locations.

Or there may be only one secret location to give up.